THE
ARKANAUT'S
OATH

Other great stories from Warhammer Age of Sigmar

THE
ARKANAUT'S
OATH
A DREKKI FLYNT NOVEL

GUY HALEY

BLACK LIBRARY

A BLACK LIBRARY PUBLICATION

First published in 2022.
This edition published in Great Britain in 2023 by
Black Library, Games Workshop Ltd., Willow Road,
Nottingham, NG7 2WS, UK.

Represented by: Games Workshop Limited – Irish branch,
Unit 3, Lower Liffey Street, Dublin 1,
D01 K199, Ireland.

10 9 8 7 6 5 4 3 2 1

Produced by Games Workshop in Nottingham.
Cover illustration by Veronika Kozlova.

A CIP record for this book is available from the British Library.

ISBN 13: 978 1 78999 476 6

See Black Library on the internet at

blacklibrary.com

Find out more about Games Workshop
and the worlds of Warhammer at

games-workshop.com

Printed and bound by CPI Group (UK) Ltd, Croydon, CR0 4YY

The Mortal Realms have been despoiled. Ravaged by the followers of the Chaos Gods, they stand on the brink of utter destruction.

The fortress-cities of Sigmar are islands of light in a sea of darkness. Constantly besieged, their walls are assailed by maniacal hordes and monstrous beasts. The bones of good men are littered thick outside the gates. These bulwarks of Order are embattled within as well as without, for the lure of Chaos beguiles the citizens with promises of power.

Still the champions of Order fight on. At the break of dawn, the Crusader's Bell rings and a new expedition departs. Storm-forged knights march shoulder to shoulder with resolute militia, stoic duardin and slender aelves. Bedecked in the splendour of war, the Dawnbringer Crusades venture out to found civilisations anew. These grim pioneers take with them the fires of hope. Yet they go forth into a hellish wasteland.

Out in the wilds, hardy colonists restore order to a crumbling world. Haunted eyes scan the horizon for tyrannical reavers as they build upon the bones of ancient empires, eking out a meagre existence from cursed soil and ice-cold seas. By their valour, the fate of the Mortal Realms will be decided.

The ravening terrors that prey upon these settlers take a thousand forms. Cannibal barbarians and deranged murderers crawl from hidden lairs. Martial hosts clad in black steel march from skull-strewn castles. The savage hordes of Destruction batter the frontier towns until no stone stands atop another. In the dead of night come howling throngs of the undead, hungry to feast upon the living.

Against such foes, courage is the truest defence and the most effective weapon. It is something that Sigmar's chosen do not lack. But they are not always strong enough to prevail, and even in victory, each new battle saps their souls a little more.

This is the time of turmoil. This is the era of war.

This is the Age of Sigmar.

NOTES ON THE DUARDIN LANGUAGE

For long ages, the duardin of the Eight Realms spoke a language known as Khazalid. Although there were many varieties and dialects owing to the huge size of the Mortal Realms and the spread of duardin civilisation, the language was more or less mutually intelligible across all its variants, as Khazalid is famously resistant to change and the duardin innately conservative.

However, at the end of the Age of Myth and the shattering of the old Khazalid Empire, the duardin were forced into relative isolation, often in new environments, which encouraged the development of fresh cultural forms.

The development of many novel technologies and practices by the Kharadron Overlords has led to a linguistic divergence between the variety of Khazalid spoken by them and most other duardin. This new, young dialect, known as Kharadrid, is still largely comprehensible to non-Overlords, but its evolution is as rapid as that undergone by Kharadron society, and the differences only continue to grow. As time passes it is becoming more difficult for other nations of the duardin race to understand their aerial cousins.

It is likely that most duardin would follow much of a Kharadron Overlord's speech, although they would almost certainly find it abrupt, as the Overlords have a reputation for impatience, and spare little time for the polite circumlocutions of traditional Khazalid. But it is in the technical and mercantile realms where whole new categories of words have been coined, to the extent that even the most accomplished engineer of the Dispossessed would find himself completely lost during a discussion on these matters.

While speaking the common, human languages of the realms, the Kharadron are more willing than their cousins to sprinkle their speech with their own terms, so in the following story, certain words used by the duardin have been provided with translations in the form of footnotes. Whether these are unique to one or common to both dialects is clearly indicated in the text.

CHAPTER ONE

BAVARDIA

A poet spoke. This is what he said:

'Rain pounded. Cold gathered against the tops of the Fourth Air. Bavardia suffered bad weather as a matter of course. For those abroad on the street, atmosphere wrapped meagrely about the body, failing to warm, failing to nourish labouring lungs. Everything was thin there – air, prospects, life, love. Only the rain was thick, thicker than beards, thicker than oaths, thermals thrust up from the lower airs, flattened by the chill into thunderheads that lashed the town with oily, unpleasant waters.

'Drekki Flynt, Kharadron privateer, came into port. His crew weathered the rain like rocks do, grey, silent and stoic. They were grim. Nobody liked Bavardia.

'Bavardia was a young place, a lawless place, one of a dozen towns budded off great Bastion, the last remnant of ancient, shattered Achromia. If hope for the future had established Bavardia, despair of the present ruled it. Heirs to a venerable empire, the citizens brought ambitions with them that they could not fulfil. Their dreams were beyond their grasp. A young place with an old soul, Bavardia was filthy as infants are, soiling itself, unsure of its limits, creeping up one crag, then up another, always on the verge of catastrophic tumbles, never settled, uncoordinated, wild with the potential and vulnerabilities of youth. Built upon ruins, reminders of what had been, sad, lost, and yet full of hope. Bavardia! A town of–'

'Oh put a sock in it, Evtorr Bjarnisson. On and on all the bloody time with the bloody poetry!' Drekki Flynt said.

The flamboyant ancestor face that fronted Drekki's helm was known across the Skyshoals. Then there was his drillbill, Trokwi, skulking head down on his shoulder. He usually gave the game away, and if the little automaton was still insufficient a clue, the massive axe Flynt carried on his shoulder was equally unmistakeable. For the truly unperceptive, the ogor plodding through the water in front of him cinched the deal. No one flew with Gord the Ogor but Drekki Flynt! Say Drekki's name aloud of a night and astound a bar. *'I've fared with Drekki Flynt!'* was a common enough boast. But just then, there was no one to see. No one to hail Drekki or to curse him.

To call the streets 'streets' was a generous lie; they were yellow streams pouring from the hills behind the town. The flood cut the earth of the unpaved roads, leaving hollows and rounded stones to take feet by surprise. Tall Gord was untroubled, the water foaming about his tree-trunk legs. For him this was fun. The others struggled on in his wake in varying levels of misery.

'Do we really need the running saga about how filthy this weather is in this filthy town, when it's all running down my bloody trouser leg?' Drekki went on. Rain rattled so hard off his closed helm that he had to shout over the noise.

'But, captain!' Evtorr protested. 'I'm chronicling your latest adventure. It helps to say the words out loud, so I'll remember.'

'Thanks, but no thanks. No amount of poet's polish is going

to put a shine on this bilge pit, so stow it in your deepest hold, Evtorr, and keep it there,' said Drekki.

'I'm supposed to be *Unki-skold*,'¹ protested Evtorr. 'Couplets and rhymes is what I do, captain.'

'You're ship's signaller, too. Stick to that. You've more talent there,' chided Drekki.

The others in Drekki's party chuckled. Evtorr's verses were an acquired taste, one that no one had yet acquired. Evtorr's helm drooped. He had spent good money having its moustaches inlaid with silver, so all would know he was a poet. Never had his metal mask looked so woebegone.

'Yes, captain,' he said.

'Now now, don't sulk, write it down later, and torture us with it when it's finished,' said Drekki. 'You never know, you might pen a good one yet.'

'Doubt it,' piped up Evrokk Bjarnisson, ship's helmsduardin, and Evtorr's brother. 'He's been trying all his life. Not got there yet!'

'He left me out and all,' grumbled Gord. 'All stout duardin. I'm stout.' He slapped his massive ogor's gut. 'But I ain't no duardin!'

He laughed at his joke alone. The crew were too busy avoiding being swept away to find it funny. Being duardin meant being shorter than a human, broad across the shoulder, with powerful, stocky limbs and large hands and feet. Beards. All the usual physiognomy of the children of Grungni. Their form was suited to life underground, as ancient history attested, and surprisingly well fitted to life in the sky, as the more recent Kharadron nations had proven, but rather poor for swimming. Heavy-boned duardin sank and drowned more often than not, and a duardin weighed down by aeronautical equipment most certainly did. It was a fate they were at some risk of just then.

---

1 | Kharadrid: Ship's poet.

'Come on, stunties,' Gord said cheerily. 'Not that hard. Push on now.'

'Not that hard!' said Kedren Grunnsson, ship's runesmith. A unique appointment on a sky-ship. He was no Kharadron. You could tell by the way he moved. The crew wore aeronautical suits of design so similar they were virtually indistinguishable, but Kedren stuck out. He walked stiffly, as someone who had become accustomed to the gear rather than born to it.

'Over there! Way up's on that side,' said Gord. They waded to the side of the street.

'Look at this. Ropes!' Kedren said incredulously, tugging at the lines anchored to the buildings. They were at human height, for it was mostly humans who dwelled in Bavardia. 'What good are ropes? What about paving? What about drains? What about choosing a better site for their town rather than this piss-filled bathtub!' He grabbed hold just the same.

'You're no fun, ground pounder, too *grumbaki*[2] by half,' retorted Adrimm Adrimmsson, who was dragging himself along behind the smith.

'Is that me you're calling grumbaki, Adrimm? The grumbliest duardin alive? There's a cheek!'

'Now now, my lads,' said their captain, who had it a bit easier, being safe in the ogor's lee. 'We'll soon be out of the rain and into the dry. Ales all round. Some meat! That much I can promise.'

Adrimm didn't take the hint to shut up – he rarely did – and continued to moan at Kedren.

'I could have stayed on the ship,' said Adrimm.

'What, and miss all the fun in this sewer?' said Kedren. 'That's the fourth turd that's slapped into my gut.'

'I keep telling you aeronautical gear has its benefits, Kedren,'

---

2 | Khazalid/Kharadrid: Old grumbling duardin.

said Otherek Zhurafon, aether-khemist, and Kedren's long-standing friend. 'Sealed in. Turd proof.' He rapped a knuckle on his chestplate.

'Proof? Pah! It will take forever to get the stink out,' said Kedren. 'I hate this place. I hate this *funti*[3] weather.'

'Listen to the oldbeard,' said Drekki. 'Evtorr was right about one thing, at least – *nobody* likes Bavardia.'

Offended, the rain redoubled its efforts to wash them out, and they were forced to cease their grumbling for a while.

'Keep on, stunties, keep on!' bellowed Gord. 'Nearly there.'

The crew reached a set of steps that led off the road to a raised pavement.

'I suppose we'll be dry now,' said 'Hrunki' Tordis, who would have had a monopoly on optimism in the crew, were it not for Drekki.

'Dry? Dry?! All this pavement is is a shoddy substitute for good civic planning,' said Kedren.

Gord stepped aside to let the duardin up. Buffeted by the flow yet untroubled by it, he shepherded his crewmates with care. A good job too. Although Drekki mounted the steps all right, Gord was obliged to catch Kedren to stop him being whirled away.

'Grungni-damned, Grimnir-cursed stupid *umgak*[4] city,' growled Kedren as Gord deposited him on the pavement. One after another the crew scrambled up, shedding filthy water. Buildings covered the pavement over, forming a sheltered area, though to duardin sensibilities it looked like it had been done by accident rather than by design. Buildings of stone leaned on buildings of wood, propped up over the pavement on wonky timber posts and rusty iron girders.

---

3 | Kharadrid: A common Overlord curse. Best left untranslated.

4 | Khazalid/Kharadrid: Human-built. Also: shoddy.

'This place was surely built by *grobi*,'[5] said Evrokk. There was a sense of wonder in his voice. 'You couldn't design a collapse better than this if you tried.'

'You say that every time we go to an *umgi*[6] town!' said Evtorr, still peevish at his brother.

'Worth saying, that's why. Unlike your verse, brother,' said Evrokk.

'Come on, come on, beards straight! Keep your aether shining,' said Drekki. 'Umgi build as they will, and bad weather we have, but good beer awaits.' Even Drekki didn't swallow his own bluster. His jollity was entirely forced.

There were a few folk around up above the flood but they hurried on by, heads down, eager to escape the weather, and not one recognised the captain, to his chagrin. The crew trudged into tottering alleys as water and shit surged down the streets below. A rat's maze to be sure, but it could not defeat their beer-sense. A duardin can find his way to a pub all turned about and blindfolded.

Drommsson's Refuge was the sole duardin-built place in town, with four square walls and a roof of precisely engineered bronze plates. Old Drommsson hadn't trusted human foundations and had cut his own right through the clay until he hit rock. Old Drommsson didn't like human beer, so served only the best duardin ales. Old Drommsson didn't like humans at all, but always seemed to find himself among them. Old Drommsson was a host of contradictions. Old Drommsson was a lot of things, but most of all Old Drommsson was dead.

'Fifty *raadfathoms*!'[7] Drekki said, recalling the old publican's words. 'Do you remember that?' He elbowed Kedren. 'He boasted long and hard about the depth of the pilings he had to put in. He

5 | Khazalid/Kharadrid: The common species of grots.

6 | Khazalid/Kharadrid: Human.

7 | Kharadrid: Standard measurement of distance.

always used to say that, remember? Fifty raadfathoms! Good old Drommsson. Eh, lads?'

He turned about. His duardin were subdued, aetherpacks steaming, rain plinking loudly from the brass.

'Well, a more miserable line of skyfarers I never did see. Show some spirit! You're Drekki Flynt's swashbuckling crew, not a bunch of half-drowned skyrinx. I've got an image to think of!'

Nobody spoke.

Drekki sighed into his helm, a noise like a night wind teasing the rigging. For a moment, he wished he were back out at sky. 'All right, lads. First round's on me.'

The crew perked up remarkably.

Behind the Refuge's roof the great copper sphere of the brewery vat swelled invitingly, not dissimilar in appearance to a Kharadron aether-endrin globe.

'Now there's a promise of beers to be drunk, eh, lads?' said Drekki.

They reached the doors. They were sheathed in bronze, and decorated in beaten, geometric designs of the sort that once graced the gates of the ancient mountain karaks.[8] Very inviting, but Drekki stopped, and turned to face his crew.

'Hold it right there, lads,' Drekki said. 'Before we go in…'

'Can we at least get out of the rain before you give us one of your interminable pep talks?' Adrimm moaned.

'Eh? Interminable? Pep talks? You stow it, Fair-weather,' said Drekki, using the nickname Adrimm hated. 'This is important. We've got our rivals. We have our friends. There might be either in here tonight. We've a delicate job ahead of us. Our client does not want a fuss, of any sort. Keep yourselves below the aethergauge.

---

8 | Khazalid/Kharadrid: The mountain fastnesses of the old Khazalid Empire. Most were overrun in the Age of Chaos, and remain ruined to this day.

I don't want a lot of notice. Certainly not like last time, right, Umherth? Umherth? Are you listening? That was embarrassing.'

'If you say so, captain,' said Umherth, not at all abashed. Hrunki, his constant companion, sniggered into her helm.

'A low profile, right?' said Drekki, wagging his finger. 'All of you. Low profiles. So low, I don't want to see your heads over the bar. Got that?'

A rain-sodden chorus of 'aye, captain' came back.

'Right then,' said Drekki. He rubbed his hands together. 'Beer time.' He took a step, stopped, and looked up at Gord.

'Actually, you'd better go first, Gord. Just in case.'

'Right you are, captain,' said Gord. He covered three duardin strides in a single, decisive step, both hands out. They banged into the doors like battering rams, flinging them open with a metallic boom and revealing a big entrance hall, full of lockers for sky-farers' kit. From the atrium, inner doors led into the common room. Gord strode right in and pushed those open too.

Warmth, light and laughter streamed out. Someone was playing an aether-gurdy. Badly.

Gord stopped in the middle of the bar.

'Oi!' the ogor bellowed. 'Clear a table! Captain Drekki Flynt's in town!'

The noise faltered. When the hubbub returned, it had a different flavour. Urgent, excited, somewhat annoyed.

Drekki grinned. 'Say what you like about our ogor,' he said, 'he certainly knows how to make an entrance.'

'I thought you said low profiles all round, captain?' said Evtorr sharply. He could nurse a sulk like no one else.

'Hush now,' said Drekki. 'You're spoiling it.'

CHAPTER TWO

HIGH TIMES AT
DROMMSSON'S REFUGE

An unmissable sign was built into the wall over the inner doors. Letters cut from steel proclaimed in seven different tongues that there were no weapons, absolutely no weapons, NO WEAPONS AT ALL allowed inside.

'You've all read Drommsson's words,' Drekki said. 'Kit off, guns in boxes. He was insistent about that. Respect the wishes of the ancestors.'

'Aye,' they said, though Old Drommsson was no ancestor of theirs.

'In memory of Old Drommsson!' Evtorr said. 'A finer duardin there never was, a purveyor of beer and wine! Step in feeling badly, step out feeling fine!'

This time, no one told him to stow it. Several of them touched their foreheads at Old Drommsson's portrait hanging to the left of the doors, as shock-haired, furious and beady-eyed as he had been in life.

Trokwi shook out metal feathers and gave out a sad peep.

'You fear rust? I'll oil you back on board,' Drekki soothed. 'A proper oath that, my little friend.'

The glass-fronted kit cases lining the walls were big enough for the aetherpack, helm and heavier parts of an aerosuit. It was a Kharadron pub, after all, and built for their particular needs, although the lockers displayed several other kinds of duardin gear, and that of humans besides. There was an attendant on duty behind a low steel counter, more for the show than the necessity, as Drommsson's was a classy place, and the locker room was fully automated, each kit box opened by means of tokens bought from a vending machine whistling steam in the corner.

Drekki shot the attendant a grin and a waggly-fingered wave. The attendant shook his head disapprovingly and went back to reading his news-sheet. Drekki was well known in those parts. That wasn't always a good thing.

As the crew unburdened themselves of their gear, sighing with relief at the reduction in weight, Gord was poked back out of the common room by a pair of po-faced guards armed with aether-shock poles. Gord had his hands up, but he was growling, tusks bared.

'So it *is* you,' said the elder of the guards, when he caught sight of Drekki. He was missing an ear, had a peg leg, an eyepatch, and a grizzled beard; the living definition of tough. 'I was hoping this was someone else's ogor.'

'Tish, Fronki! Who else flies with the likes of Gord but Drekki Flynt?' said Drekki.

'I dunno, another annoying pirate?' offered Fronki.

'Very droll, my friend, but I'm no pirate,' said Drekki.

'Everyone flying Barak-Mhornar's colours is a pirate in my book,' said Fronki. 'Not only my book neither. Pirates, the lot of you.'

'Is it really Drekki Flynt?' said the other guard. He was a little starry-eyed.

The elder nodded. 'Aye, it is. Don't get excited. The stories about Flynt are better than the reality. The reality's a pain in the *dongliz*.'[9] He gave Gord a warning eye. 'Now you, ogor, weapons stowed, or you're not coming in.'

Gord grunted, but unbuckled his gun belt just the same. His aetherpack thumped hard to the floor. His helm was big enough to bathe in. All off, his kit took up two lockers.

'Come on, lads!' Drekki exhorted the crew. 'You're looking a little glum still. Spines straight! Little bit of swagger please, as if we're fresh into port with riches aplenty!'

'But we're not, are we?' moaned Adrimm. 'We're poor.'

'Shhh!' said Drekki. 'Beer today, riches tomorrow.' He lifted off his helm, revealing a shaved head, long snowy beard tipped with gold, and a dark-skinned face he thought handsome.

The crew combed out their beards, set their shoulders straight and walked into the common room with the rolling stride of seasoned sky-farers. It was cosy after the chill of the Fourth Air rains, full of lamplight and thick with the comforting smell of pipes, beer, sweat, and flatulent duardin. The furniture and walls were clad in hygienic copper, which gave the place a comforting glow not too distant from that of a forge.

Drekki pointed a finger at the proprietor.

'Dromm Drommssonsson!' he shouted with a beaming smile. 'Did you not hear my ogor? My usual table, if you please!'

'Call that a low profile?' grumbled Evtorr. 'Because I don't.'

Drommssonsson was the spitting image of his dead old dad, right down to the furious scowl, but he nodded all the same, and prodded a couple of Dispossessed prospectors out of Drekki's favourite corner. He polished the booth until the copper cladding gleamed, then beckoned them over.

---

9 | Khazalid/Kharadrid: The parts a duardin finds impossible to scratch.

'Drekki,' he said.

'Dromm,' said Drekki. They exchanged tight nods, as much emotion as duardin acquaintances will show before they've had their ale.

Dromm Drommssonsson looked the ogor up and down, as if he hoped he'd have shrunk to a respectable size since their last meeting.

'Still too big, Gord,' said Dromm with a shake of his head.

'Not big enough,' said Gord, slapping his gut. 'I want to be bigger. Feed me.' His nose was twitching at the smell of meat drifting out of the kitchen.

'I'll get your special chair,' said Dromm, managing to make it sound like the world's greatest inconvenience. 'What do you want to drink?'

'Meat,' said Gord.

'To *drink*,' said Dromm sourly. 'And gods let someone answer who can count.'

'Well,' said Drekki. He did a quick head check. 'There's Otherek, me, Kedren, the Bjarnisson boys, Umherth, and Hrunki...'

When Drekki called her by her nickname, 'Hrunki' Tordis Trek-kisdottr saluted and grinned. She was missing her front teeth and had bigger muscles than the males. Beardless, she was, but fierce.

'Then there's Gord, of course. So that makes eight. Let's say Gord counts for four, for he is an ogor when all's said and done...' He muttered sums quietly under his breath, the integers of intoxication. 'How about we keep this light and just start off with, say, a single firkin? That's only sixty-four pints. We don't want to overdo it. I've got an important meeting on.'

'Firkin it is,' said Dromm. 'And meat for the ogor,' he added grudgingly.

'Meat for all of us!' said Drekki. 'It's been a trying voyage, and we're hungry.'

It didn't take long for the crew to shake off the rain and their trudge through Bavardia. Nor did it take them long to finish off that first firkin. As they dried, a rich smell of dirty water and unwashed skyfarer rose around them, adding to the convivial fug. Soon they were red-nosed, twinkly-eyed and sentimental as only ale-filled duardin can be. When Kedren and Evtorr started singing songs of the old karaks, the rest of them joined in, and then they were definitely having a good time. Gord never sang; instead he worked his way methodically through the roast ox Dromm provided, happy in his own way.

Happiness calls to trouble, as they say in the Kharadron baraks.[10] It's right to be suspicious of it.

'Where's this lord, then?' asked Otherek. 'Who is it, Lerarus? Human?'

'Lerarus, and human,' confirmed Drekki. 'I've no idea where he is.' He shrugged. 'No telling with umgi. They can't keep to a straight schedule for the life of them. We're here, as promised, and he's not. But eh!' He elbowed Otherek tipsily. 'That just means more time for drinking beer.'

'He better show up,' said Adrimm. 'I'm sick of being poor.'

'You're rich, Adrimm, as long as there's ale in your belly and more in your pot!'

'Hurrah!' they shouted, except Adrimm, who rolled his eyes.

Drekki tipped the barrel over Adrimm's mug, trying for a flourishing refill, but found instead the last dregs of booze. He frowned at the cloudy trickle.

'Typical,' said Adrimm.

'I'll get more,' Drekki said. He swayed a little as he got to his feet. Trokwi spread his wings to keep balance. By then the crew were making more noise than any other party in the place. Drekki's

---

10 | Khazalid/Kharadrid: Port. All the Kharadron cities are baraks.

stomach grumbled. He pulled a face and let out a long, ripe burp. 'That's better!' he shouted.

The lads cheered.

'Shhh, shhh, shhh!' Drekki said, waving his hands. 'Low profile, remember?'

His crew giggled, then stopped. Drekki frowned. They were looking behind him.

Drekki followed their gaze around, and found himself chest to chest with another skycaptain. Drekki was tall for a duardin, and had to squint down to see who it was.

'Yorrik Rogisson?' he said in puzzlement. 'What are you doing here?'

'To give you this, Drekki bloody Flynt!' Yorrik shouted. His fist followed swiftly, connecting hard with Drekki's nose. Drekki fell backwards into the table, spilling beer everywhere. His crew scrambled to their feet. Chairs scraped on the flagstones. Perfectly laid, of course.

All noise in the pub stopped, suddenly, completely, the kind of silence that intimidates pin-drops. Eyes flicked back and forth over the rims of pint pots. There were a lot of Kharadron in Drommsson's from a lot of different crews. A lot of grudges. Calculations were underway on the merits of settling one or two.

'That's for stealing my sister,' snarled Yorrik.

Yorrik had company. Behind him, arrayed in a loose line, were several duardin of his own. They stood with their chests thrust forward, beards bristling, broad hands hooked into broad belts, elbows out. The Kharadron had left their subterranean origins behind, but they acted like tunnel-dwellers still, puffing themselves up to fill the space around them.

The tension creaked up a notch.

Drekki shook his head and got back up. He wiped a hand across his nose and moustaches, bringing it away streaked with crimson.

'Ah,' said Drekki, as if surprised that he could bleed. 'How many times, Yorrik? Aelsling came of her own free will.'

'Don't you talk about my sister,' said Yorrik.

'Your sister, my wife,' said Drekki. 'And you started it.'

'Ex-wife, you *unbaraki*,[11] preening, cheating...' he spluttered, looking for further insults. 'Overly tall, Grungni-damned sky pirate!'

Drekki let out a weary sigh.

'Tall? That's an insult? Try harder, Yorrik. You've a worse way with words than Evtorr here.' He jerked a thumb over his shoulder at Evtorr, drawing Yorrik's eye away from the pint pot he was snagging with his other hand. 'And I'm not a pirate!'

Evtorr scowled.

'There's bad blood between me and you, Yorrik. There needn't be.' Drekki held out his arm. 'Let us embrace instead, like brothers should.'

'You're not my brother, Drekki Flynt.'

'There's no weapons in here, no violence. Remember the wishes of Old Drommsson, that this be a refuge from the travails of life in the open airs, where skyfarers can come together, and be safe, and warm, for a little while, and find comfort in company. It is a hard life in the sky,' he declaimed with theatrical feeling. 'Why make it harder?'

Murmurs went around the pub. 'To Old Drommsson!' someone shouted, though knowing the clientele, the toast was an excuse to start drinking again when everyone else had stopped.

'Go on, give me a hug, just a little hug, for Old Drommsson's sake.'

Yorrik gave the kind of smile that cruel, petty men like to use.

---

11 | Khazalid: Oathbreaker. The worst insult in the old karaks. The term is less wounding to the more pragmatic Kharadron than it is to their Dispossessed kin.

The kind of smile from the kind of person who knows they are not particularly clever, and wishes to make the world suffer for it.

Gord continued to eat, but even his chewing slowed. He swallowed, loud, moist. It disturbed some ephemeral equilibrium. An odd noise to start events as it did, but there we are.

'Old Drommsson can go hang,' yelled Yorrik. 'And so can you!'

'Fair enough,' said Drekki, and swung his pint pot with all his strength.

A duardin-made pint pot is a hefty item. Iron-bound wood connected with Yorrik's face. His head whipped round, and he fell backwards. A single tooth arced from his mouth, up, up, a perfect parabola, trailing spit and blood. All eyes were on it. It landed in a pint with a definite plop.

'Get 'em, lads!' one of Yorrik's bravoes called.

There was a roar akin to an avalanche, and the pub erupted into violence. Gleeful duardin pounced on one another, punching and kicking. Faces were yanked forward by firmly grasped beards. Eyes were blackened. Jaws cracked. The duardin with the aether-gurdy started a frantic jig. A few old scores were settled, but many friends fought also, for the sheer, reckless fun of it. Emotions pent up on hard voyages were released in a giant, drunken, bearded explosion.

Drekki ducked a swing from one of Yorrik's men, bowed low, and tackled him about the chest, bearing him back into a table. Mugs went everywhere. Beer flooded the floor. The duardin sat there leapt up and started beating Yorrik's lad, and Drekki, and each other. Drekki's lads followed their captain in a beer-fuddled charge, meeting Yorrik's crew head-on, in some cases literally.

Hrunki was the terror of them, swinging a mug in each hand, taking blows to the face that would have felled a male, scaring back her opponents with her fortitude as she laughed at their feebleness. But it was Gord who greeted the melee most joyously.

He put his meal carefully to the side, got off his oversized chair, wiped his hands, then gut-barged the mob of brawling skyfarers, knocking them aside like skittles. Gord lifted up one of Yorrik's crew, his enormous hands nearly meeting around the duardin's ample waist, then tossed him the length of the room. He landed on a table and broke that in half, the copper sheathing wrapping around him like a blanket while rivets went pinging everywhere. Pint pots scattered. Beer fountained up from the impact. The fight spread like a fire. In moments, everyone was slipping about on spilled booze, throwing punches.

Chandeliers were swung from. Candelabra misappropriated for use as weapons. The few duardin who tried to keep out of it found themselves very much in it, yet the fiercest combat was around Drekki's crew. Oldbeard Umherth, bald-headed and crazed of eye, had two of Yorrik's lot in a double headlock, and was repeatedly ramming them into a partition, making his nose ring jump. Gord snatched up a barrel onto his shoulder and swigged from it in between knocking random patrons flat. Even Kedren Grunnsson and Otherek Zhurafon, too wise for such shenanigans ordinarily, waded in, fists hardened by years of toil ringing skulls like bells.

The aether-gurdy player played faster, harder, louder, until someone got sick of that and broke the instrument over his head.

Drekki was on the floor, one hand wrapped tight in Yorrik's flight suit, the other methodically smacking him in the face. Yorrik had no fight left in him. A punch-drunk grin was his only defence.

'Thought you'd wait until I was in my cups, did you, you devious cove?' shouted Drekki. 'You'll never beat me, Yorrik. I'm Drekki Flynt!'

An aethershot boomed out loud. If it were intended to bring the fight to a close, it was unsuccessful, so there came another, and another, until notice was taken.

'Cease!' a loud voice yelled. 'Cease!' Plaster pattered to the floor.

The fighting stopped in fits and starts. Duardin got up off the ground, woozy from the blows and the beer. Arkanauts who were fighting seconds before dusted each other down and slapped each other on the shoulders, giving bloody grins of thanks for fun well had.

The crowd parted, opening a lead to the door. A line of Grundcorps in the bright bronze and red of the Ossmith Company stood across the entrance. One, whose aethergun still smoked, pointed.

'He's there, ma'am, that's Drekki Flynt.'

A human woman walked into the room. Drekki hazarded a guess that she was young; it was hard to judge the years of so short-lived a race. He was a good judge of quality cloth though, and she was dressed very finely, in a tight-fitting doublet and trousers flared over knee-boots. The doublet was sleeveless, showing a pale yellow silk shirt beneath. Her clothes were otherwise a variety of deep reds. Together the red and yellow gave the impression of flames over embers. Her jewellery was likewise fancy and reminiscent of fires, a large ruby at her neck, an arrangement of topaz and carnelian on the pins holding her long red hair back. Rich, then, noble certainly, but very practical were her clothes, he thought. A woman of action, he guessed.

Her nose wrinkled at the smell of so many duardin skyfarers crammed into so confined a space, and she looked behind her, to someone else in the hallway.

'Is this really the best you could find me?' she said. She sounded haughty. More than that, she sounded disappointed.

'You'll find he'll suffice, Lady Lerarus,' said a voice Drekki knew only too well.

'Funti drukk!' Drekki moaned. He'd been slow to catch on. Yorrik and the Ossmith Company should've given it away, one being the son and the other the guards of one Rogi Throkk.

He blamed the beer.

There was a hissing of machines. A walking cane came first, all of brilliant blue crystal, flawless, a sky-port's gross domestic product in one turned gem. Compressed aether-gold shod and topped it. The hand that gripped the finial was wholly mechanical. The right foot was booted in tooled leather, adorned with all manner of rich elements. The left foot was an artificial replacement, made of brass and steel, like the hand, and the leg, and the arm.

'Throkk,' said Drekki, somewhat lamely.

Throkk's expression of distaste was even more pronounced than that of the woman.

'Were you expecting Grimnir, perhaps?' he said. 'Or Sigmar?' Throkk was as famously broad as Drekki was famously tall, so wide of shoulder the joke among the apprentices at the Throkk Aetherworks was that he had to negotiate the doors sideways. They didn't say that in front of him, naturally, not when Throkk's temper was as legendary as his breadth, and he was so monstrously strong.

Monstrously monstrous with it. An accident had taken his left arm, leg, and his eye. The finely wrought mechanisms that replaced them were lit from within by aethershine. A starburst of scars radiated across his face. His hair and beard were still black as oil, even at his age, though where burning aether-gold had touched his dark skin all those decades ago, patches of his cheek, head and chin were bald and shiny pink.

'Release my son, Drekki,' said Throkk.

Drekki glanced down at the unconscious Yorrik. He had quite forgotten he had hold of him. He let him go. Yorrik's head hit the floor. He took in the Ossmith Company.

'No weapons in here,' said Drekki. 'Best tell your hired guns to set them down.' He pulled his most reasonable face. 'Then maybe we can have a drink, straighten this out?'

'Rules don't apply to me, you honourless dog. Now get up. Slowly,' said Throkk. 'You and your crew, on your feet. Everyone else, back off.'

Nobody moved.

'Now!' shouted Throkk. He rapped his staff on the floor. The Ossmith Company levelled their guns. Hammers clicked. Shuffled compliance followed. Drekki and crew wiped themselves down.

'Before you take issue with this, let it be known to all that Yorrik Rogisson started it,' said Drekki.

'I know he did, Drekki.' Throkk's natural eye moved briefly to his unconscious son. The look Yorrik got was altogether annoyed. 'I told him not to come before the meeting, but he does love his sister. You must forgive him, as must I. He still has not forgiven you for stealing away Aelsling.'

'As I told Yorrik, she came freely.' Drekki lowered his hands.

'I haven't forgiven you either,' said Throkk.

'Now,' said Drekki, wagging a finger. 'I did wonder why you kept trying to kill me. That clears that up. Thanks for letting me know. I promise not to do it again.' He grinned. 'I'll be going now.'

Drekki took a step towards the door. Three aether-rifles moved to cover him.

'Or maybe not,' he said, eyeing their black-mouthed muzzles. 'Look,' he said to Throkk. 'If you're after Aelsling, I have no idea where she is.'

'Of course you don't,' said Throkk. 'She always was more intelligent than either you or Yorrik.'

'Then I suppose you've come here to kill me?' Drekki's mind was awhirl, looking for any angle of escape. He could see none. Even if he and his crew could deal with the Ossmith Company, and that particular Grundcorps were very, very good at what they did, they wouldn't be able to fight off the whole pub. Throkk's money would ensure they would have to try.

Throkk smiled, and it was an exact replica of his son's wicked smirk, only imbued by a deep and powerful intellect.

'Oh no, it's far worse than that,' Throkk said. He leaned forward onto his cane, covering his metal hand with his hand of flesh. 'I've got a business proposition for you, Drekki, and you're going to say yes.'

'I am?' said Drekki.

Throkk nodded sombrely. 'You are. If you don't, I will invoke my grudge rights, and you know what that means.'

Throkk looked meaningfully at an aether-rifle, then dragged a finger across his throat.

'*Skwick!*' he said.

'*Skwick?*' said Drekki.

Throkk nodded again.

Drekki smiled back. It did no good to show fear to people like Throkk.

'Business, you say? Always up for a bit of business. Lead the way.'

CHAPTER THREE

A FAMILY REUNION

Dromm Drommssonsson showed Drekki, Throkk and Lerarus into a private room. Throkk called for ale. Dromm bowed and scraped his way out. He was the kind of duardin who was impressed by the likes of Throkk, and probably scared of him too.

'Really?' said Drekki. 'You were in on this, you snake.'

Dromm scowled back. 'I show Master Endrineer Throkk respect, and he respects me. The likes of him don't show up and wreck my pub, Drekki,' he said, and closed the door behind him.

That wasn't completely true, thought Drekki. There were several fresh bullet holes in the ceiling thanks to Throkk.

'Still making friends wherever you go, Flynt?' said Throkk.

'I'm known for my charming personality,' said Drekki. 'That's why your daughter liked me so much.'

Throkk tugged the leather glove off his organic hand and folded it, then tucked it into his belt.

'Aye, *liked* is the operative word, eh, Flynt?' he said. His tone was hard enough to slice sigmarite.

Throkk laid his hand on the table. His skin there too was covered in pale scars. His clothes were high-necked, long-sleeved, always concealing. Drekki had once seen Throkk stripped down to his *grundeez*.[12] His burns were extensive. He liked to keep them hidden.

'Business,' said Throkk. He took a document pouch off his belt, put it on the table, then gestured with mechanical fingers at the human. 'This is Lady Sanasha Lerarus,' he said. 'She's a mage. You're going to do a job for her.'

'I see,' said Drekki. 'This was your idea, right? Getting her to write to me to trap me? What's in it for her?'

The mage said nothing. Tiny sparks danced briefly in her eyes.

'You would not have come if I had written to you,' said Throkk. 'Besides, it is her who needs your service. I am merely a broker here.'

'So the commission you wrote to me about is real, my lady?' Drekki asked. 'This isn't a trap?'

'It's a trap all right,' said Throkk evilly.

'The commission is real,' said Lady Lerarus, annoyed by their interplay. A fiery temper to match the outfit, Drekki thought. 'But I'm not so sure we should proceed. There's bad blood here, which you told me nothing about, Master Throkk. I will not get mixed up in a feud. You duardin take your grudges too far.'

'You want to be careful saying things like that,' said Drekki. 'We don't like our shortcomings pointed out by umgi. I might get offended.'

Throkk's jaw tightened, so much that Drekki fancied he'd break his own teeth.

'Are you offended?' Sanasha Lerarus asked. She had a hard, hot stare.

---

12 | Khazalid: Typical duardin underwear – high to the chest, wide-waisted, and long to the knee.

Drekki smiled. 'I've a feeling I better not cross you,' he said, pointing a finger at her. 'I'm not offended. I've caused more grudges than I've borne. You're a no-nonsense kind of human. I think I like you.'

She made a dismissive noise. 'I don't care what you think. I care if you can do what I need you to do,' she said.

'But I need you to care!' said Drekki, with mock hurt.

'Is this clown really the best for this job?' Lerarus asked Throkk.

'He is,' said Throkk. Not taking his eyes off Drekki for a second. 'Not least because he is entirely expendable.'

'I wouldn't say that,' said Drekki. 'I'm one of a kind. Rare.'

One-handed, Throkk opened the document case and unfolded it. Inside were a number of decorated papers all bearing the seal of the Kharadron Geldraad Admiralty Courts. Throkk spread them into a fan, and it was wide.

'These are my grudges against you, Flynt. I'll not bore the Lady Lerarus with the detail, but they are a litany of theft. Theft of my daughter, theft of my prototype, theft of my ship.'

Drekki counted counterpoints off on his fingertips. 'Your daughter's not your property, the gun prototype I designed and built, the ship you illegally constructed and held. The court found in my favour on all charges.'

'Because you bribed the Admiralty with my ship!' Throkk's temper bubbled.

'You believe that if you wish. Fact is, the *Aelsling* is Barak-Mhornar's now, as it should always have been. I'm only the assigned captain.'

'That's what you think. You're as much an annoyance to them as you are to me. You neglect that they judged my grudge-making legitimate, Flynt. I can kill you, perfectly legally.'

'You can kill me only as a matter of last resort. You've been trying, illegally, without even attempting to bring me into court.'

'Shut up and listen. It is true *Captain* Flynt here is a clown,' said Throkk, making the rank sound more an insult than the actual insult, 'but the *Aelsling*, *my* ship, named after *my daughter* is the fastest in the Skyshoals, and this duardin for all his uncountable faults is among the most gifted captains, endrineers, and navigators I've ever met. I'll give him that.'

'You're praising him. A moment ago you wanted to kill him,' Lerarus said.

'He's my father-in-law, as you'd count it. It's a family dispute,' explained Drekki. 'He still loves me really.'

'I'm sure because I trained him,' said Throkk. 'His skills are beyond doubt, it's his morals that are questionable.'

'Wind past the globe,' said Drekki, flapping a hand. 'Gone and done.'

'Not for me, Flynt. I've got an offer for you, and saying no means death, so listen well. Lady Sanasha represents House Lerarus, one of the nine Great Families of Achromia. Her father, Duke Lerarus, is going to pay me an obscene amount of money for your labours.'

'Of course, I get the larger share, being the actual doer,' said Drekki.

'Of course, you'll get not a waft of aether-gold, being an ungrateful, thieving wretch,' snarled Throkk. 'What you don't get is shot.'

'That's a bad deal, I say,' said Drekki. 'What's in it for me?'

The two duardin leaned forward, bulbous noses almost touching.

'If you do this job, I will forgo my right to reparations from you,' said Throkk. 'My grudges against you will be struck from the Skarenoffri Damakronn[13] at the High Admiralty Court in Barak-Nar.'

---

13 | Kharadrid: The Kharadron's official book of legal grudges. Lit. 'Open Blue [sky] Grudge Book'.

'The assassins you keep sending after me will stop?'

'They will stop,' said Throkk. 'You and I will have no further business with one another, ever.'

'Fair enough,' said Drekki, though he was far from convinced that it would end at that. 'What's the catch?'

Throkk grinned. 'You're very unlikely to survive,' he said. 'If you do, it'll be by the guidance of the ancestors alone. I chose you because you have the perfect mix of talents to succeed, but if you die, nobody will care, least of all me. It's perfect. For me.'

'Options?' asked Drekki.

'None.'

'Alternatives?'

'Death.'

'If I run?'

'I'll send every sellsword in Chamon after you. If you think your life has been hard since you betrayed me, you'll find I've hardly started.'

'It's been ten years!' protested Drekki.

'I've a long memory,' said Throkk. 'And I am exceptionally patient.'

Drekki sighed. 'Then you better tell me what the job is.'

The bargaining concluded, they both sat back.

At that moment, Dromm Drommssonsson backed through the door into the room. The noise in the pub had returned to the levels before as if nothing had happened: another brawl on another night. Dromm was bearing a tray with a large ale jug, two of his best pewter tankards, a bottle of wine and fine goblets grown from multicoloured minerals. Throkk looked on impatiently as young Dromm poured the ale, showed the bottle to a disinterested Lerarus, then uncorked and poured that with an unnecessary flourish. He folded his cloth over his arm, and clasped his hands obsequiously.

'Will there be anything else?' Dromm asked.

'Yes – go away,' said Throkk.

Dromm bowed and scraped away again, appalling Drekki with his servility.

'My lady?' said Throkk.

Lerarus' eyes narrowed. There was a whiff of sulphur about her when angered. For a second Drekki thought she might leave, but she didn't. Desperate, then.

'Have you ever heard of the Talismans of Achromia?' she asked.

'No, should I?' said Drekki. He took a long pull of ale and gasped at the flavour. 'Grimnir's flaming beard, this is far better than Dromm's usual! How do I get hold of this for the galley?'

'Not be an annoyance or a pirate,' said Throkk, banging his mechanical hand on the table so hard the tankard jumped. 'Don't digress. Don't interrupt.'

'I'm sorry,' said Drekki, not sorry at all. 'Beer is a serious business.'

Throkk actually growled.

'Though not so serious as this,' Drekki added. 'Do go on.'

After a moment's hesitation, Lerarus continued. 'It's easier if I show you,' she said.

She moved the fingers of her left hand in a particular way and spoke quiet, aelfish words of power. The candles in the wall sconces danced, lengthened, twisted into long skeins of fire. The room dimmed by their antics, the threads of flame attenuated and arched over the table, where they split and reformed, creating a golden image of Bastion.

Drekki and Throkk leaned forward, entranced. The fiery model was exact in every regard. There was the central island of the Citadel, the Portsisle close by. There were the palaces on the Duke's Tor looming over Eyeward, menacing the slums beneath. There were the Gunnery Districts. The highest metalith of the

Aphelion; the Lowerward, which skulked beneath all the others; Outerbounds and Everywhere, flying picket on the fringes. Lakeholme, with its reservoirs and odd spiral towers.

Even the suspension bridges and chain roads that joined the city into a whole were reproduced by little curling sparks, as was the traffic. Vessels from all over the shoals and beyond came and went, came and went, streams in both directions never ceasing. The departing boats reached some outer limit of Lerarus' spell, where they extinguished themselves, but until that point it was as if they were alive, with tiny sailors of dancing flame, and billowing sails of smoke.

Drekki gasped as a gondola swept by his nose, complete with a gas dirigible represented by an orb of fire, and a tiny gondolier made of sparks bending his back to wide-finned oars.

'The city of Bastion,' Lerarus said.

'I'll say it is,' said Drekki. 'It's perfect!'

Lerarus' expression softened a little. 'Are you familiar with the Great Machine of Bastion?' she asked.

'Achromia's finest mechanical miracle,' said Drekki dramatically, making Throkk scowl. 'The finest product of the thaumaturgical sciences in a nation famed for the same. It shields the city, preventing any form of dark magic or daemon from gaining entry.'

'That is so,' said Lerarus, and as she spoke a pale skin of energy, flame stretched as thin as it would go, enwrapped the model. 'It is the only reason Bastion survived the shattering of Achromia. The only reason we withstood the Age of Chaos, when all the rest of the old empire was broken into pieces or consumed by Change magic. What you don't know is that the machine is powered by a number of talismans, up to nine.'

She made a circle in the air, and the city was swept aside. One by one, nine heraldic beasts appeared in the air, snarling, champing and roaring.

'The talismans are artefacts from the days of the old Achromian Empire, one for each of the Great Houses. When the end of the Age of Myth came, seven of them were hidden away.' Seven of the beasts faded out. 'Two were left to us. One failed twenty years ago.' Another beast, a screeching raptor, faded, leaving a gryph-charger all alone. 'We are down to one,' she said.

'Dangerous, I'll bet,' said Drekki.

'Yes.' She blew on the gryph-charger and it too went out. 'If it should fail, Bastion will be defenceless, and therefore it shall fall.'

'Then get a new talisman,' Drekki said. 'Make one. I don't know.'

'The old knowledge is slow to be regained.'

'Then find one of the old ones!' he said.

'The rest were thought lost…' She paused.

'Ah, and now they're not?' Drekki said. 'I see why I am here.'

'One has recently come to light,' Lerarus admitted. 'It is vital that we retrieve it, and that it does not fall into the hands of our enemies, for the sake of all who dwell in this part of Chamon.'

'If you secure it?'

'Bastion will stand for another five hundred years, and the Achromian Empire will rise again.' She sounded keen about that.

'I hear Sigmar's lot have been making overtures to Bastion recently. I wonder what the Azyrites have to say about the rebirth of Achromia?'

Lerarus stared at him. A sore point there. 'It is in Azyr's best interests that no foe of Chaos should fall.'

She took up a chart case from the table, popped the top off, and drew out a map. It was two-sided, presenting several lateral views and two from above of the vast, shifting archipelago of metaliths that made up the Skyshoals. She smoothed it out, and put one finger on a section out a way from the central vortex of the Eye of Testudinous. The region she indicated was incompletely mapped, but he saw a large island group. A substantial land at the centre was surrounded by twin discs of material slowly accreting into solid ground. He knew it by reputation.

'The talisman is here, at the site of the city of Erulu.'

Drekki stroked his beard. 'The Erulan Archipelago is infested by grots, and they're thickest on the main island. Those discs make approach to the ruins really quite chancy.' He made a show of thinking. 'No thanks.'

'Scared of grobi, Flynt?' said Throkk.

'I'm not scared of *a* grot,' said Drekki, 'but the ruins there are crawling with them. Thousands of them. Hundreds of thousands. A lesser captain might call this madness.'

'Which is why you're going, and I'm not,' said Throkk.

'There are no extant plans of the city, either,' said Drekki.

'I have plans. The vault is below ground, in the undercity,' said Lerarus. She reached for another map, but Throkk waved his hand.

'He's no need to see it now.'

'Then how do I know you have it?' said Drekki.

· 'I have it,' said Lerarus.

'The undercity, eh? That makes sense,' said Drekki. 'Many duardin lived in Erulu, back in the Age of Myth. But even if we can narrow the location down, we'd need an army to retrieve it. Do you have an army?'

'We don't have time to raise one,' said Lerarus. 'We have to leave immediately. We only discovered the talisman two weeks ago. The wards that have hidden it since the fall are failing. Because my family has been searching for the missing talismans for centuries, we will have been the first to see it, but it will not be long before others notice. It probably has already been noticed.'

'By the grots?'

'Others with less noble aims,' the wizard said.

'So, not only grots, but also hostile parties have to be avoided.'

'Some of the noble houses of Bastion do not wish for the

talisman's return.' Lerarus looked troubled, tired; the bearer of too much responsibility for one so young. 'The political situation at home is difficult. The families are divided into three main parties. Those of the Integrationist Party have money and influence through trade, and fear the diminishment of either should Bastion turn its back on Azyr. They think if we bring the talisman home now, then we will anger the Azyrites. They say the time when we should rely on ourselves is gone, that the machine has done its duty and that we'd be better looking to Sigmar for protection. But they have eyes only for their own wealth.'

'What's everyone else say about such naked self-interest?' said Drekki, causing Throkk to snort and shake his head; it was a little rich for Drekki to call out others for self-interest.

'The others are the Restorationists, who wish to see Achromia rise again. The Pragmatists look at both sides of the coin. They could go either way.'

'Seeing as you want this talisman back, I'll guess you're a Restorationist, and you want to push these Pragmatists into your camp.'

'My aims are not relevant. Your participation is.'

'Well, it all sounds an awful lot like politics to me, and I'm not fond of politics,' said Drekki. 'Politics puts a dampener on your endrin.' He shrugged. 'Tell you what, let me sleep on it.'

Throkk stabbed a metal finger into the table, denting the surface. 'You either go or you'll be getting a one-way trip to Shyish. I'll then start proceedings against the band of incompetents you call a crew. I'll grudge-mark the lot of them. You'll die knowing that you ruined them all. Even your low morals won't cope with that. As for you, I'll have you shaved and hung from the gibbet cages outside Mhornar until you starve, as a warning to other treacherous dogs.'

'I thought you were just going to shoot me,' said Drekki, who was more than a little taken aback.

'Don't give me reason to get inventive,' said Throkk.

'No need to be hasty.' Drekki gave a little laugh. 'Come now, you know how much I would love to see the old empire rekindled. We're all citizens of the Skyshoals together, umgi, *elgi* and *dawi*.[14] I've always been a patriot, me.' He clapped his hands together. 'Well then, seeing as I've no other choice. When do we start?'

Throkk's cold smile broadened. 'Right attitude, Flynt.'

'I'll need a little time to gather supplies and recruit more crew. We lost two good arkanauts on the way here.'

'You sail tomorrow evening, when the off-breeze is strongest, no later,' said Throkk. 'Or our agreement is void.'

'Right you are,' said Drekki. He finished his pint and reached for the jug. Throkk moved it back.

'I see. Like that,' said Drekki. He closed his empty hand. 'Fine. I shall take the mage to our ship and begin preparations immediately.'

'Arkanaut's oath, Flynt,' growled Throkk. 'Swear it.'

Drekki's mouth set and he put his hand on his heart. 'Arkanaut's oath.' He stood. 'My lady, if you will follow me?'

Lerarus got up. She seemed relieved the meeting was over.

'Gladly,' she said. 'The sooner we start, the better. We have no time to lose.'

Throkk refilled his own tankard. 'Don't mess this up, Flynt, or I will have your head.'

Drekki bowed. 'It's a delight to be working with you again, master endrineer, or dare I say, my dear father-in-law?'

Throkk's lip curled. 'Get out of my sight.'

In the common room order had returned. New tables had been brought out. Wet patches on the floor where beer had been mopped

14 | Khazalid: Humans, aelves and duardin.

away was the sole evidence of the brawl. There was even a fresh aether-gurdy player, with a fresh aether-gurdy.

'Got to hand it to Young Dromm, this place is slickly run,' said Drekki, taking in the quiet patrons. The Grundcorps had vanished, as had his crew. 'Banished outside, I expect,' he said.

They walked through the crowd, where Drekki counted an equal number of scowls and salutations coming his way. He waved and twinkled at both.

'I saw only a handful of your men here,' said Lerarus. 'Was that all of them?'

'The rest are back at the docks. The *Aelsling*'s fast and small. Crew of fourteen, ordinarily.'

They went into the locker hall. Drekki ignored the attendant's surly eye as he fetched his gear. Lerarus went for hers. Drekki put his pack and armour back on. He flicked toggles and the generator kicked in, burning aether to make the burden bearable. 'They're ready to make a quick getaway if needed, which actually was needed, if I think about it for half a second, but we didn't get away, so there you are.'

'Wise,' she said.

Drekki grinned at her. 'My dear umgi, there's not a port in these isles that doesn't despise and celebrate me in equal measure. It's not *wisdom*, it's *habit*.'

Lerarus put on a long duster and a broad-brimmed hat, both deep shades of crimson, almost purple, like the last embers in a fire. She carried a slender staff of warm orange wood. Not just the colour was warm either, it gave off a palpable heat. Nevertheless, if he had not known, it would not have been obvious that she was a mage from her gear.

'You don't really go for the full on wizard look, do you?' he said. He waved his hands at her. 'Very few esoteric accoutrements.'

'I don't like to advertise myself,' she said, as she buttoned up her coat.

'You don't give much away either.'

'Why should I?'

'Short answers all round, eh? We *are* going to have fun together. Fine. I get tired of listening to other people talk, anyway.'

'I'd gathered that you prefer the sound of your own voice,' she said.

'That's better!' he chuckled. He checked her clothes over. 'That gear's good for fair-weather sailing, but you'll freeze in the higher airs, and the lower have nasty spots that'll eat right through that. You'll not have breathing apparatus, I reckon.'

'No. I don't.'

'Few umgi do. That's one thing we'll have to secure.' Drekki finished doing up his buckles. 'Come on then.'

They went outside. The rain lashed all but a thin strip of the pavement, about thirty *grunti*[15] wide, where the crew miserably huddled.

'You took your time,' said Adrimm.

'That you did,' said Kedren.

'Yes, yes, apologies one and all,' said Drekki. 'A lot happened. The short version is that this is the Lady Sanasha Lerarus, she's a wizard, she hired Throkk, who hired us to do a job for her. We're doing it, and she's coming along. That's about it.'

Lerarus turned to address the crew, her voice commanding. 'As your patron, I intend to be firm, but fair. I expect you to listen to me carefully, and obey my instructions. If you do this, you will find me a gracious employer. First, we must go to your ship and begin preparations...'

The crew looked at her so incredulously she trailed to a stop. The brothers Evtorr and Evrokk exchanged shrugs.

---

15 | Khazalid: Forty-two grunti make up an *ufzhen*. One hundred and twelve ufzhen make up a raadfathom.

Drekki put a hand on her arm. 'Now now, wizard, slow down,' he said. 'There's two things you need to know right away. The first is that it's me that gives the orders. This is my crew. I'm the captain, wizards or money or whatever else don't count. The other is that there will be no preparations or whatnots or anything yet.'

'But you told Throkk–'

'Never you mind what I told Throkk.'

'Don't interrupt–'

'We have drinking to get in, y'see,' said Drekki.

The crew's backs straightened.

'We're not going back to the ship?' said Evrokk.

'Now you're talking Khazalid,'[16] said Kedren, and laughed.

'What? You think that was it? We've got a whole night here!' said Drekki, holding up his arms. 'Why waste it? Young Dromm might have had enough of us, but so what? My credit's good at the Black Harkraken. Trokwi!' Drekki turned to his drillbill. Trokwi chirruped. 'Fly down to the *Aelsling* and get the rest of the lads. I've a feeling nobody will be interfering with our ship while we're in port, not while Throkk and his Grundcorps are about. They'll be watching the ship to keep us in line, so we might as well make use of 'em and have them do our job for us. We could all use a good night out.'

The crew cheered.

Trokwi launched himself off Drekki's shoulder, flapped furiously against the wind before his metal feathers got purchase and he vanished into the night.

Lerarus was not happy. Drekki wasn't surprised. Umgi did not understand duardin ways. Since when did humans properly care about beer?

'Captain, this is not the best of ideas–'

---

16 | Kharadrid: Expression meaning to talk good sense.

'Ah now', said Drekki. 'The Black Harkraken mightn't be the best tavern in the shoals, but it does a very nice Ulgu porter.'

'That's not what I meant. I am paying you–'

'Another thing you need to know', said Drekki, interrupting yet again. 'Never interfere with a skyfarer's shore leave.'

'He interrupts everyone, you know', said Evtorr, who, as poet, got interrupted more than anyone else. 'It's not personal.'

'In your case, it is personal', said Adrimm.

'Besides', Drekki said, walking into the night as if it were the finest ever. 'If you were paying me, I might let you tell me what to do, but you're not, you're paying Throkk, so I'll do as I please. If you really want me to risk my life for your quest, the least you can do is let me get drunk first.'

CHAPTER FOUR

WELCOME TO THE AELSLING

A night of sticky tables followed. There was a total of four taverns in Bavardia. Drekki's crew had a jolly good try at drinking them all dry. They caroused. Songs were sung. There were a couple more fights. Gord, as usual, spent all his share on food. Whenever they departed, the ogor left behind a pile of dirty platters taller than most duardin.

Lerarus bore it a while. She gave up trying to convince Drekki to return to the ship after half an hour of yelling in the Black Harkraken, where a blaring steam-organ killed all but the most dogged conversation. Drekki pushed on through the night. His crew wanted their fun, and their duardin bodies could take far more booze than any umgi's. With luck, she'd give up, or pass out, and he could do a runner.

It was a transparent plan, to be sure, and Lerarus saw right through it. She stuck with them, sipping abstemiously at wine while the duardin necked whole kegs, until the break of day, when bleary patrons stumbled out of bars to squint at the dawn as if it were a new and entirely perplexing event.

The weather had taken a turn for the better during the night. Away from the constant fluff of grey clouds wreathing Bavardia's hills, the sky was clear. The streets had drained and were streets again. The surfacing crews were out, manfully plugging the worst of the potholes with spadefuls of gravel, knowing full well the next downpour would wash all their efforts away.

'That was the last tavern,' said Lerarus. 'No more. A new day is upon us. We sail this evening. I'm not taking "later" for an answer.'

Drekki's head buzzed. It was both euphoric and unspeakable to be drunk at the rising of Hysh. 'Dunno what you're moaning about. We'll be off. Don't you just wait and shee. See.'

He hiccupped. Time to focus. Skyfarers were stumbling all over the streets, gathering together, flowing towards the docks in fuddled rivulets. He began to take a tally of his lads. He got to eleven. It took him a while to remember who was missing. When the name finally arrived it was such a relief he belched a noisome mix of old beer and dubious curried goat.

''Scuse me. Hey! Hey! Has anyone seen Urdi?' he shouted.

'No, captain,' said Evtorr.

'Ah, Evrokk, I'm sure he'll be back,' said Drekki. 'Don't worry.'

'It's Evtorr, captain. Evrokk's my brother,' Evtorr explained, unnecessarily, because everybody knew whose brother he was. 'And it was you that asked where Urdi was, not me.'

Drekki squinted and hiccupped again.

'Right you are, Evrokk.' It was a bit of a struggle, this walking business. One foot in front of the other was the principle, but both Drekki's feet seemed keen to explore all the holes they could find. 'Bloody umgi can't even build their downhills downhill!' he complained.

Drekki was hungry. The market was setting up for the day, stalls cramming the raised pavements. Food vendors were firing up their grills, more cheerful than usual on account of the finer weather.

It was still cold, their breath pluming into the smoke, but the sun brought up everyone's mood. They saw Hysh too rarely in Bavardia.

'Breakfast,' said Drekki decisively. He wiped dribble from his beard.

He took an abrupt turn towards a stall where skewers sizzled on a griddle. He nearly capsized, righted himself, and moved unsteadily over, heeling like a zeppelin in a storm wind.

He grabbed at the stall, shaking it.

'I'll have them,' he said.

'How many?' said the vendor, a greasy-looking human.

'All of them,' said Drekki, puzzled. 'Did I not make myself clear?'

Lerarus buzzed around him, annoying as a mosquito.

'Begone, pest,' he said. For reasons that eluded even himself, he found this enormously funny, and giggled.

'Captain, this has gone on for too long. We need to be underway. For the amount my father has paid–'

'Paid Throkk, not me,' Drekki reminded her. 'Breakfast,' he said again, very carefully, in case the word tried to escape.

The meat stand was the first stop. The crew meandered shorewards over the next hour or so, stopping to eat hot pastries and to sup tea from disposable clay cups. The market came to life around them, and soon the crew were a sight more sober, and bore packets and bags. Evtorr and Evrokk carried a barrel of ale between them. Gord had one under each arm. Adrimm staggered under a huge sack of grain, green about the gills and burping stale ale. Others were similarly burdened, and similarly hungover.

Lerarus fumed at the delay.

'This isn't just breakfast,' Drekki explained. He was now feeling more like himself, the forge hammer working the anvil of his brain aside. 'They're supplies. Need them for this voyage, see? Why waste time doing it all with ledgers and plans and rushing about when you can pick it up on the way back from the pub?

We'll be ready to fare with the tide, mark my words.' He tore meat from his kebab stick.

'You don't behave like most duardin I've met,' she said. 'You're disorganised, insolent.'

'That's because I'm not most duardin,' he said, mouth full. 'I'm Drekki Flynt.'

They left the muddy byways of Bavardia, coming to its sole paved road. Slabs the size of ogor dinners leaned downhill in the direction of the docks. There were still no drains, and the road was slippery underfoot, coated with water-loving weeds that thrived in the outflows of the town. Lerarus looked where she walked and picked her way carefully past mounds of unidentifiable filth. Drekki didn't bother. The whole port was a revolting hole. There were no good places to walk.

They came to the edge. High stone wharfs lined a sheer drop that went down forever. A hundred sky-ships were docked. Kharadron skycraft predominated, but there were also the armoured dirigibles of the Dispossessed, delicate human vessels of wood and sail, and those of less common races. Balloons and magical carriages were tied up by ships whose idling aether engines put out glittering smogs. Teams of web-winged lesser drakes screeched at their tethering posts. Jetties suspended from chains jutted into the sky. Stevedores of all species were humping goods to waiting holds. The better moorings were equipped with steam and aether cranes, and these swung their booms over gaping holds, depositing goods inside.

Lerarus headed towards them.

'No, we're this way,' said Drekki, catching her arm and turning her around, away from the well-built wharfs to the tatty-looking fringes.

They trudged through the mud, skirting the edge. It stank, and Lerarus covered her nose. Sewage trickled through the silt. Crustaceans crept about on this aerial foreshore, nibbling at unnameable scraps, taking flight on rattling wings when disturbed by the crew's approach.

They reached a place where rickety walkways spread out in all directions. Drekki stopped and arranged his crew. The least hungover he gathered for a hurried conference, from which he pointedly excluded Lerarus. He sent them away to fetch things that couldn't be picked up in the market. Otherek went to the labour exchange in search of fresh arkanauts. Bokko the endrinrigger, who alone had a completely clear head, went off to find breathing gear for Lerarus. The rest hauled their loads up iron ladders, rusted thin, onto the boardwalk.

Lerarus was displeased. Drekki guessed she equated the rundown lower docks with the quality of his ship, which just wouldn't do.

'It is a little insalubrious down here,' Drekki admitted as he climbed. 'The lower docks cost less, you see. I am thrifty, despite whatever first impressions you might have formed of my other, ah, qualities.' Drekki got up onto the wharf and held out a hand. Lerarus took it, and he helped her up.

'Throkk has a reputation for straight dealing. This would be over already if he didn't,' she said. 'I don't trust you.'

'Then you must be desperate indeed,' said Drekki. She glared back. She really did have the most penetrating stare. 'I jest. Seriously. Throkk and I do not see eye to eye, for he is shorter than me, and has only the one...'

The stare grew harder.

'All right! He hates me, but he is right, you've a better chance with me than with any other captain.'

She hesitated.

'Come on.' He beckoned. 'Come on! Nearly there.'

The foul airs of the dock helped swab out Drekki's head. Not for any chemical reason; the effect, by rights, should have made him feel worse, but the stink heralded the adventure to come. In hours they'd leave behind all the reek of civilisation and be out on the wild air. His heart quickened at the thought.

They passed a gap in the moored ships. The infinite skies off Bavardia opened up offshore, golden in the morn.

Drekki stopped to admire the view.

'Glorious, isn't it? Have you done much skyfaring?' he asked.

'A little,' she said.

Drekki nodded. 'It is unavoidable in these parts, to be sure, though I bet you've rarely been this high. I like it up here. The Fourth Air is less densely blessed with metaliths than the lower strata. Finer faring,' he said. 'Yet you can still breathe, just about, though the upper reaches are too rare,' he added with great gravity, gesturing to the heavens. 'Dangerous, you know.'

'You are enjoying mocking me,' she said.

Drekki grinned. 'Madam, I enjoy everything. That is why I am so good at what I do.'

'What is that exactly?' she said.

'Being Drekki Flynt!' he said, holding his arms out. He winked.

'I suppose you think you're charming.'

'Aren't I?' said Drekki. They rejoined the crew, the wharf bouncing with heavy duardin steps. 'Then forget about me, and look at my ship, and still your trembling heart. Here we are!' he said, and gestured expansively. 'The *Aelsling*, registered to the navy of Barak-Mhornar, but mine in every respect otherwise. Fastest sky-cutter in all the Skyshoals.'

'That's it?' she said, surveying the boat. Her voice was flat. Was she dismayed? Disappointed? Feeling contempt? Drekki suspected all three, but it was hard to tell with humans, their faces were so small and flat.

'That is, indeed, it,' he said, a little put out.

She took in the bronze figurehead of Aelsling portrayed as a duardin shieldmaiden, hammer outstretched, winged helm half-competently realised. Despite its roughess, Drekki was pleased with the statue. It almost looked like his wife. Lerarus' eyes moved onto the medium-bore aethercannon in the turret upon the forecastle, then the run of the deck to the poop, where the cockpit was swathed in tarpaulin. Both half-decks were raised over the run of the main high enough to accommodate doors below, but in general the *Aelsling* was a slim, trim vessel. Drekki loved her almost as much as he did her namesake, so he was eager to impress the wizard.

He swung himself up onto the metal shrouding holding the fore endrin. 'She might look fragile compared to the ironclads, but she is very fast. We've two aether-endrins of the same capacity,' he said, knocking the bronze casing of the fore. 'Gives us unparalleled manoeuvrability, and great power to the airscrews. Which are doubled, by the way, for extra chop. You want a job done quickly, then this is the ship for you. We've plenty of space below decks, though it might not look it. A perfect ship for fast runs and raiding, this is, and that's the kind of mission we're on.'

All she could see were the dents, and the hurried repairs, and the hull scraped so regularly for aerial fauna that the colours of Mhornar were blue streaks on bare metal.

'It looks like an accident waiting to happen,' she breathed. 'What is Throkk trying to pull?'

'Ah, well, accidents have happened,' admitted Drekki. 'The important thing is that we're all still here, no? I've a good crew. A skilled crew. Loyal to the last, every one.'

Adrimm stamped past muttering blackly.

'Here's one of the coves!' said Drekki with exaggerated cheer. 'Adrimm! Adrimm, come here.'

Adrimm turned around without slowing and headed back the way he'd come with a deep sigh. He was still carrying his sack.

'What do you want now?'

'Captain,' said Drekki.

'Captain,' said Adrimm, with narrowed eyes.

'A witty one, is Adrimm,' said Drekki. 'Show the Lady Lerarus to her quarters, why don't you?'

'Right you are,' said Adrimm. 'This way.'

'Ask to take her bags.'

'She don't have any, captain,' said Adrimm wearily. 'And I am carrying this heavy sack.'

'Appearances, Adrimm,' said Drekki. 'You're supposed to ask. When we take passengers, there is a certain etiquette to adhere to.' He smirked. Adrimm needed annoying. He was annoying enough himself.

Adrimm sighed again. 'May I take your bags, my lady?'

'I don't have any bags, Adrimm,' said Lerarus.

'Right we are, then,' he said. 'This way please.'

With hardly a moment's hesitation, Lerarus stepped down from the dock onto the deck and strode unerringly to the cowled door leading below. She'd made her choice, Drekki thought.

Cargo-master Velunti Runk, all long black ringlets and earrings, blew his ship's whistle to welcome the mage aboard. Drekki caught Adrimm before he could follow her, and pulled him in close.

'Try to keep her happy, eh?' he said. 'A lot of money riding on this.'

Ah yes, the money. He'd avoided that topic with the crew. No harm in a little bending of the truth. There was money involved, only none of it was his. He had a plan, anyway. There'd be money in this if it killed him. Which it might.

'Aye, captain,' Adrimm said.

'And cheer up yourself, Adrimm,' Drekki admonished. 'Anyone would think your beard had fallen out.'

'I dunno,' Adrimm moaned. 'Second highest rating from the academy at Barak-Mhornar and I'm reduced to lugging sacks and playing steward.' He jogged to catch up to the mage, and led her below decks. Drekki watched until she was safely stowed.

'Humans,' he said thoughtfully. 'Throkk,' he added. 'Bastard.'

There were things to do. Gauges to check. Aether pellets to load. Pressures to calibrate. Drekki admitted many faults: managing his ship down to the last ball bearing was one. It drove his endrin-rigger to despair.

He and Bokko Dwindonsson had the cover off the aft endrin. Bokko was an honest sort, almost naively so, and his face reflected it. He had a round little countenance, a round little nose, and round little cheeks. All the duardin of Barak-Thrund had dark skin, but it was often greyed and cracked. Bokko's was as blemish-free as a beardling's, so smooth it looked like soft brown velvet. He had no tattoos and wore no jewellery, and seemed so young in appearance that the expressions of concern he exhibited in the course of his duties had a faintly comical air. He was wearing such an expression then. Output from the rear endrin was turned down low, so the strain of supporting the ship fell on the fore alone. Drekki was in the guts of the sphere, while Bokko handed him tools and nervously checked the gauges.

'Ideally I'd like a day more for this,' Drekki grumbled. 'That secondary condenser is a little too frisky for my liking.'

'This feeder conduit worries me more.' Bokko pointed with his spanner at a metal pipe. 'It looks all right from the outside, but the glass inner is overdue a replacement. It's gone brittle. I fear one good knock will break it.'

He was right. Bokko always was. If anything he was playing things down. The *Aelsling* needed a refit. There were a lot of patches on the globe in front of them. A few more, thought Drekki, and soon there'll be more patch than ship.

He covered his worries with bluster.

'Now, now, Bokko, we've not had the time, the funds, or the parts to run to the strict Code. The regulations are written by nervy sorts anyway. It'll last this voyage out, then we'll have the money to get it replaced.'

'Yes, captain,' said Bokko reluctantly. He started to say something, then thought better of it. The few times the endrinrigger lost his temper with Drekki was always over the cost of parts. When he did, it shocked Bokko as much as it shocked those he was mad at.

Bokko wanted Drekki to go away and let him get on with the job. But Drekki wanted to do this himself. He was an endrineer by training, after all.

He leaned back on the spanner and tightened the valve. 'That'll do the condenser, I suppose.'

'Captain, please,' said Bokko. 'You've other tasks to attend to. Let me finish up here.'

Drekki reluctantly looked into the innards. He really wanted to stay, but Bokko was right.

'Aye, my lad, I do,' Drekki said, and clambered up out of the hole. He slapped the spanner into Bokko's hand. 'Get rigging, then, endrin-rigger.'

With unconcealed relief, Bokko set to work.

Drekki was at home up on the endrins, crabbing around the grab rails bolted to the surfaces. He went to the observation cupola, and slid in. Otherek spent a deal of time up there when they were searching out aether deposits. The khemist was meticulous, even for a duardin, and every surface was spotless, highly polished. The input ports gleamed. Drekki left an oily smear upon a rail. He tutted and rubbed it away carefully. Otherek's fastidiousness showed him up.

Below the endrins, the crew worked to prepare the ship for sailing. Tools clattered and shouts echoed over the docks from other ships. They were all racing to get ready before the off-wind blew.

The *Aelsling*'s hold covers were locked upright. Velunti was guiding a mobile crane to lower in a pallet of crates. He always managed to find a crane. He always managed to find cargo. Drekki was glad of the extra money. There wasn't one of his crew he'd swap, not even Adrimm, who moaned all the time. Or Urdi, who was habitually late, and still hadn't returned to the ship. Or Evtorr and his dire line in poetry. He recalled one particularly awful effort and sniggered. Poor Evtorr. Amazing signaller, though. Read a message through the thickest fog, he could.

Drekki looked up to the higher wharfs, past the bigger, fancier ships. Throkk's men wouldn't deign to tread the pauper's dock. They were still up on the highest level, eyes fixed on the *Aelsling*. Drekki made a show of busyness.

'Captain! Captain Flynt!' Otherek waved from the wharfside. Two arkanauts in full gear stood behind him, their kitbags and hammocks slung over their shoulders.

'Back from the labour exchange,' said Drekki to himself. 'Let's see what little fish your net has snagged, master khemist.'

He slid down the side of the globe and landed sprightly on the deck, planting his fists on his hips.

It always paid to make an entrance.

'You're back, I see, master khemist,' said Drekki, giving it his full captain's swagger. 'Who are these jolly fellows, come to join my crew?'

Before Otherek could speak, the first arkanaut put himself forward, set his gear down, and took off his helm.

'Ildrin Gothrik,' he said gruffly, offering a gauntleted hand. 'Arkanaut second class.'

'Years of service?' Drekki enquired.

'Six, captain,' the arkanaut said. He was reserved, this one, but that was fine. Drekki had limited tolerance for flamboyant characters. The *Aelsling* was his stage.

'Ah well,' he said. 'Not a great many, but not straight out of the academy either. This is a young crew, a young ship. You'll fit right in. And you,' he asked the other. 'What's your name, my lad, what's your service?'

The second arkanaut hesitated, and left their helm on.

'Straight out of the academy, sir. Three months.'

The voice was high, the cadence…

'Female?' Drekki asked. He looked to Otherek. The khemist nodded his weighty helm. 'Well, well, well! A young *kvinn*[17] out for adventures in the *skarenoffri*!'[18]

'I'm not alone,' she said, defensively. 'One-fifth of my class were kvinn.'

'I'm not saying you were. I'm not saying you are,' said Drekki. 'You'll not be alone on my ship, at least. Hrunki[19] will be happy.'

'Hrunki?' she said.

'Tordis,' said Drekki. 'Our other kvinnarkanaut. She'll show you the ropes.'

'So, this is not a problem?' the woman asked, gesturing down at her body. She seemed hesitant.

A female arkanaut, newly qualified, right the way out here? There was a story there, for sure.

'A problem? Why would there be a problem? Let's have a look at you, my lass.'

Reluctantly, she took off her helmet, showing a reddened face. Most of Drekki's crew were born in Barak-Thrund, up in the high airs of the Shoals, where the endless skyscapes baked them. They were dark-skinned, white beards predominating. This kvinn was pale, red-haired. The kind of complexion that easily colours.

---

17 | Khazalid/Kharadrid: A young female duardin, a maiden.

18 | Khazalid: Sky.

19 | Kharadrid: Roughly 'reliable', used principally for engines old enough for the flaws to have worn away and to have reached peak efficiency. Lit. 'burr-free [mechanical] action'. Also employed as a term of affection for senior, valued family members.

'You hail from the mother port, Barak-Mhornar?' he asked.

'Barak-Thryng,' she said.

'The conservatives.' Another chapter of her tale slotted into place.

Her eyes pleaded with him. She'd suffered a knock recently. Behind that, there was defiance. More layers. She looked like she expected him to reject her. He'd kept her hanging too long.

'I'm sorry,' he said severely. 'Aren't you going to shake your captain's hand?'

'Aye, captain!' she said with relief.

He reached out, she took it firmly.

'Now give me your name for the rolls,' he said.

'Khenna Grondsdottr,' she said.

'Welcome aboard, Arkanaut Second Class Khenna Grondsdottr,' said Drekki. 'Velunti Runk, our cargo-master, will see to you. He's over there. The ugly duardin with the silly hair.' He winked. 'Then speak to Evtorr, our signaller. He handles the contracts. Any trouble you two have, speak to Gord.'

Drekki pointed. Ildrin's eyes widened.

'An ogor in service, in Kharadron gear?' said Ildrin. 'That ain't the Code.'

'I think you'll find it is, if you look in the right places,' said Drekki. 'And he's right useful. Now shoo,' he said, flapping his hands. 'I have captain's business to attend to. You know, important stuff.'

The two bustled off, Ildrin far more confidently than Khenna.

'Let me guess, Otherek,' said Drekki. 'The girl there. A hard life, a fight to prove herself, a hidebound captain, a mishap, an abandonment.'

'That's about it, Drekki,' said Otherek. 'Stranded by Captain Khuzudrar Aftor.'

'That old sky-dog,' said Drekki.

'I've seen her papers. She's got good grades, and the right attitude.'

'As good as Adrimm's?' asked Drekki.

'Second highest grade from the academy in Barak-Mhornar,' they both said together and laughed.

'I don't care if she ain't got no beard,' said Drekki, 'so long as she can sail.'

'She can sail all right, or so her records say, and we can count on the eighteen per cent kvinn mark reduction from those miserable sods in Thryng, so her grades will be better than they seem,' said Otherek. 'They don't like their maidens up on the ships.' He came a little closer, as if about to share a joke, but the voice echoing in his breathing tubes took a serious turn. 'There's something else you need to know. When we were up at the exchange… You know those ratty little shacks on the north part of the square?'

'Aye, I do.'

'There was someone there, watching me.'

Drekki was unsurprised. 'More of Throkk's lot, or Lerarus' mysterious rivals?'

'Whoever it was, they were umgi. Trying and failing to be inconspicuous.' He tapped the side of the metal nose cast into his helm. 'Might fool my eyes, but you'll never fool this. Too perfumed to be a local. I caught him looking our way more than once.'

'Hmm,' said Drekki. 'Umgi. Not Throkk's style to rely on the unreliable.'

'Aye, this was no dockside bravo either. Too refined, I'd say. Rich, even. Throkk likes his thugs thuggish.'

'Another coordinate to plot. Throkk's got us under close scrutiny already. Why'd he need to tail you?' His eyes flicked up to the stone wharfs, where the gunners looked on. 'The wizard wasn't exaggerating, then.' He scratched his shaved head and stroked at his beard. 'This is getting complicated. Best we leave now, don't you think?'

CHAPTER FIVE

CASTING OFF

Quiet words were had in cautious ears. The activity on deck picked up. Items were stowed. The screws were cleared of debris and hull-clinging life: skywrack, stray bits of line, irascible snapping-mussels. Bokko sealed up the aft endrin and moved on to check over the fore. Arkanauts worked huge spanners on the endrin shrouds to balance the tension. Gord lent a hand wherever his strength was needed, shifting cargo in the hold, pulling hawsers taut, thumping out dings from buckled plates. The grumbling Adrimm was lowered on a rope below to knock the skeg free of barnacles and driftweed.

'Hurry,' Drekki told his crew quietly, 'but don't look like you're hurrying.'

They were nearly all done. The last few bits were tidied away. The final adjustments made. Drekki had Bokko bring up the endrins to pre-faring burn, and the ship hummed with power.

'All aboard, captain, and ready to go,' said Gord. 'Except Urdi. He ain't back yet.' The Maneater cast an eye over the deck. He was counting his shipmates. Drekki could tell from the look of strain on his face, and the way his thick lips were moving.

'Still?'

'Sleeping it off, I bet,' said Gord.

'There's sleeping it off, and dereliction of duty.' Drekki checked his pocket watch. 'Where by Grungni and Grimnir is he?' Hysh was well over the fore globe. He wondered about Otherek's sentinel. Urdi wasn't so observant or so smart as the khemist. Could he have been got at by unsavoury sorts?

'There he is!' said Gord. 'Captain, look!'

Urdi was hurrying down the main road to the docks. He vanished behind the rigging of a tall, human-built schooner, then reappeared on the shore.

'About time too,' muttered Drekki. 'All hands, the straggler rolls in. Prepare to cast off!'

'Prepare to cast off, you laggards!' roared Gord. His voice was so loud, faces all over the docks turned to the ship.

'Aye-aye, captain!' the crew responded.

'Bokko, bring the endrins up to faring power!' Drekki shouted. 'Evrokk, get the screws turning.'

'You, Fair-weather, over the side to the wharf!' Gord yelled at Adrimm. 'You too, new lady stunty,' he shouted at Khenna. Briskly, she obeyed.

'Cast off!' Drekki commanded. He jumped up onto the gunwale and hung off the fore shrouds.

Urdi reached the boat to cheers from his mates. Umherth hauled him aboard.

'Where you been, lay-a-bed?' Umherth leered. The giant silver ring he wore through his nose glinted. 'Found yourself another kvinn?'

Urdi grinned sheepishly. His romantic adventures were the talk of the crew. Hrunki cackled at his expression.

'Sorry I'm late, captain,' Urdi called. 'Got into a drinking bout with some outland human. Plied me with exotic wines, but I drank him under the table!'

There were more cheers.

'Now now, it's not so impressive,' Drekki admonished. 'Since when did out-drinking umgi count as a feat?'

'Sorry, captain, but it was potent stuff, captain. Sore head, captain,' Urdi said. 'Slept in an alley, captain.'

'A likely story. Now get to work!'

'Haul in the bow lines!' Gord shouted.

'Haul in the bow lines!' Velunti passed on.

Windlasses rattled. Lines slithered in. The crew sang a sky shanty to coordinate their work flipping switches and opening valves. The endrins thrummed. The deck quivered as if tickled. The airscrews came up to power. Drekki drank the moment in, finding it more refreshing than the finest ale. The glint of Hysh from the globes. The smell of reacting aether, the stink of the docks, the clank and clamour of other ships getting ready for their own voyages, all less swiftly than his own, which was just cause for gloating.

Lerarus joined him, groggy from a day sleeping.

'Ah, wizard! This is it!' Drekki said to her. 'At times like this, I'd not change my life for all the aether in Barak-Nar. The moment before departure. The second before life resumes!'

'It's noisy,' she said, and grimaced.

'Your heart not in it? Too bad,' said Drekki. It was obscurely pleasing that the night had had an effect on her, after all. 'Are your quarters not to your liking? You have our best cabin.' He paused. 'Well, apart from mine it's the *only* cabin.'

'I can't stand up straight nor lie stretched out flat.' She rubbed her neck. 'And I banged my head on the ceiling twice.'

'You are a tall race and this is a duardin ship,' said Drekki. 'There's not much I can do about that.'

She checked the angle of the sun. 'I thought we were leaving later,' she said. She lifted her face to the land. 'There's no wind.'

'We're leaving now because everyone will be expecting us to leave later,' he said. 'The off-wind's not necessary. When the air cools, the land stays warm, so the off-wind blows out. Gives you a turn of speed out of dock, does the tide, and saves on fuel, but that's all. We're not like these human sailboats, we don't have to use it. We can leave under our own power. Still, nothing flies faster than a zephyr, so we'll catch it off shore for a boost and be well ahead of our opponents.'

'Opponents?' She sharpened up at that.

'Aye, we're being watched.'

'Who?' said Lerarus. She was scanning the dockside.

'I thought you'd know better than I,' said Drekki.

She looked up at the Ossmith duardin on the high wharves.

'No no, not Throkk's goons,' said Drekki. 'They're not hiding. My khemist was followed up at the labour exchange, a human, like you. Conspicuously inconspicuous.'

'Damn it all,' she said. 'I thought we'd have more time.' She rounded on Drekki. 'You made a show of yourselves last night.'

'It's you that's been noticed, madam, not us. A wizard in Bavardia, in your fancy, fiery dress, in the company of Rogi Throkk no less?' He tutted. 'The news will have been on the streets the week before you got here.' He walked down the deck to the cockpit. Evrokk tensed. 'Steady on, helmsduardin, I'll not meddle today. Are you ready to take us out?'

Evrokk nodded. 'Aye-aye, captain.'

'Then let the *Aelsling* sing. Let the world know Drekki Flynt is faring the airy blue!'

By the railings Evtorr scowled. If his way with words wasn't good enough, Drekki's was worse, that was his opinion.

Evrokk pulled a lever. The *Aelsling*'s aether-whistle shrilled.

The last of the mooring ropes wormed themselves around their capstans. Adrimm jumped back on. He held out a hand to Khenna, but she ignored him, instead lowering herself into a crouch, ready to sprint.

'Come on,' Adrimm said. 'We're pulling away!' He leaned out further.

The gap between ship and shore widened. Khenna waited until two hundred grunti of clear air yawned.

'Arkanaut Grondsdottr!' Adrimm said, dismayed.

She chose her own moment to run at the ship, clearing the gap with her leap, and slammed onto the deck.

'I need no help, thank you,' she said, leaving Adrimm hanging. The crew whooped.

'All aboard!' yelled Gord.

Dock stewards pushed at the prow with poles. Duardin aboard matched their efforts, pushing back at the wharf. The ship swung round, until they were free enough to use the bow thrusters. Aether-heated air blasted out, and the turn quickened. That peculiar moment occurred when it appeared that the world shifted around the stationary boat and not the other way round. The ship moored in front pivoted away, then the figure of Aelsling was facing empty skies, her hammer raised in salute to the noonday sun.

'Arkanaut Bjarnisson, bring airscrews up to full thrust, if you please,' Drekki said.

'Full thrust!' Gord repeated.

'Aye, captain!' Evrokk depressed wide pedals with his feet. The screws chopped at the air, and the *Aelsling* pushed forward, slowly at first, then gathering speed. The dock fell behind them. In minutes Bavardia was small and unreal, a model world; hard to credit they'd spent the night there. The stench of the city was replaced by the sharp, healthy cold of the Fourth Air.

'Course, captain?' Evrokk enquired.

'That, we're about to determine,' Drekki said. 'Until you have your orders, keep us going aslant Torven's Island – it'll be coming round Bavardia now. We'll catch the wind there. Let's get some distance between ourselves and this hole first of all. Past Torven's, lose five hundred raadfathoms in altitude so the lady don't freeze.'

'Aye-aye, captain!'

'Gunterr, keep your eyes peeled.'

'Aye, captain,' said the master-at-arms.

'And get Hrunki out of the turret. I need her particular kind of advice.' Drekki cupped his hands around his mouth. '*Trommraad!*[20] he called. 'I call the trommraad for counsel! My cabin, if you please! You too, Lady Sanasha Lerarus,' he said to the wizard. 'Bring your maps. Let's all have a little chat about this here venture.'

---

20 | Khazalid/Kharadrid: A council of elders. Lit. 'bearded council'.

CHAPTER SIX

TROMMRAAD

Otherek and Kedren shared a look. Umherth was purple, making his nose ring seem even bigger than normal. Only Hrunki Tordis thought it funny, and she laughed around her pipe, billowing smoke through the gap in her teeth like a dragon.

'Drekki Flynt,' she said. 'You've done it now!'

'You've agreed to do what?' spluttered Umherth.

'It sounds to me like he's agreed to sail into the jaws of death with no sure profit in sight,' said Otherek. His wise old face was creased with concern, wrinkling up his tattoos.

'It's sounds to me like he's an idiot,' said Kedren. His hair was uncommonly blue. His brows, sunk with concern, looked like clouds in a winter sky.

'Don't look at it like that,' said Drekki.

'Then how should we look at it?' said Umherth.

'Our wages will be adventure!' said Drekki.

Umherth shook his head, and buried his chin in his beard. They all had their helms and packs off. All but Kedren had at least a couple of piercings. Rubies and gold glimmered. They scowled to a duardin, except Hrunki, who was slapping her thigh, helpless with laughter.

Drekki took a deep breath.

'Look,' he said. 'I'll be fathom-plumb straight with you. There ain't much choice for me in this matter.'

'You could just cut and run,' said Kedren. 'That's the way you sky-beards do it, isn't it?'

'You're not thinking of fulfilling the deal, surely?' said Otherek.

Their eyes slid to Lerarus. The duardin were thinking evil thoughts.

'Over the side of a ship in the shoals, it is said, you fall forever,' said Umherth. 'You'd not be raising a stink for the captain if you took yerself a little flight.'

Lerarus stiffened. Her eyes blazed, literally, with fire leaping in the dark depths of her pupils. 'You might try it,' she said. 'You would fail.'

Hrunki broke the tension. 'Shame on you, Umherth!' she said, and punched Umherth in the shoulder. He winced. Hrunki was powerful strong.

'The idea appeals to the worst of me, but I've taken the contract, which is as good as an oath.' Drekki directed this to Kedren. 'And I'll tell you what appeals more.'

'Oh, Grungni and Grimnir. Not fame,' said Kedren.

'Yes! Imagine it, Drekki Flynt accomplishes the impossible, again!'

'Fame fills no purses, nor repute bellies,' said Kedren.

'You'll lead us to peril to burnish your reputation?' said Umherth.

'Not quite, not quite,' said Drekki, waggling his hand. 'There is money. Will be money. I think.'

'How?' said the others, almost perfectly in unison.

Drekki leaned in conspiratorially. The others did the same.

'Listen here, for I'm going to tell of a marvellous profit. This talisman lies in the vaults of Erulu, which was the second city of the old empire.' He searched his map rack on the wall, poked at a few. 'Here we are,' he said, selecting a case. He pulled it out and unfurled the contents on the table, holding it flat with snotling-skull paperweights.

'Erulu is here,' he said, jabbing his finger into the map. It was more complex than Lerarus' chart, being skyfarer made. Kharadron charts of the shoals were covered in directional arrows and miniature diagrams of seasonal shifts, air currents, monster migrations, and the annual perils of Chaos incursion. 'Deep, deep in sky-grot territory. But that means that it ain't been plundered like many old places since the end of the Age of Chaos.'

'Nah. Grots'll have had it all,' said Umherth. 'Thieving grobi.'

'Since when did grots know the proper value of anything?' said Drekki. 'Since when did grots have the brains to break into a warded vault? Likely as not, this place will be stuffed with treasures, my friends. Treasures we'll sell to the highest bidder on the black market.'

'If the retrievals guild don't swoop in on 'em,' said Hrunki.

'As if they've ever caught old Drekki Flynt,' said Drekki.

'What if this vault doesn't exist, Drekki? All we'll have is broken statues and the like. That's what we'll find. Grots ruin everything. It's their nature,' said Kedren. His voice simmered with hatred.

'True, but I'm not relying on that alone, because there's a detail I think has been left out, eh, Lady Lerarus? Why don't you tell us a little about this vault,' said Drekki. His smile hardened just a touch. Time to pull some more of the truth from the wizard.

The air was bluing with smoke from Hrunki's pipe. Kedren pulled out his own and filled it thoughtfully. Lerarus was out of place there, Drekki thought, head bowed to avoid the ceiling. Though tall, she lacked duardin solidity, their presence. Lerarus was thin. Lanky. There was nothing to her. It was a wonder to Drekki that humans bred so prolifically. There was nowhere in that skinny body to fit a baby, even a scrawny human one.

Drekki raised his eyebrows. 'Go on.'

Lerarus' lips thinned. She was weighing her options. Finally, she spoke. 'It's a Stormvault,' she admitted.

'Aha!' said Drekki, pointing a finger. 'I knew there was more to this than you were letting on. It wasn't Achromia who hid its treasures, was it? It was Sigmar's lot.'

She nodded. 'The coming of Chaos and the death of Testudinous was foreseen by the mages of Azyr,' she said. 'The ancient Achromians were warned, but all the land was in uproar. They were bloody days. But did the Azyrites aid us? No, they took it upon themselves to save the future, and damn the present. They bullied our leaders into sealing half our treasures away, and after that their sorcerers stole our best warriors.'

'Are you sure that's how it went?' Drekki said. 'The ancient Achromians must have had a hand in this.'

'There was division between the Great Families,' she admitted. 'Back then, as now, whether to follow the Azyrites or not. Achromia was powerful. Some of us didn't see the need to follow their lead, believed that we could stand on our own and should use the full power of our machine to protect ourselves. There was a vote, and the decision to seal up most of the talismans was taken, for the sake of the future.' She paused, then added harshly, 'But the ones who agreed were deceived. The Azyrites closed up their realmgates and left us to our fate. With only two talismans, the Great Machine could save Bastion but nowhere else. They knew what would happen. They knew our empire would be shattered. Now the Azyrites have come back with hammers openly displayed, and daggers behind their smiles, saying they want brotherhood. I won't let them betray us again. The talisman is ours and should be held by the people of Achromia against foreign aggression.'

'The plot thickens,' said Drekki.

'Ten to one, Azyr won't like that,' said Kedren.

'Should we be going against Sigmar?' Otherek asked. 'There's a treaty between the Geldraad[21] and Azyr.'

'Captain's got a privateer's marque. Code says we're free agents. Profit first,' said Hrunki. She wagged a blunt finger. 'We can do what we like.'

'Aye, so long as there is profit,' said Umherth. 'Don't sound like there's any in this.'

'Let me get this straight,' said Kedren. 'The treasure is in an Azyrite Stormvault?'

'Yes,' Lerarus said.

'They're not amenable to being cracked, those vaults,' said Kedren.

'This one is failing.'

'Failing, not failed?' said Kedren. 'In case you don't know, lassie, I'm a runesmith of the true kindreds, not one of these ludicrous aeronauts. You'll not pull the wool over my eyes so easy.'

'Pfft!' said Drekki. 'He's far too cautious.'

'Am I now?' said Kedren with a gimlet stare. 'I know magic. I work magic. Nobody gets into a functioning Stormvault. A failed one is dangerous. A failing one more so.'

'It will be dangerous,' Lerarus admitted. 'But I am a mage.'

'I know runes,' said Kedren. 'Don't make me the equal of Sigmar's thaumarchitects. What's so special about you?'

'Because I know the deactivation spells,' she said. There was fire again in her eyes, that flash of power, swiftly buried.

A grim and thoughtful silence fell. The trommraad turned in

---

21 | Kharadrid: The ruling council of the Kharadron, made up of representatives from all the major sky-ports.

on themselves, a circle that excluded Drekki and Lerarus. There they muttered to one another, weighing up the pros and cons. When they took too long, Drekki spoke up.

'You're forgetting something, my venerable friends,' he said. 'The grots will not have got in there, not yet. So even if the city's despoiled, which I admit it will be, I remind you that this thing will be stuffed with magical treasures. Have you ever heard of a Stormvault with just one artefact in it? Especially here, in Achromia, the home of marvels in the Age of Myth?' An enticing smile shone in his beard. 'We'll be heroes. Doing the impossible! Freedom of the skies! Any job we want.'

'Not tempting enough,' said Umherth.

'And we'll be rich,' Drekki said.

The trommraad conferred in low, hurried voices.

'I thought I was buying your service?' Lerarus said from the corner of her mouth.

'Throkk's got me bound over a barrel, so I am yours,' Drekki said. 'But a venture this risky don't get done without the say-so of the elders, whatever the captain's orders. They could even vote me out and replace me, if they were of a mind to. I suppose Throkk didn't tell you that part, before you handed over your money.'

'All right,' said Otherek eventually. 'We've agreed. Let's do it. There were many of our people in Erulu back in the great days, so yes, that might mean rune treasure. That area's also yet to be surveyed for aether-streams. There's potential aplenty here, and if you say it will get Throkk out of your beard, captain, then...' Otherek shrugged. 'We're all for it.'

Lerarus nodded, as if it were all a foregone conclusion.

'How, then, that's the question,' said Kedren.

'We sail quietly, keep a low profile,' said Drekki. 'The wizard has a map of the undercity. It shouldn't be too hard to puzzle out where the vault is. We sneak in, and sneak out.'

'First we have to get there,' said Umherth. 'You reckon we'll be followed?'

'If so we'd be best hiding among our own kind,' said Hrunki. 'Strength in numbers, and a bit of anonymity.'

'That's right,' said Drekki. 'Well said, Tordis. That's why we're going here.'

He unfurled another chart atop the first.

'In the Second Air, not far from here, the Krund and Riksson Mining Company have a major operation, out by the Sodium Blights,' he said. 'Metalith detonation. Major aether-harvesting from the rubble. They're running regular kronvoys up to Barak-Thrund. They're offering good contracts for privateers to guard the ships, more at the moment now the shoals are pulling at the Perimeter Inimical, and the Season of Change is coming around.'

He waved his hand over the map. The Skyshoals were close to Realm's Edge, and their irregular shape had them brush close to the magic-saturated outlands of Chamon. When that occurred, Chaos incursions were common.

'More profit,' said Otherek approvingly. 'That's a major trawl going on there. Lots of aether-gold. Riksson and Krund have struck it big. I heard from my cousin that three-quarters of the skycaptains from back home are signed up.'

'Risky. We've not done kronvoy escort before,' said Umherth.

'Only because of Throkk,' said Drekki. 'There's nothing to stop us signing on now. We can spin them a tale about an accommodation between he and I. It's mostly the truth, as it happens.'

'Doesn't Krund hate you?' said Otherek.

'He does,' admitted Drekki. 'He's a bad diamond player and a worse loser, but Rikko Riksson is an old friend. I can talk him round.'

'Rikko refuses to play diamond with the captain,' cackled Hrunki. 'So they're still talking.'

'Let's hope it's him there, not Krund,' said Kedren.

'It's a grand idea, Drekki,' said Otherek. 'We'll be out of sight among the fleet, and if anyone's coming for us, they'll never dare take on the full might of Barak-Thrund.'

'It's settled then,' said Drekki. 'We'll make all speed to the mine. I'll sign up. We fare with them back home, then move on. It'll get us a good part of the way there.'

'How many additional days will this take?' Lerarus asked.

'Another ten at least,' said Otherek.

This angered the wizard. The temperature in the room rose noticeably. 'That's too many. The vault began failing two weeks ago. We'll get there and find it ransacked.'

'Listen, lass, it's better we get there slow than not at all,' said Otherek. 'If they're chasing us, they're not chasing the vault.'

'Who,' said Kedren, taking his pipe from his mouth and pointing with the stem, 'are they?'

'Rival lords,' said Lerarus. 'The Integrationists. Money's worth more to them than honour.'

'You sound like Kedren,' said Drekki. 'Doesn't she, Kedren?'

'Nowt wrong with honour, lad,' said Kedren.

'Money's better,' said Drekki. 'So I see their point. I digress. Trommraad, are we all in agreement?'

Otherek spoke first, then Hrunki. 'Zhokri-ha,' they said with a nod.

Umherth hesitated, until Hrunki nudged him. 'Oh stop it, Tordis!' he snapped. She gave him a mild, admonishing look. Umherth looked at the floor. 'Zhokri-ha,' he said, abashed.

'Kedren?' asked Drekki.

The old runesmith stared long and hard at Drekki.

'Aye, if you say so, though I've a feeling I'll not live to regret it,' he said. 'Zhokri-ha it is.'

* * *

Orders were passed on. Evrokk made the necessary course adjustments. Life on the ship assumed its familiar rhythms and the day went on.

Hysh sank away below the floating isles of the shoals. It would erupt from time to time, finding gaps in the islands, until it circled around, and up, and the great continents of Chamon got in the way. The main body of the Realm of Metal was a shifting mass of giant terrestrial plates, the Skyshoals writ large. When Hysh went behind them, night came.

The crew divided into two watches, according to a rota drawn up by Velunti. The half on duty headed below to sleep, except Gord, who snored mightily atop a pile of canvas and rope by the foredeck. Drekki put himself on the first watch.

Lerarus, not being crew, was free to do as she pleased. Drekki found her by the prow as the last shreds of evening coloured the dark, her hood up against the cold. They'd come down into the top of the Third Air, but night was still chill at that altitude. By the larger-than-life rendition of Drekki's wife, the mage seemed slighter than ever. A stray gust of wind could carry her off. Maybe she thought so too, because although she was admiring the view, she kept back from the rail.

'Peaceful night, eh?' Drekki said.

'Yes,' she said. It's never easy to guess the mind of a mage, but she appeared calmer than usual.

'It's not always like this, mind. It'll be rougher further in.'

Lerarus turned to look at him. 'It will be worth it. The fate of all I believe in rests upon this voyage. Achromia must rise again.'

'Maybe,' said Drekki. 'Are the Azyrites really so bad? You could live like we Kharadron. We're federated – together, but apart.'

'Sigmar does not intend to give the peoples of the realms such freedom as your ports enjoy,' she said.

'Are you sure? I've been to the free city of Tabar on the mainland.

It's good to see life return to the wastes. There's much to be done, and many dangers, but Sigmar is bringing civilisation back slowly.'

'To what was once Achromian sovereign territory,' she said.

'It was dead for half a millennium.' He became unusually grave. 'Worse than dead.'

'Your people would know. Azyr was not the only one to abandon us. You watched from the clouds as we died. It must have been a spectacle.'

Her rancour was deep. Drekki chose his next words carefully.

'My lady, my people did what they thought right. Most of our kind was wiped out too, our old empire is gone as well. I'm only saying the Azyrites are bringing life back where there was none.'

'No. They come to us with their honeyed words, after having abandoned us. They want to put a Stormkeep into Bastion. If that happens, they'll rule in all but name.'

'Better peace than endless war,' said Drekki.

'Why exchange one form of tyranny for another?' Lerarus countered.

'You know, it's a long way to Erulu,' he said. He sucked in a breath through his moustache. 'Maybe we should try not to argue about this.'

They were quiet for a space.

'Look!' Drekki leaned upon the rail, eyes fixed on the sky. 'Aha! Fine timing, my friend.'

'What?' she asked.

'Whaleen, off in that moisture bank.' He pointed to a stack of clouds lit up gold from beneath. 'Watch him surface. Now.'

She followed his broad finger, and gasped as a great aerial mammal rushed up through the vapour. Its flotation bladders pulsed, its flukes swiped lazily through the air. From afar they heard its wailing song.

'Hunting air-krill,' said Drekki. 'Many a magnificent beast

around here. Some, like him there, are friendly. Seeing one is regarded as a good omen.'

They walked around the ship to watch the whaleen. It flitted through the clouds, breaking them apart, four-part jaws open, feathery sifters spread wide.

They reached the stern, where the heat of the rear endrin took the bite from the air, and the chop of the airscrews was loud. The cloud bank receded. The golden light faded. Night was spreading from the edge with serious intent. The whaleen reared one last time, pirouetted, and plunged down into the evening, trailing song and mist behind.

'A fine end to the day,' said Drekki.

'What's that?' Lerarus asked. She pointed directly astern to a yellow light. 'A star?'

'Too low, and Azyr's in the opposite quadrant,' said Drekki. 'Hmm. That's not good.' He took out his glass from his belt. Trokwi hopped aside as he extended it. 'It's a ship, and it's right on our tail.'

'More of your people?'

'I don't think so. It's moving wrong. Probably an air-barquentine. I see sails. Umgi… Humans. Your pursuers, I'd wager,' said Drekki. 'Found us quicker than I'd have liked.' He stomped into the middle of the deck. 'Evtorr! Douse the navigation lamps! Adrimm!' he called, for it was he at the helm at that hour. 'Increase speed. Drop another two thousand raadfathoms, then have Evrokk take the wheel.' He turned back to Lerarus. 'Evrokk is the best of my pilots. We'll need his skills if we're to shake them.'

Drekki moved off to attend to his crew.

'How many more days will that add if we dive?' Lerarus called after him.

Drekki pretended he couldn't hear, and clambered up to the observation cupola. Cold air teased his beard, froze his cheeks. As the last rays of the sun went, the light vanished. Reflections, then, off the pursuing ship's hull. No navigation lights. They were hiding too.

The *Aelsling* ran quiet and dark, no lights, whistles or shouting, every bit of faring conducted with exaggerated care. The hum of the endrins seemed loud nonetheless, and the chop of the screws like axes in wood. When Evrokk came up and took over he burned aether at as high a rate as he dared, and dropped them further into the Third Air, risking collision on the reefs that choked those parts. All the while Drekki kept watch, well past his shift, until, in the chill before the dawn, he finally fell asleep.

He came awake with a gasp as the light of the returning Hysh slapped him warmly in the face. He steadied himself on the railings of the cupola and put his glass to his eye.

The pursuing ship was still there.

'And they're getting closer,' he said to himself.

CHAPTER SEVEN

THE SECOND AIR

Evrokk stayed at his post all night and had not slept a wink. Drekki had to order him out of the cockpit, and even then Evrokk didn't rest but joined the others at the stern, watching their pursuer. It had crept near enough that they could make out the details. A high prow in the likeness of a long-necked fowl arched from a hull of light wood. Long bags woven of aerite at either side held buoyant gases. Sails of the same flexible metal bent under a strong wind from three masts.

'It's just an umgi barquentine. How are they still gaining?' said Evrokk. 'I don't understand it. No wooden sailing ship should keep pace with the *Aelsling*.' He looked at the aft endrin doubtfully.

'She's in fine shape, Evrokk,' Bokko said, annoyed at the implication he wasn't doing his job properly. 'I made sure of that.'

Drekki snapped his telescope shut for the fiftieth time that day. It was becoming a nervous tic. 'Dashed confounding,' he said.

Khenna made a noise, about to speak, then thought better of it.

'Have you anything to add, arkanaut?' Drekki asked.

'What's she going to add? She's so new to the sky she's got dirt on her boots,' grumbled Adrimm.

'She's on my crew and she's permitted to speak, junior or not,' said Drekki. He gave Adrimm a hard look. 'Go on, Arkanaut Grondsdottr.'

'Wind mages,' Khenna said. 'They're using wind mages in Bastion. Aelementalists tutored by the Hurakan Lumineth in Hysh.' She looked about her fellows. 'It was part of my academy training,' she explained. 'Non-Kharadron means of aerial transit. The umgi are getting better at it.'

'What kind of abilities will their mage have?' asked Kedren. He watched the ship thoughtfully. 'It'd be good to know what we're up against, even if we don't know who they are.'

'I can't say,' said Lerarus. 'But if that mage has kept up their spell for this long, they're skilled.'

Drekki slapped his telescope into the palm of his hand.

'Right, lads,' he said. 'Wind they might have, and magic behind them, but they're only umgi in a little wooden tub. They're fragile. We're not.' He looked round the crew. 'Who's up for a bit of adventure?'

'Grungni armour us against skybeard foolishness,' said Kedren. 'Not another "adventure".'

Trokwi fluted uneasily.

'Get ready to dive. Take it low into the Second Air, into the reefs. If that don't get them off our back, naught will. Evrokk, you get some sleep, we'll need you at the wheel again right soon.' He looked at the rest. 'All right! Get to it! You all know what to do, don't stand there sucking your beards. We might have to fight. Gunterr, make all ready.'

'Aye, captain,' said the master-at-arms.

'Bokko, sort out the wizard with her protective gear.'

'I got some back at the port, madam,' said Bokko, his round, honest face looking more reassuring than ever. 'It's made for our kind, but I've been working on it to make it fit you. I'll be right back.' He hurried off. Always in a hurry, was Bokko.

'Why will I need breathing gear?' said Lerarus suspiciously.

'I did say you'd need some,' said Drekki.

'But why will I need it now? What's down there?' She looked uneasily over the side. Not for the first time, Drekki thought she was discomfited by the drop.

'Chemical fogs and the haunts of beasts,' said Kedren darkly.

'Don't listen to him, he was born in a hole. There are many reasons we Kharadron are overlords of the skies, and good breathing kit is one. We can go where other sky-ships can't. That includes them back there,' he said, jerking a thumb at their tail. 'Do you have training in their school of magery? The aelemental stuff? I've guessed you're all about fire, but if you can, it might be an idea to throw a few counterspells their way, slow 'em down. Then we could stick to the more clement airs and the question of air tanks and such becomes academic. Save time too.'

'I am not an aelementalist,' she said. 'If we were closer I could attempt a disspellation, but I don't have the expertise to undo their wizard's craft at this distance.'

'Shame,' said Drekki. 'Monsters and peril it is then.'

'What is your specialisation, lassie?' Kedren said.

Lerarus gripped her staff. Her expression was fierce. 'Battle magic of the Aqshian Colleges.'

'Battle magic?' said Kedren with a wide grin. He began a chuckle that turned into a hearty guffaw, then Otherek started up, and Drekki joined in.

'Why's that funny?' Lerarus asked.

'I wanted you to drop their wind, now you tell us you can blow them out of the sky,' said Drekki. 'That's a little more useful, don't you think?'

The *Aelsling* descended rapidly, yet the air-barquentine gained on them all the while. Gunterr Borrki got Hrunki into the turret and had the better marksduardin manning the two swivel carbines that poked out of the hull behind the *Aelsling*'s prow. A careful watch was set all round the ship. Adrimm at the stern, Urdi up front. Evtorr was sent down below to watch from the ventral porthole set before the skeg. Otherek went up on the endrin tops to the observation cupola, dragging his khemist's gear with him.

'Might as well keep a survey up while we're here,' he said. 'No one's charted these parts for a while.'

'With good reason,' said Umherth. 'These airs teem with harkraken.' He swung his volley gun back and forth, squinting at every strand of cloud, as if expecting tentacles to slap on the endrin spheres at any moment. 'Giants they be, break the back of a ship with a blow!'

A discomfort in their ears marked their crossing of the Third Air pressure line. Bokko brought out Lerarus' breathing kit. It was a stripped-down version of arkanaut gear, yet she struggled to get into it, disliked the mask, thought it was heavy and hot and found the view restrictive. She told Drekki so. Repeatedly.

'You'll grow accustomed,' he said. 'Or if you prefer you can perish without it.'

'I can still breathe this air,' she said.

'Right now, but the Third Air is a tricky place,' he said. 'Fly into the wrong sort of cloud and you'd be dead in seconds.'

Lerarus rubbed at fogging lenses. 'I cannot see a thing.'

'And stop that, all the moisture is on the inside. Breathe through your nose, not your mouth, that'll sort the problem.'

She muttered bleakly, said a word of power, and a flash of fire in the helm burned off the mist.

'Novel,' he said, 'but if it works…' He shrugged. The atmosphere was thickening. Drekki worked his jaw to pop his ears. It was getting hotter. Evrokk took over the helm.

A cry came up the speaking tubes from Evtorr, then a second shouted by Urdi at the stern.

'Fogs to fore and below!' Urdi called. 'Ware, ware!'

'All crew, switch to breathing gear,' Drekki ordered. Gord repeated his orders loudly. 'Take us in, Arkanaut Bjarnisson, steady as she goes.'

The air around them was clear as still water. The first sign they were over fog was the sound of the airscrews reflected back up at them. The constant chop became louder and flatter. Wisps of vapour appeared over the gunwales, wormed through the shrouds, tickled the globes of the endrins. Then they were swallowed at once.

In the pearly mist, the buzz of the endrins redoubled. Small, sharp noises became huge, piercing the fog like knives do flesh, but from further than a few feet, dull sounds were swallowed. Behind them curled vortices that reached and prodded with unnerving life.

'Master khemist, readings if you please,' Drekki said.

'Only water vapour, captain,' Otherek responded. He sounded far away.

'That's something,' said Drekki.

'My ears hurt,' Lerarus said.

'It takes a while to adjust. Might affect your spell casting. You can equalise pressure by swallowing until the pain goes. Now, if your suit gets ruptured, hold your breath and get below. Quickly.'

'Is there anything else I should know?'

'Try not to fall overboard,' said Drekki. 'I think that covers it. Stick close to me, and Gord.'

'There's going to be a fight!' said Gord enthusiastically.

'That is not comforting,' said Lerarus.

They stood in silence awhile, ears straining for sounds of pursuit. Drekki's breath rushed in his ears. The hum of his suit's aetherworks foiled his hearing.

Suddenly the *Aelsling* pitched. A black shadow came out of the fog right at them.

'Metalith, dead ahead!' Adrimm hollered.

Velunti Runk put out a twin-blast evasion whoop from the horn. 'Brace! Brace! Brace!' he yelled.

'Curse it, cargo-master, show some sense! Less noise!' yelled Drekki. 'So much for silent running,' he grumbled. He locked his boots' magnetic soles to the deck and grabbed Lerarus' hand. 'Hold on,' he said.

The *Aelsling* tipped violently to the side. The crew's boots kept them more or less upright, but Lerarus fell, dangling from Drekki's grip as the ship dived almost perpendicular. The metalith sailed noiselessly past them, tall and black, an orphaned cliff.

Evrokk was good, but no one is that good. He clipped the rock. The *Aelsling* rang. Loosened stones bounced over the gunwales, ricocheting off the deck and punching holes into the fog. Drekki waited for the raw, metallic scraping that would signify a serious collision, but it did not come The metalith sailed on its lonely course. The ship righted itself.

Lerarus got her balance back. She was breathing quickly.

'All right?' Drekki asked.

She nodded tentatively.

'Stay close,' he reminded her. He marched over to the cockpit. 'A near miss.'

'Aye,' said Evrokk. He was intent on the instruments. 'There'll be more of them about, for sure. These airs are murderous with reefs.'

'Aye, aye, I know,' said Drekki. 'Can you scry?' he asked Lerarus.

'No,' said the mage.

'Then it'll be down to Trokwi and Otherek,' said Drekki. 'Get up there, little chap, scout around, get us a picture of this shoal.' The drillbill nodded its metal head, and flew off. 'Take us slow, Evrokk, just in case.'

'Aye-aye, captain.' Evrokk threw levers. Pressure bled off from valves near the stern. Steam plumes glittered with spent aether.

A boulder rolled out of the fog. It struck the forward engine plangently.

'Blasted luck,' said Drekki. 'There's another already, and where there are two there are lots. Crew! Skyhooks and gaffs, get to the prow gunwales, ready to fend. Bokko, up top please. Adrimm, go with him.'

A clatter broke the sodden silence. Arkanauts snatched poles from racks on the gunwales and crowded the prow.

'Not a one to hit the statue of my Aelsling!' said Drekki.

'Thirteen degrees off the edgeward board!' yelled someone. Ildrin, Drekki thought.

A boulder the size of a gargant came out of the murk, twisting on its axis in nervous pirouettes. As it passed it sprayed water on the deck. Evtorr poked it away, swearing loudly as the rotation twisted the gaff in his hands.

More dark boulders followed. Some were the size of ogors, and bald, others were large enough to support copses of trees or hosts of dripping ferns. One floating by at head height was crowned with tightly furled leaves. In each was a cupful of water, and a resident frog staring out.

Hushed calls passed back and forth between the crew as they relayed instructions to one another.

Drekki looked up suddenly. 'Anyone else hear that?'

A rushing sound, a captive wind. Air displaced by a hull.

Otherek came shimmying down a line from the aether-tops. 'It's them. The pursuit. I saw their keel disturbing the mist. They came right over.'

Drekki rushed from one side of his ship to the other, head tilted, thinking fast. 'The rocks are moving slowly relative to us,' he said. His whispered commands were sharpened by the fog. 'Everyone, not a word. Evrokk, dead stop, no signal!'

A massive wall of stone appeared ahead, no more than fifty raad-fathoms away. Hushed commands were passed on by Gunterr, and the crew lined up around Aelsling's statue, skyhooks presented like a wall of pikes. Drekki could forgive them jostling the figurehead this once.

The airscrews cut dead, then reversed. The *Aelsling* slowed.

'Brace!' Gunterr hissed. 'Prepare to take shock!'

The cliff loomed up. A shadow at first, then features resolved, planes and angles, plants wedged in cracks, trickles of water, until they were so close the coarse grain of the stone leapt out clear as day. Drekki gritted his teeth.

The *Aelsling* coasted, no more than a few grunti a second. The endrins hissed.

Hooks and points clinked on the rock. Duardin muscles strained. Muttered curses disturbed the air. The figurehead's hammer touched the stone. It bent by several degrees with a drawn-out, angry squeak.

The *Aelsling* stopped.

Drekki let out his breath.

'By the pantheon,' Lerarus breathed. 'There are rocks all around us. What have you done?'

She wasn't wrong. The mist was now full of rocks and the shadows of rocks. Although a few floated back past the ship, as they were moving slightly slower than the others, they were all heading in the same direction, caught in the circular currents of the Second Air, and now so was the *Aelsling*.

'Aye, well, they didn't name it the Skyshoals just 'cause they felt like it,' breathed Drekki. 'We'll be safe here. We're part of the reef.'

The rushing of the captive wind blew in, so close the fog stirred. Drekki heard voices. He strained his ears, failed to catch what they said. He did a quick reading with his suit aethometer. The air was soupy but breathable, so he risked taking off his helmet to hear better.

Men were shouting. The rushing sound continued. Maybe they couldn't drop their sorcerous wind. Maybe they struggled at this depth.

'Whoever's at the helm ain't no Kharadron, that's for sure,' he said. 'They're moving too fast. They're at risk of foundering if they keep that up.'

Their wake cut above, so perilously close they all saw the rippling fog this time. The crew held their breath.

Then the ship sailed past, heading deeper into the reefs. The noise dwindled. The dance of the vapour died.

Drekki let out a breath he didn't realise he'd been holding, prematurely, as it happened.

'They're coming back round!' said Urdi.

The rush of wind came at them again. The first explosion followed shortly after. Bright balls of white light roared through the fog, sending it into wild perturbations. Where they contacted solid matter, they detonated in polychromatic explosions. Three hit the metalith the ship sheltered behind. Rock showered over the ship. They came down to the left and the right, rocking the *Aelsling* with shockwaves. Drekki flinched as a fireball howled past the ship, turning cold fog into hot steam. It missed them by a handful of raadfathoms.

The one that followed was directly on target.

'Ware! Ware!' Adrimm called.

'Prepare for impact!' Gunterr roared. He said something else that the fireball's approach obliterated.

Ancestral memories of rockfalls gripped the duardin. They tucked in their heads, each one becoming a small boulder of flesh. Only Gord and Lerarus remained upright, the ogor gaping, childlike.

Lerarus went into action.

The fireball exploded. No fire, no pain. Drekki unfolded.

Gord was looking up, his jaw slack in wonder. 'Cor!' he said. 'Look at that!'

A dome of pale flames held back the charges. Lerarus had her staff held above her head horizontally. Her free hand traced lines of fire. Muffled incantations sounded behind her breathing mask.

The fire boiled out, then in, sucked to the point of implosion.

The *Aelsling* rocked, but gently. The enemy sailed on.

Lerarus set her staff back on the deck. She leaned on it heavily. 'That,' she panted, 'falls within the remit of my mastery.'

'Impressive,' growled Kedren.

Ball lightning dropped like rain to the stern. Flashes lit up the cloud bank. The enemy turned about again.

'They'll find us. They'll hit us,' said Adrimm up front. 'We should run!'

'Hold your tongue, Fair-weather!' said Drekki. 'Nobody move a muscle.' He cocked his head, following the enemy's progress. The explosions came nearer, but none hit. The barquentine passed off the coreward board. He nodded. 'Aye, as I thought. They're quartering the reef, seeking to flush us out. They've done this bit. They won't be back over here. They're sailing blind.'

'Maybe Adrimm's right. Might be time to dash,' said Umherth. He gripped his gun tightly. 'They could have seen the wizard's fire.'

'We wait,' said Drekki. 'They'll not get us now, you'll see.'

A few minutes of magical bombing passed. It suddenly stopped. Directionless sounds of distress filled up the fog: cracking wood, rending metal, and panicked shouts.

'There we are,' said Drekki. 'That's not a mistake I'd ever make, dropping bombs into a treacherous reef like that. Keeps you from looking where you're going. Hey, Bokko,' he called softly. The endrinrigger came immediately. 'Into your endrin and up you go, scope 'em out. Don't let them see you.'

Velunti and Khenna helped Bokko into his one-duardin dirigible rig: a miniaturised endrin globe dangling a stiff harness. Once secured, Bokko rose up and vanished into the mist, the aether-endrin puttering.

'Where's your mechanical bird?' whispered Lerarus.

'He'll be fine,' said Drekki. 'He'll be back soon to let me know the extent of the shoal, where it's thick, where it's deadly. Once we get Bokko's news we can plan our next move.' He lowered his voice. 'Adrimm is right, we do have to run, but when is the trick. He'd dash out now, and then we'd be seen.' He shrugged. 'That's why I'm captain and he'll never be.'

Sure enough, Trokwi returned a few moments later. He twittered into the captain's ear.

'Evrokk, get this down,' he said to the helmsduardin. Evrokk pulled up a notepad that was attached by a chain to the cockpit.

'Ready!' he said.

'Depth below, one hundred twenty,' said Drekki. 'Width three hundred. Height above, ninety-eight. Large rocks to the fore, some substantial under the skeg, lighter swarms below that.' He paused to let Trokwi tweet a little more. 'Gravel tail behind bent corewards five hundred raadfathoms long. We've dropped deep in, right into the middle of this reef.'

'What now?' said Lerarus.

'We wait and see,' said Otherek.

Bokko came back. He put down on the stern. Drekki went to him. The endrinrigger pulled off his helm, showing a gleeful face.

'They've run aground, captain! Venting gas from one of their floats. It'll take them hours to get off that rock, and they'll be limping when they do. Their chasing days are done.'

'We should go in for the kill,' said Lerarus. 'Eliminate them.'

'Yeah! Listen to the wizard lady,' said Gord, who still hoped for a fight. 'Smack bash.' He ground his teeth within his helm. 'Then chomp.'

'Your advice is noted,' said Drekki, who hadn't the faintest intention of taking pointers from Gord. 'Bokko, what's the tactical view?'

Bokko sucked his teeth. They were very white, and very broad. 'I dunno, captain. There's a whole bunch of them. Look well armed. Ship's carrying cannon too, five to a broadside, look like *don hundraki*.[22]

'They'll not get through our hull,' said Otherek.

'Arrr, but fighting will call any harkraken that might be around, to be sure, if that bombardment did not,' said Umherth. 'They're everywhere round here, everywhere, I tells ye!'

'Umherth! Less of the monster talk,' said Drekki. 'Stop rolling your eyes like that. You look mad.'

'He is mad,' grumbled Adrimm.

'Then we fight,' said Gord.

'No we don't,' said Drekki. 'It's too risky. One bit of damage in the wrong place on the *Aelsling*, and the whole thing's off. We go deeper. Bokko, go over the side again, help Evtorr guide us from below. Last thing I want is a hard landing on a large isle. Though we can weather a few little lumps, a crash is not on today's menu. Semaphore only, no shouting! Urdi, Ildrin, watch coreward and edgeward boards if you please.'

'Aye, captain!' they responded.

Drekki marched to a bank of speaking tubes and pulled the cover off one, letting it dangle on its little chain. 'Evtorr! Eyes peeled to the prow, we're going lower.' Finally, he called out to Evrokk. 'Reduce lofting power by thirty per cent. Sink as fast as you dare. Listen to your brother and Bokko.'

'We'll be lucky not to strike and put a hole in the hull,' muttered Evrokk, moving to obey just the same.

Drekki grinned.

'You've been with me long enough to know just how lucky I am, Evrokk Bjarnisson. We'll not hit anything, because I'm Drekki Flynt! Now dive!'

---

22 | Kharadrid: A hundrak is slightly more than a pound in weight. Don is ten in both variants of the dwarf speech. Don hundraki therefore refers to cannons that fire cannonballs of about eleven pounds.

CHAPTER EIGHT

AN UNWELCOME ENCOUNTER

Laughter filled the great cabin. The captain's bed was folded away. The long table was out, laden with meat and ale. The benches had been pulled up out of the floor, and on them the duardin sat elbow to elbow, Lerarus slotted like a sheet of paper between Umherth and Drekki.

'You needn't look so uncomfortable, wizard,' said Otherek, waving a roasted drumstick at her. 'You're our guest. We're a welcoming crew.'

'Aye,' said Kedren. 'They even let me, a ground pounder, stay.' The crew laughed.

'That dome of fire!' Adrimm said with a beaming smile. 'What a sight! I thought we were goners.'

'You always think we're goners,' said Drekki. More laughter. Adrimm scowled.

'To the Lady Lerarus!' Evrokk shouted. He raised up his mug.

'Aye, she's useful all right,' said Hrunki.

'Lerarus!' they all cried, and clanged pewter together. There was a period of silent guzzling, then they laughed again, and again, at the slightest of things.

'They're drunk,' said Lerarus, who hardly sipped her ale. A disapproving expression had settled on her face, and did not seem apt to shift. 'Are you always drunk?'

'They're duardin, and they're letting off steam,' said Drekki. Lerarus frowned at the unfamiliar metaphor. Industry was the preserve of few places. 'Calming down,' Drekki explained. 'That episode today was enough to rattle the most level-headed of duardin.'

He picked up some meat and tore at it with his teeth. The crew were joshing and joking and taking offence. Chatting about old deeds and tall tales. They laughed and stroked their beards. But whatever they were doing, they drank.

'This isn't a crew,' Lerarus said after a few minutes' observation. She was beginning to feel the ale despite the poor measure she had drunk, and she spoke with philosophical certainty. 'You are a family.'

'We're more than that,' said Drekki, tossing the bare bone aside. He wiped his beard and gulped his beer, then finished off with a burp. 'Family is important to duardin. For we Kharadron, bonds of crew and corporation can take the place of clan blood, but it's the same thing. This is a small ship. Everyone has to pitch in, even my officers have to work the endrin tops. You get to know each other almost too well. Every one of these hard-heads would die for the others. It makes me proud.' He picked up the leg of another unfortunate fowl and set to work.

'Even Gord?' said Lerarus. She looked out the open door. Gord sat on the deck, too big to come inside, back against the cabin wall. He was working on a long iron skewer of roasted birds, equal to those consumed by all the duardin combined.

'Even Gord,' said Drekki. 'Even Adrimm, that moaning grumbaki.' He pointed him out with his chewed drumstick.

'Why do you call him Fair-weather?'

'Because when it's going well, he's all "Captain Flynt, my hero", like now, and when it's not, he's the first to complain. Isn't that right, Adrimm?' Drekki shouted.

'What?' Adrimm said, taking his ale away too quickly, spilling foam down his beard.

'Fair-weather, aren't you?' Drekki shouted.

'Aye, captain!' Adrimm shouted tipsily.

'That's all right though,' shouted Umherth and staggered to his feet. 'Because he's got...'

'The second highest rating from the academy at Barak-Mhornar!' everyone bellowed together and laughed uproariously. Adrimm hunkered down and muttered.

'Oh yes! I'd forgotten that, seeing as he never mentions it,' said Drekki to more laughter. 'So, wizard, maybe some introductions. You don't know everyone yet.' He cast about for the right place to start. 'We've Velunti Runk, who you know. Silly hair, remember? Third mate and ship's cargo-master, also serves as purser. Raise your pint, Velunti!'

Velunti saluted. 'Purser and cargo-master? Surgeon, third mate, and cook too. I do everything round here. Maybe you should pay me more,' he said. The others cheered.

'More money? More beer!' they cried. 'More beer!'

'All right, all right.' Velunti staggered up, nearly knocking Adrimm off the bench. 'I'll fetch a cask, if it's all right with you, captain?'

'Aye, lad,' said Drekki. 'More ale for all of us!'

More cheers. Velunti bustled out.

'Who've we got next?' Drekki said. 'Evrokk! Yes, Evrokk. The helmsduardin, brother of Evtorr, who is out on watch.'

'Evtorr's the poet?' said Lerarus.

'The terrible poet,' Drekki corrected. 'They look a lot alike, it doesn't help they wear their beards in the same plait. Next to

Evrokk is Otherek Zhurafon, oldbeard, first mate and aether-khemist, then Kedren Grunnsson, our Dispossessed runesmith.' Kedren was pale yet ruddy-skinned, his beard tinged blue, with a shock of unruly hair of the same distinctive colour, so he stood out from the largely dark Kharadron.

Drekki continued around the table. As he introduced them they acknowledged the mage according to their character – a discreet tip of a pint pot, a roar of laughter, a mocking bow, a belch. 'Gunterr Borrki, master-at-arms. Next to you is Umherth Davrok, a madder old duardin you'll never find.'

Umherth bared his teeth, growled, hammered the table with both fists, and barked like a dog.

'Then that's Hrunki, her name's Tordis, but only Umherth ever calls her that.' Drekki leaned in and whispered loudly, 'They're definitely not sweet on each other.' He winked. 'Then Urdi Duntsson, our romantic adventurer. If he offers to tell you any stories, don't accept. Some of them are… well, questionable. The worst of them would make your beard fall out, if you had one.'

Urdi grinned. 'Shall I tell the one about the aelven maid and the–'

'No!' everyone shouted.

'Now, did I leave anyone out?' said Drekki.

'You left this out, captain!' Umherth let out a ripping fart. The duardin cheered.

Velunti, bearing a keg on his shoulder, walked right back into it. He flapped at his nose with his free hand. 'Umherth! Find some manners, we have guests.' He put the barrel down and tapped it.

'No fear, my chamber's empty. If you want another round you'll have to give me more ammunition!' Umherth cackled and waved his pint pot around his head, causing the others to duck.

'Nobody wants another shot of that,' said Adrimm.

Lerarus wrinkled her nose. The stench was quite something.

'First time among a lot of duardin, eh?' said Drekki. 'Some of you umgi find us uncouth, and we're skyfarers, proper fighters and carousers, not like those soft-bellied Dispossessed that live among men.'

'Oi!' shouted Kedren. 'That's me you're talking about!'

The others laughed. Drekki shushed him with a flap of his hand, got up and waved his pot around. 'We're the farers of Barak-Thrund, the children of Barak-Mhornar, the worst of the lot!'

'*Khazuk!*'[23] they all bellowed, and guzzled their ale. A quiet of gulps and happy sighs followed. Velunti bustled about. He had a cloth folded over his hand like Drommssonsson, and made a mock of courtly fuss as he collected up the pots and refilled them.

'So you best get used to it, wizard,' Drekki said. Velunti gave him a fresh drink, which he drained straightaway. He slammed the vessel down. 'Right. Business calls. Time to relieve Ildrin, Khenna, Bokko and Evtorr. As much as I can't abide his poems, he needs to eat sometime.' He smirked. 'I'll relieve them, then I'll relieve myself.'

'I'll come too,' she said.

'Need some air?'

'Something like that,' she said, eyeing the increasingly rowdy crew.

'Suit yourself,' Drekki said. 'Cold out, mind. Though we're cruising the upper Second Air, high currents plunge and stop here, brings the upper chill with it.' He stopped at the door. 'Hrunki, Umherth, Adrimm, finish your ale and gobble your meat, you're out on next watch, which starts' – he ostentatiously consulted his pocket watch – 'right about now.'

'Aye, captain!' they said, and wolfed down their food.

'What about me? I'm on rotra... on rattro...' said Evrokk. He frowned. 'I'm on the plan.'

---

23 | Khazalid/Kharadrid: Time-honoured duardin toast.

'You're a loose endrin globe right now, Evrokk. Too drunk. Stay in here. You've earned it.'

Evrokk burped, to general hilarity.

'I'll go instead,' said Urdi, and set out immediately. 'I have to fetch my kit. I'll meet you on deck.'

'A little earthy, aren't they?' said Drekki affectionately.

'That is a way of putting it,' said Lerarus.

Drekki picked up his massive two-handed aether-axe from where it was propped up by the door. 'You can never be too careful,' he said, and they headed outside.

Lerarus shivered the moment they stepped through the door. It was a lot colder outside the cabin's fug. She half looked like she wanted to go back in, but there was another uproarious cheer and she stepped away, nearly tripping over Gord.

The ogor was content, eating the birds, bones and all. He was so absorbed with his food that he didn't hear them approach.

Drekki rested a hand on Gord's shoulder. 'You all right, my giant friend?'

Gord looked up and grinned greasily. 'Aye, captain,' he said.

'Why do you follow him?' Lerarus asked.

'Why do you want to know that?' said Gord, puzzled.

'You're an ogor. Up in the sky,' she said. 'I've not heard of that before.'

Gord chuckled. 'Not so strange. I know other Maneaters who sail the sea or sail the air. I know ones who travel the realms in great wheeled castles!' He stuck a fat finger into his mouth, wiggled the nail in a gap in his teeth, drew it out, and sucked a strand of gristle from it. 'It's not about where, or who, or why. Maneaters follow the mawpath. It's always for the eating. The Gulping God demands a life of feeding,' he said. 'Food is worship. The Gulping God says so. When the captain saved me, he showed me that the shoals is the biggest mawpath of the lot. So much to eat! There's never a bad meal with Captain Flynt, and such tasty variety.'

'Something for everyone up in the shoals,' said Drekki. 'As you were, Gord.' They moved off.

'You saved him?'

'I did. Kind of. From hobgrots. It's a long story. Another time, maybe.'

'He seems clever for one of his kind.'

'He is,' said Drekki. 'But don't get excited.' He dropped his voice. 'He can be shockingly dim.'

'Isn't he your friend?'

'He is! One of the very best.' Drekki wrinkled his brow. 'Do you think I'm being cruel, being honest?' he said. 'I'm not. I have to know everyone through and through. Their strengths and weaknesses, what makes them happy or sad. What motivates them and what stokes their fury. Everyone has to give their best here, Lady Lerarus, whatever that is. You must know that. You're the mistress of your own life, I can see that. You were born to command.'

'It's not quite like that,' she said quietly.

They went to the helm. Drekki tapped Bokko on the shoulder and told him to eat. Khenna and Evtorr were next.

'Where's Ildrin?' he asked the poet.

'Last I saw he was patrolling the deck, captain,' said Evtorr. 'Heading to the prow.'

'How long ago?'

'Three minutes, I'd say.'

'Strange,' said Drekki. 'He knows it's change of watch. Is he still there? I can't see anything in this fog.'

'He's there,' said Lerarus.

She pointed out a dark, duardin shape knelt at the prow. It looked over its shoulder, face cowled, saw Drekki and Lerarus, then hurried off, disappearing in front of the turret.

'Ildrin? Ildrin! What are you doing?' Drekki called. The fog deadened his voice.

Ildrin appeared at the edgeward board.

'I'm sorry, captain… I was coming in but I thought I saw something,' he said, looking out into the fog. 'Movement. Gone now. It could be harkraken.'

'Down at the prow?'

Ildrin frowned. 'I wasn't down at the prow. I was over by the gunwales. The movement was that way, off the edgeward board.' He pointed.

'Weren't you now,' said Drekki suspiciously. He stared at Ildrin. 'Captain?'

'By the prow.'

'No, captain. Like I said, I was by the turret. Captain, is everything–'

'Go eat,' said Drekki.

'Thank you, captain,' said Ildrin, and hurried off.

'Something funny about that one. Why did he lie?' said Drekki.

'Did he lie?' said Lerarus. 'He got here very quickly, if it was him down at the front.'

'Prow,' Drekki corrected automatically.

Lerarus made a noise of annoyance. 'My point is, it was probably someone else. It would have taken him at least a few more seconds to get here from there.'

'Maybe. This fog plays tricks on the eyes,' said Drekki.

'I don't like it,' said Lerarus, and shivered. 'I could burn it off. I might.'

'Don't,' said Drekki. 'This fog is our friend. We can't be seen. When it forms, it's stable, predictable. The Second Air meets the high plunging Third, one warmer, one colder, so you get fog. It's the best hiding place you could wish for.'

'Anything could be out there.' She looked into the uncertain night. 'Ildrin said he saw movement.'

'Are you worried about harkraken? Ha!' said Drekki. 'Ildrin is spooked. He's been listening to Umherth with his bellyaching about sky monsters. Don't you start too. I've not seen a harkraken at this altitude for years. We'll be fine.'

Lerarus took a step back. 'Really?' Her eyes went wide.

Drekki turned around to see a long, silent tentacle descending at speed. He leapt forward, tackling Lerarus around her skinny middle, and bore her down to the ground.

The tentacle hit the deck with a resounding boom, then withdrew.

'Fine, in the face of the evidence I'll admit I was wrong,' said Drekki. He drew in a deep breath. 'Harkraken!' he bellowed.

A slobbering, screeching, clashing rattled off the hull, and a score of tentacles erupted skywards, wrapping themselves around the shrouds, pulling at the fittings. Delicate pieces came free as the biggest harkraken Drekki had ever seen hauled itself out of the murk.

The crew stumbled from the great cabin. They snatched up their guns and opened fire as they emerged. They were drunk, and aimed poorly, but enough bullets punched into soft, molluscan flesh that the tentacles reared back like a nest of snakes, each for itself, divided and alone. Where they withdrew from the metal their toothed suckers left scratches.

A good many of the bullets spanged from the endrin globes, and Drekki called a ceasefire.

'Try to aim straight!' he hollered. 'An unlucky shot in the endrin and we'll all be dead. That goes double for you, Gord!'

'Nothing happened last time,' said Gord, which was true. The patch from his wayward shot was there, bold as the brass it was stamped from.

'Not helpful!' said Drekki.

They waited, tense. The rigging ran with condensation.

'What is it?' asked Umherth. He hurried out last; it had taken time to get his volley gun prepared.

'Harkraken,' said Drekki.

'I told you! I did tell you!'

'Shh!' said Drekki. 'It's gone underneath.'

An impact shook the ship, staggering the crew.

'It's coming up!' Drekki shouted. 'Prepare to fire!' Then he added, 'And shoot straight!'

The harkraken's bulbous head rose over the side of the *Aelsling*. Giant, yellow eyes with slot pupils rolled in a boneless face. A long beard of tentacles hung from the front of its mantle, each thick as a duardin is stout, and rolling with a ceaseless motion. Flotation sacs of thin skin patterned with veins pulsed at the rear of the head, in front of which a pair of fleshy nozzles protruded either side, puffing air to direct the beast's flight.

The harkraken's limbs crashed down in a writhing knot, sweeping across the deck and swatting duardin aside. Evtorr was knocked unconscious. Gord was turned about, tottering like a high-wire artiste on the point of losing his balance. Otherek slammed into the rails, only just catching himself before he tumbled over into the depthless sky. Umherth let off an uncontrolled burst of aether-fire as he was flipped head over heels. A line of wet explosions stitched up the harkraken's face, and it gave out a sucking screech. Bullets ricocheted from the forward endrin, each one leaving a deep indentation, like a finger punched into dough.

'For the love of Grungni, Umherth, be careful!' Bokko shouted.

Adrimm dragged the stunned Umherth back under the forward endrin. A tentacle struck the deck where he'd lain with a slap that lifted up rivets. The tentacle convulsed, dragged back, and the thing hauled itself forward, until it was half onto the deck, bending the rails and tipping the ship edgeward. The unconscious Evtorr slid towards the creature, jamming fast under the rail on the brink of the drop.

Lerarus sent a blast of fire at the beast. It seared the thing's flesh, filling the air with the smell of seafood. It was not discouraged.

'My brother, my brother!' Evrokk yelled, and dived for his kin. A tentacle found him, rolled itself around his waist and lifted him aloft. Evrokk shouted, and with a wriggle managed to draw his arkanaut's cutter, but bad angles meant he struggled to get in a blow.

Gord roared and punched his daggerfist into the root of a limb. That seemed to hurt the harkraken, for a whistling rasp sounded from under its webbed skirts. Propelled by rage as much as by the foul air gusting from its siphons, the creature came further onto the ship, causing it to list even more, and Gord was pinned by its muscular skirt. He carried on punching, until the flesh around him was in ribbons, and he was dyed black with blood.

Gunterr rounded up the crew with a series of powerful shouts, and had them set up a crossfire. The beast was impossible to miss. Glowing aether-bullets smacked into rubbery hide, but seemed to do little more than annoy it. Lerarus yelled searing words and slammed another line of fire into the head. Golden eyes swivelled in her direction. A tentacle snatched her from the deck. Her staff clattered away, her incantations reduced to useless, breathless gasps.

'This is a job for axes, not guns,' said Kedren, pulling his handaxe from the loop on his belt.

'I concur,' said Drekki, hefting his own, aether-powered twohander. 'Trokwi, go for the eyes!'

The drillbill speared at the harkraken's face, drill spinning. Tentacles waved all over the place, smacking duardin aside. Drekki watched them move, seeking a pattern, timing his strike.

'On my mark, ground pounder.' Drekki counted out the sways of the limbs. 'One… two… three… Charge!'

The duardin ran at the beast. Runes flared in the foggy night on the blades of both weapons. Kedren swung at the tentacle crushing Evrokk, severing it with two blows. Splashes of black blood sprayed up the globes and sizzled on the hot metal round the cooling vents. Evrokk and the severed tentacle fell hard; the limb uncoiled, and tossed about on the deck.

Drekki went after Lerarus. He hewed the tip from a tentacle questing for his head, ducked another, jumped a third. Lerarus' struggles were growing weaker. She strained desperately, trying one final time to free herself, then drooped unconscious over the crushing coil.

The harkraken was being driven back by the efforts of the crew. The tentacle holding Lerarus withdrew over the void. In a moment it could be gone. It was not unknown for harkraken to conduct lightning raids for food, leaving a ship a few crew lighter.

'Oh no you don't!' Drekki said. He jumped clear over the gunwales, axe back. His legs pedalled thin air, trying to extend the range of his leap. Shreds of fog sped by. Below him was nothing, nothing at all.

With a cry, Drekki slammed his axe into the tentacle, burying the head up to its butt. Runes burned into the harkraken's flesh, cooking the fluids welling up from the wound. He used the axe as a handle to haul himself up onto the limb, and wrapped his legs about it.

The tentacle swung wildly, attempting to dislodge him. His beard blew back up onto his face and he spluttered it aside. 'Grungni alive, what do I do now?' he said. He hadn't planned this far ahead.

Gord squirmed free, and commenced punching the beast over and over. As often happened, he'd forgotten his pistol in the excitement. Umherth staggered back onto his feet. Adrimm helped brace him against the tilt of the deck. So steadied, the oldbeard opened fire. A storm of cerulean and gold blazed around the monster's face, the light flashing off Trokwi's metal feathers as he dived repeatedly at its eyes.

The mantle of the harkraken rolled aside, showing more of the pulsing bags behind its head.

Drekki cupped a hand around his mouth. 'Go for the flotation sacs!' he shouted. 'Knock it out of the air!'

Umherth was roaring and firing, old maniac that he was, but Adrimm caught the command, elbowing the oldbeard until he stopped then gesturing at the sacs. Drekki had to get the mage before Umherth burst them.

'Now or never, Drekki old lad,' Drekki said. He wrenched out the axe. The beast hissed. The tentacle whipped back and forth. Drekki clung on so hard his thighs ached, crawling up until he was within reach of Lerarus. She was pale, hardly breathing. He reached back with his axe, and swung, cutting at the tentacle. Runes carved into the bite of the blade shone. Runes of sharpness, cutting, speed, fire and hardness: gifts from Kedren. The flesh parted, skin peeling back, showing alien anatomy. A final swipe, and the tentacle fell.

Drekki lunged for Lerarus. He caught her by the shoulder, his hand bunching in the fabric of her clothing. The severed tentacle squirmed around the mage, the weight of it dragging at Drekki's muscles; then it fell away, and his load lightened by a half.

'Now!' shouted Drekki.

Umherth opened fire. Blue trails thwacked into the skin of the harkraken. One of its eyes exploded as the trail of gunfire moved up the head. Umherth had found his aim.

The sac closest to Drekki collapsed. Acrid gas billowed, and the beast went wild with pain. It reared up, webbed skirt spread in a threat display, exposing its clacking beak. The tentacle stump Drekki clung to swung over the deck, then back, then in again, smashing the captain against the shrouds of the aft endrin. Lerarus' coat slipped in his fist.

The harkraken's siphons were roaring jets of stinking air. Clouds of gaseous ink spilled into the fog, turning the pale night to utter darkness.

Again the tentacle smashed against the shrouds. The harkraken was trying to wipe Drekki off. He did his best to keep the mage free from the impact. Human bones broke so easily.

Drekki tried to launch himself towards his ship in a manner he hoped would be dramatic, but with Lerarus weighing him down, all he managed was a flop off the tentacle. He swung wildly with his axe at the side of the ship. It connected with the shroud, parting the metal horizontals with teeth-jarring twangs. Kedren's runes were too good, and the axe sliced its way through them all, and he fell.

Drekki clenched his fingers around the firing lever for the axe's built-in harpoon and squeezed, sending it upward as he and the mage dropped.

For a fraction of a second, Drekki thought his luck was done, and he would fall with the unconscious Lerarus through the Skyshoals forever, though actually, the much-mentioned forever was probably fanciful. They'd die in any number of interesting ways: eaten by sky beasts or birds, dashed to pieces on a metalith, choked on poisonous air, or if they were really unlucky, sucked into the Eye of Testudinous and whatever in Grimnir's name that did to you. All these fates and a few more besides raced through Drekki's mind.

The harpoon arched up, and down, hit the rigging and whirled itself around and around, each revolution faster as the line shortened. With a wrench, Drekki came to a stop. He dangled from the haft, Lerarus dangled from him. He gave a wild whoop.

'I'm not falling! I'm alive! I'm Drekki Flynt!'

With great care, he used his little finger to flip the winding switch. The small aether-motor beneath the axe head growled, and the cable wound in, hauling him and Lerarus back up to the ship.

As they emerged over the gunwales, Urdi saw them and rushed to help, pulling Drekki's sleeve. Together they got Lerarus up, and soon Drekki was back on the deck, shaking, aching, but alive.

'You all right, captain?' Urdi yelled, for the battle was still noisily proceeding.

'What a ride,' Drekki said. He got up. Lerarus moaned. 'She's alive then. Good.'

He assessed the situation. The harkraken was panicking. Pseudo-pods everywhere. The beak rattled.

'Why doesn't it run?' he shouted. 'Why doesn't it try to... Oh.' The ink in the air was clearing. Now he saw. 'Gord.'

The ogor had hold of one of the tentacles. He'd wrapped it around his midriff like an anchorman in a tug-of-war. He was leaning back, feet planted firmly on the deck, and for once it looked like he'd remembered his magnetic boots. His fingers dug into the flesh. The beast was going nowhere through no choice of its own.

'Good eating on this, captain,' grunted Gord. 'Not letting that go. Harkraken rings are best deep fried,' he added, smacking his lips. 'My favourite.'

'Fair enough,' said Drekki, his profiteer's mind already esti-mating the amount of meat he could salvage and pickle. Fifty barrels? Fifty, he confirmed to himself, then got on with tot-ting up the value. He liked what he calculated. 'Skyhooks!' he commanded. 'Harpoons! Hold it fast. Gunterr, plug it in the head with the cannon. Let's get this done. Fish dinners for all, after this.'

He searched about for his master-at-arms. Gunterr was ahead of Drekki's thinking, and was already boosting Hrunki into the turret.

Bokko brought out a heavy harpoon launcher. With a thump of aether-charged gas it launched, spearing the creature squarely in the face. The harkraken shrieked, grasped the shaft with a tentacle, but could not tug the barbed lance out. Bokko reeled the line tight. The crew swiped at its limbs with hooks tied to ropes, sinking them deep, hauling on them, pulling tentacles taut.

Gunterr was at the turret's side, shouting something that couldn't be heard over the harkraken's gurgling. The gun whirred round, pitched down.

'Ha ha!' cried Drekki, shaking his fist. 'You'll rue the day you ever crossed the path of Drekki–'

The gun boomed. Aethershot screamed through the air, a hardening gold streak that blasted into the head, which exploded.

Offal of a most disagreeable kind showered all over the ship. Flat rags of flesh slapped hard against metal. Goop sloshed out through the deck drains, but not before Drekki was doused in it, head to foot. Harkraken blood, brains and bile.

'Flynt,' he finished weakly.

CHAPTER NINE

THE KRUND AND RIKSSON MINING CO.

Rocks floated out into the pebbly swarm thousands of raad-fathoms wide that surrounded the Krund and Riksson Mining Company operation. A sphere of empty space quarried out of an archipelago of metaliths, leaving a sky orange with dispersing chippings and dust. Aether-gold was so thick on the air everyone could smell it, not just Otherek. Flotillas of fat-bellied trawlers swept slowly across the mining ground, filters extended. Others, already full-laden, fared in lines towards a kronvoy of immense krontankers waiting miles out for loading, their volatile cargoes well clear of the blasting zone.

'Fare steady,' Drekki told his crew, scanning the scene with his telescope. He was looking at a huge metalith off at the edge. Kharadron demolition ships clustered around it, tiny by the side of the rock. The ale bubbles of one-duardin dirigible rigs bobbed around. Aether-torches flickered up the cliffs. Strings of lights plotted lines of access for blasting crews.

It was good land. There was a forest atop of the metalith. Nobody was paying much attention to that. Duardin hearts were set on the wealth within. A ring of small platforms bore flashing beacons and tolling bells to warn shipping off.

'They're prepping that isle for detonation. Keep a good hundred raadfathoms between us and those platforms,' Drekki ordered. 'Still can't see the operations base, mind.' He tutted. Last thing he wanted was to spend all day cruising this dusty waste.

'This is where you get your magic gas from,' said Lerarus.

'Aether is the produce of science,' said Otherek, affronted.

'It is,' said Drekki. 'Take a look.' He handed his telescope to the mage.

'They're going to blow that whole island up?' she said. 'That's... frightening.'

'They are,' said Drekki. 'Quite soon, too. We're in for a show.'

'Your people are getting too ambitious,' Kedren said, putting his own scope away. 'No race should wield such power.'

'What about magic?' asked Drekki. 'That's pretty destructive.'

'There are few runes struck that could level a world,' said Kedren.

'I suppose you agree,' said Drekki to Lerarus. 'But you're a mage, all the flash and bang you like.'

'Magic is an art,' she said. 'It took me years of study to learn my skills. Only a gifted few can wield it. The kind of person that could break an island like that is born once in a thousand years. Our rarity limits the damage we can wreak. This is...' She lowered the telescope. 'This is indiscriminate.'

'We have to go where Grungni's breath is,' said Otherek. 'Once the air seams are exhausted, the only way to get it is to blast open metaliths. Deposits inside hold them up, you see.'

'Aye, and then the rock loses buoyancy and falls through the shoals, causing who knows what havoc below.' Kedren shook his head. 'Reckless.'

'There's nothing down there,' said Otherek.

'Could be. Duardin have survived in stranger places,' said Kedren.

Otherek put a hand on his friend's arm. 'All the old karaks are gone, Kedren. You saw the last one, your ancestral home. They're all like that now. There's nothing below but the Second Air and the toxic clouds of the First.'

'Magic should not be industrialised,' said Lerarus.

'It's not magic!' protested Otherek. 'It's just a resource, like coal. Aether is a vital element to our civilisation. Without it nothing would function. This appears destructive, but no aether-gold, no Kharadron. Think of the progress we've made. It's of benefit to us all.'

Kedren harrumphed. 'There are other ways to fly,' he said.

'Not better ways,' said Drekki.

They came closer to the blast zone, within easy distance of the beacon platforms. A horn blared, and a Grundstok gunhauler undocked from one of the larger ones, moving quickly to intercept them. The boat soon drew alongside. The guild gunner manning the turret connected a megaphone to his helm.

'You are entering an active mining site,' he hailed. 'Power down your endrins and halt.'

'Best do as he says, Evrokk,' said Drekki.

The *Aelsling* slowed. The gunhauler swooped round over the prow, and doubled back.

'Prepare to be boarded!' the gunner hailed.

'Right, sonny, by one of you? Big talk,' said Umherth.

The hauler came in quick. The gunner got himself out of the turret and threw across a line. Drekki's crew pulled it in and tied off the boat alongside.

'Permission to come aboard?' the gunner said. Now he wasn't bellowing at them through a megaphone, he appeared nervous.

'Do I have a choice?' said Drekki.

'No, well,' said the gunner, even more nervously. 'Not really.' The rail gate was opened. He leapt across, nimble as his craft. 'I'm going to need your name,' he asked.

Evtorr held out Drekki's warrant papers. Drekki took them and presented them with a flourish.

'Captain Drekki Flynt.'

The gunner's grin was obvious in his voice. '*The* Drekki Flynt? I knew it was you! You're really Drekki Flynt? The thief of the egg of Ladonirkir, the dragon-speaker, the grot-scourge?' He took the papers. His hands were shaking.

'The one and the same,' said Drekki, and struck a heroic pose, legs wide and belly out. 'You recognised the ship, didn't you? Go on, you did.'

The gunner became bashful. 'Well, the *Aelsling* is unmistakeable, isn't she? What with the figurehead, and the ogor.' He bowed solemnly. 'It is an honour to meet you. We were keen to come out and beat the others, isn't that true, Vana?'

The pilot looked up from her instruments.

'Grungni and Grimnir, you are embarrassing,' she said. 'Do your job! This isn't some privateers' meet and greet.'

'Yes, yes, sorry. Only I love the stories.' He shrugged. 'Umm, Vana not so much.'

'Some of them are even true,' said Drekki, twinkling as hard as he could through a quarter of an inch of reinforced steel. Nobody ever gave him enough credit for being able to do that.

The gunner went through his papers, stamped them, pressed his aether-seal to them, then pulled out a form from a pouch and had Drekki sign.

'They all appear to be in order, Captain Flynt,' said the gunner. He handed the papers back and saluted. 'And, if I could... Could you...?' The gunner pinned his gun under his arm so he could scrabble about in his pocket. From it, he produced a small autograph book, which he held out hopefully. 'Only if it's no bother,' he added hurriedly.

Kedren tutted at him.

'Let the ground swallow us all up now,' said Vana.

'I'm with you on that,' Kedren said.

'Of course! Of course!' said Drekki, delighted to be recognised. He opened the book and flicked through, looking for a blank page. 'I see you've some of the most famous skycaptains in here.'

'Only one or two…' the gunner said modestly.

'No, really,' Drekki said. 'Some of these are almost as well known as me. You've even got…' He stopped dead. In front of him in tight, painfully straight runes was a very familiar signature. 'Aelsling's mark,' he wheezed.

'Yes! If you could sign it right there, next to Aelsling's. Drekki and Aelsling Flynt, on the same page, together again!'

'A rare combination. You could sell that. It's very special,' said Kedren, with a heavy ladling of sarcasm. 'A fine profit for you, youngbeard.'

'I could never do that,' said the gunner, with a level of earnestness only the truly starstruck can attain.

'What's your name, lad?' asked Drekki.

'Sedrik, captain.' The gunner saluted, provoking another groan from his pilot.

'Get on with it, you wazzock!' she shouted.

'Then I dedicate this inscription to you,' said Drekki. He wrote *To Sedrik* in minuscule runes, then flamboyantly signed his own name four times the size of Aelsling's.

'This is such an honour.' Sedrik clasped the book to his chest. 'Blessed be my ancestors.'

'Most unduardinlike display,' grunted Kedren.

'Tell me, Sedrik, what did Aelsling say when you mentioned our bold captain?' asked Otherek.

'I met her in Barak-Mhornar. She was happy to sign my book,

as you like, but when I mentioned Drekki here... Sorry, can I call you Drekki, captain?'

The captain graciously inclined his helm. 'That is my name. You may use it.'

'She just stared at me. On account of your painful separation, I assumed. Er, I thought she was going to hit me, actually.'

'Painful separation?' said Gord, puzzled. 'But didn't you get–'

'Thanks, Gord!' said Drekki briskly. 'Ah, alas, we always miss one another. The call of adventure, you know. Someday soon we shall be together again.'

'Can we go now, Sedrik?' Vana called. 'Unlike you, I have got other things to do. Things that people are paying me for!'

Sedrik attempted a parade-ground salute, but fumbled his gun, losing what little professional composure he had until that point retained. Which, all being said, wasn't very much. 'They'll be blowing the metalith in twenty minutes or so. You need to stand off another five hundred raadfathoms until it's done. After it's blown, wait for the ejecta to fall, it takes longer than you think. Then you can proceed to the site offices. Over there.' He pointed downwind, to the edge of the zone. A metalith larger than the other remnants nestled in clouds of floating debris, the gleam of metal Kharadron structures visible on its surface.

'That's where it is!' said Drekki. 'My thanks, young Sedrik. May your faring be blessed by open skies and fine days.'

'This is such an honour,' jabbered Sedrik.

'It'll be the last you ever see, if you tell anyone about this before we're gone, do you hear?' said Kedren.

'Secret business,' said Drekki. He tapped the side of his ancestor mask's nose.

'It's not bloody secret any more, is it?' grumbled the runesmith.

Drekki shook his head. 'I'm sure it will stay so. Of the most sensitive nature, right, Sedrik? Dimsson's the name, got that?'

'Yes, Captain Flynt. I mean *Dimsson*! Captain Dimsson. I won't tell a soul,' said Sedrik.

'I suppose you want paying,' said Kedren.

'To be involved in one of your adventures is payment enough for me. Not a soul, on my oath.'

Sedrik stumbled his way off the ship. Vana gunned their engines and the gunhauler pulled away. They could hear Vana berating him until they were out of sight. Drekki and his crew waved, some more ironically than others.

'Lost love,' said Otherek. 'One day, you're going to have to own up that she left you, Drekki. It's dangerous misleading people like this.'

'I'll win her back, you'll see.'

'I'm more worried about the news of this voyage getting out,' said Kedren. 'So much for being discreet, you and your bloody hunger for fame.'

'Shut up and wave, the pair of you,' said Drekki. 'Just shut up and wave.'

The lights of aether-torches winked out on the doomed rock. Demolitions duardin flew their dirigibles back down to the waiting ships and hooked themselves up to dangling cables for a tow. Shrill whistles cut through the smog, starting a ripple of motion in the launches and lesser boats, which cut wakes in the dust. Heliograph flashes blinked from the cordon of beacon platforms, answered by the trawler fleets waiting at the perimeter. These gathered in a tight-packed rectangle, five abreast and six high, waiting to begin extraction.

'They're calling in the harvesters,' said Evtorr, interpreting the signals. 'They'll blow it now.'

'About time,' grumbled Kedren. He was determined not to enjoy this display of dangerous innovation. Instead he sat on the deck with a jeweller's loupe flipped down over his eye, carving minuscule runes into buckshot for his blunderbuss. He took great pride in enchanting each and every piece of shrapnel, and liked to vary the effect.

'Evrokk, get us ready to move,' said Drekki.

The endrins of the demolitions fleet flared, the telltale witch-light of burning aether shining through their globe ports. They hurried away, as if before a storm. When they reached a thousand raadfathoms, mournful klaxons wailed across the site.

'Here we go,' said Drekki. He nudged Lerarus. 'This is a privilege, you know. Not many humans get to see this.'

She stayed silent. She was staring at the forest atop the metalith. They were always on about fertile land in Bastion, seeing each patch of green earth in the Skyshoals as theirs by right.

Signalling flashes went back and forth between the beacons and the ships. They ceased after a pattern of three long blinks, three short ones.

'Boom,' said Evtorr.

'It's good when you keep your poems short,' said Drekki.

'One day, you're going to upset me,' said Evtorr. 'But a poet's heart is bold, a poet's heart is strong! I shall weather the outrageous things and insults of ill-fortune you cast my–'

'Wow,' said Gord.

They saw the ignition before they heard it. Plumes of dust puffed out from locations spaced two hundred raadfathoms apart on the rock, following a horizontal path around the centre and up several vertical lines. A series of pops followed a good four seconds later.

Bigger explosions ensued. Detonating aether flashed blue, like lightning. Deep scoops of material were ejected silently from the sides of the metalith, tumbled rocks pushed out by spreading showers of gravel. Again sound chased sight, and a tremendous booming hit the ship.

With a musical, rending moan, the metalith broke into pieces. Huge lumps of it flew out, almost as far as the perimeter of beacons, before gravity dragged them into steepening curves, and they plunged down through the sky. The forested top collapsed into itself, shooting up clouds of rubble with volcanic force. The sides welled out, the explosion so thick with dust it seemed the metalith was expanding. It was an illusion that lasted only a few seconds, as the billows spread and dispersed, and what seemed solid was revealed as diffuse. Land became rubble.

Boulders rained down. Some retained enough aether-gold to remain buoyant, and tumbled away in every direction. If they escaped, they would find orbits around larger islands, perhaps adding mass and aether to new lands, new continents, but most would be sucked in by grinding ships and crushed to harvest their precious, gaseous lodes.

Otherek pointed excitedly. In the clouds of dust, golden gases sparkled. Plumes of liberated aether gushed from the dirty spall of rock. Even as the explosion continued to spread, the trawlers were already moving in.

'How many of these islands do your people destroy in the course of a year?' asked Lerarus.

'A good question,' said Otherek, failing to catch the ice in Lerarus' voice. 'Maybe fifty in the Skyshoals annually. This kind of strip-mining is a new venture. It's not proved itself economical yet against standard air-seam harvesting, but as the seams were scattered during the Necroquake, they're getting thinner and so competition gets greater. It'll pay off. It's the future, they say. I hear there are big plans to scale it up.'

'Fifty lands that could be reclaimed,' said Lerarus.

'Well, maybe,' said Otherek.

'Perhaps we have more enemies than we thought,' she said.

'Steady now,' said Drekki, who did understand how she felt.

'We have a common goal. The rights and wrongs of aether-gold mining are a problem for tomorrow. We've a talisman to retrieve, in case you had forgotten.'

A shower of grit rattling off the endrins preceded the all-clear. Drekki had them underway before the echoes of the explosion died.

The headquarters metalith was a sad and dusty place, with a top planed down to a uniform flatness. It was bigger than it appeared from a distance, with most of the buildings clustered at one edge like wary animals, the rest of it occupied by piles of spoil. The port made a second group of buildings half a mile from the little town. Drekki opted to walk. Lerarus insisted on coming with him.

'You're only making yourself obvious,' he said.

She was in no mood to argue with him, and stood firm, reducing her responses to single syllables, 'no' predominant among them.

'Stubborn as my old ma,' Drekki remarked, and let her tag along. 'Fine. Just keep your breathing mask on. The dust in this air will grate your lungs to a pulp.'

At a booth at the end of the primary jetty, they signed various forms, and paid an outrageous harbour fee. Drekki was asked what his intention was, to which he spun a lie about corporate deals and need-to-know.

'I want to surprise old Rikko,' he said to Lerarus when she asked why he didn't just announce himself.

'You're too reckless,' she said. Grundstok gunners roamed the wharfs, looking for things to shoot. Drekki waved at them as he and Lerarus passed the port fence, and set off for the company town.

'Bah, no bother,' he said. 'It's just a joke. Live a little! Have a little fun!'

'This isn't to get around some sort of issue, is it?'

'This time, no,' said Drekki.

'It's dangerous, not telling him straight.'

'Could be.'

'Why is your fun all so dangerous?' she said.

'Because it's the most fun of all, cocking my nose at Nagash,' he said. 'He always gets his due in the end, you've got to take your chance to snatch delight from in front of his face while you can, the bony old *grindazdok*.[24]'

Lerarus grimaced. She was walking with difficulty, and leaned onto a fence post for support.

'Your land legs will come back soon enough,' said Drekki. 'It's a big old difference being on the ground after faring,' he said. His own gait was broad and rolling, good for keeping him upright whether on the deck of a storm-lashed sky-ship, or drunk as you please in port.

Aether-powered vehicles rumbled by, crunching fallen rock into yet more dust. Everything there was geared for industry. Huge sheds with rock crushers pumped out choking clouds, giant vacuum pumps sucking out the last little wisps of aether-gold. The noise was tremendous, a hammering, roaring, grinding, hissing clamour of aether production that shook the whole island.

Krund and Riksson's headquarters was a shabby, corporate place of corrugated tin buildings housing the khemists and krond-counters needed to keep the business running. But as is the way of such things, the foreman's building was far more stately, a stout mansion in the old Khunzuk style, surrounded by mani-cured stone gardens fenced in iron. There were sharp points on the poles, and sharper signs on the gates.

---

24 | Kharadrid: The most determinedly miserable of all duardin, whose spirits cannot be lifted by the finest ale or sky-ship.

'The rewards of enterprise are shared only as fairly as the entrepreneurs deem fit,' said Drekki. 'Give me a life in the air any day.'

The effect of this fortress of wealth was spoiled by a thick coating of rock dust on every leaf, stone and tile, so that it blended more readily with the town than the architect would have liked.

'No matter how fancy your mining hat, when you swing a pick, you're going to get dirty,' remarked Drekki. Lerarus didn't say anything, but Drekki had to explain. 'Old duardin saying,' he said. 'It means–'

'I get it,' she said. 'It is hardly the most taxing of metaphors.' She frowned. 'There's no one at the gates,' she said. 'All the gunners are at the port.'

'That's because this mansion is not the kind of place those who are not allowed to go will go,' said Drekki, pushing it open with brazen disregard. 'But you're right. All the real wealth is in the warehouses. Social convention keeps this place safe. Pah!' he said. 'That won't keep grobi sky-pirates out now, will it? When I get my mansion, there will be regular patrols. Volley guns. That kind of thing.'

He marched down an ornamental gravel path, which was almost obscured under layers of additional grit put out by the mine. Everything was flour-white. The steps were, the porch was, the door and its knocker. When Drekki took it and knocked, dust sprayed all about.

The door opened upon a solemn duardin in a butler's robes. He had a butler's face. The sort that said, 'Clear off, riffraff, it's time for lord whatsisname's tea.' Drekki smiled right into it.

'Hello there, my good duardin. I am Captain Dimsson. This is my mage.'

'A mage? A human mage?' The butler did not approve.

'In the kind of business I'm in, a bit of magic never goes amiss, whether umgi or dawi,' said Drekki. 'Speaking of business, I've come to offer Rikko Riksson my services.'

'All skyfaring affairs are to be conducted at the docks,' said the butler. He pointed behind them. He was already shutting the door. Drekki's foot stopped it closing.

'Not business like this,' he said. '*Special* business. He and I are old friends. I assure you.'

The butler looked down his long nose at Drekki, then went with provocative slowness to a bank of speaking tubes set into a wooden board. He picked one up, pulled it out, uncapped it, cleared his throat. He made quite the pantomime of the affair.

'I've seen snails move with greater alacrity,' Drekki murmured to Lerarus.

'There is some kind of… pirate here to see you,' said the butler loud enough for Drekki to hear, and with a contemptuous glance. 'Says his name is Dimsson. Shall I send him away, sir?'

Drekki chuckled at the expression on the butler's face. Very deliberately, the butler hung up the tube.

'Master Miner Riksson will see you now. Apparently,' he said. 'The suiting room is to your left. Leave your' – he gave them a slow up-and-down look – 'workwear in there. Master Riksson you will find in his office. The door at the end of the hall. And wipe your feet.'

But Drekki had already stomped past, showering rock dust onto the immaculately polished floor.

Drekki hung up his helm and his pack in the suiting room. While Lerarus did the same, Drekki smacked his lips and ground his jaw from side to side.

'Grit in my teeth and grit in my beard. Terrible business, this exploding of isles.'

Such implied disapproval did nothing to improve Lerarus' mood. She was boiling inside, he could tell.

He shrugged. 'Suit yourself.' He ruffled his beard and cackled at the dust he left on the floor.

Drekki went into Riksson's office without knocking. The duardin himself was sat behind a desk as wide as an open prairie, carved from a single block of green stone veined with gold.

'Hello, Drekki,' Rikko Riksson said without looking up from his writing.

'Hello, Rikko,' said Drekki. 'Didn't fall for my little ruse, then?'

Rikko looked up from his papers. 'Dimsson? That old alias from way back when? I knew you were here, the minute you arrived.'

'I have to try. Life's too dull without a little theatre.'

'Theatre? I sometimes wonder if you're a duardin at all, Drekki Flynt.'

'I have a beard, don't I? I'm short, aren't I?'

'Not that short,' said Rikko.

Drekki sat, gestured to a chair for Lerarus. They were made for duardin, low to the ground, hard as stone. Lerarus ended up with her knees by her ears. She fidgeted all the while.

'You have a bloody cheek, is what you have.' Rikko got up and went to a drinks cabinet, pouring dark liquor into three square glasses. He handed them out. 'What happened to you? My harbour master tells me the *Aelsling* is pretty beaten up.'

'Ah, a little run in with a harkraken,' said Drekki. 'But it is dead, whereas we're merely dented, so Drekki Flynt wins. We've got a good chunk of it pickled. I'll sell you a few barrels, if you're interested.'

'Always on the make!' Rikko said. 'Sure, Drekki, sure. We've a need for supplies on an operation like this. Hungry work. Thirsty work. I don't suppose you've got any ale in the hold? My workers are grumbling, and an extra drink would drown their complaints. We're nearly done in this field, and our next resupply isn't due until we've moved the HQ to the next blasting grounds. That's in a week. You know how it is when there's ale rationing. All duardin moan like grumbakz born.'

'No ale to spare, I'm afraid,' said Drekki. 'We're here for the work. The meat's a side trade.' He sipped his liquor and smiled. 'You know, you could house your duardin in something other than tin sheds. That might make them happier.'

Rikko waved a ringed hand. 'Too expensive. The margins in this game are too fine. They know that.'

'You look like you're doing all right,' Drekki said mildly. 'You realise your workers can see this mansion too?'

Rikko gave him a low-browed frown, then changed the subject. 'And who is this?'

'This is my mage, the Lady Sanasha Lerarus. Battle wizard. Fire school.'

The brows rose up again. 'So you're running with umgi as well as *ogri*[25] now? You're getting a reputation, my friend.'

'I'm an inclusive kind of captain. Gord's got talents, so has she, who cares if they've a few extra feet in height and no beards? Now, Rikko, to business. First, before we deal, I'd rather keep my being here on the quiet.'

'Throkk on your tail?'

Drekki waggled his head. 'Not quite. We've reached an accord, but I want to get some money together while he's feeling well disposed. See if I can buy him off for good. Life would be easier if I'm not being chased down all the time by my, um, other acquaintances while I'm trying to turn an honest coin. And, you know, scouting seams isn't paying so much right now, which I'd say is sort of the fault of your mining ventures, so you owe me.'

Rikko barked out a laugh. 'You can't argue with progress, Drekki.'

'I think you'll find I can.'

'Fine, old friend. I can get you onto the escort. The *Aelsling*'s a fine ship, you're good in a fight, although you're lucky I'm here and not Krund. You're not his favourite duardin.'

---

25 | Khazalid: Ogors.

As Rikko bent to open a drawer, Drekki winked at Lerarus. *See, lucky*, he mouthed.

'I'm taking a risk with this,' Rikko said. 'Knocking around with ogri and umgi isn't the only reputation you're getting.' He pulled out a scroll of terms and conditions.

'Oh really, what's this other reputation?'

'Unreliability. I need to know you'll see this through.' He handed the scroll across the table. Drekki took it with a winning smile.

'I intend to go right to Mhornar and see Throkk's agents, don't you worry.'

Rikko gave him a long look. 'This all might be true. I don't care. I need the ships. There have been attacks – pirates, grobi, orruks, sky beasts… you name it, so if you bail on me, I'll hold it against you.'

'We'll do our part,' said Drekki. 'I swear.'

'Then I'll have my clerks draw up a contract of employment, and give you a down payment. A quarter now–'

'Come now, half!' said Drekki. 'Half's usual.'

'Aye, but you're not usual. Unusual fees for unusual fellows. A quarter will do.' Rikko raised his glass. 'Welcome to the Krund and Riksson Mining Company, Drekki Flynt. Don't try to cheat me.' He smiled.

'Would I do that?' said Drekki innocently.

'Yes,' said Rikko, his smile vanishing like an extinguished candle flame. 'Yes, you would.'

CHAPTER TEN

THE KRONVOY

Drekki watched the mansion dwindle astern as the *Aelsling* sailed to join the flotilla. Rikko had gone the way of most of his friends, he thought. Young once, adventurous too, pushing the edges of the possible, until they'd found a sure way of making coin and become set in their ways. They were obsessed with wealth, not with profit, and they were not entirely the same things.

The ships mustered at the edge of the mining zone. More than half the duardin joining the kronvoy were Grundcorps of various companies, and their gunhaulers swarmed the tankers. The balance of the fleet was made up of privateers, which was only to be expected, as Mhornar and her holdings infamously favoured their use.

Being a fast ship, the *Aelsling* was assigned picket duty. See anything amiss, they'd try to get word back to the kronvoy. Drekki's lot were thus stationed several thousand raadfathoms coreward from the main group.

Drekki proudly pointed out the chief vessels to Lerarus.

'Krontankers,' he said. 'Among the very largest sky-ships in all existence, and the arteries of the Kharadron economy.'

The tankers were immense, dozens of times bigger than the *Aelsling*. The bulk of them comprised vast cylinders grouped into twos and fours, fastened to a large, open frame. Into these tanks the harvested wealth of the Skyshoals was poured.

'Each one of them can hold millions of cubic grunti of aether-gold,' Drekki explained. 'There's more money in this flotilla than you'll ever see again. If you were to go to Azyr and sit in the jew-elled halls of Sigmar himself, you'd not see as much wealth as this.' Drekki was salivating with avarice. Aether multiplied the gold fever of the duardin a thousandfold. Several of the crew lifted their helms to dab the dribble from their beards.

Gord was unimpressed, and pointedly went about the limited tasks he was allowed to do on his own.

'Can't eat it,' he said. 'Gold's no good. I want to see a *food* tanker.'

No one tried to put his wrong-headed opinion straight. Paying Gord in food meant bigger shares of aether for the rest of them.

Large superstructures were perched near the tankers' sterns: castles guarding fortified command centres. A walkway led down the spine of each ship over the cylinders, with shorter crossways at regular intervals. Each intersection and terminus sported its own tower bristling with cannon. Units of Grundstok mercenaries patrolled the decks, neat squares of duardin tiny as blocks of ants.

More arresting still was the kronvoy lead, the *Thrandi-Zhank*, a Khrundhal-class battleship. When it cut through the clouds of grit and headed for the lead position, Lerarus leaned forward. Though much smaller than the krontankers, its nature as a man-o-war gave it a presence they could not match. The duardin chattered excitedly with each other, reeling off its specifications and exploits. The *Thrandi-Zhank* was a true warship, thick of hull, parent to a swarm of lesser flying machines, its stepped decks crammed with turrets sporting the most powerful cannons in the Kharadron arsenal, and that meant the most powerful in all of the realms. It was the pinnacle of aether technology. A ship from a different age. A ship that spoke of the future.

'You had all this,' Lerarus said, 'and you did not help? For five hundred years Bastion held off the forces of Tzeentch, alone. We believed that we were the last people in all the realms, and you had this?' She was dazed by the thought.

'Actually, the Khrundhal is a new design,' offered Bokko, too bedazzled by the sight of such engineering to catch the tightness in Lerarus' voice. 'The class is only four decades old. It's interesting how it developed from the–'

'Shush, shush, shush, Bokko,' said Drekki, flapping a hand behind his back. The way his crew kept misreading the wizard's mood could get them all in hot water. 'Now's not the time, there's a good lad.'

Bokko's mouth formed a surprised yet understanding 'O', and he went off chattering about jobs to be done.

Lerarus didn't speak after that. Drekki beat a tactful retreat, leaving her at the rail.

The *Aelsling* reached her station and held position. A chastened Bokko assembled a work crew to continue with the ship's maintenance. Evtorr set up his portable aethergraph on the rail facing the fleet. While he waited for the signal to depart, he composed poetry in a little book. The hopeful looks he shot at passers-by were ignored. Evtorr would wilfully interpret a blink as a sign of interest, and use it as a pretext to declaim some of his verse. Nobody wanted that.

Mustering took time. It was the best part of a day before all the ships were in position, until, finally, a drawn-out blast from the *Thrandi-Zhank* drew signallers to their posts across the kronvoy. From golden, aether-gilt mirrors messages flashed.

'That's it, the order to depart!' Evtorr reported.

'Excellent,' said Drekki. 'Return signal. Received and understood. Evrokk, get us underway. Bokko, keep an eye on the rear endrin, would you.'

'Aye-aye, captain!'

Lerarus glowered, her mood as fouled as a rarely scraped hull. Drekki dithered. In the end he tackled it head-on. If you have to have a wizard on board, he thought, best make sure it's not an angry one.

'Look,' Drekki said to her. 'I can see where you're coming from. It ain't a good thing to realise you've been left high and dry by those you consider shipmates. Maybe we should have done more, but we were trying to survive too.'

'You did nothing.' She turned aside. Drekki followed her round so he kept in her eyeline.

'Besides, if we take the sins of my ancestors as a given, they're not me, and I'm not them. Is it fair to lay the blame for what they did at my cabin door? And the crew here, we're us, not just Kharadron, but individuals. I don't hold with labelling folks. I don't hold humanity's shoddy construction and flighty, inconstant nature against you, do I? So you don't hold what my folk did or didn't do against us personally either. We're doing our best to get you what you want. We're in this together. Can't be achieving new goals if you're bothering bygones all the time.'

Lerarus stared fixedly out over the sky.

'All right then,' Drekki said. That was as emollient as he could be. He was at a loss at what to say. 'Fine.' He drummed his hands on the rail. 'Well, with the likes of the *Thrandi-Zhank* sailing with us, we're not likely to be attacked now, are we? Good plan this, if I say so myself.'

It was not the first time Drekki had spoken too soon. It would certainly not be the last.

* * *

It was a few days after and getting dark when Evtorr hollered, 'Storm rolling in from edgewards!' Adrimm was half a second later with his warning from the prow lookout, and by that time Evtorr was rappelling down the endrin globe to signal the fleet. Drekki was proud of his crew. They were quick, first off the mark with the signals. Evtorr was already well into sending the code on his aethergraph before those on the other ships blinked into action.

The kronvoy lit up with signal flash. A river of stars twinkled as the Kharadron urgently communicated.

Drekki snapped out his telescope. A wall of black clouds was rolling in from Realm's Edge on legs of multicoloured lightning. Magical discharge flashed within. Drekki already knew what they faced before Otherek and Kedren joined him at the rail to give their opinion.

'That ain't no natural storm,' Otherek said. He sniffed at the gathering wind.

'Aye, it isn't,' said the runesmith. 'Charged with magic, that is.'

'Velunti! Wake up the first watch,' Drekki commanded. 'Best we're all ready for this.'

Lerarus was first out, bleary-eyed, half-dressed and still in a temper.

'There's a storm coming,' she said. She had to duck to get under the endrin. 'So that moaning one told me.' She meant Adrimm. A fine description.

'It's coming in fast,' said Drekki, still scanning the horizon through his scope. 'Out edgewards.' The direction wasn't really necessary; the storm was a thick black line in the sky, linking horizon to horizon. You'd have to be troggoth-thick to miss it.

Lerarus stiffened, stopped midway in putting her duster on. 'That's no natural storm.'

'Aye. We'd already got there.' Otherek sniffed again. 'I smell magic. Bad magic.'

'Sigmar curse us all,' she said, but Drekki got the idea she wasn't very surprised.

'Something you're not telling us?' Drekki said.

'Give me a minute to think.' She watched the storm, already only ten thousand raadfathoms away, a high wave of cresting cloud, gaining fast. 'This will be rough.'

'You're telling me that a storm will be rough? A magical storm is still a storm, and we have all the appropriate warding.'

'This one will be rougher than any you've ever known,' she said. She shrugged her coat on, smoothed it down, tied back her hair and pointed. 'Look closer. There are daemons at play in the wind.'

Drekki swept his telescope around to follow her finger. It took him a moment to find them, and when he did, he growled: a visceral, unconscious reaction to the unnatural. Long-limbed creatures danced in the lightning, manifesting, beginning to fall as gravity caught them, then being atomised by stabbing arcs of power to materialise elsewhere.

Kedren squinted. 'Stuff and nonsense. I've seen the like before, they're lightning spites in the sky. It's early in the season for daemon incursion. The Trailing Isles are too far from the Perimeter. Chaos doesn't have the power to show itself this time of year.'

'I tell you they're not spites,' said Lerarus. 'They are daemon heralds, the vanguard summoners. They're breaking through the veil of the real to let the others in.'

A device at Otherek's belt began to rattle and ping. He picked it up and looked at it very carefully. He made a couple of little ums and a couple of little ahs and twisted a couple of knobs. They were the kind of sounds endrineers made when an aether-condenser is on its way out and they're going to have to charge you a lot to fix it. Coming from a khemist, they were bad sounds to be hearing.

'She's right, Drekki. If I'm reading them this far out, they're coming in force.'

'They must really want you dead,' said Drekki, with a sidelong look at Lerarus. 'Whoever they are.'

'I've got some stuff that might help us here,' said Otherek. 'I'll fetch it.'

'I thought you didn't do magic,' said Lerarus.

'Aether science,' Otherek said, 'can counter magic.'

'And I need my staff,' she said.

The two of them set off briskly, discussing tactics, despite Otherek's insistence their disciplines owed nothing to one another.

Kedren took the moment for a quick smoke before mayhem descended, taking off his helm, stuffing full his pipe. He had the motions down piston-smooth, and was puffing blue in a moment. 'She didn't say anything about daemons when she came aboard, but she don't seem too surprised either.'

'So you think it is something to do with her too?'

'Aye, well, if you're looking at restoring a major artefact to the single civilisation in these parts that managed to resist Chaos for five hundred years, you can be sure the gods will be interested. Question is, did she expect this?'

Drekki snorted. 'Of course she did. She and I need to have a bit of a chat about exactly who is opposing her. I don't like being surprised.'

'There's a thing to consider here, Captain Flynt.' Kedren only ever called Drekki 'Captain Flynt' when he was angry, or when matters were looking grim. 'You might want to think about running again.'

'So we can be caught alone by a horde of daemons? Maybe not,' said Drekki.

Thunder rumbled. Drekki thought he could hear wild laughter behind it.

'Grungni's dongliz,' Kedren said.

The wind slapped the *Aelsling* with unpredictable blows. The endrins rang. The rigging hummed. The first veils of rain hissed on the metal. Alarm sirens wailed across the kronvoy. There was movement on every ship as the Grundcorps prepared to repel boarders. They were regimented, professional, more like clockwork mechanisms than duardin of flesh and blood.

'All hands to battle stations!' Drekki roared.

Boots thumped. Gunterr Borrki unlocked the arsenal cabinet and handed out the bigger weapons. Hrunki dropped into her turret seat and slammed the hatch shut.

Trokwi rattled his feathers. Drekki loosened his gun, Karon, in her holster.

'There's going to be fighting!' said Gord. 'Nice.'

'Nothing to eat after though, first mate,' warned Drekki.

'Oh yeah, I'm not stupid,' said Gord conversationally. 'Had a friend tried to eat daemon once. His head turned into a table. Have to be harkraken for dinner again.' He pulled out his pistol, thumbed the hammer. 'I like harkraken. I'm by your side, Drekki.'

The black torrent raced in, ready to consume the ships. There was a respite of a few seconds, a misjudgement of distance on Drekki's part. It was a little further out than he thought.

And then, it hit.

CHAPTER ELEVEN

DAEMON STORM

A storm in the Skyshoals was not to be sniffed at. Hurricane winds ran ships into islands. The metaliths themselves were not immune. Whole groups could be picked up and shifted, their stony sides acting as sails; in the worst of tempests they could be broken apart, cracked under strain or crashing into one another. There were the usual perils of lightning, rain and gales, but in that part of the realm of Chamon weather was not limited to wind and water. The complex airflows between the layers held up all manner of debris, from glass-pitting stone to molten metal. Aelchemical discharge from aether-rich clouds could fry an endrin completely. Wild aelementals rode on the winds, and they didn't care much for organic life.

Daemons were worse than any of that.

Churning clouds of dark grey and black swallowed the kronvoy. Deadly cumulus lit with bursts of magenta and blue; louring, impenetrable as stone. Rain fell harder, constant, coming on full, drenching everything, cutting visibility even before the clouds struck the *Aelsling* and swallowed up the sky. Drekki got a glimpse of the first ships caught on the outer edge. They rode up, turned about, tipping dangerously. He saw tiny figures lit by lightning falling from a foundering ship. An aether-endrin exploded. Flashes in the clouds shone through leering, daemonic faces, their brilliant mouths outlining airborne daemons surfing the winds. He saw shoals of manta-like Screamers, and twisted figures riding on discs. They gesticulated wildly, calling magic from the storm and directing it howling at the ships.

The clouds rode over the first krontanker. The daemons descended to the deck. Aether-fire flicked out from the deckcastles, competing with the furious display of magic unleashed by the boarders.

The rain angled, blew horizontally. The lenses of Drekki's helm streaked with it. The wall of black swallowed the line of the tankers. He caught sight of the *Thrandi-Zhank* coming about, implacable, the endrin-ports on its massive quadruple endrins blazing, great cannon already firing into the swarms of daemons. The scale of such aeronautical power stunned him. He'd seen Khrundhal-class vessels many times before, but they were always in dock, or on patrol, a deterrent rarely unleashed. In ten years he'd not witnessed one in action, not even at the heights of the *Garaktormun*.[26] They were an 'I dare you' to the foes of the Overlords.

The *Thrandi-Zhank* was faster and nimbler than he'd expected, turning in a twisting ascent within a radius of only a few hundred raadfathoms. And the amount of firepower! Timed shells exploded within the swarms of daemons, shredding their supernatural flesh. There must have been whole companies of Grundcorps aboard, judging by the straight-line streaks of aether-rifle fire coming out from the shooting decks. The first wave of creatures to attack the krontanker nearest the battleship were obliterated in short

26 | Kharadrid: The Necroquake.

order. But a second wave followed hot on their heels, bursting out of the clouds, led by a pair of avian-headed greater daemons, who hurled bolts from their staffs that fizzled and burst on the *Thrandi-Zhank*'s aetheric wards.

The storm front closed over the battleship, obscuring her struggle. The clouds picked up speed, racing towards the *Aelsling*. Pressure built before the tempest.

Kedren calmly extinguished his pipe, stowed it, and popped his helm back on. Umherth flicked the toggle switches on his volley gun, setting it to rapid fire.

'Brace for impact!' Drekki roared. He let his axe head thump to the deck and gripped the rail.

The storm hit like a fist. The *Aelsling* heeled. Drekki leant into the tilt, his boots clamped to the metal. Trokwi's claws scraped over his suit fabric. Drekki let go of the rail and grabbed him before he was snatched away by the wind. Kedren was on his knees, elbows bent around the railings, fingers locked together. Umherth laughed into the storm. The other crew, where he could see them, were in similar straits, holding on for dear life. The wind was visible, a stream of black particles, like soot, but not, something much worse – a living darkness that nibbled at the edges of the soul. In the cockpit Evrokk fought with all his might against the rebellious tiller. The ship bucked. An aether-endrin, broken free from the rigging of some other, less fortunate vessel, spun over them, spraying sparks from its ruptured shell like a feast-day firework.

The *Aelsling* was going the same way, the stern lifting, likely to be flipped and broken.

'Get her nose into the wind, Evrokk!' Drekki hollered. His voice stayed trapped in his helm. The wind wouldn't let it out.

Evrokk didn't need to be told. He was a good helmsduardin, and put all his weight on the wheel, dragging down. He wedged it with his shoulder, his hand moving over the banks of switches that controlled the endrins. The ship moaned. Metal screams before it breaks, like an animal, or the damned. It was screaming now.

Clean aethershine blazed. Otherek came out from below, his khemist's staff radiating a calming light. A clear flask of live aether slowly discharged through apertures at the top. Lerarus worked beside him, channelling the power given off by the aether. The light plunged into the storm, edged with flickering flames. The strands of black vanished. Magic dispersed into the rigging as harmless foxfires.

They had a few crucial seconds. The wind was still there, but with its blizzard of magic dispelled, it was only wind. Evrokk got the ship level, prow pointed into the storm. The deck heaved, hull lifted by waves of air, plunging down, hawsers thrumming under strain. They were being driven backwards by the gale. There were flashes and bangs within the clouds. Tzeentch had roused the sky to war. The duardin fought back. Who would win, Drekki would not have dared to wager.

'Otherek and I can't keep this up for long!' Lerarus screamed. Drekki could just about hear her. 'We need to flee!'

Thunder cackled around them. Faces wrought of cloud grinned at them. Fingers of lightning pointed, flashed, flashed again. Drekki threw up his hands to his lenses to protect his eyes. When he lowered them, there were things bounding across the deck. *His* deck. Rotund, barrel-shaped monsters with splayed feet and oversized hands held up on knobbled arms. Weird fires burned around fingers hollow as reeds. The things had faces set directly into their chests, and they were pink, pink as a pale umgi's newborn skin, pink as roses. Pinker.

Horrors. Ridiculous, but deadly.

'Daemons! Daemons aboard!' Drekki roared.

Umherth howled with delight. His volley gun drowned out his shouts.

Drekki had heard the stories, but he'd never fought daemons himself. The stories were bad. The reality was worse. They moved unnaturally, flicker-jumping from one spot to the next, capering and laughing as if at a dance. The sight of them hurt his eyes, hurt his soul. He squinted hard, trying to pin them in place by will alone, drew Karon and opened fire. Umherth's volley gun spat multiple shots, bullets streaking from multiple barrels. Karon put out a spread from each of her three mouths. Gord's oversized handgun belched. An aether-bullet the size of a cannonball exploded a daemon. Together, the weapons put out a wall of shot that shredded Tzeentch's children.

A gibbering daemon leapt at Drekki, and he drilled it right in the face with a spray of bullets. It hit the deck and flopped over, rubbery skin heaving, hide sinking in as if its insides had suddenly liquefied. Blue arms thrust out of its mouth: one, two, then three and four. A pair of smaller things burst from the daemon's decaying remains, these blue and miserable where their melting parent had been pink and manic. They advanced with sour faces, slower than their forebear; no less menacing for it. Those felled by Umherth and the others gave up similar progeny.

'Like that, is it? Singles for pairs? If I were gambling I'd be a happy duardin,' said Drekki. He levelled his gun. 'I don't like to gamble with my ship,' he said, and blew the blue grumblers apart.

Blue flesh disintegrated under the lash of aethershot, split again. Two blue daemons became four dancing fire imps, burning hot. Their touch blackened metal, made it glow. From the dozen daemons that boarded initially came a throng: blue, pink, and living fire. Screaming flames blasted from the hands of them all, setting metal alight.

Gunfire could only slay so many. The daemons moved into

cutter range. Huge, spatulate hands raked at the skyfarers. Velunti took a blow that staggered him back, clutching his chest, and Drekki feared him dead. He lost sight of the others. Daemons crowded him. Rune magic flared as Drekki's axe disjointed them, taking off arms at the elbow, legs at the knees. He finished two this way, heaving them off the deck when they were crippled, denying them the chance to divide.

'Get them off my ship!' he shouted. 'Hurl them overboard!'

Gord thumped a Pink Horror between the eyes, stabbing it with his bladed fist, then used his weapon like a pitchfork to flip the daemon shrieking back into the storm. Otherek's aethercraft dispelled them with a scything beam of focused power. Lerarus invoked ancient spells of purifying flame. Under both, daemons popped like soap bubbles.

The deck was suddenly free of the larger foes. Daemon corpses fizzled, brightly coloured flesh turning to black sludge. Lerarus, Otherek and Kedren moved up the deck, extinguishing the last of the fire sprites lurking in the rigging with rune, aether and sorcery.

Drekki strode through the rain to the cockpit. The muck of battle sluiced from the drains. He kept his feet as only one raised on a heaving deck can. 'Evrokk, bring us about, get us out of here!'

Cannon fire vied with thunder in the storm. The wind remained high.

'That'll be a black mark against us with Krund and Riksson, captain,' said Evrokk.

'Let me worry about that. Our first duty is to Lerarus. Code says so.'

'Code also says breaking a contract is grudgeworthy. How many more black marks can your book take?'

'Contract be damned or we will be,' said Drekki. 'Bring us about. Full power to the endrins. Get the wind behind us and use this storm against itself. That'll hurry us on.'

'Aye-aye, captain,' said Evrokk reluctantly, but he spun the wheel surely. Again the ship pitched heavily as the wind caught it broadside. The duardin swayed in their magnetic boots. When the prow was away from the storm, the *Aelsling* settled. Evrokk pulled on lines to increase the aether-burn fore and aft, and the airscrews chopped harder. The wind picked them up and sped them away.

A tremendous explosion boiled in the storm's heart. Golden light. Blue light. Figures of daemon swarms and ships embattled were silhouetted against the cloud.

'Aether explosion,' said Otherek. 'A big one.' He sniffed the air. 'A lot of aether-gold! One of the tankers has gone!'

Shockwaves disrupted the storm front. Clouds parted, curtains opening on disaster. Firelight bathed the crew of the *Aelsling*.

'Funti drukk!' Drekki swore.

A krontanker was ablaze from stem to stern, dropping ponderously out of the kronvoy line, smoke and aether trailing from ruptured tanks. Tiny figures leapt from the sides, some ablaze.

One of the containers went up, venting precious cargo in a gold-hued explosion. A haze of spilled aether surrounded it, aglow, discharging its power in short-lived displays of lightning. There was so much of the gaseous metal on the wind it burned their noses.

'The wealth of a barak, gone up in smoke,' someone wailed. Gunterr, perhaps. It was hard to tell, their voice was hoarse. Few things will make a duardin weep like wasted wealth. Drekki's own eyes prickled at the tragedy of it. He tried to imagine all he could have bought with that much aether. He failed, and he had a broad imagination.

A hot wind, the dying shockwave of the dying ship, buffeted them.

'At least the others are getting away,' said Otherek. He was positively funereal. But it was true, the storm had spent itself. Duardin vessels proceeded, harried by thinning flocks of daemons. Fewer lightning strikes troubled them. Fewer daemons flashed into being upon their decks. The *Thrandi-Zhank* cruised around with seeming impunity, the overwhelming firepower of its cannons seeking out the larger daemons. Each one slain saw a drop in magical charge. The supernatural storm was becoming a natural one. 'They're giving up.'

'Snap out of it, snap out of it!' growled Kedren, who cared far less than the others for the loss of gas. He strode about, slapping his crewmates with a gauntleted hand, making their helms ring. 'They're not giving up. They're not going after them because they're coming after us!' He pointed aft.

'A cloud?' said Adrimm. His voice trembled.

'Only if you're an optimist,' said Kedren, who said that word as if it were the direst insult. 'Look again!'

'Uh-oh,' said Drekki.

Otherek's eyepieces whirred. A sharp breath followed. 'Uh-oh doesn't even begin to cover it.'

'Uh-what?' said Gord.

'More of them, coming in fast,' said Gunterr, who had his gunnery sight pressed to his helm. 'Screamers and disc riders.'

The cloud broke into a thousand shapes.

'Why are they after us?' moaned Adrimm. He positively drooped. A sorry sight, all gooey with daemon ichor.

'If we survive, we'll find out. Time for the guns to show their worth,' said Drekki. 'Evrokk! Disengage all limiters. Push the *Aelsling* as fast as she'll go.'

'We'll die if we do that!' said Adrimm.

'We *might* die if we do that, Fair-weather. We definitely will if we don't. To the rails! All guns outward.'

Shapes took form. Manta-like Screamers led the way, surging at play in the wake of the ship. Disc riders followed. The Screamers could have been mortal beasts, if one pretended hard enough. The discs were in no way natural. Some were fleshy pads with tiny mouths, fringes ringed with teeth. Some appeared as artificial conveyances, with upholstered surfaces and fine brass rails around the periphery, until sticky eyes opened, and tongues lolled out of hidden orifices. If those were disturbing, their riders were worse, freakish and offensive to the senses in every respect. Lizardy beasts. Emaciated men with five arms. Pillars of shrieking crystal. Two screaming women sharing a single pair of legs, conjoined at the waist, bifurcating like a tree, their faces waving bouquets of infant's legs. A thing with a head like a grotesque moon led them, a jester's marotte gripped in one claw waved wildly about its face.

Reality warped around these things. A wash of Change rinsed everything filthy.

'Evrokk, more speed!' Drekki ordered.

'I'm giving it everything we've got!' the helmsduardin replied.

'Then find some more!'

The disc riders commenced a long-range bombardment by sorcery. Lerarus' fire shield turned their spells aside while they remained that far away, but every second saw a little gain.

'They're coming!' Gunterr shouted.

They were.

Screamers caught up to them first, the fastest of their number weaving behind the stern, then drawing level with the side. They swooped in at the ship, ring mouths wide, giving the cries that gave them their name. Each daemon beast carried an array of spines. They angled these at the crew. Guns barked. One of the Screamers went for Gord, attempting to bite him. The ogor smashed it out of the air with his dagger fist, near cutting it in two. Umherth took himself up to the back, and sprayed a display of shot into the wake. The hull carbines angled as far back as they could, blasting explosives into the flights of Screamers, discouraging them from attacking, while Hrunki loosed opportunistic shots with the main gun.

'Drive them back!' Gunterr shouted, firing off his paired pistols.

The beasts shrieked past, spines clanging off the shrouds and hawsers.

'Ha! Can't get at us, can you, you stupid fish!' Adrimm crowed.

'Stow it!' Drekki yelled. 'They're not after us, they're trying to sever the links between the hull and the endrins.' Clangs from overhead indicated attempts to break the endrin housings.

The *Aelsling* eased ahead. The disc riders were dropping back. Screamers surged and fell behind, surged and fell behind, until only a trio of faster individuals remained, then these too were outpaced.

A final effort came from the moon-faced jester leading the daemons. He knelt on bony legs and slammed the butt of his marotte into the top of his disc. Sparks shot from his mount's rear, propelling it far ahead of its fellows.

The daemon-jester gesticulated with his puppet-topped wand. No joke accompanied the gesture, but a blast of magic that ripped up a section of the deck, melting the metal, turning it into a field of waving fingers. Umherth was nearly hit. Turning the disc in, now dead and aflame, the daemon skidded across the broken section of the ship, ripping up the newly sprouted digits. The ship bled. The rider stepped lightly free, the dead mount sliding to a stop by the gunwales. A fresh spell at the ready, Moonface advanced, grinning, jabbering in an unknown tongue. A skin of magic around it absorbed aethershot. Crackles of power burst from every impact. None got through.

Gord went in first, swinging a punch with an ogorish roar. He was thrown back for his troubles so hard he almost flipped over the gunwale. The daemon-jester walked past him, fixed on the helm. A shrieking bolt of Change streaked at the terrified

Evrokk, but Lerarus stepped in the way, staff aloft, and the bolt was deflected by a spinning disc of fire.

They entered into a duel, mage to sorcerer. Sparks and fires fountained everywhere.

'Grungni's beard,' said Drekki. 'I'm glad it's just the one. Otherek, Kedren, a little support on the aether front, if you please.'

'Aye-aye,' said Kedren. He spat on his gauntlets, and gripped his axe harder.

'As you say, captain,' said Otherek, all business, and his staff vented a magic-damping mist of aether towards the fighting wizards. The combat lessened in ferocity. Sorcery flickered out.

'Now you and I, runesmith,' said Drekki.

He and Kedren went into action, running past Lerarus to attack the daemon. A tongue of lightning that spoke sweet blandishments flew at Kedren as he swung. The runes on his axe blazed, and broke the spell with a loud bang. Drekki followed close behind, his two-handed aether-axe humming. Duardin steel parted daemon head from daemon neck. The moon-faced head dropped onto the deck, where it grew legs and scampered about.

'Funti drukk!' Drekki yelled, and punted the head over the side with his foot.

The daemon's body swayed, blindly spraying rainbows of magic. The crew dived aside from rays and bolts.

Lerarus advanced, face set. A fireball roared from her staff and struck the daemon in the chest. When the fire boiled away, only ash remained. It blew away on the wind.

The battle was over.

The storm was well behind them. Towering thunderheads topped themselves out against the Fourth Air high, high above. Lightning still flickered, but the thunder that followed did so at some delay. The daemons were gone.

'Well done, everyone,' Drekki said. 'Any casualties?'

Velunti Runk took a headcount. 'A few scratches, none dead,' he reported. He was subdued, nervy.

'What about you?' said Drekki. 'You were in the thick of it. I saw you take a blow to the chest that should have burst your ribs.'

'Got lucky, I guess,' Velunti said. 'I'm fine.'

'Are you sure? You look terrible.'

Velunti's face had gone an ashen grey beneath his extravagant hair, but he shook his head and puffed out his cheeks.

'It's the daemons. That's all. They put the fear in me. I'll be fine. I... I'm sorry. I've got things to do, captain.'

'Haven't we all,' said Drekki. 'Get to it, lad.'

Bokko hurried around, worriedly checking the damage. When he got beneath the rear endrin, which was radiating a fearsome heat, he shouted up to Evrokk.

'Ease off! Ease off!'

'A small miracle we lost no one,' said Drekki. He looked at the deck. Most of the flesh had turned back to metal, though it kept its new form. The edges were puckered lips. He could see into the cabins below. 'That's a mess, and no mistake.'

'It's not the worst, captain,' said Bokko, skidding to an undignified stop. Somehow, he'd gathered up an assortment of tools and parts. 'Endrin two!'

Drekki frowned within his helm. Now it was pointed out to him he could hear the stutter of an unhappy machine.

'The bloody tube! I bet it's bust,' he said. Bokko was already scampering up to the endrin tops. 'Do what you can, I'll be up soon,' Drekki said. 'Where's the mage?'

'She's here, captain!' Hrunki shouted.

Lerarus was down in a swoon, her helm hanging loose by its pipes. Hrunki was crouched over her, daubing foul-smelling unguent onto a welt over the mage's brow. Lerarus opened bloodshot eyes.

'Good work, Lerarus,' Drekki said.

'I didn't do much. We'd be dead if it weren't for you and Kedren,' she croaked painfully.

Hrunki shot Drekki a black look. He ignored it. He'd make his own mind up whether Lerarus was fit to talk.

'That's an unusual weapon for a Kharadron,' Lerarus said.

'An axe? This axe,' said Drekki. He rested the butt on the deck. The blade was clean; daemon blood never stayed manifest for long, but the metal was dulled by the contact. 'All duardin like axes, and this is Kharadron made.'

'A Kharadron axe with runes on it, is what I meant,' she said. The runes were faded, but just visible still.

'Ah, yes, Grunnsson's axe,' said Drekki. He turned the blade in the light. The built-in harpoon glinted. 'Kedren struck the runes. He's good at axes, bad at names. Call it duardin cultural exchange.'

She nodded, leaned back, eyes closed. She wasn't feeling on top of things, that much was for sure. Hrunki's scowl was beginning to bore into Drekki. Time to go.

'Take it easy,' he said.

'I will if we're clear. Are we clear?' she asked.

'For now, but we've other problems.'

'Don't be bothering her with those now, Drekki!' scolded Hrunki.

Lerarus wouldn't let it lie. 'Problems like what?' she said.

Drekki tugged off his helm. He puffed out his cheeks. 'Technical issues, like that moon-headed *kaztronk*[27] turning a strip of my deck into fingers. More pressing, there's a problem with endrin two, and I'm not entirely sure where we are, if I'm completely honest.'

Black sky roiled around them. Visibility was down to a few ship-lengths in every direction. Otherek, Umherth and Kedren joined them. They looked worried.

---

27 | Kharadrid: Freak.

'There's more woe,' Otherek said.

'And what would that be?' sighed Drekki.

'Think about it,' the khemist said softly. 'We were followed when we left, and we were found. Those daemons came right after us just now. I wouldn't put that harkraken incident down to chance either.'

'What are you saying?' asked Umherth.

'Open your lugholes and put your head into action, oldbeard,' said Drekki. 'Can't you see? We've been marked.'

CHAPTER TWELVE

A DUARDIN ACCUSED

The *Aelsling* limped through empty, lemon skies. There was naught to see but a line of metaliths bumping along a turbulent stream a thousand raadfathoms up, but Drekki was taking no chances, and a constant watch was posted.

Ammunition was down. Aether was low. Then there was the damage. It was worse than they feared. Bokko turned up all agitated again, so Drekki told Otherek and the others to wait while he went to speak with the endrinriggers.

'It's that bloody pipe,' Bokko said. 'The glass inner's bust. Leaking everywhere. I've stabilised it, but we've got to keep the endrin down to forty per cent output, captain, or we'll blow the whole assembly. I could jiggle a little more out of her, if we were willing to risk it, but it really needs stripping, and a proper glass weld doing. Ideally I'd replace it.'

'No jiggling to be done till we're assured of safety,' said Drekki. 'How long would a weld take?'

Bokko shrugged. 'How long's a braid of beard? You know as well as I, you can't tell what the inner's like until you've slid the outer off. If we put in somewhere for a day or two, we shut the endrin down... I could do it then, quickly too.'

'Not likely, my lad. Can't it be done on the fly?'

Bokko gave him Bokko's special look. It was a look that said, in this instance, *I told you we should've put that pipe right.*

What actually came out of his mouth was, 'Tricky for most who aren't us, but you and I could.'

'Then we do it on the fly,' Drekki said. 'Time's short.'

'I'll get on it.'

'Wait for me, you can't do it alone. See to the deck now you've got the endrin stable. Get it closed up. One good downpour and that's us all flooded out and losing height with the weight of water.'

Bokko nodded. Drekki caught his arm.

'The *Aelsling* is getting distressed,' he said quietly. 'I'm feeling it keenly. This is more than our usual scuffed paint. Put right as much as you can. It's bad for morale.'

'Aye, captain.'

Onto the other, more urgent matter. Drekki went back to his magic users. Hrunki scowled all the harder at him for dragging the human mage into his business again. Her scowl deepened into fissures in granite when he reached out his hand to help the wizard up.

'You shouldn't get her onto her feet. The lass ain't right yet,' she said.

'Let's see what the *wizard* has to say on that score, shall we?' said Drekki. 'Are you right?' he asked.

Lerarus took his hand. When she got to her feet, she swayed and looked like she was about to fold in half. She gulped air, nodded, and steadied herself on the rigging.

'That amount of magic is draining to perform. I'll be fine in a minute.'

'There you are, Hrunki, if she says she's all right, she's all right,'

Drekki said. 'Right then, how are these sky-dogs finding us? We're marked, right?'

Lerarus nodded tiredly. There was agreement on that from all.

'Runes?' asked Drekki.

'Nay, lad, I'd know,' said Kedren.

'Then something else. An amulet? A scratch? The mouldering corpse of a wandertross nailed upon the bow?'

'Only a spell would lead daemons to us so certainly,' said Lerarus. 'Something potent.'

'And what form would that take?'

'Anything's possible,' said Kedren. 'Magic's a broad art.'

'Look for paint, scratch marks, something of that kind,' said Lerarus. 'Something on the fabric of the ship, that can be done by a non-wizard.'

'No other wizards aboard?' asked Drekki.

'Not that I can feel,' she said.

'Nor me,' said Kedren.

'Or me,' said Otherek.

'So it has to be something physical. I wouldn't use an object. Not if I wanted to be sure. An object can be found and tossed overboard. A mark can be more easily hidden, but it might need to be renewed. Marks scuff. Paint runs. That's the drawback of that approach.'

'Right,' said Drekki thoughtfully. 'Then I think I know where this mark will be,' he said, and marched the length of his ship to the prow. The others followed. 'Just here. Am I right?' He pointed under the gunwales, off to the right of Aelsling's heroic back. Her hammer was still bent. Seeing his sweetheart so discommoded provoked a pang of hurt in Drekki.

Lerarus levelled her staff. A muttered word, a little grunt of pained effort, a brief blaze of light. Her staff twisted in her hands so forcefully she nearly dropped it.

'Steady, lassie,' Kedren said. He reached for a pouch at his belt.

Lerarus shook her head, jaw clenched tight. 'Put your runes away. I'm done.'

Painted words appeared on the metal.

Lerarus fell back, released from some unseen pressure. Gord's gut cushioned her stumble. His massive hand steadied her. Being grabbed by an ogor was not comforting, and she did her best to shake him off. It was an uneven struggle. She stayed where she was.

'Those words weren't there yesterday,' Gord said slowly.

'They were,' said Lerarus. 'We just couldn't see. They will have been there since the start.' She raised her voice and shrugged hard. 'Let me go, Gord.'

Gord kept hold. His puzzlement blocked up his mind. All his brain was engaged with thinking on the words. There was not enough power left in his skull to unclench his hand. Lerarus continued to struggle in his sausage-fingered grip.

'Let me free!' she said. She heel-kicked his shin.

Gord blinked slowly, then released her. 'But it wasn't there this morning...'

'What's it say?' interrupted Drekki. There was no time to coax Gord's wits out of first gear. He looked closer. Trying to read the writing hurt his eyes.

'Look away,' said Kedren. 'Bad magic, that. Very bad.'

'Listen to the smith,' Lerarus said. 'This is one of the dark tongues of Chaos. Daemon tainted. Damnation follows understanding.'

'Sure as night and day,' said Kedren. He spat to ward off ill-fortune.

'Rather after the fact, that spitting, don't you think, seeing as ill-fortune's ridden our beards all the way out here?' Drekki said, eyebrow raised. 'Can you read it, Lerarus?'

She was offended. 'You think I'd damn myself, captain?' said the mage. 'But I do not need to read it to know it as a spell.' She shaded her face with her hands, as if the tortured writing glared, though it was simple paint, black on the metal.

'Then get it off my ship,' growled Drekki.

'We will, lad,' said Kedren. 'Precautions are needed first. It must be denatured, dispelled, then scrubbed off carefully by someone with the right pair of gloves. Very long. And extra thick,' he said significantly.

'I can bleed off the magic,' said Lerarus.

'I'll douse it with aether,' said Otherek. 'That'll nullify most of it. Aether beats magic every time.'

'This has been refreshed.' She squatted down to get a better look, but screwed up her eyes in pain while she did. 'It can't have been more than a few days ago.'

'Then there's a spy aboard,' said Kedren.

'Do you have any clue who might have done this?' said Lerarus.

Drekki looked around. Some of the crew were gathering, curious. Otherek shooed them back.

'Not out here,' said Drekki quietly.

'Then you do have a clue,' said Kedren.

Drekki gave the slightest nod. 'How long will it take to get rid of it?' he asked.

'An hour, maybe more,' said Lerarus. 'Less than two.'

'Then we call the trommraad now,' said Kedren. His tone brooked no disagreement.

'Then we call the trommraad after,' said Drekki, disagreeing anyway. 'While you deal with this mark, I'll take a look at the endrin. Have Velunti make everyone work in pairs. They've all seen this now. No one is to go out of sight of their shipmate. I don't want anyone trying anything while we're occupied.' He looked up at the stuttering endrin, and blew out a long breath. This was proving to be a trying day. 'I'll also try to figure out where the dreng we are.'

* * *

'Bokko is right, this is bad,' Drekki said to himself. He poked about under the casing, checking over Bokko's temporary remedy. There were a number of problems. 'Bent holding pins. Misaligned ring feed, broken shut-off valve, and that cracked aether conduit,' he muttered. 'At least that secondary condenser still works.'

He sent Trokwi in to make sure. The drillbill stalked under the fizzing workings of the endrin, and reported back with affirmative warbles. The cracked conduit was the worst of it. The protective metal outer pipe was still intact, so the glass beneath had to have failed, just like Bokko said it would, because aether was pouring out of a broken weld. The leak lowered the pressure at the injector, where the aether was mixed with air and forced into the core reaction chamber. Less aether meant less power. Less power meant less speed.

'Funti drukk,' Drekki said.

The outer pipe would convey the gas into the engine only for a while: steel didn't hold up long in the face of pressurised aether. Bokko had wrapped the weld in bandages impregnated with plaster, which remedied things somewhat, but it was still leaking.

However, the leak wasn't gushing, so the crack couldn't be all that bad. Drekki reckoned a simple glass repair job would see it right until they were in a place they could do it properly. Awkward but achievable. But it would need the two of them to fix, not least because once that metal cover and the bandages were off, it'd be spewing aether right in their faces, because they couldn't shut it down on account of the broken valve. Bokko would need to bleed the aether off.

Drekki was sorely tempted to dive right in; it would feel good to get his hands dirty, put all the thoughts of leadership and decision making out of his mind.

'Endrins are so much simpler than people,' he said to Trokwi.

The bird-facsimile's jewelled eyes clicked open and closed. Did he understand such talk? Simple tasks and surveying he managed with aplomb, but the abstract nature of being? Although Drekki had made Trokwi with his own hands, what went on in the drill-bill's clockwork brain was a mystery to him. An artisan put life into an object. Once it was in there, it did its own thing.

'I suppose it'll keep,' he said. Bokko's stopgaps were holding for the time being. He went over to the observation post, and climbed in. Easier to take their bearings from there. On the deck below him, Bokko's cutting torch hissed as he sliced away the tainted plates.

Adrimm led the call in a sky shanty, Evtorr and Velunti sang the responses. Gord's basso enriched the sound. The hold was open, they were hauling out sheets of replacement metal for the repairs. It was almost like a normal day. If the smell of hot steel and aether hadn't been disturbingly cut with roasting flesh, it would have been relaxing. Duardin find peace in work.

Drekki couldn't relax. He hummed and hawed over his instruments. He was as skilled as a league navigator, or so he liked to think, but he could make no sense of what he saw. Pressure readings suggested they were in the middle currents of the Third Air. Everything else was confusing. His compass wandered. There were no identifiable islands in sight. All around, the sky was that strange, uniform lemon colour, opaque as a light mist, shrinking the world in on the *Aelsling*, so that far horizons stole worryingly close while he wasn't looking. Light-scatter readings were therefore of little use. He put his prismatic gauge away.

'Maybe good that we're running slow,' he said. 'Don't want to race into trouble.' He didn't believe that. What if they were attacked? What if they needed speed? But it did well to keep a good shine on a situation, he held. 'Optimism slays more daemons than despair,' he said. 'Come on, Trokwi. Time to talk to the others.' He frowned. 'Though I don't think they're going to like what I'm going to say.'

* * *

'You better take that back, Captain Flynt!' Spittle flecked Umherth's beard. 'Urdi's been on this vessel with us since you rolled into the Grey Rat and shot your mouth off about fortune and glory, why, seven years gone now!'

'Now, Umherth, that's not what the captain's saying! Listen to him, it's just that he can't be sure,' Hrunki said, half-scolding, half-soothing. Neither approach caught.

'Urdi's my second cousin's nephew on my mother's side,' Umherth snarled. 'He's clan!'

'Aye, and you're crew,' said Drekki with an authoritative point of his finger. 'And you're a trommlord, so keep your bloody voice down. Aboard ship, crew's tighter than clan. Has to be. I need you on this, you old toothless *bozdok*.[28] Head before heart, so cool your cannons.'

'Urdi's been with us from the start,' repeated Umherth.

Drekki responded with perfect calm. 'So have you, and you've a thicker beard and more inches on your belt, so you should know better than to jump to the most obvious conclusion.'

Umherth spluttered. His face contorted into a series of odd expressions. His skin darkened around his nose ring.

'I'd cool it yourself,' said Kedren into Drekki's ear. 'The little vein is going in his temple. Bad sign that.'

'Don't care. Calm down, Umherth,' said Drekki.

Umherth made a throttled noise. Hrunki pulled at his arm. He wrenched it free with an inchoate shout. His fist clenched. A punch hovered, waiting to be unleashed.

'All finished?' said Drekki.

The atmosphere was denser than beer, practically foaming with tension.

'I still say it's Ildrin,' said Umherth. His fist lowered slowly.

---

28 | Kharadrid: Hard-headed fool.

The fight left the room, unfought.

'I'm the one as saw him,' said Drekki. 'Whoever it was. There was a hooded figure by the bow. Ildrin came past a moment later. That doesn't mean it *was* him. Khenna, Evtorr and Bokko were on watch with Ildrin too.'

'Then it could've been any of them,' said Umherth.

'It could, it could, but as Urdi went out before me to start on the watch change, it could have been him too.'

Umherth settled into a traditional grumbling stance, chin down, beard swallowing his face, arms crossed. 'I don't see how all this matters. You saw this person after we were followed. Too late for them to have painted that hell mark on. Gah, who even knows that's it? It could be a prank.'

'It is not a prank, it is a signal to the followers of the Changer,' Lerarus said. They'd almost forgotten she was sat there in the corner on the floor, where her head was safe from the ceiling, watching the council with young yet wise eyes. 'The ship, the harkraken, and the daemons, it could have brought all of them down on us.'

'The ship came first,' said Umherth.

'It does, but a spell like that needs renewing. That could have been what the captain saw, a renewal, not the first painting.'

'Stuff and nonsense!' said Umherth.

'She's right, you know, Umherth,' said Kedren. 'Magic like that needs a touch up, lest it fades. This isn't runecraft carved in stone.'

'Just because you don't want to admit Urdi might be implicated, you're dismissing the facts,' said Otherek.

Umherth's spluttering set up again. Drekki warded it off with raised hands.

'Look, I'm not saying it definitely *is* Urdi,' said Drekki. 'It probably isn't. I'm just saying it's not *definitely* Ildrin.'

'What about the others?' said Kedren.

'I'm inclined to rule out Evtorr and Bokko,' said Drekki.

'The poet and the endrinrigger are only as good-hearted duardin as Urdi!' said Umherth.

'Don't interrupt, Umherth. That's my vice, not yours. I'm going down the list here, shush,' said Drekki. 'They are good-hearted. Khenna too. She seems straight as a driveshaft to me. I can tell the good from the bad, you know that. But gut feeling is not the cornerstone of my opinion here. Fact is, I know exactly where they were. I met them all and relieved them all before I saw this other personage. Only Urdi and Ildrin were unaccounted for at that exact time, so it has to be one of them. I'm poking at the pertinent here.'

'What about a stowaway?' said Hrunki.

'Another duardin? Hiding aboard? Really?' said Drekki. 'We've searched the ship stem to stern. Otherek would have sniffed them out.'

'There's no one else aboard, captain,' said Otherek.

'Then they've got to be in the crew, haven't they? So. Speculations. Number one is Ildrin. Ildrin's new, we don't know him at all.'

'He's a grumbler,' said Umherth. 'Urdi's not.'

'If grumbling were a crime, you, Adrimm and Kedren would be in the gibbets outside Mhornar docks with razorbills pecking at your dead eyes,' said Drekki. He spread his fingers. 'That being said, grumbling don't play into his favour, I admit. Urdi, on the other hand, was missing all night before we sailed, out drinking he says.'

'He'd never betray us,' said Otherek. 'I'll side with Umherth on that. He'd certainly never turn to the Dark Gods.'

'Everyone has a price,' said Drekki, provoking a pained moan from Umherth. Drekki shot him his captain's look. 'All right, all right. What we need is evidence.'

'Any evidence will be overboard,' said Kedren.

'Not so,' said Drekki. 'This spell needs renewing, right?'

'Yes,' said Lerarus.

'And this paint is special?'

'It's not just paint,' said Kedren. 'And I'd use "evil" rather than "special" as my descriptor of choice, but broadly, you are correct.'

Drekki nodded. 'Fine then. Find the evil paint, find the turn-coat duardin. That'll be our evidence. Vote.'

Zhokri-ha, unanimously, even from Umherth, though he did mutter a bit.

They had their evidence in minutes, Ildrin too, clapped in irons and held by Gord, squirming wrathfully before Drekki's judgement outside the cabin.

'What's this then, Ildrin?' Drekki asked, lifting up a jar filled with a gloopy black liquid. He wore a glove of the kind used to load aether fuel rods: thick, woven metal, proof against ninety thousand *milli-khar*[29] of aetheric radiation. He could feel the sick vibration of the stuff through the glass, even so.

'I ain't never seen it, captain.' Ildrin wriggled in Gord's iron grip. 'I swear!'

'That so, is it?' said Drekki. 'How come then it was in your locker? Why is it there's black muck and burns on your hand? Otherek says there is, don't deny.'

'Show him, Gord,' said Otherek.

Gord forced the fingers of Ildrin's right hand open. There was indeed the aforesaid muck and burns marring Ildrin's hand.

'I don't know! I don't know how it got there. I don't know! It was like that this morning, when I woke. I couldn't get it off! I thought it was oil or something!'

'A likely story,' Umherth sneered.

---

29 | Kharadrid: One hundred and eleven thousand milli-khar is equal to one *aethrigen*. Five aethrigens will kill a duardin stone dead.

'Down to the brig with him,' Drekki said.

'Right-ho,' Gord said. He whistled a tune as he dragged Ildrin away. His mind was on something else, probably dinner.

Ildrin, on the other hand, was entirely invested in the situation.

'I'm innocent! I've done nothing! Curse you, Captain Flynt! Curse you!'

His voice was cut off by a door slamming.

'That settles it,' said Umherth happily.

'Does it, now,' said Drekki to himself. He stroked his beard, as duardin are wont to do when troubled. The gold cappings he wore on his braids jangled.

The trommraad filed out, all except Kedren, who tarried.

'You don't look sure, lad,' he said.

'I'm never sure till I'm sure,' said Drekki. He had a faraway look in his eyes. He was thinking. Deeply. 'When ale's in the pot and the pay chest is full, that is when a matter's concluded, not before.'

'We've got our culprit, what's the problem?'

'If it's not him, then it's not him.'

'You did the right thing.'

'He's safest locked up, I agree, but I don't like to be wrong.'

'We're not wrong,' said Kedren.

Drekki shrugged. 'Maybe. I'd have had Urdi banged up too if you lot could be counted on to vote. So I say, we watch everyone closely. Maybe someone will pull something rash and settle the matter for good.'

'What, like this mission?' said Kedren.

'I'm going to ignore that,' said Drekki.

'All right, lad,' said Kedren. 'I'll see to Ildrin's hand. It doesn't do to have that stuff on you. If he's innocent it'd not be fair if he turned into something unpleasant. He's had a bad enough day already. I've got the right salves and runes to get it off and stop any rot.'

Kedren left. Bokko entered.

'Ah, Bokko, good news, I hope?'

'Well, er, I know where we are now,' said Bokko, who didn't look happy at all.

'Excellent!' said Drekki, clapping his hands together. 'Things are looking up.'

'Not excellent,' said Bokko apologetically. His eyes were downcast. He twisted his oily hands around his spanner. 'In fact, you could say far from excellent, as it were.'

Drekki raised a quizzical eyebrow.

Bokko was grave. 'Best come and see for yourself, captain.'

CHAPTER THIRTEEN

THE EYE OF TESTUDINOUS

The sky stopped some hundred miles away. As any skyfarer will aver, that's bad news in the Skyshoals, where the sky generally goes on forever. It only doesn't go on forever in two places. One of those places is the Perimeter Inimical, where the realms give out and pure magic begins. The other place is arguably worse – it's moot, for sure, as nobody has survived either – but that other place is bad, and it is…

'The Eye of Testudinous,' said Drekki.

He snapped his telescope shut. He didn't need it to view the immense vortex turning before him, for it filled the airs from First to Fifth, but magnified detail seemed a little less terrifying than the whole of the thing. 'Dongliz. Funti *dongliz*.'

A group of the oldest gathered at the prow, Gord and Lerarus alongside. Ahead, the lemon skies turned a fizzing orange, as if reality were compressed so greatly little bubbles of it were trying to escape. Who knew, that could have been the case. Where the eye turned, the laws of physics became fuzzy. Titanic energies were at play, perhaps even gods. Maybe worse things. Almost certainly, worse things. Drekki did not know. Nobody did. This was fresh territory for Kharadron science.

'How did we end up so far in?' Evrokk said.

'The storm,' said Drekki. 'It must have displaced us halfway across the shoals. Bloody magic.'

'We should turn back,' said Otherek.

'We'll be too late to Erulu,' said Drekki. 'We're in a bit of a race here, lads, in case you need reminding.'

'Stuff Erulu,' said Otherek, unusually forthright. 'My advice as aether-khemist is to turn around right now.' Serious situation, if Otherek was citing his rank.

'It don't matter,' said Evrokk. A grin sick with fear tugged his mouth out of shape. 'We're being sucked in.' He went to the gunwale, leaned out on the rigging, and scowled up. 'Without that second endrin we don't have the power to fare free, sure as sure. We're in the orbit of the Eye. In its pull. Worst density mass in the shoals, and we're being sucked into it,' he repeated. 'Sucked in!'

'We're still faring slow,' said Kedren. 'Can't we just turn around and fly the other way? Is it really that powerful?' For once, no one mocked him for his lack of skyfaring knowledge.

'Slow to start with.' Evrokk gave a bitter chuckle. 'It looks safe enough, but you wait till I try to turn us around. Think of it like a waterfall in a river. Look up there.' He pointed now, past the endrin globe bleeding its fuel in a way that it shouldn't, up at the line of metaliths queuing for annihilation. 'They're going in. Slow at first, then fast and dead. Like us.'

Adrimm was eavesdropping. They should have known he'd heard. His hammer taps were suspiciously absent. His nut-brown skin went grey when he heard.

'This is it, we're going to die.'

'You said that the day before yesterday, Fair-weather,' said Drekki. 'And a few weeks back, but we're still here.'

'Yes, but that's the Eye! The twisted heart of the shoals. Nothing that goes near that gets out.'

'Just because nobody has ever come back doesn't mean they die,' said Drekki. 'This could be an opportunity.'

'The evidence suggests otherwise,' said Otherek drily.

'Yes, yes, but think!' Drekki said. 'Going in would be insane, but going around it…' He held up a finger, as if he had made the winningest point in the world.

'There's no round, there's only directly *in* or directly *away*,' said Evrokk. 'And I think I just said we can't go directly away.'

'Not so,' said Drekki. 'If we get around it, then we'll be closer to Erulu. We'll make such good time, we'll go so fast we'll arrive before we left.'

'If we get around it,' said Gord, catching on to the gravity of it all. His expression went blank. Half of him understood. The half that didn't was in charge of his face. If he was against it, Drekki's plan really wasn't promising.

'Saved time's no use to the dead,' said Kedren.

The duardin fell to arguing in baffling, technical terms, switching to Khazalid when the Azyrite tongue ran out of useable words, then to the Kharadrid argot. Lerarus lost understanding and then lost her patience. She split the air with a lance of fire. That silenced them.

'Speak plainly so I can understand! Is it possible to get past?' Lerarus asked.

'Impossible,' said Evrokk.

'*Improbable*,' corrected Drekki. 'Not impossible.'

'If we do what you say, captain, how many days will it shave off?'

The duardin shuddered and exchanged hunted looks.

'What's all that about?' said Lerarus.

'Never say "shave" to a duardin, lass,' said Kedren.

'I reckon if we chance it and come out smiling, we'll be on and at Erulu within three days,' said Drekki. 'That's seven days ahead of schedule.' He grinned. 'Now what do you think of that?'

'I think you've gone mad,' said Kedren.

'I ain't ready to face Nagash!' wailed Adrimm. A bold heart beat in that breast. Throw him without warning into combat or the fiercest storm and he'd be all right. Show him death from a little ways off, though, when he had time to think on it, and Adrimm got the wobbles.

'We'll be all right. If we fare at it hard, we'll accelerate really fast, and I mean really, really fast. We keep in at an angle, then put all power in, and our momentum will sort of slingshot us on our way, like a big flywheel flinging off dirt, if you will,' said Drekki, making heroic gestures with his hands, as if success were a certainty.

Kedren shook his head. 'Skybeards.'

'Maybe he's right.' Otherek stroked the metal tubes on the front of his mask. 'Could work.'

Evrokk looked halfway to acceptance, then shook his head hard. 'We'll not get up enough speed to break free. We'll be trapped in a spiral orbit, going faster and faster, until we're dragged in, and then...' He waved his hand at the Eye. 'Then whatever happens when you go into the Eye will happen.'

'We won't if we get that second endrin going,' said Drekki. 'With that running, we'll be laughing. Go as fast as we can, right at it.' He jabbed with his hand. 'Switch course, curve around the maelstrom. Reach the correct velocity, then blam!' He clapped loudly once.

'Airscrews won't give us enough push.'

'I'm not talking about airscrews,' said Drekki with a smirk.

'Oh no,' said Evrokk. 'No.'

'If we vent the aether directly through the overspill vents, we could use it to fare right past, faster than any duardin has ever been before.'

'Or dead as a lot of other duardin before,' said Kedren. 'I reckon "blam" covers it.'

'Hear him out,' said Otherek. 'Venting the aether's a ticklish proposition, but it could work. We get up a ferocious clip, then vent from the coreward bleeds. If we keep it lateral, we should shoot off, like he says. Do you have the calculations?'

'As a matter of fact, I do,' said Drekki.

'Your father's, I'm guessing,' said Otherek.

'His father?' said Lerarus.

'Aye, Bazherek Flynt dabbled with this. Notorious for it, he was,' said Otherek.

'Hang on, hang on, the same father who vanished trying to find the lost sky-port of Barak-Minoz, and went missing with your brothers?' said Adrimm, giving up all pretence of work and shouldering his way among the oldbeards. 'Went missing right about these parts, in fact, after employing said calculations?'

Drekki waggled his hand. 'More or less.'

The clattering of hammers had just about stopped. Everyone was listening now. Only loyal, diligent Bokko kept on with his job.

'That's great, that's just great!' moaned Adrimm.

'Velunti?' Drekki called to his cargo-master. 'Can you get rid of Adrimm for me please?'

Velunti Runk hurried over, and herded Adrimm away with many a 'Yes, I know,' and 'It'll be fine! Captain Flynt's got it all in hand.' He put him to work on the far side of the ship then came hurrying back.

'Thanks, Velunti. I can't bloody think with that *wazzock*[30] grumbling on,' said Drekki. 'Lads, lads! Brave hearts. We can do this.'

---

30 | Khazalid: Ancient insult of uncertain meaning and provenance.

'The nav-guild didn't approve your father's charts or your father's calculations,' said Evrokk.

'Which is why I'm not in the nav-guild,' said Drekki. 'They're too timid by half.' He turned around to face the crew. 'I'll not dip this in honey, this is going to be tough, but if we pull it off, we'll have a fortune in nav-data and we'll snatch the talisman from under the noses of villains. They'll be singing songs about us in every barak in the sky. You'll be rich and famous, every one of you. Who's with me?'

His need to give a more detailed speech about the coming venture was obviated by practically everyone aboard having had a good listen in for the last five minutes. A curious duardin is hard to put off.

'Zhokri-ha!' shouted Umherth, beating his helm ring with his fists. The thump of gauntlets on brass encouraged several others. Umherth's fervour had that effect.

'Aye, captain, we sail where you go!' they shouted. And: 'I ain't no coward.' And: 'Will there be an extra ration of gunrum?' And: 'And shares for danger pay?' That last was from Velunti, who among his many other jobs was also the *Aelsling*'s chief representative of the Skyfarer's Union.

Not all were so enthusiastic. A few raised their voices in opposition. Drekki calmed both sides of the argument with a gentle downward push of the hands.

'I'll see what I can do. If you want bigger shares and more booze as well as being the most famous of the Overlords, then I'll fix it.'

'Hurrah!' they shouted again, more enthused than before.

'Better get him to write that down first,' grumbled Evtorr.

'Maybe in blank verse?' Urdi quipped. Everyone laughed. Evtorr scowled.

'Right then,' said Drekki to his inner circle. 'First things first. We've no chance of either passage or escape without that endrin fixed. That stays bust, so do our chances. Bokko, suit up. I'll need you in the air. The aether will need bleeding once we get the outer casing off that broken tube.'

'Aye-aye, captain!' said Bokko.

'I've got an idea,' said Kedren. 'I think I can help. May I?'

'That you can, master runesmith,' said Drekki.

'You get on then,' said Kedren. 'I'm going down to my forge. I'll be up with you soon.' He set off at a determined pace.

'Evrokk, you've got the helm,' Drekki said.

Evrokk had gone pale, a different shade to Adrimm's ashen colour; there was a hint of green to him. He dropped his voice.

'Please, captain, this faring is beyond me. I can't do it!'

'You can, you can! Confidence!' Drekki slapped him on the back. 'If anyone on board can pull this off, Evrokk my lad, it is you.' He paused. 'Well, I could do it, but I've got an endrin to fix. So you'll have to do it instead.'

Second best wasn't so bad. So far as Drekki held it, it was flattering. Evrokk was not convinced.

'What are you waiting for then? To work!' shouted Drekki.

The sound of hammering recommenced to a more desperate beat.

They got the deck closed up with riveted plates as the wind was picking up speed. The turning of the Eye dragged at the sky, pulling the air into hard-toothed currents. The *Aelsling*'s passage was mightily perturbed.

'Get those clasps on the cannon properly! Tie down that tarpaulin, get this ship locked down!' Gord strode about the deck with Gunterr Borrki, repeating the master-at-arms' shouts at ear-splitting volume. The wind was louder. Gord's voice cracked in competition. Velunti Runk performed a similar role, rushing about with Urdi getting the hatches battened. Giant pins were slid into the retaining loops over the cargo hold and threaded through with steel cables to hold them fast.

Evtorr shut up his lamps, took them down, and stowed them in padded cases. Umherth checked the shrouds. Hrunki was with Khenna tightening the hawsers, until Hrunki saw that Khenna could do it just fine alone, so she went off to help Gunterr. Everyone had their own responsibilities to attend to. It kept their minds off the growling tornado of magic swallowing the world ahead of them.

Evrokk had to concentrate the hardest. He sat in the cockpit, trying to keep his hands loose on the wheel; he could react better that way. He was trying not to be daunted by the power of the Eye. The name was purely poetic. The Eye looked nothing like an eye. It was a huge vortex, a yawning, sucking hole in space and time. A slot. Or a hole. Probably. It depended which way you looked at it.

Opinions differed as to what the Eye was, and to where it came from. There was the legend, everyone knew the legend, but was that true? There was no time to think on veracity while staring reality down, and poor Evrokk was doing a lot of staring.

Close, and getting closer, the Eye was a funnel of orange light, whirling round and around. Like thick, flawed, molten glass, it was translucent, but not transparent. But actually it was, then it wasn't again. Shadows raced round it, then didn't. There were *things* inside, looming huge and black, which then went to nothing: a promise of the destruction the ship could expect if it kept its current course. There was no choice. They had to keep going. The Eye had the *Aelsling* in its grip.

The Eye was unstable. It bent about in the middle, so the throat of it tracked across the sky, this way, then that. In, then out. This perturbed the wind, and therefore the ship, and the faring was rough. Lightning was wrung from thin air. Forks stabbed in all directions, seeking down and finding only the pull of the Eye. The accompanying thunder was subdued, hollowed out, gone before it fully rumbled, like inappropriate laughter stifled a second too late. Clouds spun into wreaths that were ripped into shreds. This went for the solids too. Metaliths. Bigger lands. Immense animals. A pelting cascade of things. A dead whaleen tumbled past, end over end, flaccid as dough, spine shattered. It was going so fast. Forty seconds later they saw it explode, a mote of black against the orange glow transmuted into a bouquet of sparks. A sizeable metalith bearing a dead village spun by, the casualty of a raid somewhere, the buildings set to the torch and the island itself sent off on a course of total destruction.

The Eye spoke to them over the wind's howl in strange whoops, and it showed them things: foreboding flashes, projected huge upon the vortex's rippled sides; disturbing visions, yet so fleeting the crew could not be sure what they saw.

Otherek had a ringside seat, sat up in the observation cupola atop the second endrin. He was scared. Duardin are brave as a rule, but not immune to fear. He used focus in spades to bury his terror, smothering it in work, taking rapid notes from his machines, all of which were going crazy.

Still, he could see the potential. Drekki had been right. If they got out of this mess, there'd be money to be made from the data.

Meanwhile, on the far side of the rear endrin globe, Drekki and Bokko laboured on the damaged mechanism. This was advanced endrineering, under high stress. A Grade Five Severe Plus task, and there wasn't a higher grade than Five Severe Plus.

Drekki rested a moment. His back needed stretching out. Overhead, Bokko bobbed about under his personal endrin, straining his three-line anchor. The lines twanged. He was up high with a draw wire and dispersal funnel, leaching the aether from the endrin so Drekki could work in something close to safety. Bokko glowed with discharging aelchemical energy, bright as a gheist on a moonless night.

'Are you all right up there?' Drekki hollered at him.

Bokko couldn't hear.

'Are you all right?' Drekki shouted again. Still he was not heard. He banged his free hand on the nearest of Bokko's lines and gestured. The endrinrigger got the gist, nodded and stuck up his thumb.

Back to the task in hand, back to the endrin casing.

The work Drekki was attempting was fiddly under ideal conditions. These were not ideal conditions. Now the pipe cover was unscrewed, opened out and off, he could clearly see the crack in the glass. An outgassing of vaporised aether, so very, very hot, hissed in his face, and that was with Bokko drawing off most into the tempest. His helmet was getting uncomfortably warm. Sweat dripped off his nose and gathered in the bottom. His lenses were misting up. In those hypothetical, ideal conditions, the endrin would have been deactivated for the repair. Rapid death by unknowable vortex would have been the consequence of doing that currently, so active it stayed.

Inside the endrin, Trokwi held on to the workings with his clawed feet, bracing his head against flexible copper tubes to keep them clear of the repair site. This allowed Drekki to get deeper than he could otherwise without dismantling the lot. Already, Drekki had fixed a few of the other problems, and quite well, if he said so himself, but that damned tube would stay broken, wouldn't it?

He reached inside again, one hand holding his arc torch, the other a stick of welding silica. He needed both hands in there, in a space that barely accommodated one. The contortions of his shoulders hurt his back.

'*Krundit vhon,*' Drekki swore as he eased back in. 'Bloody endrin.'

Wind buffeted him. It seized him then let go, seized then let go, each gust threatening to peel his magnetic boots from the globe. His safety line yanked against his belt, tormenting his back. Gods alone knew what stress the storm was putting on the clasp, the belt staple and the bar on the globe underneath him.

So many things that could break and send him off to his death. Just one would do it.

He turned up the arc welder, bent his elbows nigh on backwards to get the silica stick close to the tube and the glowing tool tip.

'Nearly there...'

The wind was strong enough to ruffle metal feathers, and Drekki feared for Trokwi, but the little drillbill held stoically on, keeping his workspace clear.

'Almost got it.'

The ship bounced.

'Funti drukk!'

Drekki snatched his arc welder away to prevent him pile-driving it through the pipe. He cursed endrineers and aether-khemists alike for not finding a more durable material than glass to convey the aether-stream.

'Toughened, my scaly behind,' he growled. 'Bloody liability!'

Maybe I could have come up with something better, if I hadn't abandoned a promising career as an endrineer to run off for a life of adventure, he thought.

'You can shut up too,' he told himself.

He tried the weld again. The crack was tiny, delicate, half hiding itself around the back of the tube. The leaking aether was infuriating, the space for manoeuvre small, and the lurching of the ship large. He blobbed melted silica everywhere it was not supposed to go.

Maybe this wasn't such a good idea after all. He had put the ship at risk. Maybe this was one reckless gambit too far.

No time for doubt, it wasn't his way. He breathed deep.

'Concentrate, Drekki, get it fixed,' he said. The welder descended again. 'Dreng funti von!' he swore, as another shake sent the tip of the instrument skating over the tube. An angry orange line cooled into a black scar. Another couple of those and the tube would shatter completely. Grungni, his shoulders and back were screaming!

Vibrations from behind announced someone coming up the access ladder. He pulled up his arms, loaded his lips with a rebuke for Kedren for being late, but it was Evtorr.

Looking up, he got a better view of the danger they were in. The Eye had swollen into a wall of racing orange lines, all sense of its circular nature lost. He had half an hour at best. Trails of power coming off the vortex raked the *Aelsling*, eager fingers dancing on rails, searching for something or someone to snatch. Each caress left molten welts. A minor metalith went spinning past, becoming a black speck against the hot-glass glow of the Eye.

The poet rested his helm against Drekki's. Touching, the vibrations of their voices could pass through the metal.

'My brother wants to know when he needs to accelerate.' Evtorr still had to shout. He sounded distant, false, like those experimental sound recordings they were doing up at Barak-Nar.

'Not yet,' Drekki shouted back. His breath misted up his lenses even more.

'He says,' Evtorr said, pulling lungfuls of breath from his tanks, 'that we need to do it soon. We're getting very close. He says we're approaching the point of no return.'

Yes, yes, thought Drekki. If that wasn't blatantly obvious, thank you, Evtorr. 'We can't increase power until I've patched this conducting tube,' he said.

Evtorr peered in the hole. 'Tricky,' he said.

Drekki swallowed his annoyance. A lot of harsh words went unsaid.

The ship bounced hard. A swarm of boulders streaked by at the tips of fiery trails. All three duardin waved their arms, trying to regain their balance. For a second, the bleed wire Bokko held lost contact with the broken pipe, and Drekki took the full brunt of the aether leak. His suit temperature rose dangerously.

Evtorr got in there, rammed the wire back home.

'Right, thanks, Evtorr,' said Drekki. 'Now back up. This needs fixing.'

Evtorr nodded. He made to descend, but then Kedren finally came huffing up. He climbed awkwardly on the endrins at the best of times, but now, for some reason, he was holding out one arm far from his body, his clenched fist clad in a thick leather smithing glove over his aeronaut's suit, and that made him more unstable than ever. Evtorr leaned over to help him.

Drekki went to resume his work, but Kedren was waving his arm about, so he waited. Kedren joined Evtorr and Drekki in a conclave of touched helmets.

'Where have you been?' Drekki asked.

'Getting this ready,' Kedren said. He opened his double-gloved fist.

Inside was a small clasp, the sort of thing used to repair cracks on pipes. It was still cooling from the forge. A rune stood prominently at one side.

'This fit the problem?'

'What?' said Evtorr. 'You can't seal cracked glass with a copper clasp. It'll do nothing. The gas will just leak out round it!'

Drekki moved his head around a touch, so he could look Evtorr right in the eye. 'I've fared with this ground-thumping trommlord on more than a few voyages. Don't underestimate the runecraft of the ancestors. Old Kedren here might just save our beards.'

'Rune magic?' said Evtorr excitedly. The glories of the ancients were a favourite topic of his.

'Aye,' said Kedren, and bent to his task. He got his hands in the hole. Evtorr relinquished his space so Drekki could watch the runesmith clasp the band around the pipe. Kedren was not a maker of machines, yet he had the rune band in place quickly and efficiently, far faster than Drekki could have.

His helmet clanged on the endrinsphere as the ship bounced through another air pocket. He grabbed Drekki's shoulders so their visors could stay in contact.

'Give me that welding thingy,' he said.

Drekki handed it over.

For all his grumbling about new-fangled Overlord ways, Kedren showed no difficulty working the torch. When he was done, a soft, golden glow emanating from the rune joined the blue of the aether coursing through the pipe. Again, their helmets touched.

'Rune of repair,' he said. 'It'll take about three minutes to convince that glass to knit itself back together.'

'Oh, the glory of the karaks will save us from disaster, when I see a shiny rune I'll be happy for ever after,' Evtorr began in his special recitals voice. It was booming and self-important, and also very annoying.

Drekki pushed him away so he couldn't hear the poem.

'It'll be cutting it tight,' he said.

Kedren shrugged. 'It's what we've got.' He pulled out a pocket watch and depressed a button. One of its many hands switched to countdown mode. 'This reaches twelve, we hit the pedal or whatever it is you skybeards do to make these contraptions fly, and get out of here.'

'Right,' said Drekki. He gestured to Trokwi to stay safe in the globe before bolting the cover back in place. He dragged Evtorr, who was still declaiming to himself, back in close. 'You, shut up and listen. Stay up here with Bokko. He has to stay bleeding the power off the fracture until Kedren's magic has it closed. You need

to keep your feet clamped tight to the sphere, and your line on.'
He clipped his safety line onto Evtorr's belt. 'Feel for the engine
opening up, you'll not hear it. Then get Bokko down. He won't
be able to bring himself in under these conditions.'

'I'll keep him safe, captain, I promise.'

Drekki patted his arm. 'See that you do, Evtorr. You're a lousy
poet but a fine duardin.'

Out on the syrupy walls of the Eye, another metalith vanished
in a flash. That would be them, if the repair didn't take. Nobody
needed to be told.

Evtorr got up and waved at Bokko.

'And you can recite as much poetry as you like in this noise,
once I've gone,' said Drekki, though Evtorr could not hear.

Drekki beckoned to Kedren, and together they went down to the
deck. The shrouds were singing with the strain. The ship dipped,
jouncing them off their footing. Unpleasant harmonics built in the
steel, making a choral moan. The staple ladder thrummed under
their hands. A peculiar, violent energy ran over the fabric of the
vessel, causing their palms to itch and their nerves to jump. They
reached the deck shaken.

'I don't want to do this again,' Drekki said, by necessity to himself. The voice of the Eye destroyed all other sound except the
racket it raised in the ship. He clipped a safety lanyard to his belt
and then to Kedren's. Together they swayed up the deck to the
cockpit.

Burning debris raced past. Larger chunks of matter tumbled
overhead, unrecognisable, surfaces afire. Whatever they had been,
all was reduced to the same embers by the force of the Eye. Musi-
cally they plummeted to their destruction, coming apart into
showers of nothing before they hit the glassy vortex.

With a mid-length skyhook I could touch that, Drekki thought.
They were way too close.

The deck was clear, every item secured. Evrokk was alone at the wheel, leaning hard on it towards the edgeward board, straining to keep the ship pointed forward. The strain in the rudder could be felt through the ship. They were in the death spiral now, on a rotary course, picking up speed, prow still forward to the eye. Gravity pulled on the fluids of their bodies, making Drekki's blood pool on his left-hand side. What with the wind, their velocity, and the Eye's fatal attraction, it was difficult to move.

They reached Evrokk as Kedren's watch counted down to the point of escape.

They were nearly done. There were seconds to spare once the repair took, no more. After that, no amount of thrust would set them free. They were already travelling at tremendous speed.

Drekki waved at Evrokk. The ship was shaking ferociously, blurring vision and making it hard to see. Kedren held up his hand. Five digits splayed. He curled in his smallest finger, the start of a visual countdown.

Four.

Drekki's teeth rattled. He grabbed at the rail round the cockpit. His arm shook until it went numb.

Three.

Glaring streaks of molten matter curved in towards the Eye, exploding into pure energy when they hit some horizon that reviled solidity.

Two.

Evrokk was moving. He was pulling levers, opening valves. Drekki lunged for the wheel and grabbed it, steadying it while his helmsduardin prepared to make the *Aelsling* race.

One.

Evrokk wrapped his arms around the guard rail, hanging off his elbows, his fingers locked together. He had his foot on the aether release pedal.

Venting aether was a risky business. It depleted the fuel fast, risked damaging the endrins, and it often exploded. These were just a few of the many reasons sky-ships didn't use aether jets as their primary form of propulsion. Not yet, anyway. It had been tried. The results thus far had been unfavourable.

Ordinarily there would have been a thorough safety check before attempting something like this. The crew might even debark to a towed skiff. It was that dangerous. All Drekki had in his favour was a duardin in the air holding up a wire, another with his foot on the pedal, and his crew below hanging on for grim death and wishing hard for success.

This better work, he thought, or Nagash will kill himself laughing when we line up before him.

Can atomised bodies line up? he wondered.

Zero.

Kedren's closed fist was all the warning Drekki got. The vibration of the deck, the tremble of aether working underlying all the stresses exerted by the Eye; it all changed when Evrokk's foot stamped down. Drekki gave a cry and put all his weight on the wheel to bring the prow away from the Eye.

Acceleration was instant and savage. The roar of evaporating aether outdid the song of destruction. Blue light washed the deck. Evrokk slammed another lever home. Mag-boots squealed on the deck. Drekki's blood, so cruelly dragged from his left-hand side, now wanted to gather in his backside. Pressure squeezed air from his lungs. His eyes hurt. He clung on for dear life, knowing that to release the wheel was to release life.

It was working. The *Aelsling* was moving alongside the Eye, picking up speed, the prow turning surely towards open sky. The ship burst through showers of embers. It was licked by storms of lightning, but still the sky-ship accelerated, going faster, and faster. The Eye lost all sense of form, so did the ship, and Evrokk. Drekki's limbs spread out into a strange and disturbing smear. The Eye was an angry orange smudge, then it slid past them and away from them. Drekki's head rang, his organs were compressed, he couldn't breathe, but they were away, pushed off from the Eye by the venting, and catapulted forward by the vortex's intense attractive force. Black spots danced in front of him. He felt himself going faint.

Truly, they were going faster than any duardin had ever gone before.

A hand fumbled past him, groping for the aether shut-off. Drekki leaned back to let it grab the lever.

Grungni's second-best hammer, this hurts, thought Drekki, before blacking out.

First thing Drekki knew, something was screeching around the ship. Sunlight shone directly into his eyes.

He was on his back. Uncomfortable that, in an aeronautical suit with the backpack beneath you.

'Mmmf,' Drekki said. He sat up woozily. 'Ah, my head,' he added. He tugged off his helm and let it crash on the deck. He put his face into his hands. 'Like a hangover without the fun.'

They were in calm skies. The *Aelsling* was moving at a steady clip, under airscrews again. A young Hysh gave out pale light. It was morning, somewhere.

The something screeched again. Drekki looked up and saw there were birds all around the ship, in a great flock, diving in to peck off aerial fauna from the hull.

'Sawfeathers,' said Drekki. 'Huh.'

He got to his feet. They were faring past a group of green islands that teemed with life. There was no sign of civilisation of any kind, just birds in the sky, and green treetops swaying in a clean breeze.

Weeping blended with the sawfeathers' screeching. Drekki looked around. He was dizzy. Nauseous. He belched. That made him feel better. The crew leaned heavily on the gunwales. Gord lay on the deck, a peculiar wheaten hue. It wasn't him crying, though the ogor looked like he wanted to die.

Drekki got to his feet. He swayed, took a step, swayed again, then shook it off. Everything hurt, but at least he was upright.

Evrokk was sitting cross-legged beneath the forward endrin, helm off, face buried in his beard. He was the one weeping, openly and freely in great, gulping sobs. Bokko was nearby, out of his suit, dressed in his vest and his grundeez, a blanket wrapped round his shoulders. A deep cut ran across his face from temple to jaw. Blood caked his beard. Some quickly recovered soul had fetched a mug of hot ale that Bokko cradled with shaking hands. His dirigible rig was broken, and dangled off the side of the rear endrin by its safety lines, casing burst and blackened.

Otherek was close by Bokko. He also had his helm off, and his hair and beard were all over the place. When he moved, little jags of static crackled from them, earthing on the lock ring for his helm.

'What happened?' Drekki asked.

Otherek was dazed. It took him a moment to focus on his captain.

'I saw it happen, from up in the observation cupola.'

'Saw what happen?' said Drekki. But he had a stone in his chest where his heart should have been. He already knew.

'It's Evtorr,' Otherek said. 'Bokko's endrin exploded. Evtorr pulled him in. But, the weight was too much. He… Bokko's safety line broke. He…'

'He fell into the Eye. He died saving me,' said Bokko thickly.

'He's gone. My brother. He's gone!' wailed Evrokk.

'Oh, Evrokk,' said Drekki. 'I'm sorry.' He put his arm round the helmsduardin's shoulder.

Evrokk wept the harder.

Later that day the crew broached a cask of ale in Evtorr's honour. Drekki led a service of mourning under glorious skies. Evtorr's bravery, conscientiousness and ability as a signalduardin were praised.

At the close of it all, Drekki read one of Evtorr's poems aloud. They agreed it was one of his best.

CHAPTER FOURTEEN

THE ERULAN ARCHIPELAGO

Behind them the Eye became an amber line in the sky, then a glow, then a distant yellow patch on the shoals, before vanishing altogether. The *Aelsling* sailed calm skies back into the greater swirls of the islands that slowly, slowly orbited their way around the violent centre.

'We've kissed the Eye and lived, lads!' Drekki told the crew. Despite their brush with mortality and Evtorr's death, the arkanauts were buoyed a little, for the boast was a good one.

For the next few days, Drekki spent much time closeted in his cabin, poring over his charts. Evrokk insisted on flying, though he spoke very little. Drekki gave him bearings every six hours, taking the helm himself when he thought Evrokk should rest. Khenna was given a watch at the wheel, under supervision. Adrimm too.

'Just remember those bloody spiders and what happened to Brok, all right?' Drekki said, before he relinquished the wheel to Adrimm. 'A place like this could hold any dangers. Stay sharp.'

Their course took them deep into the middle of the Third Air, where the spiral arms of metaliths that made up the Skyshoals crowded together at their thickest. It was in this globular cluster that the Erulan Archipelago could be found.

Those altitudes were highly conducive to life, yet Erulu was a region largely unexplored in modern times.

'A tricky proposition, captain,' Velunti Runk said to him.

'Aye,' said Drekki. 'The density of land fragments makes faring perilous, and foundering is far from the greatest risk. Grots are the main danger.'

'I'll post lookouts,' said Velunti.

It wasn't long before they spotted the first signs of the greenskins.

Upon a metalith denuded by fire, a totem had been erected: some orrukish god as tall as a tower, with a tiny body, much of its height being taken up by a smirking, round face painted a shocking red. A scare beacon, intended to warn off interlopers.

'This is it,' Drekki said, as they fared by. 'This is where the hard part begins.'

Three days they traversed the archipelago. Each metalith was an island alone, but some were large enough to pull their fellows towards them, so that they formed stable constellations. In those hot, tropical climes they teemed with life, and in several places they saw networks of vines that bound boulders into three-dimensional forests as rich as any coral reef. Rain-fed waterfalls plunged from the largest isles, watering those below, so that rivers made short, dashed courses over several metaliths, before taking a last tumble and blowing to spray. Airfish sported in these deluges, where long strands of vegetation in the flow provided aquatic nesting sites.

Evrokk took it steady. Collision with loose rocks was a constant danger, let alone the perils of grots. Lookouts stood at prow and aft, edgeward and coreward, ready with skyhooks. Drekki changed them regularly – attentions wandered otherwise – though Otherek insisted on pulling endless shifts in the endrin observatory, and would not be coaxed down, even for meals.

Trokwi spent the days scouting.

The channels narrowed. The atmosphere thickened with jungle scents. Moisture beaded the ship in the morning. Mist snaked through the isles. Ancient, pre-shattering charts showed the city of Erulu on the coast of an ocean, and the environs preserved something of a maritime air. Water was plentiful. As such, forest grew from every surface.

On the fifth day, Kedren knocked on the door of Drekki's cabin.

'We're getting nearer, Drekki,' he said, and jerked his head outside. Drekki rolled up his charts and followed him out.

They had come to a place of overgrown ruins. Broken streets ended in sheer drops. Half-buildings perched daintily on floating outcrops. They were weirdly intact, though choked with jungle. Some showed signs of recent despoliation.

Several were occupied by armies of chattering monkeys. The creatures gathered in belligerent troops to hurl sticks, rocks and their own dung at the ship. Drekki bore it good-naturedly, chuckling at their antics, though Adrimm required a dressing down when he decided to respond in kind.

Lerarus became thoughtful.

'Not enjoying the voyage?' Drekki asked her.

She shrugged. Her face carried the rosy blush of sunburn. It had caught them all, baking the duardin of Barak-Thrund almost black. Drekki liked to be tanned, it showed off the brilliance of his beard to its best effect.

Drekki sniffed deep. 'Come on, this place is a natural marvel. Crawling with life, air's thick and clean, no sign of corruption.'

'We fare through a graveyard,' she said. The tottering remains of a temple rose over them. Hysh shone through empty windows. Colossi of gods slowly being throttled by creepers stared severely out from alcoves next to broken stairways. 'These were the richest lands in Achromia. Many of my people died here. They had no way out.' She gave him a pointed look.

'Not this again,' he said. 'Listen, we can map this place, open it up to your folks now they're streaming hither and yon out of Bastion again. That's something, isn't it? New lands here for your reborn nation. Old treasures for the taking.'

'If your people don't blow it all up to suck out the soul of the earth for your ships,' she said darkly, 'we might be able to prosper.'

'And not that again either.' He sighed. 'You're a charmer, no mistake.'

Then she did something he didn't expect – she apologised.

'I'm sorry,' she said, and seemed to mean it. 'We're getting close to our goal. I'm nervous. My father is depending on me. I've spent years working towards this. I can't fail. If I do, I'll have wasted my life. What if our pursuers got there before us? What if the Stormvault is empty? What if we die opening it?'

'What if, what if, what if? You really didn't strike me as a "what if" kind of wizard.'

'Circumstances,' she said. 'We all have doubts.'

'I don't,' said Drekki.

'I don't believe that,' she said.

'Don't, then.'

A chirruping cut through the air. 'Ah look, Trokwi's back,' Drekki said. He squinted against the remorseless sun. 'Excited too. It looks like he's got news.'

The drillbill swooped around the boat, metal plumage flashing. He brought up his feet, spreading feathers, coming in for a graceful landing on Drekki's outstretched hand. The automaton twittered a fluting song so fast they could hear the miniature pipe stops in his chest clicking.

Drekki listened intently.

The little machine concluded his message, and hopped self-importantly onto Drekki's shoulder. Drekki tugged his white beard, rattling his gold ornaments.

'Hmm,' he said.

A gaggle of sunburnt, expectant faces gathered behind him.

'Well?' said Kedren. 'What did he say?'

'Trokwi's found something interesting,' said Drekki. 'Prepare to change course!'

'We don't have time for excursions,' Lerarus said.

'Oh, we've got time for this one,' said Drekki. 'You'll see.'

CHAPTER FIFTEEN

THE WRECK

Carrion feeders riding the thermals gave the position of the wreck away. At Drekki's command the *Aelsling* slowed and turned towards the column of birds and airfish.

Close in, the ship became suddenly, obviously apparent, as a white splash of debris on the rocks. Two isles had crushed it: arid, middling things, free of everything but the sparsest scrub. Empty gas bags draped over the smaller, upper isle like burial shrouds. Silver aerite rippled in the wind. Metal thinner than silk pressed tight to stone, coyly revealing the rounded features beneath, then lifting again. A tangle of sails and rigging entwined the bags with the wreckage below, stopping the bags from blowing away, and thus the wreck from falling.

'Does that look like the ship that was dropping charges on us?' said Gord, surprising them all with his insight. 'It does to me.'

'Indeed it is, my ogor friend,' said Drekki.

There were mutters of agreement from the crew. Various features were pointed out as proof.

'There's not much left,' said Otherek. 'Those two rocks must have come together hard to smash her like that.'

Smashed was the operative word. Splintered timbers poked up in every direction, hardly holding the shape of a ship. The masts were snapped at a uniform, almost deliberate angle by the overhang of the upper rock, like the islands were a single set of teeth. Shards of wood littered the stone. The masts were pulverised where the metaliths met, but the pressure of the locked islands and the tangle of rigging kept the ship in place. Shreds of sails flapped from the last, attached spars. The movement did nothing to deter the ravens, lammergeiers, silverfins and scrounge-eagles picking over the remains of the crew. Birds hopped about, chasing off the airfish, waiting for the wind to lift the metal cloth off some unfortunate or other so they could peck up a morsel of flesh.

Evrokk had the ship down to a snail's pace. They got a very good look at the wreckage.

'We don't have to worry about them beating us to the vault,' said Kedren.

'Indeed,' said Drekki. 'Looks like they found another pressing engagement.'

Nobody laughed.

'We still need to check,' said Otherek. 'They might have been and gone. They might have the talisman aboard right now.'

'Wouldn't that be fine, saving us all the bother,' said Kedren.

'They don't have it,' said Lerarus with irrefutable certainty.

'You know this?' asked Drekki.

'I am sure,' said the mage.

'How so?' asked Otherek.

'Magic. I could sense it, if it were there. It is not.'

Otherek checked his gauges. 'I'm getting nothing thaumaturgical, that's for sure. She's not lying.'

Ah, but she is, thought Drekki. He had a nose for such things;

just as Otherek could sniff out aether, Drekki could sniff out a lie. There was something she wasn't saying.

'That's reassuring,' said Drekki. 'What's not, is that they could have got off in a jolly boat, and be heading off right now, talisman included.'

'They'd not get far, would they?' said Urdi. 'We can chase them down, captain.'

'They'd still be getting somewhere. And we can't chase them down if we don't know where they are,' said Drekki. 'This island group is big. They could have gone to ground. There are plenty of places to hide around here. We need to check, make sure we're on the right course. We can find out who's after us, that sort of thing. Lerarus, Gord, Kedren, you're with me. Bokko, Adrimm, Umherth, keep an eye out. Scare off those buzzards and whatnot while you're at it.'

'Aye-aye, captain,' said Bokko. He went to fetch his gun. Adrimm and Umherth followed, arguing about the merits of the captain's plan. As usual, Adrimm was not in favour.

'Hey, Lerarus, you got any flying spells or such that would waft us down there?' asked Drekki.

'No,' she said.

'I get a lot of "no" out of you. Fine. We'll do it the old-fashioned way. Hrunki, Khenna, Urdi, fetch some ropes. Evrokk, bring us over the lower rock.'

Lerarus looked nervous. 'You want to dangle me over the edge?'

'Dangle? Not dangle. What we're going to do is *rappel*,' said Drekki.

Gord grunted with delight.

'It'll be fun. Gord likes it, don't you, Gord?'

'Yeah. Dangle dangle weeeee!' he said.

Lerarus paled further.

'What's wrong, wizard?' asked Drekki.

She stood stiffly, too proud to speak. 'I am not fond of heights,' she admitted reluctantly.

'You've been on my ship all this time and you're telling me that now?' He employed a laconic tone. He'd figured it out a while back. She'd been looking nervously over the edge since the day she'd come aboard. Only battle or magic or peril seemed to focus her. All other times she kept noticeably far from the gunwales.

'There's a difference to being on board your vessel, and hanging off it on a piece of rope,' she said. 'A *thin* piece of rope.'

'I see. Then can you tell me whose ship that was without going down to see?'

She peered nervously over the edge at the smashed timbers. 'I cannot,' she said.

'Then you're coming,' said Drekki. 'Don't worry, it's all perfectly safe.'

'You keep saying that.'

'Do I?'

'Yes. It's always perfectly safe. But it never is.'

'We're still alive.'

'Evtorr's not, is he?'

Drekki's good humour vanished like smoke on the wind. 'That's low,' he said.

'The company I keep is having a bad influence on me,' said Lerarus primly, then she caught sight of Drekki's sullen face.

'I'm sorry,' she said. 'I'm scared. It makes me snappish.'

'Don't be,' said Drekki. 'You are right. Come on.'

The *Aelsling* hove to. Adrimm hurled the anchor over the side, waited for it to clang on the stone, then reeled in the chain until it bit fast. He stuck up his thumb at the away party waiting by the open section of the guard rail. Drekki nodded.

'Now then, like I showed you,' he said to Lerarus. 'Holding this bit of the rope lightly in your hand.' He tugged at a line lashed to the side of the ship. 'And this bit of rope tautly under your backside. Want to go down, then let this rope slide through this here belay ring.' He tapped a loop of bronze the rope went through. 'Simple. Do you want a demonstration?'

'I'll demonstrate!' shouted Gord. The ship rocked as he ran and leapt overboard. He left behind the sound of running rope and a fading cry of 'Waheeeeey!'

'All right, like that,' said Drekki. 'Only not exactly like that. You know what I mean.'

Lerarus hesitated.

'I'll go first.' Kedren stepped up to the edge, threaded the line through his belay hoop, and took the rope in hand. 'I don't like this aerial foolishness any better than you do, lass. Trust me when I say it's fine.'

'I still don't understand why a duardin like you is keeping company with duardin like them,' Lerarus asked.

'Ah, now that is a tale and a half, no mistake,' said Kedren, and stepped off the side. He went down with significantly more caution than Gord.

'You next, wizard,' said Drekki.

He had to push her off the edge, she dithered so long, then slung his axe across his back and followed.

They made it down safely. The drop looked bigger from below. They always did. Lerarus shuddered.

'See? Fine. Never look up, never look down,' said Drekki. 'Only ahead, that's the skyfarer's way.'

She looked at the wreck. 'I'm looking ahead right now,' she said.

'Hey, that won't happen to us,' Drekki said. 'They were umgi farers. You're flying with duardin. You're practically an arkanaut. Honorary, of course.'

They picked their way over the island. It was rough, wind-sculpted. Grit gathered around knee-high eminences. Air-shore creatures scuttled out of their way. Neither metalith was big, the upper a hundred paces maybe, and the lower three times the size.

It was unusually dry, and vegetation was restricted to a few patches of Third Air samphire. Guano streaked the stone. Across a large tract, piles of twigs were stacked at uniform intervals.

'Nesting ground,' Gord said, going from nest to nest. To his disappointment, all the piles held were empty eggshells. The birds had been scared off by the wreck. Scavengers had done the rest.

'No eating now, Gord,' said Drekki. 'I need you focused, in case any of these here coves are still alive.'

'Right you are, captain,' said Gord. He stuffed a handful of twigs into his mouth anyway.

'You recognise it yet?' asked Drekki.

'Only that it's from Bastion,' said Lerarus.

The ship was completely mashed from prow to amidships. The bird figurehead was unrecognisable. Bits of wood were scattered about, so thoroughly shattered they'd be no use for anything but kindling.

Woven aerite flapped. A stiff, warm wind rolled over the isles, spreading the scent of death.

Drekki went to a corpse, kicking a vulture off the chest with a steel-toed boot. He knelt beside the dead man, gave him a poke.

'Dead at least four days,' he said. 'Flesh is blackening.' Not that there was much flesh left; bone gleamed from exposed ribs. The face was a pecked-out horror, white teeth grinning at their own ruin. 'Does he look familiar?' Drekki asked.

'Not funny,' said Lerarus.

'Check his teeth. Rich man's, those. That's something.' He crouched down. 'Aha! Here's a part of the puzzle.' He picked up a black-fletched arrow dislodged by the feeding of birds. 'Sky-grots,' he said, holding it up so the others could see.

'Aye,' said Kedren. 'That's as grotty an arrow as I've seen. Dross and rubbish.'

'Still deadly, if it hits you in the right spot.' Drekki tossed the arrow aside and strode the last few yards to the crushed ship. He looked over the edge.

'The stern's intact,' he said. 'And here are more clues,' he added, pointing to holes made by cannon, more arrows, and a crudely made grapnel dangling broken rope.

He rested his free hand on his hip.

'Between grots and islands, they've made a real mess of this ship,' said Drekki. 'Either of you got any ideas whose it is?'

Kedren shook his head. 'Compared to most umgak construction, the quality of this is pretty high. But I can't see any badges, no heraldry, nothing.'

'It's a standard design,' Lerarus said. 'A pursuit barquentine. The navy of Bastion has scores of these.'

'Why would the triumvirate be chasing you?' asked Drekki.

'Why indeed? They're avowedly neutral in the matter of the talismans. You can also find ships like this in the private flotillas of every one of the major noble families,' Lerarus said.

'Then there's only one way to find out whose it was,' said Drekki. 'We're going inside. We'll have to climb down, under this overhang.' He pointed to where the boat was pinned by the rocks.

'Hmm,' said Kedren.

'Hmm? What's with the hmming?' Drekki asked.

'I know rock.'

'Course you do, you spent most of your life living under one, before you saw sense.'

'This is not stable.' Kedren put his hand on the stone and cast his eye over upper and lower rocks.

'Isn't it?' said Drekki with deeply sarcastic surprise. 'It's two floating islands jammed together by the wind. Tell me something I don't know, runesmith.'

'This is no time to be cocky, Drekki! I mean it is *really* not stable,' said Kedren. 'Look.' He gave the upper isle a push.

The islands shifted grittily against each other. Sand pattered. The bags wrapped around the stone rasped. A woody groan rose from the remains of the ship. The splintering of timber followed.

'It wouldn't take much,' said Kedren. 'These islands are sliding along each other. They haven't finished with this boat yet. There's a lot of tension in this rock. The wind is pushing on this smaller one in a way that makes it want to roll. If it breaks the rigging tangling it, it's going to flip, and it will, if the wind keeps up.'

'Air? Pushing? Rigging? Wind? Why, Kedren, we'll make an arkanaut of you yet!'

Kedren shot him a filthy look. 'All right, all right, rib me, you bozdok, but when it goes, you don't want to be in the way.'

'I'll force it apart,' said Gord, wrenching a broken spar free and jamming it into the crevice between the two. 'That'll fix it. Get in easy that way.'

'No, no, no!' said Drekki. 'You do that, and the ship will fall out.'

'Or the rocks crash back and finish the job,' said Kedren.

'Or that,' said Drekki.

'Oh,' said Gord. He dropped the spar.

'My plan stands,' Drekki said. He put down his axe and started stripping off the heavier elements of his arkanaut's gear. 'Trokwi, stay with Kedren. Warn me if things look dicey.'

The automaton trilled and flapped onto Kedren's shoulder.

Drekki piled up his gear and went to the edge of the rock. He hammered pitons into cracks and began rigging a rope.

'Stay up here, you two,' said Drekki. 'We'll be back soon.'

'By you two, you mean those two, not me?' said Lerarus.

'That's right. I said you're needed. You're going down there with me. There's a way in through the cargo hatch. We'll find the captain's cabin in the stern, yes? Crammed full of things, captain's cabins are.'

'It's not safe!' Lerarus protested.

'Then we better be quick,' said Drekki with a grin.

Stressed wood moaned around them. The barquentine was a tumbled mess of objects. Compartments to the prow were crushed to letterbox width. They trod gingerly on a shifting ladder of wreckage, stepping down to what had been the stern, now a chute over a bottomless drop.

There were corpses in there. The smell of decay was choking. Rustling down in the ruin revealed the furtive feeding of rats. Drekki and Lerarus had left their helms up top, so they breathed through their mouths. They tasted the dead.

Creaking, scuttling, the cawing of scavenger birds. None of these sounds put them at ease. Drekki resisted the urge to hurry. Going fast at the wrong time was worse than going slow. One misplaced foot and the whole thing would collapse like a house of cards.

He was thinking light thoughts all the way down to the cabin.

'I'll go first,' he said, lowering himself in. The door creaked sadly from its hinges, betraying slight movements in the wreck. He marked that; tiny motions dislodge precarious objects. A valuable warning.

Heavy feet landed on the edge of the captain's desk. The table was balanced on the windows at the back: a huge, many-paned run that would have afforded fine views to the ship's master, currently looking queasily upon the plummet of the shoals. The glass was covered in a gentleman's impedimenta: books, silverware, thaumaturgical instruments. An orrery of layered continents depicting the whole of the realm of Chamon was wedged in one corner.

Nice piece. I'll have that, if it's going, thought Drekki.

Transoms creaked under Drekki's weight. Some of the few uncracked panes of glass cracked. He tensed, balanced on his toes, spread his arms. The creaking stopped. No death happened. He grinned.

And there was Lerarus not liking heights.

'Remember, no looking down, if you can help it,' Drekki said. He helped her into the room. 'Don't step on the table edge!' he insisted. 'It won't take the weight of both of us.'

She swung with difficulty to the side of the cabin, where she wedged herself into a bookcase.

'Now what?' she asked.

Drekki cast about. 'I want to know who's behind this,' he said. 'Books, logs, captain's records. That kind of thing. That's what we need.' He looked at the window. 'Hmm. It's all down there on the glass.'

He considered the spidered glass. He stroked his beard thoughtfully.

'You know,' he said conversationally. 'You are a lot lighter than me, slip of an umgi kvinn that you are...'

'Oh no,' she said. 'I'm not standing on that!'

'It'll be fine, I'll loop this rope about you, get myself braced. If you fall, you won't fall far.'

'I don't want to fall at all.'

The ship groaned ominously. It shifted a touch. The hanging door creaked.

'Come on, up and at 'em,' said Drekki, holding out the rope.

'For the love of Sigmar,' she protested, but came forward and took it.

Awkwardly, they swapped positions, he going up and out again, so he could sit on the wall with his short duardin legs dangling through the door, she taking his place on the edge of the desk. With exaggerated care, Drekki looped the rope under her arms. She gave him a hard look.

'Come on, this is a big adventure,' he said. 'I thought wizards loved adventures.'

'This is just a big funny game to you, isn't it?' she said. Very carefully, she lowered herself down the table. Drekki took the strain. 'I'm not doing it for adventure,' she said, whispering up at him as if too loud a noise might shatter the window. 'I'm doing it because I have to!'

She placed her feet on the upright mullions, avoiding the thinner transoms and the glass. A discouraging crackling spread across the window nevertheless, right to the very edges. She swayed, and said the kind of rude words that Drekki did not associate with lady wizards.

'All right down there?'

A sharp rejoinder, equally blue. 'I'm not going to die because of you,' she said.

'You're not going to die at all,' he said. 'Because I've got a hold of you.' He gave the rope a gentle tug. He meant to reassure, but she gasped in fright.

'If this glass breaks, I'm going to get very badly cut,' she said. 'And if that happens, you're going to get badly burned.'

Drekki thought that likely, so changed the subject.

'Can you see anything? Pick up some of those books. Start with that one.' He pointed one out.

'Don't let go of the rope!' she hissed.

'Stop complaining, and go and get it,' he said.

Tottering like a circus acrobat on her first day on the job, Lerarus bent over and snagged one of the books. It wasn't the one he'd pointed at, but no matter. She found her balance, and flicked through it.

'Anything?' asked Drekki.

'I think it's a lading book, it's full of figures.' She opened it right at the front and held it up. 'No crest or owner's mark.' She put it down. Gingerly.

'Try another,' he said.

'What do you think I'm doing?' she snapped. She moved across the window. A pane broke with a loud, icy snap. Pieces of glass fell. 'I don't like this, I don't like this.'

'You can face down a daemon but a little height upsets you?'

'I know how to deal with daemons!' she said. 'I can't fly, can

I?' She found another book. 'This one's encoded. Bastion letter cipher. It's a journal, I think.'

'Sounds promising. Can you read it?'

'I would be able to, if I weren't standing on a breaking window over a bottomless drop in a wrecked ship crushed between two giant rocks with nothing but a sarcastic pirate holding me up!'

'Always with the pirate. I'm not a pirate! Toss that book up here.'

'Really?' she said.

'It'll be easier to climb with both hands.'

'If you don't catch this, and drop it, this window will break.'

'Then I won't drop it, will I?' he said.

Muttering more foul language, she bent for a slow throw, and tossed the book up. Drekki caught it with ease, the covers snapping together crisply in his hand.

'See?'

She swore again.

'Now where did a high-born lady like you learn language like that? Surely not off the aelves in their fancy magic school.'

'You'd be surprised,' she said. She stopped, and bent down. 'Now hang on… That's interesting.'

'What is?'

'Teacup.'

'Teacup? How are crocks interesting?'

'It has a crest on it.' Again she bent with the utmost care and picked up the object. She squinted at the underside. 'House Crave, that's strange. They're not daemon friends. Very much not.'

'How much not?'

'Lord Crave is Bastion's Witchfinder-General. The Craves have held that office for centuries.'

'Means nothing,' he said. 'Strong denial is often a sure sign of deception. Many witch hunters are witches.'

'And you know that for a fact, do you?'

'It's a widely held opinion.'

'Your kind is so opinionated. How do you...'

'Square that away?' said Drekki. 'The saying applies to umgi and elgi, not dawi. One of us gets unreasonable, he's just being stubborn, but one of your lot does, ten to one he's hiding something.'

'You know,' she said, 'you've a lot of opinions about humans that aren't very flattering.'

'Then try to be better,' said Drekki.

'It's prejudice,' she said. She poked about a little more, wincing every time a pane snapped.

The ship creaked loudly. They both froze.

'All the tableware and the silverware has the crest of House Crave. I'm done here,' she said hurriedly, stowing the teacup. 'I've enough proof to satisfy myself, and enough to raise some pointed questions back home. Pull me up.'

'Not so fast,' he said.

'What?'

'You see that orrery over in the corner?'

Lerarus looked over. Her shoulders slumped, and she made a pained noise. 'Yes.'

'Get it for me, would you?' he said.

She gave him another pained look.

'Please?' said Drekki.

'Is it important?'

'Very,' said Drekki solemnly. 'Who knows what clues it might reveal?'

'All right,' she said. 'All right!'

She crept over the window. Every piece of it crackled. She bent down and put hands on the orrery.

'Got it?' Drekki asked.

'It's heavy!' she said.

'Just pick it up, I've got a tight rope. Everything's fine.'

Swearing freely, Lerarus heaved the mechanism off the glass and clamped it to her chest.

'There, that wasn't so hard, was it?' said Drekki brightly. 'I'll haul you–'

The boat dropped a foot. Lerarus swayed. Cracks raced across the window.

'Drekki…' she said. She looked up with eyes round with terror.

The window collapsed under her. She screamed. Drekki braced. Books, silverware, furniture and papers dropped in a glittering fall. The rope jerked as Lerarus reached the end and bounced. The boat groaned, slid further with the sudden movement, then halted.

Lerarus was on the end of the rope, spinning slowly. She'd kept hold of the orrery, though. That was pretty impressive.

'Are you all right?' Drekki called.

'Of course I'm not bloody all right!' she yelled.

'Just hang on, I'm pulling you up now. Got to take it slow. Sudden movements are very much not to be attempted.'

Presently, she was up through the door, standing on the outer horizontal wall of the cabin, shaking, white, but alive.

Drekki took the orrery and strapped it to his back. 'Many thanks for that. Now we go. Climb gently!'

'What do you mean, "climb gently"?'

'This whole ship is about to drop,' he said. 'It needs no encouragement to do so quicker. So, gently, yes?'

They began their ascent. There was a scraping along the hull that grew louder, more insistent.

Something gave. A convulsive shudder burst planks. Rock pushed its way through the ship, snapping timbers. Drekki climbed faster, gentle tread forgotten, dragging himself up the shuddering fittings of the craft as the metaliths ground it to nothing.

They got to the aft cargo hatch, and the rope they'd left dangling there.

'Get a hold!' he said, and thrust the end at Lerarus.

They both grabbed it. Too late. The upper metalith scraped along the lower. The aft hull collapsed inward. Rock rolled towards Drekki. The hatch frame exploded.

He closed his eyes. He had the impression of huge weight. At least it would be quick.

He opened one eye, then another. He was still in the ship.

'Not dead then,' he said. A wall of heatless red flames shone a few handspans from his face. The upper metalith had rolled right over them, and was moving slowly off into the shoals. 'Lerarus?' he asked. Looking down at her, he saw lots of bits of ship falling through the sky. A good chunk, all broken up, remained hanging from the rock. If that fell, they'd be dead, magical shield or no.

The mage had wrapped the rope around her forearm and was clearly uncomfortable, but she kept her fingers spread. She grunted, and clenched her fists. The light went out.

'That's the third time that little trick has saved me.'

'You're welcome,' she said.

'Would you like a job?'

Kedren's head appeared over the edge of the rock. 'Captain!' he said. Kedren was not a habitual grinner, but he grinned now. 'You're alive!'

'Of course I'm alive,' said Drekki. 'I'm Drekki Flynt. Take more than a little rock to crush the life out of me.'

'Get up quick,' Kedren said. 'The rest of this is going to fall.'

They scrambled up. With the smaller isle sailing away into the shoals, sunlight was free to scorch the whole of the metalith, leaving them feeling more exposed than before.

Gord leaned right back, so the rear of his head almost brushed the stone. A crude harness of ropes strained around him, supporting the remains of the wreck.

'Good effort, Gord,' said Drekki. 'But you can let go now.'

'Can't... let... go...' Gord gasped. His face was bright purple. He was being dragged across the metalith surface, heels raking gravel from the stone.

'I'll sort you out.' Drekki scrambled up. He snatched up his axe from the pile of his gear. Runes flared, the aether generator puttered, and he swung. Hot metal burned as much as cut the makeshift harness away.

Relieved of weight, Gord fell backward, thick ogor skull clashing on the ground. The ground came off worse.

With a relieved, creaking sigh, the last of the ship slithered down the face of the metalith, timbers shivering, hull disintegrating, until it reached the isle's limit and fell into air, and there was a sudden, profound quiet.

Drekki broke it.

'You were supposed to warn me,' he said to Trokwi, who was perched on an abandoned nest. The bird trilled apologetically.

'Any luck?' asked Kedren.

'Some,' said Drekki. 'Clues,' he added.

'That orrery better have been worth it,' said Lerarus. 'Getting that nearly killed us.'

'Yes. It'll look very nice in my cabin,' said Drekki.

'Nice? Cabin?'

'Very fine, don't you think? It'll make me look like a captain of serious means.'

'You mean you didn't need it?' said Lerarus. Drekki wondered how many more levels of incredulous the human possessed. He had the impish desire to find out.

'Need is too strong a term,' said Drekki. '"Want" probably fits better.'

'And you say you're not a pirate.' Lerarus gave him a look that could have melted stone.

Gord laughed.

CHAPTER SIXTEEN

LORD CRAVE'S JOURNAL.

Night wrapped the archipelago in its embrace. From every island came the hooting of animals, the buzz of insects. The endrins hummed. The airscrews chopped. Drekki strode the length of the deck, back and forth, back and forth, pacing out his thoughts. Lerarus was in her cabin, working on the journal.

Evening shone up from below. Hysh was under the realm of Chamon, halfway through its daily circumnavigation of the sky. He wondered how fast it must go to cover such distance. Very fast, he concluded, after a few swift calculations. Better duardin had worked that problem over before, though, he thought. Past a certain scale, science disintegrated into metaphysics. No matter how much Otherek Zhurafon insisted that all things were knowable, some things really were not. Hysh moved because Hysh had to. Its speed was that required to light up the day and usher in night, no more, and no less.

Urdi approached. 'The wizard says she's ready for you now, captain. We're finished.'

Drekki nodded. Unfortunate that, Urdi getting his mitts on the book. He'd rather have kept him away from the wizard and this sensitive business. But it turned out Urdi knew Bastion letter cypher better than she.

'Right you are, Urdi,' Drekki said.

He went below. Ildrin was singing tunelessly from the brig near the stern, kicking the wall to beat out time.

'Knock it off, Ildrin!' Drekki hollered. Predictably, Ildrin did not, but sang louder and kicked harder. Drekki shook his head, and knocked on Lerarus' door.

'Come!' Lerarus called.

Drekki entered. There was just enough room in there for the two of them, if he stayed back by the door. There were rumpled blankets on the bed where Urdi had been sitting. Lerarus had made best use of the cramped space, finding a pallet to lift her up so she could sit cross-legged at the tiny desk – it was far too low for her to use the chair. She had the book open before her.

'I hear you've had some luck with that journal,' Drekki said.

'Yes,' she said, 'thanks to Urdi.' She flipped it closed and rubbed her face tiredly.

'Not good?'

'There is no such thing as good tidings, not in this world,' she said.

'Share them with me,' he said. 'Good or bad.'

'The Craves were chasing us. According to the crest in the front here, this book was written by Alois Crave, Lord Crave's nephew by his third sister. In it, he outright says he was commissioned to come after me.'

'Let me guess,' said Drekki. 'If they're smearing ships with dark magic gunk, they're not playing on the side of good any more.'

'It's not that,' said Lerarus. 'I don't think it was them who painted the ship, but I do think they want the talisman for themselves.'

'I see. Why? Are they of the Integrationist sympathy? Could that be it?'

She shook her head. 'Not publicly. They've been scrupulously neutral, right the way through. My father believes they're looking for favour from whoever emerges out of this in charge.'

'Then maybe they're not daemon worshippers,' said Drekki.

'I don't think they are,' said Lerarus. 'There's this here that–'

'Although I wouldn't rule it out just yet,' Drekki interrupted. 'You say they've been witchfinders for centuries. Proximity to evil corrupts. People change path slowly, little by little, each step taken justifiable, until you find yourself somewhere you never thought to go.' He rapped a steel rib with his knuckle. 'We Kharadron are a case in point there. Nothing changes, then it does all at once. The pivot of history turns on the backs of a few men and women, so our philosophers say.' He paused. 'Well, they also say a lot about steam engines, working hard until you drop dead, the correct length of beards, good metal, respecting your elders, never trusting aelves, aether, and gold, but that's not all.' He became thoughtful. 'Sorry, you were about to say something?'

'Well, I was about to give you the proof of why they haven't turned,' said Lerarus with withering levels of sarcasm. 'But you interrupted me so I thought I'd let you talk, seeing as whatever you have to say is so much more important than what I might say.' There were flames dancing in her eyes again.

'Ah,' Drekki said. 'My apologies. Do go on. What does it say?'

She shook her head. 'Well, you understand, not "we don't love daemons".'

'I see we are making our first attempts at humour,' said Drekki.

'Maybe hanging around with an inveterately flippant duardin is rubbing off on me?' she said. 'They were sent out to stop me. Listen.' She read aloud. '"Fifthday. L and conveyance tailed from Bavardia. Pursued into area of reefs. No contact. Magical bombardment attempted. Minor collision resulted in cessation of pursuit. Target escaped." That's when they followed us into the fog.'

'L being you?'

'That seems likely, doesn't it, unless you've cheated them too, and they can't spell terribly well?'

'Ouch. Harsh.'

'Now listen to this. "Orders renewed. Conveyance certainly compromised by enemy cultists." It's that part that says they're still doing their jobs,' she interjected, then continued to read. '"Pursue at all costs. L cannot be allowed to secure the talisman. G insufficient measure."' She flipped through some pages. 'These following entries are about them hunting for us, then we get to this. "Firstday. No sign of L or conveyance for three days. No contact with G. Argument with Captain X. I am for attempting the vault ourselves. Captain X against. I prevailed – we go to secure the talisman directly, for the greater glory of Achromia. Sails set for Erulu." Then there's more about them sighting the island. Nothing after that.'

'Nothing about finding the talisman once they got here?'

'No.'

'Then I'd say they failed,' said Drekki. 'Crave probably died. The ship made a run for it, got caught by grots.'

'That also looks likely.'

'Who or what is G?'

'I don't know. I'd hazard a guess they've had someone spying on you as well as watching me? Or maybe G is their adviser? There was that man Otherek saw at the docks. Urdi mentioned it to me. That could be G.'

Drekki stroked his beard. 'But no mention of a spell, or such-like manner of chicanery.'

'They didn't paint the mark. Someone else did. Probably. Ugh!'

She rubbed her face again. 'This is hard to make sense of. If only my divination was better, then we'd know for sure.'

'We should broaden our pool of brains,' said Drekki. He tapped the end of his nose with his finger and winked. 'We Kharadron know a thing or two about laws and codes, and therefore plenty about trickery. Let's take this to a couple of experts, shall we?'

Drekki asked Lerarus to read the whole journal to Otherek and Kedren. Though the book was slender, it took a while to get through, especially with the cypher, and the oldbeards butting in with their questions. When Lerarus was done, most of the night had passed, Drekki's cabin was misty with pipe smoke, and ale pots sat in silent ranks around them.

'I can see why you think they're still on the side of Order. But my advice is not to jump to any conclusions where Chaos is concerned,' said Otherek. 'They were definitely chasing us. Seeing as they bombed us, it's probable they've been willing to use force to stop us from the beginning. On the other hand, we can't prove they've been using dark magery to find us, nor that they definitely want you dead, wizard, nor that they're playing for the other side. They might think you've been tainted. They might have other reasons they don't want you to get the talisman.'

'If they do think I've turned, it wouldn't be the first time they've been wrong,' said Lerarus. 'They've sent plenty of innocents to the fires, my great-grandfather included. He did nothing. The Lord Crave of the time just wanted him gone.'

'But what about you, lass?' Kedren asked. 'Are you pure?'

'Really? Do you really believe that I would turn against my own city, that I'd go to all this effort to make it more powerful and keep it safe only to betray them?'

'Is that what your plan is?' said Kedren.

Lerarus' eyes flashed.

Kedren raised his hands. 'I'm just covering all the possibilities, lass, no offence.'

'Fine,' said Lerarus. 'At the very least, whichever way you look at this, attacking the *Aelsling* was an aggressive act by one Great House against another. That's something. I've enough to challenge them when we get home.'

'Do you think so?' said Kedren. 'Your courts will not take your testimony at face value. It's our word against theirs. I know you umgi. Your lords are as slippery as eels. They'll demand more than a cup with a crest on it or your say-so to damn one of their own. They'll say it's a plot to discredit House Crave. They'll imply that it's a plot by the Lerarus family. Your clans aren't close allies, I bet.'

'None of the Great Families trust the others,' admitted Lerarus, 'and my father hates the Craves, after what they did to his grandfather.'

'Thought not. And these people, they're witch hunters, right?' said Kedren.

'The foremost in the city,' said Lerarus, whose expression suggested she was grasping the scale of the task ahead. 'Lord Crave is the Witchfinder-General.'

'Powerful office, last I heard,' said Kedren.

'So you've an irreproachable man and a book with no mention of the spellmark, or of daemons,' said Otherek. 'How do we link them together? In one of our courts you might get a charge of assault to stick, but daemonology? Not a chance. The Code is clear on that. It's a serious charge and needs serious evidence. Bastion's courts are no different.'

'Right,' agreed Kedren. 'So you're going to go in there, wave that book about, flash your little teacup and on the basis of that accuse one of the most powerful men in the city, whose entire reason for being is to root out the agents of Chaos, of being an agent of Chaos. Pffft.' His circling pipe put out a fume of smoke. 'You'll be laughed out of there in a moment, or worse.'

'Playing Teclis here,[31] this amount of proof would be enough for the Admiralty Courts to order an investigation,' said Drekki. 'If the Achromians choose to investigate, they might find more.'

'I think you'd have a time of it convincing our Admiralty Court, to tell you the truth,' said Otherek. 'An umgi one would never listen to us.'

'Remember who'll be doing the investigating,' said Kedren. 'I'll bet there exists no agency beyond the Family Crave's reach that could poke into this unmolested, not if they've held this office for so long. These people are no duardin. They do not think like us. They do not have the same consistency of thought. Even among their own kind, there is no common bedrock to umgi souls. You skybeards have been isolated too long. You think you can pull one over on the people with your Code and your double-dealing promises? Do me a favour. You've caught them unawares. You've dealt with the middlemen. These human high-ups are cunning, they're flexible in a way we're not. One of you clever-clever cloud fondlers might bend the truth and think yourselves smart. Umgi will outright lie to your face.'

'Aye, I believe it,' said Otherek. 'If the Craves have turned, it wouldn't be the first time evildoers hide behind rectitude, or the upright and pure become corrupted by the very thing they're seeking to destroy. I know how easily hearts can be swayed.' He pointed emphatically with his pipe stem. 'What I'm saying is that it isn't going to make a jot of difference when you've got Lord Fancy-Pants standing up in front of his peers, denouncing you as the outsider, as the renegade, and rubbishing every word you say.'

---

31 | Common duardin expression meaning to employ pointlessly subtle, gratuitously contrary arguments that defy good common sense just to show how clever one is.

'Goes double if they put in a counter-accusation,' Kedren continued, 'claiming the Family Lerarus is deliberately trying to discredit them, and that they're the daemon worshippers. They'll say that's why they're after you in the first place, and to be honest, we don't have any proof ourselves – other than mutual respect,' Kedren added, 'that it is not the case.'

'See, wizard?' said Drekki. 'You've got something to learn of courtly intrigue, it seems.'

'My father handles that side of things,' admitted Lerarus. 'It's hopeless, then.'

'Perhaps not,' said Drekki. 'What I find interesting is that there is no mention of the spell. No mention of "other means" or anything at all that even obliquely references the other attacks on us.'

'Are you driving right at the silver seam here?' said Kedren.

'I am,' said Drekki. 'Just because they attacked us in the clouds, it doesn't mean they were behind the other assaults. I agree with what you said in your cabin, Lerarus. I don't think they're on the wrong side. I mean, they're not on our side, but they're not serving Chaos. The question is, why are Bastionite witch hunters chasing us? What do they know that we don't?'

'The captain saw Ildrin marking the ship after we were bombarded,' said Otherek. 'Maybe the mark wasn't being renewed after all, but newly applied. Who is he working for? We could put it to him.'

'All he does is sing, kick the door and protest his innocence,' said Drekki.

'And it might not have been Ildrin,' said Kedren thoughtfully.

'Don't start on Urdi again. That's settled for now,' said Otherek, 'and I wouldn't go letting on to Umherth that you think otherwise.'

'We still may have another problem,' said Kedren.

'Aye,' said Otherek. 'We know for sure that there is more than one group of people after us. Question is, why? Chaos attacking us makes sense. The Craves doesn't, unless they believe the talisman's return will do evil to their city, or they are making a naked play for power?'

'Politics,' growled Drekki.

'The Craves might be trying to manage the timing of the talisman's return,' said Lerarus.

'Then why didn't they speak to your father?' Kedren asked.

'Maybe they did,' she said bitterly. 'He doesn't tell me everything, and like I said, he hates them.'

'Brilliant,' said Kedren. 'Half the world on our tails, and we don't know why.'

Drekki grinned.

'Not to worry,' he said. 'I'm used to being unpopular.'

CHAPTER SEVENTEEN

A LITTLE BIT SNEAKY

They came upon the city of Erulu soon after. The isles got bigger, and closer together, until Drekki spied the pair of flat, circular discs of debris that were marked on the charts as surrounding the principal island.

Drekki spent some time peering at the debris, then at a chart tacked to a board he jammed level against his stomach. He marched a compass divider across in stiff-legged, rotary steps, then back again, jotting numbers down in his notebook. All the while, the rocks in the discs scraped on one another and banged together loud enough to be heard from miles away.

When he was satisfied, he sent for Lerarus.

'We're nearly there,' he told her. 'This region is poorly mapped, but the discs are a sure sign. It's a rare phenomenon, new lands forming out of the old. The mass locus is the largest chunk of land, where sits most of the ancient city of Erulu. If this is anything like the other mass aggregations I've seen, they'll funnel in at the centre, but until then the gap between should be deep enough to navigate. We'll soon have your talisman.' He gave it some dramatic flair.

Lerarus' face remained stony. 'How many days?' she asked.

'Not days, hours,' he said. 'Measurements of these discs disagree on their extent, but seven hours at most, I would say.' He pointed forward, between the clashing debris. The sun was blocked from above and below, and it was cavern-gloomy between the discs. With Hysh sinking, a few stray beams punched through the lower disc, but these were so bright and so infrequent they confused the vista, so that the heart of the mass stayed lost in shadow and glaring shafts. 'It's in there, at the very centre.'

'Then we'll reach it by nightfall.'

'Should do,' said Drekki. 'That couldn't be better. It'll cover our approach. I'd rather not fly into battle if I can help it. I'll send Trokwi ahead a bit to see what's what.'

'Do we have something akin to a plan?' asked Lerarus.

Drekki nodded. He pulled out the second map Lerarus had brought with her, the one depicting the old duardin undercity. It was very old and he treated it reverentially, smoothing it flat on the board, pinning it in place with clips.

'It is a lovely thing,' he said, more to the map than to her. 'You said the Stormvault was under the centre.'

'Yes,' she said. 'As far as I can tell. I mean, I'm almost certain that's where it is. When the wards drop, it's hard to miss, if you're looking for it. I get the sense it is underground.'

'We duardin were always thorough when it came to making up charts. But the Stormvault isn't on this map, as you'd expect, what with it being secret and a late addition and all. However, because it must have been built before the city fell, if they wanted it to remain a secret, they couldn't have just carved up huge chunks of the place to install it. And that means...' He invited an answer.

'They chose somewhere that was big enough to house it that already existed?'

'Exactly. That means it can only be in one of a few places. These are the old subterranean docks, here, built into the cliffs that fronted the sea.' He tapped at angular wharfs butting faded blue. A dotted line away from them showed the overhang of the city above, as it was in ancient times. 'Or, we have the Underking's Hall, where the duardin lords of Erulu dwelt.' His finger moved. 'There are the forges here, the Great Feasting Hall here, though that is a little small, and the warehousing complexes here. There's also the Merchants' Hall. That'd be big enough too.' He tapped his chin. 'It's a lot of ground to cover. We have to think carefully. We will be detected, so we're not going to have much time.'

'Once we are inside, I will be able to lead you to the vault. I can feel it, even now.' She looked towards the centre of the metalith discs.

Drekki continued to pore over the map. 'This whole thing could only have come off if the duardin lords were involved. The upper city council, and perhaps the Empress of Achromia must have known as well. There will have been an agreement struck.'

'Our histories say different,' said Lerarus. 'They say it was Sigmar's doing.'

'Histories aren't infallible,' said Drekki. 'They can be lost, rewritten, forged... I smell a little buyer's regret here. I've avoided talking to you about this because it obviously upsets you, but haven't you thought just a little about how the Azyrites pulled this off? Taking a component of your most potent weapon and hiding it for hundreds of years, in secret, right when it might be most needed? It doesn't strike me as very likely.'

'It's what happened,' Lerarus insisted.

'Maybe you need to stop playing the victim and think about the motivations behind it. You might reach a different conclusion.'

'Maybe you should leave the politics to me and do the job I'm paying you for.'

'You'll get your talisman, I promise. Plan is this. You, me, Gord, Kedren, Otherek, Umherth – we'll likely as not need his volley gun – and a couple of others will enter from under the rock that holds the city. We'll find a nice little open tunnel and creep in. This is the grots' main lair, so all the stories say. Ten to one, and I am a gambling duardin, says they'll be using the old docks for their sky-ships, so we avoid those. We avoid all the big places, the obvious places. We go as low as we can, approach by night, threading our way through the isles below. Then we come straight up and under, lights out, up the spiral from the lower disc. The raiding party will go in, the *Aelsling* will go hide while we work our way through the undercity. We find the Stormvault, we break in, we take the talisman. We find a way out, Trokwi will fetch the ship.' He hooked his thumbs together and fluttered his hands like bird wings. 'Then we'll make our escape, hopefully without being noticed.'

'That's a lot of ifs there.'

'I don't believe I said "if" once.'

'Probably purposefully,' she said. 'Each of these stages being successful is contingent on luck, and you know it.'

'This whole venture is your idea,' Drekki pointed out. 'I'd have rather done something less suicidal.'

'You were hired to make it happen,' she countered. 'If the success of every stage were down to fine planning then I might condone this, but you're just hoping things will go right.'

'Just hoping works fine for me, all the time. I am Drekki Flynt.'

'Not here it won't. The greenskins will have lookouts everywhere. There's no way we'll get in without them seeing us.'

Drekki grinned. 'I'm glad you've spotted that,' he said. 'Because we're going to need a distraction.'

* * *

The *Aelsling* took refuge amid the shifting rocks in the disc below Erulu. Directly below the mass of the island the rocks went up into a spiral, as Drekki had predicted. A real hazard to shipping, but a fine screen for their infiltration.

Drekki had the *Aelsling* blackened from end to end with a compound boiled up by Otherek. It smelled worse than a skyfarer's grundeez after a ten-day storm, though Otherek assured him it would wash off with the first heavy rain.

Lerarus spent most of the day upon the foredeck, drawing complicated magical symbols in chalk upon the plating and snapping at crew who tried to paint over them.

Night crept in. It became very dark very quickly in that strange, aerial cavern. By then, the ship was blackened, the aether-ports covered over, and all potential sources of noise muffled.

'Practically invisible,' said Drekki.

Lerarus was ready. The landing party was ready. Drekki gave the order to ascend. The crew obeyed in total silence.

The docks were on the coreward side of the isle. Drekki kept his ship well clear. All the duardin could see from their position were the downward fringes of the place, a shanty that made Eyeward in Bastion look expertly planned. Jury-rigged jetties and a few airboats crowded off the wharfs. Overspill from the main dock, Drekki assumed.

They all took their boots off, then Drekki had Evrokk bring up the ship on the opposite side of the funnel of rock linking Erulu proper to its attendant, lower disc, but for Lerarus' spell to work, the wizard needed a clear line of sight, so they were forced to sail around to the front of the spiral. At that point the danger was greatest, and all eyes were on the looming island above, searching for spyholes and lookout stalactites.

Lerarus began her incantation, passing her staff over the lines she had drawn. Nothing seemed to be happening, so far as the duardin could tell, until she reached a hushed crescendo, raised her slender staff two-handed over her head, shook it twice, and spoke a final, quiet word of power.

Far out, in the upper accretion disc, there was a flash. A fiery ember began to move.

'There,' said Lerarus with a tired sigh. 'Your diversion is on its way.'

The ember became a fireball. It didn't look very big to begin with, and there was grumbling about its inadequacy, but it soon became clear what feat Lerarus had achieved. A large rock, several times the mass of the *Aelsling*, was headed directly towards the docks. It was only small because it was far away, and it soon got bigger, and bigger, trailing dirty smoke and flame, moving with the inevitability of Sigmar's own comet.

They were some way away from the docks and the meteor, yet they could hear it roaring, before it hit. The duardin watched the burning rock vanish behind the stone, right at the docks. There was a pause, then a satisfyingly large explosion. A blast of fire rushed out into the night, lighting up the underside of the upper disc for a raadleague or more. Flaming beams of wood arced out, gently spinning, and fell through the sky. Tiny crisped grots followed.

'Oooh,' chuckled Gord. 'That's so pretty.'

'I wish we could see this from the front,' said Adrimm.

'We'd be seen from the front, Adrimm,' said Drekki.

'Aye, but still...' Adrimm grinned. 'Those grobi burning up like that. I'd forfeit my share to see it.' He cleared his throat. 'Well, maybe ten per cent of my share.'

Secondary explosions flashed in the sky with green-and-yellow sheet lightning.

'It must be mayhem up there,' said Umherth, with a mix of awe and disappointment that he wasn't taking more of a part.

'I'm not being critical, but could you not have done two?' asked Urdi. 'Two would definitely have burned all their ships in the dock.'

'Do you realise how hard that was?' Lerarus said. 'How tricky it is to weave a spell of that potency on this floating bathtub? All this magical machinery interferes with true wizardry. That was not easy.'

'It's not magic, it's science,' said Otherek quietly. 'I keep telling her,' he explained to Hrunki. 'I'll let it go. It's a bit beyond her under-standing.'

Hrunki nodded sympathetically. Lerarus muttered something unflattering about duardin under her breath.

'It was a good effort,' Drekki assured her. 'In fact, rather better than I hoped. Well done you.'

'You are an insufferably patronising duardin, Captain Flynt.'

He shrugged. 'Can't compliment anyone these days. Right. Take us up with a bit of speed, if you would, Arkanaut First Class Bjarnisson.'

The *Aelsling* rose quietly under the island, endrins running on the lowest setting making tiny, delicate huffing noises. The isle was black and enormous. Up there on top somewhere were the ruins of the city of Erulu. Patterns of shadow marked out fissures in the underside. Reflected firelight dappled eminences. Deeper, darker places suggested tunnel mouths or the caverns of cloven halls. It was to one of these Drekki directed his ship.

'Are we going the right way, wizard?' he whispered to Lerarus.

Lerarus, hands still tight on her staff, nodded. 'We're close,' she said.

As they neared, still unseen, they glimpsed spidery gantries of lashed wood, buckets on ropes, catwalks that wouldn't survive a good gust of wind – rickety constructions grots used as sentry posts and shortcuts between holes in the stone. There was movement up there, scrawny figures bearing torches running into the rock. Firelight blinded them to anything further than a few feet away, and so the *Aelsling* approached undetected.

Fifty more raadfathoms, and the noises of screechy grot-speak reached the ears of the crew, of flat feet slapping on creaky wood, of general panic.

'*Drengi*[32] idiots,' said Umherth gleefully. 'They're all scapering off to the dock!'

'Hush now,' Drekki said. 'Everyone, quiet. This is the delicate part.'

Drekki padded carefully to the prow, where he could look up past the forward endrin. Otherek went to the middle of the boat. Like Drekki, he carried his boots in one hand, stockinged feet silent on the plating.

Drekki squinted into the dark.

'Bring power down to fifteen per cent, gradual ascent, one raadfathom per second.' He spoke in the quietest whisper. Otherek relayed the order at similar, secretive volume.

Half-closed pipes vented glittering steam. Bokko, hanging from the aft endrin on a line, gave a thumbs up.

Drekki grabbed the rail and leaned out over the abyss. He looked up. 'Four degrees to the edgeward board,' he whispered.

'Four degrees edgeward!' Otherek passed on.

Evrokk made the appropriate adjustments. The *Aelsling* shifted very slightly to the left.

'Prepare for a dead stop in fifty raadfathoms,' Drekki said.

The order went down the ship. The *Aelsling* slowed. Drekki gestured to Adrimm to get the ropes ready. Adrimm poked Khenna into action, and they went to the side.

A fragile walkway came down past the endrins, as if lowered smoothly on chains.

---

32 | Kharadrid: Another curse, best left untranslated.

'All stop!' Drekki said. The endrins hissed. The ship coasted to a halt. Adrimm and Khenna leapt over the rails and hauled the boat in.

'All clear!' Khenna said.

Drekki looked up. They were drifting only a few handspans below the island.

'Nice work, Evrokk,' Drekki said, going to the cockpit and slapping the helmsduardin on the shoulder. Evrokk, still numb after his brother's death, only nodded.

A flurry of muffled activity ensued. Drekki and his landing party picked up their weapons from the deck. Some of them went ashore, and those on board passed equipment over. All was conducted with characteristic duardin efficiency and in near total silence.

After a few sweaty minutes, Drekki, Kedren, Lerarus, Otherek, Gord, Urdi and Umherth stood on the catwalk, boots back on. Kedren eyed the frayed rope suspending the walk with deep suspicion. His eyebrows crept up his face as his gaze reached the rusted staples holding them into the rock.

'Terrifying,' he said.

Gord shifted his belly. The whole thing creaked worryingly.

'Steady there, Gord!' Kedren hissed.

Gord grunted. 'Not going to fall.'

'What do you know about engineering?'

Gord shrugged. The catwalk swayed.

'Just stop moving!'

'Shh,' Drekki said. It was very quiet under the stone. Every sound echoed tremendously. 'Gunterr, you're in charge while we're away. Bokko, stick to the observation cupola, watch out for Trokwi. As soon as you see him, follow him in. If he gives this signal' – Drekki tapped Trokwi, who gave out a single, soft peep – 'we're goners, and you're to get out of here as if Archaon himself was trailing your wake, you hear me?'

'Aye, captain,' the master-at-arms said.

'We aim to be done by Hysh-rise. I reckon what with the overhang on this here metalith and the discs we'll get a few more hours of dark, but if the sun touches the edge of the opening between the discs and we're not returned, same thing applies – get out of here.'

'Aye, captain,' said Gunterr.

'Get to the hiding place. Don't move unless it is to flee or to collect us. Grungni willing, we'll be back soon enough.'

Hrunki stepped forward. 'You be careful now, Umherth, come back safe.'

The others giggled. Umherth nodded, embarrassed.

'Aye, I will.'

Otherek elbowed Lerarus. 'See? We told you they were sweet on each other.'

'I think you're jealous, Otherek,' said Kedren.

Hrunki winked and blew the khemist a kiss, causing him to mumble and squirm.

The *Aelsling*'s muffled bell clonked once. It sank back down, quickly vanishing out of sight.

'Right then, let's be off,' said Drekki. 'Urdi, you're up front. Otherek next, then Umherth. Gord, in the middle. Kedren, me and the wizard will take the rear. And take it slow on this bloody bridge. One loud fart and the whole thing will fall down.'

Drekki let the vanguard get ahead.

'Let's go,' said Drekki. 'For fortune and glory and lashings of beer!'

The party moved away into the dark, wincing at every creak of the wood.

CHAPTER EIGHTEEN

STORMVAULT

The walkway led them through a breach in the rock into a tunnel crafted by duardin hands. They breathed a collective sigh of relief. Stone made them feel safe. The tunnel was broad, and went off into darkness in two directions. Darker patches hinted at openings into other places.

'Let's not go back that way, eh?' said Kedren, looking back on the walkway. Even as he spoke, a bit fell off.

'Let's not rush ahead either,' said Drekki. 'Hold up a moment, everyone, I need to get our bearings.' He pulled out the map. 'Light!' he commanded.

Trokwi cocked his head and his eyes lit up, illuminating the faded lines depicting the undercity. Drekki looked about, consulted the map, looked about again.

'This must be the main *ungdrin*,'[33] he said. 'It connected the city core-to-edgewards. I need to get my bearings to tell exactly where we are, though. Lerarus, which direction is the vault?'

---

33 | Khazalid: Subterranean highway or system of the same.

'It's somewhere down there,' she said, looking away up the tunnel. 'I can sense it. It's getting stronger, and it's going to fail soon. I can feel that too.'

'How far?'

'I don't know.'

'Then we push on,' said Drekki. 'The Underking's Hall is closest. We'll try that first.'

Kedren stopped Lerarus a moment. 'Put on your breathing gear, lass. Grot tunnels have bad air.'

She nodded, and fumbled the helm over her head.

On they went. Touches of glory remained in the undercity. The ungdrin ran straight as a die. Past the height where it was easy for the grots to spoil, the ancient stonework was as clean-edged as if it had been mortared in place yesterday. Carved vaulting had the look of a forest canopy reproduced in stone and refined to geometric perfection. Where the rune lamps remained on their fixtures, they were untarnished, though dark now for lack of fresh enchantment. Kedren offered to reignite them.

'Leave 'em,' Drekki said. 'We rely on aetherlamps. If we light up the whole place, we'll be telling the grots that we're here.'

They made the Underking's Hall in an hour, and found nothing but the filth of grobi. There were some moving about in the shacks clustered around the old king's throne, so the party crept through as quickly as they dared.

More hours passed. They traversed high-ceilinged halls, marvellous gates, drainage channels, rack-and-pinion railways, the remnants of mechanisms cast in brass and steel. Such feats of engineering, even ruined, were enough to swell the heart of any duardin.

The grots had wrecked what they could; whether through malice or carelessness, the results were the same. The floor was choked with trash and grotty leavings. Bones littered alcoves. Vandalised statues sat guard over branching passages, their heads hacked off. In places, so many layers of crude, angular graffiti had been carved over each other it had gnawed the ashlar back to the bedrock, while at unpredictable intervals, grot-made tunnels broke through the run of the duardin masonry. The sight of those made the crew curse more than anything.

Seeing the achievements of their race defaced brought a grim mood upon the party.

Lerarus slowed. She grabbed Drekki's arm hard. 'We're close,' she said. 'Very close.'

Drekki called a halt, and took up his map again. Trokwi provided light.

'That's peculiar. According to this, the Hall of Merchants should be hereabouts.'

'I don't see no hall,' said Gord.

'Exactly. It's been hidden. Ergo, the Stormvault must be here.'

'What's ergo mean?' asked Gord.

'It means we've found it,' said Drekki patiently. 'Just look for a secret door.'

Gord raised his fist back to punch the wall.

'Quietly!' Drekki said. 'And on the other wall. It will be on that side.' He pointed. 'That's where the hall should be. The stonework is suspiciously whole. Looks like the grots have been discouraged from meddling here.'

'Subtle magic,' said Lerarus. 'Humans and duardin working together. Perhaps the aelves as well.'

'Ah well,' said Kedren, 'that narrows the necessaries down.' He took out a set of metal runes from his pouch, sorted clankingly through them, put most back, then cast half a dozen on the floor for a reading. Meanwhile, Otherek fed liquefied aether into a device on his staff, and slowly moved it along the wall, leaving frost trails on the stone and shifting light in the air.

'Urdi, keep watch on that tunnel there,' said Drekki. He meant a grothole opposite the investigation site, whence blew a dank wind. 'I don't like the smell of it.'

The party fanned out, fingers spread on the masonry, tools gently tapping for voids. They were diligent, but duardin secrets are made to be kept, even from other duardin.

'I can't find anything!' Umherth complained.

'Use your head,' Drekki said. 'And I do not mean headbutt the rock.'

'Shh!' Urdi held up a clenched fist. The whole group came to the alert. He cupped his hand around his ear, then pointed up the grot tunnel.

The duardin flattened themselves against the wall by the tunnel mouth. Drekki put his finger to his lips. Gord cracked his knuckles and stood ready.

The slap of flat feet came pattering out of the foetid dark. Muttering accompanied it. 'Not fair, not fair! Run here, get that, he says. Bring this, do that, he says. Not fair!'

Torchlight shone in the tunnel mouth.

'Kaptin's so mean, so cruel.' There was sniggering. 'Shame about all them pretty ships of his getting all burned. What a fire!'

A grot with a spotty red bandana tied around its pointy head emerged. It carried a feeble torch, and wore a stripy jersey.

Gord stepped out in front of it. 'Hello,' he said.

'Er, hello?' said the grot. Then, 'Eeek!' as the creature realised what was reaching for it.

Gord lifted the grot up by the neck, and bit off its head. A stomach-churning crunching followed. Gord swallowed with difficulty and dropped the body. Warm grot-blood sprayed over Urdi.

'Bony head,' he said. He burped and patted his chest. ''Scuse me. I got a bit peckish.'

A shrill squeal came out of the tunnel.

'There's another,' said Gord.

'For Grimnir's sake, stop it from getting away!' Drekki growled.

Running at the tunnel, Gord misjudged the height of the door, and smashed his forehead on the stone, nearly knocking himself out. Lerarus tried a spell, but the helm mangled her words and she produced no more than a pathetic fizzle from her staff.

'I've got this,' said Umherth, stepping into the tunnel mouth, volley gun barrels whining up to speed.

Drekki shouted for him to stop, but what exactly he said was lost under the roar of the gun. It was a brief discharge, catastrophically loud.

'Ha!' Umherth said. 'Shredded him. How'd you like two thousand rounds a minute, green-scum?'

'Umherth!' Drekki whispered angrily. 'Every greenskin within half a mile will have heard that!'

'He didn't get away though.'

'No, and nor shall we if we keep up this racket. What a bloody shower. Find that cavern!'

At the edge of his hearing, Drekki heard horns.

'Funti drukk!' he swore. 'They're on to us. Hurry up! Hurry up!'

They abandoned stealth. Hammers tapped loudly. Umherth cranked up the gain on his aether-o-matic, and sent whooping pings down the ungdrin.

It was Kedren who found the way in.

'Right here, captain!' he shouted. He pointed to a blank section of wall. His runes were on the floor in front of it, violently ablaze.

The crew gathered around.

'This should do it,' Kedren said. He plucked up a rune. 'By runes crafted, found and opened,' he announced. He pushed the rune into what looked like a crack in the mortar. There was the click of a lock, a dazzling flash that had them blinking, and a whole section of the wall vanished. Where there had been wall, a tunnel was open before them. Cobwebs stirred, disturbed by the change in pressure.

'Angdruk kanz!'[34] Drekki said. 'Everyone in!' He glanced back up the tunnel. The blowing of horns was joined by the jabber of many agitated voices, rustling, and the clatter of weapons. The draught picked up.

'There's so many of them they're pushing up the pressure,' said Otherek. He shut off his device.

Gord went in, Lerarus, then the rest.

'Can you get this shut again?' Drekki asked Kedren.

'Easy as can be,' said Kedren with a modest shrug.

'That's good. It'll buy us a little more time.'

Drekki went in. Kedren lingered. He did something by the doorway, stepped back, and the section of wall winked once more into existence.

They found themselves in total blackness, total silence. By his species' refined underground senses, Drekki could tell they were in a large space. But with all the crew breathing loudly around him it felt unpleasantly intimate.

'Someone get some light.'

'On it,' said Otherek.

'Hang on,' said Kedren, 'allow me.'

A hammer struck sparks from a rune that took on a blue glow, and a thousand chandeliers on the ceiling flashed into life, flooding the halls with concentrated starlight. A massive flock of bats burst from their roosts and went screeching about, causing Umherth to give out a thoroughly unduardin squeal.

The bats whirled around, and around, then vanished towards the far side of the hall.

'What the dreng was that?' said Drekki.

---

34 | Kharadrid: Lit. 'That's the bolt threaded!' Commonly translated as 'Bullseye!'

'I don't like bats,' said Umherth.

'The Merchants' Hall of the duardin of Erulu,' Kedren breathed.

The crew were in the tunnel gateway of a hall of some size. Behind them, the entrance was blocked by stonecraft so expertly built the joins were invisible. A small section in the centre was covered in lines of runes that glowed a warm but fading gold. It was through this magical doorway they had entered.

Columns marched in straight lines. The hall was beautifully built, mathematically perfect, the work of the ancestors, with every angle precisely cut, if a little brutal because of the duardin fondness for hard, straight lines. Once upon a time, halls like this had numbered in their thousands across the realms. Those days were long in the past.

What occupied the centre was a major departure from the duardin norm.

'That's a sight and no mistake,' said Umherth. His voice was thick with gold fever.

'The Stormvault,' said Lerarus. 'We've found it.'

A narrow pyramid of silver rose up from the plaza where once duardin merchants had struck deals and exchanged stocks. At each corner a gryph-hound the size of a horse carved from jade sat at sentry, so lifelike and attentive it looked like they would get up at any moment. Coloured light played lazily over the pyramid's skin and the statues. An air of power surrounded it, then it lapsed unexpectedly. Drekki's ears popped with a shift in pressure. The light on the pyramid's skin went out, the hall darkened and the vault became momentarily mundane. A crackling sounded from inside. The runelamps flickered with it.

'We're here just in time,' said Lerarus. 'The spells are coming apart.' She looked back at the door, whose runes had become nothing but faint marks.

'That will make it easier, surely,' said Drekki.

'Exactly not,' said the wizard. 'The vault will stay physically shut and the hall gate won't. When the spells fail the grots will be free to enter. I can hear them.'

From the other side came the faint tapping of tools on stone.

'It'll be fine,' said Drekki. 'They've been here a few hundred years and not found their way in. I'll look around. Make sure it's safe for you while you work.' What he really meant was to hunt for loot, and he was as eager as Umherth to be about it. He made to go forward.

'Wait!' Lerarus said, urgently enough to make him stop. 'It's still dangerous. Slowly, captain. Carefully.'

'I wasn't just going to blunder on in,' said Drekki, though he was.

'It will take us time to deactivate the wards safely,' Lerarus said. 'We've got to disarm the protective spells, and get the vault open before the outer wards fail.'

'How long will that take?' said Drekki.

'Don't get all hasty. I did say this would be tricky,' said Kedren. 'We'd best get started. Otherek? Wizard?'

The three of them went about some esoteric task that Drekki could not comprehend. His knowledge of aether ended at pistons and energy pumps. Otherek's aelchemical khemistry was far beyond him, and magic was another thing altogether.

'We'll keep watch,' he called after them.

The magic of the Stormvault ebbed again, plunging them into a menacing twilight.

'Stay away from the pyramid, captain. Stick close to the walls,' said Kedren, turning back. 'We're fortunate this vault is failing or we'd all be charcoal by now. Don't do anything rash.'

'Got it,' said Drekki. He gathered the others together into a huddle. 'Let's check for grots. Thoroughly, if you get my meaning.' He gave them all his captain's eye. 'And don't do anything rash, like Kedren said.' He winked.

'Treasure?' said Umherth eagerly.

'Why would I be looking for treasure?' said Drekki with wounded innocence.

'I get you,' said Umherth with a knowing tone.

'Treasure won't do us no good if we die,' said Urdi. 'We need a way out too, and this hall's sealed.'

'Them horrible bats get in and out, don't they?' Umherth lifted his helm and sniffed. 'Air current coming from that way,' he said. He pointed across the hall, past the pyramid.

'Let's check that first then,' said Drekki, 'while carefully checking everything else on the way.'

'For treasure?' said Umherth.

'For danger!' said Drekki loudly, so Lerarus could hear. 'And treasure,' he whispered to his group.

They went together: Drekki, Umherth, Urdi and Gord. The clink of gear, the whine of aetherpacks and the heavy tread of the ogor filled up the hall. There was a tremulous feeling to everything, like a bowstring about to break. Periodically the pyramid made its unhealthy noise. The light faded and flared.

Around the edges of the hall were signs of hasty conversion from stock exchange to magical vault. Piled furniture was covered in cobwebs. Broken chests spilled disintegrating ledgers. There were piles of damp dust that might have been cloth, banners maybe, or paper documents, and heaps of dead rune lamps, carelessly discarded. Tools leaned on the stone: picks, mattocks, boxes of chisels corroded into solid, ferric masses. A rusty wheelbarrow sat dead centre between two columns, like an abandoned dog waiting for an owner that would never come back.

'This is definitely not a work of secrecy,' said Drekki, looking at the tools of his forebears.

Umherth shrugged. 'Umgi. Making stories up and getting it wrong. It's because they don't write their history down properly, I heard, and no one lives long enough to remember, so they forget and argue about it.'

'That's not our concern. We'll deliver this talisman and get our reward. That'll be as far as I want to get involved in umgi politics. This is all wrong. Ildrin, daemons, secret not-secret vaults, daemon hunters!'

Gord laughed.

Urdi gave him a sidelong look. 'What's so funny about that?'

'Harkraken though, that was well tasty,' the ogor said.

Under a pile of rags, in a forgotten gap, they found a chest with an unbroken lock. Once Drekki's crew got to it, it didn't remain unbroken for long.

'A few things of worth in here,' said Umherth, rooting about with one hand and pocketing the contents with the other.

Drekki did a quick valuation. Gems in rotted bags. Square coins threaded onto currency bars.

'Good pieces,' he said, as the treasure vanished into sacks. 'None of you be hiding that away, now. It all goes into the yield. Fair shares. Pile it up so we can count it. All out of your pockets now. Ahem. Umherth? I mean you.'

'Aye, captain,' said Umherth sulkily. He emptied his pockets into the sack Urdi held out.

Gord pulled out a mouldering cloth, coughed at the dust, then went, 'Oooh!'

Beneath the cloth was a rune axe with nice High Achromian decoration. Umherth reached for it.

'Steady,' said Drekki. 'Give.' He held out his hand. Umherth reluctantly handed it over. 'I'll look after that.'

Drekki divided up the loot for them to carry, though Gord got most. They became hopeful after the chest, poking into every nook and cranny. A couple more chests turned up, all empty. Nothing but dreck and ruin to be seen.

'All the good stuff must be in there,' said Umherth, looking longingly at the pyramid. There was a note of desperation in his voice. 'I mean, can you imagine what glories could be hiding in that thing?'

They all stared at the vault.

Gord saw something, turned aside and frowned. 'Light, captain!' he said.

A strong glow came from somewhere on the far side of the vault. The little group moved cautiously past one of the jade gryph-hounds, rounding the corner of the pyramid so they could see the other side of the cavern.

The pyramid crackled. The lights went out, came back on again, half illuminating three human figures stood in poses suggesting a reaction to something fearful. A sword half drawn, a hand cast up, a body turning as if to flee.

Gord's nostrils flared and he hefted his punch dagger. Umherth brought up his gun. Drekki pushed it back down.

'They're dead.'

The little party stopped. The pyramid crackled again. A beam of cold, deadly radiance bathed the humans, calling up a dull silver sheen on grey.

Umherth squinted. He took a step forward. 'Transmuted. Looks like lead?' he said.

'Metal magic. The wizard did say the vault was dangerous,' said Drekki.

Gord sniffed loudly. 'I smell flesh. There's more dead 'uns over here, captain,' he said. 'Dead, but not lead.' He licked his lips.

By the cavern wall, three more men lay. These had all been slain by more conventional means: knives and the like, judging by the tarry pools of blood spread underneath them. A fourth corpse was leaning on the wall, legs out straight, head bowed, a black-fletched arrow near his heart.

Gord sniffed. 'Not dead long,' he said hopefully. 'A few days at most.' He reached out.

Drekki slapped Gord's massive finger aside. 'Don't even think about eating them,' he said. 'I've got to figure this out.'

'Figure what out? Which one to eat first?'

'Think with what brain you have, Gord, leave your stomach out of it. There's something fishy here.'

'I like fish,' said Gord.

'Figure of speech. I mean suspicious. Look, this one here was killed by grots.' He pointed at the man dead from the arrow.

'All of them were killed by grots, surely,' said Urdi. He was checking the men's pockets thoroughly. He pulled out a few coins and put them in the sacks.

'You'd think,' said Drekki. 'But that don't make no sense. If grots had got in here they would have pillaged the place, or there'd at least be signs they'd tried. I don't see any dead grots, do you? Just those lead umgi.'

'You're right, captain,' said Urdi.

'So he must have been shot outside but died in here, right?' Drekki walked back to the other three corpses. 'This fellow here, he doesn't have his sword out. He's been knifed in the back.' He poked at the dried-up wound between his shoulder blades. 'This fellow has a dagger, as well as his sword. Blood on the blade. I'd say he's the culprit.'

'What do you think happened then?' asked Urdi.

'Umgi politics,' said Drekki. 'Before they attempted to open the vault, these two here tried to kill off their comrades and take the loot for themselves.' He moved closer to the pyramid. 'Signs of a struggle,' he said, pointing out fresh, white sword nicks in the stone, a discarded scabbard, and splashes of blood. 'Here's another dead one.'

'One, two, three,' said Gord. His thuggish face crinkled. 'That's more than three of them! That's a lot.'

'Aye, and that fellow there is wounded.' Drekki pointed to one of the men turned to lead by the pyramid. The hard, white light flickered on and off him, showing up details. Mouth set in a scream, sword in hand, no scabbard at his belt, and a clean cut through the cloth of one puffy sleeve.

'Cutting down your fellows for the sake of some loot,' said Umherth. 'Terrible.'

'Eh, eh,' said Drekki. 'With your questionable past you're the last one to be judging.'

'I've no idea what you mean,' said Umherth shiftily.

'Captain!' said Urdi. He tossed over a medallion.

Drekki caught it. 'Crave's crest,' he said. 'It's them from the ship. Let me see. Lord Crave's nephew decides to beat us to the punch. They get to the island. This lot sneak into the city, get into a scrape with some grots, find a way in here somehow, then this group turn on each other, the ship tries to escape and fails, then we find the wreck.' He looked around. 'No sign they came the way we did. There must be another entrance into this place. Why did they turn on each other? Some effect of the pyramid, maybe? Or something else?' He tapped a finger against the beard moulded onto his helmet. 'We'll figure it out later. Let's get away from the pyramid. Let them make it safe. In the meantime, let's follow this arrow-shot chap's blood, that'll show us how they got in.'

A line of black stains led them across the hall. The draught got stronger, until they found themselves by an open door. Stairs led down in a steep, straight line. Far, far below there was a point of light. Fresh air blew up from it. There were piles of umgi gear by the entrance, ropes and a long box like a coffin that Umherth opened right away.

'Empty,' said Umherth disappointedly.

'This must be it. Handy little exit for us,' said Drekki. 'And I can't smell no grobi.'

'Stinks of bats though,' said Umherth with a shudder.

They poked about a little more. Finding nothing else of interest, they sat down for a smoke and a bit of cured meat. Gord grumbled about the size of his portion. Drekki wandered over to tell the others what they'd found, and wandered back again when they told him to get lost for a while. Then they watched the pyramid. The way it glimmered was mesmerising for a bit, until it got boring. They waited. And waited some more.

Three hours later, the others were ready to open the vault.

Lerarus worked in the centre of a circle of protective runes laid out by Kedren. Otherek's contribution was a device clipped to long loops of copper wire around the runes, but the brunt of the task fell upon the wizard, who was standing, head bowed, muttering words of power that made the air shimmer with heat as she spoke them. Having done their part, the runesmith and khemist retreated to a safe distance. They still had their hands full keeping the others from straying too close.

It was an active job. Umherth in particular was raring to get into the vault. His eyes flicked constantly from Lerarus to the pyramid. He shifted from foot to foot. He wasn't alone. All of them were impatient.

'Isn't she done yet?' Umherth said. 'I thought you said you were ready?'

'Ready to make the attempt, Umherth. She'll be done when she's done,' said Kedren. 'This isn't like smashing a lock.'

'I could try smashing it,' said the oldbeard. 'A bit of blade work might speed things up a touch. I'll wait until the lights go off, should be safe then.'

Lerarus' incantations stopped. She let out a long, pained sigh.

'If you tried that, you'd be turned to lead like the men of Lord Crave, or you'd burst into flames.' She turned to glare at Umherth balefully. 'Come to think of it, you will burst into flames if you don't shut up.'

Her threat had little effect on him.

'I could try though. Might hurry things along a little.' He patted the cutter hanging from his belt.

'I think she means it,' said Drekki, laying a hand on his arm. 'She could flambé you to a crisp with three words or less, so why don't we all be quiet now?'

'But it's taking so long!'

'It'll take a damn sight longer if you don't be quiet!' snapped Lerarus. She set herself back into position, and drew in a breath.

'Sorry,' said Umherth.

'Gah!' Lerarus shouted. 'Shut up!' A cloud of sparks flashed around her head.

Drekki shooed his followers back. 'Come on now, give her some more space.'

Lerarus placed her hands high up her staff, bowed her face, and began again.

'It won't take forever, will it?' Drekki said to Kedren, quietly enough that Lerarus would not be disturbed.

'This Stormvault is protected by layered spells,' Kedren explained. 'One turned those luckless umgi into lead. There will be more. She has to deactivate them all, in the right order, one at a time. She's tackled the minor stuff, the alarms, cantrips of power amplification, evocations of dread, all that. Now she's on to the dangerous ones. When they're done, she can tackle the lock.'

'And what's your contribution?'

'My runes give her a bit of breathing space, a bit more time to think, not much more than that. Otherek's gubbins there will bleed off any magical overspill,' he said, pointing, 'but it's mostly on her.' Kedren, who had his helm under his arm, stroked his long beard. 'She's young, even for an umgi, but she's got a lot of talent. She's brave too. I'll give her that.'

Something was happening around the wizard. Colourful flames

danced, making an ovoid shape around her. The vault groaned. A burst of lightning sped from one of the gryph-hounds' eyes. Drekki could have sworn the animal screeched. The bolt hit the fires, and burst spectacularly, splitting into a blaze of smaller jags that leapt into Kedren's runes. The ring of metal letters burned red-hot, and crackling power danced along Otherek's coils.

'Oooh,' went Gord.

'That's one down,' said Kedren.

Lerarus continued, her voice rising. Thunder rumbled from the heart of the pyramid. The groaning stopped, the vault seeming to stabilise in the face of the threat. The silvery beam that had played on Crave's men flashed from the pyramid's tip. Again, ancient magic encountered Lerarus' fires, found no way through, and puttered out, yet all around her there were glittering falls of lead as the beam of transmutation caught dust in the air.

Lerarus was shouting now, lifting up her staff. Fire ignited along the length. Drekki did not understand the words, but they were liquid, some kind of Aelfish, he guessed.

A roil of green fire burst from every side of the pyramid. It rolled out, licking up the walls of the cavern, igniting the damp dust of old ledgers and cloth so great was the heat, but on the side facing the duardin, it was sucked towards Lerarus, and into her staff. With a single word, she directed it down into the runic circle. Kedren's runes shone so brightly each one cast its own image up into the air. A potent thrum set up from the vault.

Movement rippled over the jade gryph-hounds' skin. They blinked, and stretched. Light blazed from their eyes. They got up, paced around the pyramid, screeching warningly, the way their living counterparts did when danger approached. When Lerarus did not cease, they gathered in a pack facing the wizard, stalking forward. A great wind blew up, blasting dust into the duardin's eyes, making their beards whip about. They huddled down and put their helmets back on. The gryph-hounds broke into a run.

'This is it!' Kedren shouted over the tumult. 'The last enchantment!'

The lead gryph-hound leapt as, with a final cry, Lerarus slammed her staff into the stone. A ring of bright white light raced out from the runic circle, hit the pyramid, and was reflected back. Otherek's contraption absorbed the backwash, melting into steaming puddles of molten copper in the process.

The noise stopped. The wind stopped. The gryph-hounds were jade again. The one that had leapt crashed to the ground and shattered into a million pieces that skidded in every direction. Umherth looked about, bent down and began frantically scooping up the bits.

'It is done,' panted Lerarus. 'The last protections are down.'

'Treasure?' said Umherth, looking up from pocketing jade.

Drekki gave him a look. 'Shhh!'

Lerarus leaned on her staff for support a moment, then stood straight, and held up her arms. 'Open,' she said, her voice powerful. A simple word, but so imbued with magic that it boomed around the hall.

The pyramid obeyed. Silver ran, revealing seams at the corners. The sides seemed to retract into the ground, though there was no slot for them to recede into. Slowly they vanished out of sight.

Where the pyramid had been was a square dais with gently sloped sides about forty grunti high. Upon that was a statue of a seated woman, twice life-size, and fashioned from bands of metal.

'Looks like some sort of sarcophagus,' Urdi said.

'There'll be a richly decked queen within!' Umherth said excitedly. 'Gems for eyes! Marvellous headdresses! Magical swords galore!'

The banded metal clanked and retracted, rattling together.

The duardin leaned forward, eyes wide with greed.

The metal vanished into itself, revealing a throne of silver. There were no jewels, gold or treasures. Instead, there was a young woman, the high back and sides of the throne enclosing her on every side but the front. She was garbed in close-fitting armour and white robes, half her face so heavily tattooed it was almost black, her long hair piled high onto her head.

There was a moment of appalled silence.

'Where's the bloody treasure?!' Umherth yelped.

'Yes. Yes exactly, what the hell is this?' said Urdi.

'Looks like we won't be making any extra on this job, then,' mumbled Kedren.

'Who is that?' said Drekki, turning to Lerarus.

'That is the talisman,' said Lerarus calmly.

'It's a woman,' said Drekki. 'It is not a talisman.'

'She is the talisman.'

'Where's the treasure?!' howled Umherth. 'There's no treasure, no treasure!'

'It was you who assumed the talisman would be an object, captain,' said Lerarus. She looked up. The rune lamps flickered, and each time they did, they got a little dimmer. 'We must be quick. All magic in this hall has been dispelled.'

'But that means...' said Urdi.

'The door,' said Otherek.

The lights went out.

Kedren struck a rune to illuminate a space around them. Darkness pressed in. On the far side of the room, where the door had been, many red eyes glinted.

'Funti drukk,' said Drekki. 'Grobi!'

CHAPTER NINETEEN

GROTS

Both groups were stunned to see each other, if the amount of confused blinking coming from the grots was anything to go by. Their surprise didn't last.

A squeaky cry of 'Get 'em!' started a green avalanche. Grots streamed forward, waving crude, wide-bladed cutlasses.

'Yeah?' said Umherth evilly, and opened fire.

A spread of hot blue aether-gas blasted across the hall, turning gold before it hit the first line of grots. The greenskins promptly disintegrated. Umherth hosed them down, laughing manically, killing scores. The grot charge came to a stuttering stop.

Umherth ran out of ammunition. The gun whirred to a halt. He quickly snapped the gunstock away from the barrels and changed out the gas bottle.

Grots stood whimpering in the puddled remains of their fellows. They were on the verge of running.

'Gord,' Drekki said. 'Grab the girl!'

A bigger grot shoved its way to the front.

'I said, get 'em!' It whacked the head off one of its cronies with a cutlass by way of encouragement.

With a shrill 'Waaagh!' the grots surged forward anew.

Umherth fired again. Arrows hissed through the air down onto the crew, clattering from their armour. They bounced off the throne on the dais. For the moment the talisman, or the woman, or whatever she was, was protected, but that wouldn't last.

'Clear Gord a path!' Drekki shouted. He drew Karon and added his fire to Umherth's.

Lerarus sent a wash of flame into the horde. All the duardin were firing, the Kharadron with their aether-pieces, Kedren with his rune-struck blunderbuss, whose ammunition today was enchanted with cold. Grots froze solid. Umherth's bullets shattered them.

Gord and grots surged up opposite sides of the dais at once. One shot from the ogor's huge pistol carved a cone of flying limbs and innards into the piratical horde. He roared at them, punched a head clean off a bruiser near the front. That did it. The vanguard turned and ran, thumping into their comrades. The lot of them fell over, tumbling down the dais steps in hopeless knots.

Gord plucked the sleeping woman from the throne, draped her over his shoulder, and legged it, arrows and pistol balls whistling past his ears.

'I believe we have overstayed our welcome,' said Drekki, firing Karon repeatedly. 'Out the back, lads!'

Gord made it to the huddle of skyfarers in four ogorish bounds. They run clumsily, ogors. Their legs are short for their height, but they can shift when they want to. He was away through the duardin, towards the door while the rest of the crew were still setting themselves in motion. Drekki and the rest ran after him, keeping the grots back with gunfire while Gord hared off down the stairs at a stoop.

'Go get the ship!' Drekki shouted at Trokwi. The drillbill trilled and took flight, swooping down the stairway, dodging Gord's brutish head to plunge towards the light.

Umherth's volley gun ran dry. 'I'm out, captain!' he cried.

'Then get going!' Drekki slapped him on the back, speeding him into the stairwell. Lerarus cast one final fireball back into the hall. Grots lofted upward, burning and squealing.

'I need to stay with the talisman,' she shouted.

'We'll be right behind you!' shouted Drekki.

She ran down the stairs. Urdi went next. Drekki, Kedren and Otherek held the door. Drekki's pistol banged at a prodigious rate, spitting fire from her three barrels, covering his crew's escape, until that too clicked, and no more bullets came. He put it away and unslung his great axe from his back.

'I'll handle this,' said Otherek, stepping forward. 'Hold them off for a moment.' He slammed his fist against the base of his atmospheric anatomiser. The heavy nozzle dropped out of the side, trailing a hose. He cranked up the dials to maximum emission.

Grots crazed with fear and hatred hurled themselves at the three duardin. Drekki and Kedren stepped forward. Runes burned. Aether shone. Grots dropped to swipes of the axes. A couple of them caught fire. It was a good day for burning greenskins.

'Clear!' shouted Otherek.

The bulky machine made a sad little toot, and out spewed a cloud of primal aether. It rolled out, glorious and gold, unrefined, deadly. Protected by their aeronautical suits, the duardin suffered no ill effects. The grots had no such defences. The ones nearest were flash-boiled, meat sliding from their bones as their squeals turned to gurgles. Further back, where the gas lost its heat, they choked, tongues turning purple. For a second, there was calm.

'Drengi expensive way to wage war,' complained Drekki. Grot corpses sparkled with solidified aether-gold. 'A ship's price a shot.'

'Then get out of here before I burn up my retirement fund,'

said Otherek. 'I reckon I can afford one more blast to keep them off your backs.'

Kedren and Drekki were off, into the dark. Down the stairs Drekki saw the others marked out by their aetherlamps a way ahead. Right up front, Gord was a silhouette blocking the daylight. Another whoosh came from behind, a clang as Otherek ejected the spent cylinder, and he followed after.

'Get up in front, Otherek,' Drekki said. 'Kedren and I will act as rearguard.'

Otherek's golden slaughter granted only a few seconds before the grots got their courage back and surged down the steps. Drekki and Kedren ran on until the arrows and pistol balls were clanging off their packs with dangerous force, then the Kharadron captain and Dispossessed runesmith turned to face their ancestral enemies.

Grots flooded towards them, five abreast, tongues lolling, all thoughts of fleeing washed away by their need to kill the duardin.

'This is it,' said Drekki. He hefted his axe.

'Khazuk! Khazuk! Ha!' Kedren shouted.

'Kharadror, Kharadrar!' Drekki answered.

The grots hit them. Drekki and Kedren were as solid as the walls of a mountain hold. They retreated step by step, killing as they went, allowing the others to pound down the stairs towards the light.

Strength flowed into Drekki from the runes on his axe. Never before had he been so grateful for the craft of the old ways. Without the rune magic, he would have been exhausted after five minutes hefting so massive a weapon, even with the aether boost his suit offered. Magic filled him, swelling his muscles, enabling him to swing the giant axe with ease. He half fancied there was a throng of ancestors at his back, shouting encouragement as he slaughtered the greenskins. It was like the great tunnel battles of the Age of Myth, or of more ancient days still, when pre-duardin warred with grobi in the dark of another world over the ruins of a shattered empire.

Time blurred, measured by pounding hearts and the chop of axes. Blood ran down the stairs. The grots were hindered by their own dead, but still they came on.

Drekki and Kedren fought on until they found themselves in a pool of weak grey light and with nowhere else to go. They had reached the bottom. The stair finished abruptly, the last step cleaved diagonally across into a treacherous triangle. Ropes looped round iron staples showed where the umgi had come in, but this tunnel had never been discovered by the grots. There were no wooden additions to the underside of the island. Nothing to step back onto. The disc of broken land slowly reforming beneath Erulu was so far down it was washed out, like an old painting. Drekki swayed on the edge of oblivion. The wind was strong, and it nearly took him.

The others were gone. For a second, he feared they had fallen.

Trokwi floated up beside him, riding the thermals and tweeting a greeting. The throbbing of endrins reached him then. The *Aelsling* rose from below.

'Captain, runesmith. To the left! Grab the line!' Gunterr shouted. He was up in the cupola, gesturing madly. Adrimm was crouched beside him, locked in place by line and mag-boot, sighting up a harpoon, cable coiled at his side. He fired. Something hit the stone, and to the left an aether-powered grapnel drill screwed itself deep into the rock.

Kedren cut a grot in half. Their assault was not slackening.

'Go!' Drekki shouted to Kedren. He didn't need telling twice. The runesmith caught the line and stepped off to rush away, swinging about madly, gauntlet screeching on steel wire.

Drekki slew a grot, then another. He needed to clear a space, or he'd be knifed in the back. The *Aelsling* was struggling to keep position. The wind caught her globes like sails, pushed her aside, and the line parted with a musical *pling!*

'You're going to have to jump, captain!' Gunterr shouted. Adrimm quickly exchanged harpoon for aethershot rifle and shot past Drekki's head, slaying a grot who fancied its chances while Drekki was distracted.

Distracted he was. He was a goner if he missed this leap. Taking hitting the deck as a given, it was still a goodly drop.

'A better fate than a thousand grobi blades,' muttered Drekki.

He leapt.

Despite several Kharadron generations already born in the air, a duardin is not naturally inclined to flight. Stumpy legs and thick-thewed arms make no substitution for wings. Drekki fell like a plumb weight. He hit like one too, clonging off the forward endrin. He threw out an arm, grabbed a rail for long enough to stop himself bouncing over the edge into nothingness, but his fingers were wrenched free. He tried to get his feet under him as he slid down the globe, and turned the magnetic soles on. They clicked, half-adhered. Big mistake. It only made him stand up awkwardly and fall forward. His boots ripped free of the metal. Clear air greeted him, going all the way down to the lower disc then on to eternity. He rolled over, like he was sporting in the sky like a bird, like it was fun. It was not fun. Rock rolled over him above. He turned face down. He was already falling past the *Aelsling*.

He was really quite scared.

A huge hand shot out and grabbed him by the ankle, stopping his fall with painful abruptness.

'We've got him!' shouted Urdi. 'Let's haul aether!'

The *Aelsling* plunged as Evrokk took her down in a skilful cork-screw. Grot bullets and arrows rattled off the endrin tops. Drekki swung out, arms waving. His heart was going like a piston. He was still dangling over the drop in the ogor's hand.

'For the love of Grimnir's flaming arse, pull me in, Gord!' he shouted.

'Oh yeah, sorry,' said the ogor.

The ogor deposited Drekki on the deck, where he was greeted by Kedren. The runesmith was furious, helmless, face beet-red.

'If you dare tell me that went well, I'm going to shoot you myself.'

Drekki forced a grin. By Grungni, that drop was a terror, and it was hard to conjure his bravado, but he needed to cover his fear for the sake of his duardin.

'We got the talisman didn't we?' The warble in his voice was quite evident.

'Did we?' Kedren said. He glanced at the girl. Gord had dropped her like a sack of rags upon a pile of rope. She lay there, still magically slumbering, Lerarus fussing over her. 'That does not look like a talisman to me. That looks like a girl. We've been had.'

'Never mind that,' said Drekki. He got up. Horn blasts were sounding from all over the island above. 'We can argue when we're out of this, because we're not safe in the karak yet, that's for sure.'[35]

---

35 | Khazalid: Common saying expressing the idea of safety as yet unreached.

CHAPTER TWENTY

KAPTIN BLACKHEART

Drekki recovered his wits quickly. 'Get us out of here, Arkanaut Bjarnisson!' he called back to the cockpit. 'Bokko, engines to full!'

The crew went into action, taking their places, Otherek clambering up to his spot on the tops, while Gunterr and Adrimm made their way down. For the moment, the grots at the bottom of the stair remained isolated. All they could muster was a scattering of shot, and a couple fell screaming from the pushing behind. They were hardly a threat to the *Aelsling*. That wouldn't last. There were already signs of movement on some of the other walkways. Drekki looked for the quickest way out from the discs surrounding the island and into clear skies.

That'd be past the docks...

'Can't go that way,' he said to himself.

Horns blew the alarm from every quarter. Hatches were opening in the underside of the island. The rear endrin boomed. Someone up there was dropping rocks on them.

'Best way out if you please, aether-khemist!' Drekki hollered up to the observation cupola.

'Fifteen degrees coreward,' Otherek responded.

'Fifteen degrees coreward!' Drekki shouted down to Evrokk.

'Drekki!' Lerarus said. 'I have to get the talisman below deck. I need some help.'

'Fine, then get ready to sling a few fireballs about, if you would.'

Lerarus was torn. She glanced at the girl then at the grots. 'I can't.'

'Can't? No ship, no talisman,' said Drekki. 'Just saying.'

'There won't be a ship if I don't keep her asleep. The talisman posesses a lot of raw magical power. If she awakens and loses control, grots will be the least of our worries. We have to get her below, now!'

Drekki looked at the girl, then at the wizard. She was strung out, pale from her exertions, black lines under her eyes. 'Dreng it! Very well. Someone get the talisman below!'

Velunti and Urdi carried the talisman downstairs. Her limbs flopped about, her body sagged into a deep valley, as stiff as a piece of string. She was so boneless the duardin struggled with her dead weight, and she was only taken inside with much cursing and puffing. Lerarus shouted at them all the time to be careful, the slam of the steel door cutting off her admonishments.

'Battle mage, ha! Fat lot of use,' Drekki grumbled.

'Captain! Sky-ships coming in from edgeward!' Khenna shouted.

Drekki ran to the prow.

'You've good eyes, Khenna,' said Drekki. A group of grot airboats under lumpy sacks of gas were floating down from the island and moving to intercept.

'Same to the edgeward board, captain,' Adrimm hollered. 'I knew this was a bad idea,' he added blackly.

'Stow it, Fair-weather,' Drekki ordered. He scanned the horizon on Adrimm's side. Fair-weather wasn't wrong: more ships approached. A couple of bigger ones at that.

'How many of these green bastards are there?' said Umherth.

'A great many,' said Kedren.

'Funti drukk! The only clear way out is past the docks,' said Drekki.

'It's a trap. They want us to go that way. They mean to sweep us right into their main force,' said Kedren.

'These are grots. I'd bet my last piece of diamond that they're too disorganised for that. They're all over the place. If we go full speed, we'll be past them before they're out and at us.'

'I'm not sure that's a good idea,' Kedren said, following Drekki around as he went from crewduardin to crewduardin, shouting orders and encouragement.

'Do you have a better one?' said Drekki. 'Ten degrees coreward, Evrokk,' he said upon reaching the cockpit. 'Then give it everything she's got under the safe limit.'

Bokko helped Evrokk slam levers and spin wheels. Opened valves poured aether into the endrins. The metal of the globes creaked with sudden heating. The airscrews chopped at the air with renewed ferocity. The *Aelsling* drove forward.

'Gunterr, get everyone ready for boarding. They'll try to swarm us,' said Drekki. He strode over to the turret and rapped on it. A speaking hatch squeaked open.

'Don't fire until they're on us, Hrunki,' said Drekki.

'I'll go for gas baggers.' Hrunki's voice echoed from the turret. 'I'll line them up, see if I can get a couple with each shot.' She chuckled.

'Good, Hrunki,' said Drekki.

By then, the *Aelsling* was nearing the lower side of the dock. The fire had spread throughout the grots' flimsy shanty and chunks of building were falling from the sky in flames.

'Push right through!' Drekki ordered.

'Aye-aye, captain!' Evrokk yelled. The *Aelsling*'s whistles shrilled.

'Grots off the coreward bow!' Umherth yelled.

Several skinny figures were swinging down from walkways under the rock on ropes, waving cutlasses so energetically one of them sliced through its own line and went plummeting to its doom. The rest fared no better, being picked off by leisurely aethergun fire. A grot gas bagger that attempted an approach was promptly obliterated by a perfect shot from Hrunki. Aether punched through its balloon, exploding it from within. Though these forays were easily repelled, the amount of gunfire coming at the *Aelsling* was increasing, and it wasn't just small-bore stuff any more. A couple of hopelessly aimed cannonballs sang past. All it took was one lucky shot…

The rain of fire was near.

'Full speed ahead!' Drekki hollered. 'Brace for impact!'

Burning wood and rope rang off the endrin casings as they raced under the burning shanty. The inferno crawled all over the island's belly.

'Captain…' warned Kedren.

'Keep going!' roared Drekki.

The *Aelsling* burst through the firefall. Bits of charred, broken wood hammered them in a moment of fury, then they were through and out from under the island. Huge clouds of black smoke poured from the impact site. A moment of choking darkness followed as they passed through that too, and they were out into the lesser gloom under the upper disc.

'Would you look at that!' Adrimm shouted. He was looking astern, and whistling in appreciation.

Drekki moved to the back of the boat. Kedren followed.

'That is some serious mayhem,' said Umherth approvingly. He had his volley gun couched in the crook of his arm. 'That human wizard packs a punch.'

On the poop, a good view of the receding island could be had.

The ruins of the city of Erulu topped steep-sided hills. Jagged pillars pricked the sky. Broken fortifications slanted down slopes, lazily making their way to collapse. Palaces stared with desperate black windows across the Third Air, shocked at their changes in fortune. All was of lacy stone as white as bone.

The greenskins had inserted themselves into the tumbledown city with all the thoroughness of a virus. They couldn't quite overwhelm the majesty of the broken walls, but they'd given it a spirited try. Tottering buildings filled gaps. The streets squirmed with movement. When Drekki trained his telescope on the hill, he frowned.

'Must be tens of thousands of the little green beggars,' he said. Kedren gestured for a look. Drekki handed him the scope.

What had been the port of old Erulu had been converted into berths for sky-ships. The island had retained a shoreline of sorts, with remnants of the old sea wall still clinging to the base of the cliffs. The old harbour survived, being a cove embraced by the hills. The cove was now a shallow basin of stone, its entrance protected by piers that once kept out the ocean waves and which now rebuffed the wind. Around the harbour had been districts of warehousing, chandlers, banks, company offices, magical weather machinery and other buildings of commerce, all ruined to angles of wall and heaps of rubble, all built back into grotty parodies by legions of ingenious, thieving gits.

The grots had constructed a messy honeycomb of berths over the harbour, linked together by a bewildering maze of catwalks. Lerarus' meteor had been admirably on target, smashing into the base of the structure near the old sea wall to Drekki's right. The evidence for her accuracy was conclusive, being a large, black hole surrounded by molten rock and what looked like a massive bonfire of wood. On this spinward side of the cove, all that was left was burning fiercely. Grots ran about, ineffectually flinging buckets of water onto the inferno. The ships at rest there were undergoing a short-lived career change as firewood. The flames had already crept up the hill into the city, as well as down the cliffs under the island. Large parts of the settlement were burning, or were about to.

'Now that is an impressive amount of damage for a distraction,' said Kedren, panning Drekki's telescope over the wreckage.

'Aye, but we got only half the ships,' said Drekki. 'And they're not distracted any more.'

The coreward docks were largely unscathed, though fires caused by embers and flaming debris burned in a dozen places. The greenskins weren't concerned with the blaze in that part of the bay. They'd caught sight of the *Aelsling*, and were racing to get their boats launched instead. Grots chopped tangled mooring lines with axes, so many of them hacking away that the sound of blades thunking into wood and rope outdid the furnace crackle of the fires.

The first of the ships rolled down its ramp. A cumbersome thing of wood and canvas wings, it dropped like a rock. Running down its spine was a long crank, with lines of grots facing each other along each side. As these hundred grots turned the crank, the wings jerked up and down spasmodically, then smoothly, and the whole ungainly thing began to fly.

'Impossible,' said Kedren.

'They seem to think it works,' said Drekki. He took back his spyglass. Umherth spat over the side.

It was only the first of a dozen kinds of bizarre skycraft to make it into the air. Balloons inflated. Snotling-powered paddlewheels rumbled around. The fuses of massive rockets were lit by cackling, sooty-faced grots. Smoke belched from primitive steam engines. Captive beasts were prodded into the sky with goads. The breadth of the grot race's creativity was on display, and it was breathtaking, if for entirely the wrong sorts of reasons.

Some of these things literally crashed and burned. Experimental designs entirely. Others were tried and tested: the gas baggers, the whaleen gondolas, the magically powered thaumaturgibles shooting green sparks from huge brass funnels. They raced down wooden-and-stone slipways, each one taking to the sky with a reedy shout of 'Waaagh!', and for every ship that ended with a more noisy cry of 'Argh!' another two came powering after the *Aelsling*.

'I wouldn't want to take flight in any one of them,' said Adrimm. 'At least they don't look like they've got anything to bother the likes of us.'

'*Nuntuzsprakki!*'[36] Drekki growled. 'How long you been a skyfarer?'

'Fair-weather's done it now. Look!' Umherth pointed.

Something huge was freeing itself from the inferno. A black shape imprisoned by fiery bars shifted in the smoke. Drekki held his breath, hoping it would be consumed, but it broke through, bringing half of the blackened airdocks down as it crashed out into the free air.

'You bloody have, too, you *umgdawi*[37] fool!' said Drekki. '*That* will be a problem.'

The ship was big, three times the length of the *Aelsling* and four times wider abeam. The hull, coming out backwards, was all of iron rusted to a dull maroon. A giant blimp kept it aloft. There were ballistae and cannons poking out from inconceivable places – wherever a grot thought it might be a good idea to have an artillery piece, and that was everywhere.

'That balloon's a peculiar thing,' said Kedren. 'Kind of rough looking. Like dragon skin? Is that a tail? It's got legs!'

---

36 | Kharadrid: Lit. 'Too soon speaker'. Speaking too soon is regarded as very bad luck among the Kharadron.

37 | Khazalid/Kharadrid: Unduardinlike.

'That's no balloon…' said Drekki.

The ship swivelled slowly in the sky, bringing into view a vast, surprised face upon the front. Vestigial arms and legs were held tight in by ropes, and its mouth was stitched shut, but somehow it was still alive: a gargantuan squig, inflated with who knew what to bear the vessel beneath it.

Upon the squig's brow, dead centre, was a large tattoo of a grinning orruk skull with a single eye glaring from one socket, an eyepatch over the other, crossed cutlasses beneath its bucket jaw.

'The Jolly Orruk! Grungni's oaths! I think I know who that is!' Drekki swore. 'Bokko!' he shouted behind him. 'Get the endrins ready to burn at full power. Disengage all safety stops. Full speed ahead. Battle stations, everyone!'

The crew raced about the ship.

'What's all the panic for, Drekki? It's only grots.'

Drekki jabbed a finger at the squig blimp. 'There's one grot here who has the worst reputation of them all. Only one grot who dares to fly the Jolly Orruk without fear of actual orruks pulling his head off. Only one who has a squig-blimp that big. He's known all across the Skyshoals for his mercilessness, cunning, skymanship and terrible sense of dress. I've heard the stories, but by Grimnir and Grungni, I never thought to actually see him.'

'Who?' said Kedren.

'Kaptin Blackheart, that's who,' said Drekki. 'We've got a fight on our hands.'

CHAPTER TWENTY-ONE

ESCAPE TO THE SUN

Once turned about, Kaptin Blackheart's ship pushed its way through the others lumbering out of the ramshackle port. The sky was crowded with ships, all crammed with tiny figures waving weapons.

'Cannon's fully reloaded, ready when you need, captain!' Gunterr reported.

'We can't fight our way out of this,' Drekki said. 'We'll have to outrun them, but keep Tordis ready, just in case.'

Drekki went from post to post, shouting orders.

'Full speed, all safeties disengaged. Airscrews to maximum rotation, Arkanaut First Class Bjarnisson!'

'Aye, captain!' Evrokk responded.

The bell rang. The whistle shrilled. The thrubbing of the aether-endrins shifted to a higher tempo. Drekki looked over the side. The shadows of the ships raced over the accretion discs hemming Erulu in.

Long spars were unfolding from the sides of the grot flagship.

Ropes went taut. The spars spread, opening fin-like structures. Sailcloth bellied with the wind, and the ship increased speed. He could clearly see the front now. The bow was wide, with two large gateways covered over by rolling portcullises. A rattling cut faintly across the intervening sky. The twin portcullises set into the bow pulled up. Something inside roared.

Two apish, draconic beasts shot out fast as crossbow bolts. They came to a sudden, snapping stop, restrained from escape by huge chains attached to harnesses. Wriggling, they began to pull the flagship ahead of the flotilla.

'Dreng it. He's got maw-krushas. That's Blackheart for sure. Umherth, get that gun ready,' Drekki ordered.

The wind was picking up. Airstream rushed past his helm. The *Aelsling* was close to full output. He had a bad feeling it wouldn't be enough. The clearer airs away from the broken city's heart were thousands of raadfathoms away.

Catapults twanged on the bow of the grot vessel.

'Incoming!' Otherek yelled from the cupola.

Slow ovals arced up from the artillery, reached their apex, and began to fall.

'Stupid grots,' said Gord. 'Don't see what harm rocks will do to your *Aelsling*, captain. Hurhur.'

Drekki wasn't laughing. He shaded his eyes. Stones would be expected, flung from a catapult, but grot behaviour was far from predictable, and these projectiles were moving differently to rocks.

'Those aren't rocks, Gord,' he said.

Spinning creatures fell at them, tails and legs tucked in. Each was a bad-tempered ball of teeth. A mouth on legs.

'Squigs!' Drekki hollered.

Most of the beasts were wide by a mile. A couple hit the endrins and bounced off with flubbery boings, jaws clacking as they fell, as if a show of aggression would make a difference to their ultimate fate.

One hit the deck. One could be enough.

The squig bounced hard, turned a somersault, and landed again on its feet. Black claws scrabbled at the metal.

'I got it!' Gord shouted.

He lowered his pistol. The squig pounced, enveloping Gord's gun and fist in its mouth. Long teeth sank into ogor muscle. There it remained, looking pleased with itself, until Gord roared, and the squig exploded with a stomach-turning *splatch*! Leathery flaps of squig slapped into the endrins, into Drekki, into everyone. It was remarkable how much mess one barrel-sized beast could make. It left a ring of teeth embedded in Gord's wrist like a bracelet.

Smoke trickled up out of Gord's oversized pistol. He grimaced, shaking his arm free of the fangs, drawing out with his teeth those that would not come free and spitting them at the deck like bullets.

'Right you are, captain. Not rocks,' said Gord grimly. He reloaded his gun.

'Second volley, coming in!'

'Umherth, right about now, if you please!' Drekki commanded.

'Arrr, captain!'

Umherth always sounded just a bit too keen on blowing things up.

He opened fire, volley gun spitting blinding tracers of aether into the *Aelsling*'s wake. He shook with the recoil. The noise was immense, but they could still hear the old maniac laughing. One, two, then three squigs exploded like meaty fireworks as his burst tracked across them. The rest descended upon their downward trajectory, right at the ship.

'Ready to repel squigs!' Gunterr roared.

'Don't worry, lass, they won't hit,' Adrimm said to Khenna. 'Grots are terrible shots.'

'I'm not so sure,' said Khenna. 'I've heard all about Blackheart.' She hefted her aether-cutlass. 'And don't call me lass.'

'There are exceptions to every rule, they say in Barak-Mhornar, especially when it comes to the Code. These grots are that exception,' said Drekki.

'Ten squigs, dead on target. Catapults reloading for third volley!' Otherek shouted from his perch.

Twanging like rubber balls, the squigs rained down on the *Aelsling*. Again the endrins acted as umbrellas, deflecting the creatures away. Most of them. Four made it onto the deck, where they raced around raising mayhem. Umherth kept his attention to the aft. Adrimm and Khenna punctured one with simultaneous thrusts of cutlass and gaff. It crawled around, slowly deflating, before Khenna finished it off. Urdi was caught off guard and almost swallowed whole, saved only by Gord's huge foot booting the thing off the edge.

One came for Drekki, mouth gaping, fat tongue trailing on the deck. Drekki aimed Karon, taking his time to line up his shot, but Kedren's thrown axe split its piggy face in two.

'Can't take your time with this lot, Drekki,' he shouted over the crowded deck.

The last squig was haring around the deck, snapping at everything and everyone, smashing them aside with butts of its pliable forehead, defying all efforts to corral it. Aetherguns crackled. Rounds pinged off the ship.

'Watch your shots,' Drekki commanded. 'Gord, that goes double for you.'

'Third volley incoming!' Otherek yelled.

There were squigs again, but they weren't alone. Flimsy wooden cages crammed with screaming snotlings were mingled among the attack beasts. They struck the ship, shattering on impact. Half the snotlings were dead on arrival, their tiny bodies slipping across the deck like landed fish. The rest ran about screaming, driven into a frenzy by their terrifying flight. They attacked blindly, or hurled themselves at the duardin and clung to their limbs for comfort. Some of the cockier examples cuffed their fellows into order, and went for the ship's workings. Several vanished down vents into the interior of the *Aelsling*.

'Khenna, get below. Root those little bastards out. Make sure the wizard is safe.'

The *Aelsling* yawed off course. Drekki threw out his arms to keep his balance, and saw that Evrokk was being assaulted in his cockpit. A gaggle of tittering snotlings were playing pile-on with him, and he was vanishing under the heap. Drekki stormed over, kicking the deck clear on the way. He plucked the squirming greenskins from his helmsduardin, tossing them shrieking over the side. Evrokk elbowed them, punched them, slapped them silly. The cockpit was a mess of tiny bodies. Infuriating giggling was punctuated by the snap-crack of slender bones breaking.

'Grimnir alive, they've sharp bloody teeth!' Evrokk said. They'd enough of the snotlings out of the cockpit that he could get the ship back under control, levelling the deck and turning the prow back out to the open skies. Evrokk was still obliged to stamp though, until the last were squished.

Drekki looked back. The flagship had gained on them by a hundred raadfathoms at least.

'That cost us. We can't afford to be slowed like that! Adrimm, get your grumbaki arse over here and protect Evrokk. We have to make it to the clear air!'

'More munitions coming in!' Otherek roared from above. What seemed like bats were folding their wings and stooping on the ship.

'Grots, with wings!' said Gord happily, for a seasoned traveller finds delight in all novelty.

'Doom divers!' Gunterr hollered.

Not doom divers. Not as such. These grots had no suicidal impulse for short-lived glory.

At the height of their speed the grots spread their wings with un-grotlike elegance, slowing themselves dramatically. What looked like well-practised ease saw them swoop in low, then up, deliber-ately stalling a few feet above the deck. Overconfidence proved fatal to a few, and they screamed when they realised thin air awaited their feet, not iron deck. The rest landed lightly. They shucked their wings and drew their swords.

'Slit the stunties!' shrilled their champion. 'Get the pilot! Bring it to a stop!' The creature waved its sword about, directing its cohorts.

'Get off my ship,' Drekki growled, and blew its head off.

The grotty aerial elite had grit. The loss of their boss had no effect, and they went into action. A group of fifteen formed up. Others attacked as soon as they landed, breaking up the gunfire trimming the numbers of their fellows. Crude iron swords rang off aether-blades. Pistols cracked on both sides. Gord guffawed as he fired his immense gun, each shot that hit obliterating its target. He missed just as often. More than one angry shout was directed at the ogor, telling him to mind his aim. It did no good. Gord was Gord.

Adrimm went down with a wound to his thigh from a rusty cutlass. Drekki moved on the cockpit, lopping the head off a grin-ning boarder as it leaned in for the kill.

The headless body flopped over Adrimm. Drekki pushed it off with his foot.

'You all right, Fair-weather?' He helped the grumbler up.

Adrimm almost collapsed when he put weight on his leg. Bracing himself with a hand on his bloody thigh, he winced but then nodded.

'I'll live.'

'Then get yourself sat and cover this position with your gun,' Drekki said. 'Keep Evrokk safe.'

'Aye, captain.' He leaned on his gaff and drew his pistol.

Cannon fire cracked from behind.

'Brilliant,' said Drekki. 'They've ranged their big guns.'

Cannonballs cut hissing channels to the left and right of the *Aelsling*. The ship rang like a gong as one found the stern. Not much danger so far out, but Kaptin Blackheart was gaining. Drekki took out his spy-glass. He thought he saw the infamous kaptin, stood on the prow of his boat, waving an oversized cutlass and sporting the most outrageously huge tricorn that ever graced a green head. A veil of cannon smoke drew over him. When it was gone, so was he.

'So that's him,' said Drekki.

Kedren found him. His axe-runes shone ruddily through blood.

'It's not looking good, skybeard.' Kedren raised his pistol and shot down a grot going after Velunti Runk. 'Damned grots get everywhere. Even up here. Will we ever be free of their menace?'

'Let's save ourselves first, and bemoan the fate of the duardin race later,' said Drekki. 'Blackheart's gaining now, but those maw-krushas will tire soon. They're monstrously strong in a fight but can't keep that pace up. When they falter, we'll pull away. If we can pass this press of debris, we can ascend. We just have to keep ahead.'

'All right, sounds good,' said Kedren.

'Steady now, I speak of a chance, not a certainty. If he brings us to boarding we'll be swamped,' Drekki said.

'Sounds less good.'

'Keep them off the engines, off the controls. We lose either of those, we're dead in the air. Take up the prow, runesmith. I'll cover here.'

They parted.

Squigs and grots and snotlings rained from the sky. Under their impacts, the ship tolled like a temple's carillon on a feast day. Gord bellowed and kicked many of the creatures overboard before they could figure out that they'd landed. The grots were easy prey. The squigs ferocious but manageable. It was the snotlings that were the worst. Otherek stopped his running commentary on enemy ordnance, being occupied by the little blighters ripping up the endrin covers. Bokko was sent into fits of anger by their efforts. The sound of swearing and pistols above joined that of the melee on the deck. Bits of snotling and the odd deceased goblin commando rolled off the endrins.

Drekki fought hard, Karon growing hot in his hand, his aether-axe soon slick. But the rain of living ammunition Blackheart kept up was unbelievable, and every time Drekki glanced astern the Jolly Orruk's leer and the stupefied face of the giant squig were closer. The clang of cannonballs smashing into hull plating got louder. More grots were coming down on them, from the islands themselves, dropping on ridiculously inadequate parachutes or rappelling on lines that were too short. They met predictable ends. And yet there were enough grots with sufficient intelligence to be a threat. A rare number could tell when a rope was long enough or a parachute was big enough to actually work, and some of those bold geniuses made it onto the *Aelsling*, joining the wing boys. The noises of fighting atop the endrins intensified. Strange lights played where Otherek unleashed his alchemical devices.

'Could do with that funti wizard right now,' Drekki said, but Lerarus remained below.

Drekki's eyes darted about. Kedren was embattled up front. Gunterr was blasting bloody chunks from the boarders. Adrimm sniped grots with his pistol and swept snotlings away from the cockpit with his gaff. Velunti was hanging from the shrouds, using the extra height to drive back a fistful of greenskins with his cutlass. Urdi protected Umherth, who continued to blast what he could from the air. All of them needed help. Too many decisions to make. Too much to do. His crew were beset on all sides.

A squig barrelled through the fight, knocking goblins over and turning duardin about.

'Gunterr!' Drekki roared. The beast was headed right at the master-at-arms.

Gunterr discharged his deck sweeper, the wide-muzzled gun cutting down a dozen assorted annoyances in one shot. He was reloading when the squig leapt. Drekki fired, but missed, and the gaping mouth of the creature snapped shut on Gunterr, swallowing him whole. Drekki fired again, and this time he hit. The squig, much engorged with Gunterr, went into a tumbling roll. A moment later Gunterr forced his way out, all his strength needed to prise open the dead squig's jaws. Grots went for him. Drekki did his best to keep them away with Karon's angry chatter, and Gunterr got back on his feet.

Something sank needle teeth into Drekki's leg. He roared, stamped hard, bursting the snotling scrabbling at his calf under his iron-shod foot. Another scampered past on all fours, giggling around the aetheric oscillation dampening lever it had stuffed in its mouth.

'Someone stop that snotling!' he yelled. 'We need that!'

Nobody could. Grots were pouring aboard from every side, driving back the crew by weight of numbers. Aetherguns barked, dropping the greenskins in numbers, but more rushed in to replace them. The grot flagship was drawing in to hover overhead, ramshackle cannons peppering the *Aelsling* with hails of scrap.

A barge sidled alongside. Upon it came bigger grots, cleverer grots. They worked behind the charging hordes, protected by sheet-steel hoardings. Safe under armour, they prepared broad-mouthed firearms strapped to the backs of muscular gunners. Hissing tapers touched powder holes, and the guns woofed black smoke. The charges seemed weak, pointless, until a weighted net came spinning out of the gun smoke and wrapped itself around the railings where Urdi was fighting. Another followed, whisking the fog of battle into a whirl and enveloping Velunti. A second of struggling saw him hopelessly caught. Hooks bit into his flight suit. The weights tangled up his feet. Grots shrieked and piled atop him, bashing away with belaying pins and fists. There was a howl of triumph. Velunti's helm was ripped free. A club rose and fell, and he ceased moving.

But they didn't kill him.

'They mean to take us alive!' Drekki shouted behind him. 'Hrunki, put a hole in that barge to the edgeward board!'

Hrunki, locked down tight in her turret, set the gun into motion, grinding the snotlings ripping at the workings into a gristly paste as it came about. She let loose a shot into the barge's amidships. Splinters fountained everywhere, scything down grots, cutting ropes and sending more down into the bottomless skies. The gas bag on the barge ignited with a cough of brilliant fire. A mushroom of smoke rose over it, and the boat dropped, slowly, as if gravity were taken unawares and needed to catch up, then with a murderous rush when it did. Shocked grots fell past, taking their net-mortars with them.

Drekki would have laughed, were he not so occupied. A grot pirate came at him, cutlass ready for a backhand chop. Karon chattered angrily. Shining aethershot hit the grot in the chest, flipping it onto its back. It flew into its fellows, staggering them, and it died in a puddle of its own blood.

More whoomphing blackpowder shots. More nets. Drekki looked over his shoulder. A second catch-barge was sneaking up. He glanced upward. Blackheart's straining maw-krushas flew overhead, but past them he could see the disc was thinning, and the muscular wingbeats of the monsters were laboured. They were close to freedom.

'Back to back!' he hollered. 'Get yourselves to the turret! We need a few more minutes, that's all!'

Umherth stalked backwards, knees bent, bracing himself against the ferocious recoil of his volley gun. He shouted wordlessly, a deep-tunnel roar of rage and aeons-old hatred. Grots fell down, cut in two across the chest as neatly as harvested poppies. Red blood and green fluids swilled across the deck. The greenskins were not discouraged. Replenishments swung in on ropes from the ramshackle flotilla surrounding the *Aelsling*, eyes swivelling madly, teeth clamped on crude knives. The weight of them was pushing the *Aelsling* down.

The ship was sinking.

Too late, the *Aelsling* burst out from under the disc into brilliant sunlight, a million grots on its tail.

The last of the duardin gathered around the turret, pressed shoulder to shoulder. They kept the grots back for a minute more, until, one by one, they were brought low. Gunterr went down first, a spear through his heart, dead for sure this time. He would get no chance to brag about his lucky escape from the squig. Kedren was pulled off his feet by his beard, his rune axe severing several impertinent arms yanking at him, but there were too many, and he was beaten senseless. Gord staggered around, completely covered by grots hanging from his every limb, more of them clambering onto his body until even his enormous strength was no use, and he fell to his knees, then forward, where he was quickly bound.

Grots wrenched the turret hatch open and Hrunki was hauled out. Evrokk was dragged from his cockpit. Drekki heard, but did not see. His view was obscured by dozens of grabbing, filthy green hands pawing at his weapons and his helmet. Karon opened up a brief and bloody corridor before she was ripped from his grasp. His axe followed. Trokwi escaped snatching fingers and flew trilling away.

At least that's something, Drekki thought bleakly. More stinking grots piled on top of him. He was punched until his helmet came off, and then he was punched some more. His nose burst. Stout pins thwacked into his skull. Duardin bones are rock hard, but not invulnerable. Black spots bloomed across his vision, obscuring the leering, hook-nosed faces of his assailants.

He heard a roaring bang from very far away. The grot sitting across his chest turned to look, then, all of a sudden, its head was gone. Gore fountained from the pirate's scrawny neck. It slumped over Drekki.

Drekki pushed himself up. Blood covered his face. He was pretty sure a good portion of it was his own. His head spun. His eyes blurred. Through shifting veils of light he saw grot ships exploding, raked by aether-fire. Kaptin Blackheart's ship was turning about, its spent draught beasts yanked hard into a tight circle by long reins of chain.

He braced himself on his hands. Light from Hysh shone into the gap around Erulu, silhouetting a host of stumpy, angry shapes on his ship giving the grots what for. His crew were back up and fighting! But... he didn't recall having as many as all this, and unless Bokko had built half a dozen more endrinrigs, there must be... more duardin?

He felt thick-headed as Gord. He'd imagined the spirits of his ancestors before. Now he was seeing them. He fell back again with a groan.

The face of a female duardin filled his vision. She wore an eyepatch, and her nose was squashed flat as a stoneflour pancake. She was familiar, he thought. Or maybe she wasn't. It was all terribly confusing.

'Captain! Captain!' the kvinnarkanaut shouted behind her. 'I've found him! He's over here! He's still alive!' The skyfarer turned back to him, pushing him back when he tried to get up. 'Woah now, don't you be going anywhere. Steady, steady, Drekki Flynt, I've got you. Let me help you sit.' She propped him up on a cushion of dead grots. With her arm cupped under the back of his skull, he was able to look towards the prow, where the figurehead raised its hammer into the noon.

More of that annoying, headachey wavering. The figurehead doubled, seemed to split, come alive, and step forward. Shadow rolled over this second shieldmaiden, until surrounded by a glowing nimbus of light, he saw the most glorious creature in all the Skyshoals, at least according to Drekki. A duardin kvinn, as perfect as the *valikraz*[38] of olden tales.

He grinned dopily at this divine vision.

'Beautiful,' he said.

She stopped in front of him, and let the head of her heavy aethermatic hammer thump to the deck.

'Hello, Drekki,' said Aelsling.

---

38 | Khazalid: According to some, the handmaidens of the goddess Valaya herself.

CHAPTER TWENTY-TWO

ESTRANGED

'Get those corpses over the side, you laggardly sky-dogs!' Ghisela Askisdottr had a shout like a cannon. No. Make that a broadside.

'Does she have to be so loud?' Drekki said. He felt sick. He was supping at a pot of warm ale, but it restored only a little clarity.

Aelsling shrugged. 'Is your ogor any quieter? Ghisela is the best first mate in any barak. Shouting's part of the job.'

She looked over the ship that bore her name.

'Bit of a mess you've got yourself here,' she said.

'Spot of bad luck is all,' said Drekki. 'It's your old dad's fault.'

She gave him a sharp look. Sharp words followed. 'Why do you think I'm here, you drengi idiot? When I found out what he'd done...' She shook her head.

'I don't know. I thought you might have come to your senses and come back to me.' Drekki tried to grin winningly. It made his eyes hurt.

'I came to my senses when I left you,' she said.

'That's wounding,' he said, because it was.

She sighed heavily, so much that the armoured breastplates of her flight suit rose and fell like the karaks of old. 'You're guilty of a lot of things, Drekki Flynt, but making my choices for me is not among your crimes. Dad won't listen, and you're not listening. I'm not coming back to you. We're over. Let it go.' She scowled at him, but affectionately so, thought Drekki. 'Drink your ale. You're concussed. Sit still till it passes. Maybe you can work on growing up a bit while you're about it.'

Aelsling moved off, shouting as loudly as her first mate.

Drekki's crew huddled on the deck, none of them in the mood for talking. Only Gord was on his feet, helping Aelsling's crew throw grot corpses over the side. Gunterr was dead, Bokko in bad shape, still unconscious, touch and go if he'd pull through, according to Aelsling's surgeon.

Maybe he should get a surgeon. Seeing him patch up his duardin made him think it would be a good idea. Velunti did that sort of thing, but he wasn't that good at it, and had too many jobs anyway. Actually, maybe he really should pay Velunti some more.

Aelsling's crew had taken over the ship. Duardin with hard faces roamed everywhere. One sat in the cockpit in front of him right now. Endrinriggers floated alongside the endrins beneath their one-duardin dirigible rigs, tool attachments whining. He noted she had three to his one. In fact, looking about, he saw she had lots of everything to his not very much. An arkanaut frigate kept pace with the *Aelsling*, three Grundstok gunhaulers flying in close formation beside it. Then there was her ship off the coreward board, the *Skalfi Vrundaz*, a sky-cutter like his, only bigger, shinier, better.

All of this could have been his. Should have been his. Him and his stupid heart.

'Brother gods, she's right, I am a mess,' said Drekki.

He half expected a smart comment from Otherek, a grumbling

rejoinder from Kedren, or Adrimm to get all worked up. Nobody said anything. They were exhausted, battered, sat on the poop deck, beards dangling between drawn-up knees. A beaten crew.

'At least we're still alive,' Drekki said.

After an hour Trokwi came back.

Drekki rediscovered his smile. 'Where did you get to, my mechanical friend?' He scratched under the bird's drill.

Trokwi chirruped.

'You're right. There's no point moping.'

Buoyed a little by Trokwi's return, and feeling a little less sick, he went to the rail. By that point the grot bodies were all gone. There was no sign of pursuit in any direction. The great discs of compacted metaliths around Erulu were far to the stern. Hysh was shining brightly. It was as fine a day as any.

Aelsling's riggers had put right most of what was wrong with the ship. Duardin swabbed the deck methodically of all traces of battle. A couple of them were even straightening the bent hammer of the figurehead. The ship was looking better than it had for weeks, but having it done by somebody else only made him feel worse. He thought he might lose his temper if they broke out the polish and paint, like Aelsling were a duardin matron come home to the family hold after a trip away, and found her lazy husband had feasted too hard and let everything go.

She was showing him up with this display of efficiency, and that was far from the worst. She'd come back, but she hadn't come back.

He slumped into a rare, introspective silence.

Aelsling joined him, after a while. 'I'm nearly done,' she said.

'Leaving so soon?' he said. 'You could stay for some ale at least!' He affected a cheeriness he didn't feel.

Aelsling came to the brink of her temper. 'Drekki, we've been through this one too many times already. There's no future for us. I've my own crew, my own operation.' She tried hard not to hurt him, but not hard enough. The words slipped out. 'Which is doing significantly better than yours.'

'Only because you took all the loot from the Ladonirkir job,' he said. 'Half that egg was mine.'

'Yes!' she said. 'I outright betrayed you and marooned you on a rock, and you don't get it even after that. I don't see how I can make this any clearer to you. There is no us, Drekki Flynt.'

'Right. So coming here to save me was just an act of kindness.'

'I couldn't let you die, could I?' she said quietly.

'You didn't know I was going to die,' he said. 'Come on, there's more to it than that. Admit it.' He tried his most appealing grin.

Aelsling's eye-roll was so pronounced her pupils all but vanished into the back of her head. 'Drekki! You flew in here on this funti drengi suicide mission my father sent you on. *You would have died* if I had not come here.'

'Come on, just admit that we were good together.'

She gave an exasperated growl. 'Move on already!' she snapped. 'It's pathetic. Look at that monstrosity!' She pointed at the figurehead.

He shrugged. 'I think it captures you perfectly. You should be flattered.'

'I think you're a drengi embarrassment, Drekki. I can't spend my life picking up the pieces you leave behind.' She rearranged her plaits. 'We had some times together, and I thank you for opening my eyes enough that I could see there was more for me than bringing up beardlings, but that's as far as it goes. We ran our course. We had seven good years, then the wind dropped. Aether's spent.'

'We had something,' said Drekki. He dropped his voice and leaned in. 'We could again.'

They looked into each other's eyes, her face softened, just a bit, and she squeezed his hand on the rail.

'Love's not aether-gold, Drekki,' she said sadly. 'It loses its shine.' She let go. 'Speaking of gold, four-fifths share of your loot for this job for hauling your arse out of the fire and not a single per cent less. You remember that. I want it at Barak-Thrund before the month is out, you hear? If you try to cheat me, I'll know.'

'That's a little high, Aelsling,' he said. 'Maybe we could negotiate, for old times' sake?'

'It's Captain Rogisdottr or nothing, Drekki Flynt.' She moved back a step. 'No negotiations. Four-fifths, that's my fee, and I think it's a bargain. Now, I've business elsewhere.' She looked at him and sighed. 'You look after yourself, Drekki. Not many days to Bastion from here. Once you've finished this job, at least my father will leave you alone. I owe you that.'

'We'll see if he will,' he said. He gave a little bow. 'Until next time. Maybe we could have an ale together then.'

'Next time you'll be bringing me my four-fifths share,' she said. 'Crew!' she shouted to her arkanauts. 'Pack up. We're leaving.'

She went back to her skiff, pointedly not looking at him.

'Farewell, Captain Rogisdottr!' Drekki waved and smiled for the sake of his crew, but inside it felt like the sun had gone out.

CHAPTER TWENTY-THREE

ADELIA

The best part of a day went by. The airs opened up, Erulu fell behind them. When Lerarus did not emerge, Drekki sent Khenna off to drag her up to his cabin.

'Don't take no for an answer,' he said. 'And you stick by this so-called talisman until I get to the bottom of this, clear?'

'Yes, captain,' she said.

Five minutes later, Lerarus arrived.

'Sit down,' said Drekki.

Lerarus remained standing, leaning on her staff to keep her head from banging on the cabin's low roof. 'You sound serious,' she said.

Drekki frowned. He was serious. His reset nose throbbed. Seeing Aelsling had put him in the foulest of moods. 'I think it's about time you and me had a little chat.'

'What about?' said the wizard.

'Don't come all innocent with me, umgi, you know what about. About that talisman not being a talisman and being a person. What have I got myself into here? And sit down! Stop looming over me like a bloody gargant.'

'Very well,' she said.

Lerarus propped up her staff against the wall, sat down, and spread her fingers on Drekki's table.

'I'm not happy about this. I'll not be party to depriving someone of their liberty,' Drekki said.

'I don't recall you had much choice. Would you honestly have turned down the contract if you'd known? Throkk would have killed you.'

'I'd have tried harder.'

'If it makes it better, I assure you the talismans are not enslaved. They took their roles of their own free will.'

'Right. Fine. So why didn't you tell me?'

She sighed. 'Because you've got a reputation for getting a little worked up about this kind of thing. The duardin who takes fright at obligation, who runs away from his responsibilities, who'll bore anyone who'll listen about the freedom of the skies. That's why. It just seemed easier to let you think *she* was an *it.*'

Drekki harrumphed. 'I want the full story,' he said, 'or you're going off on the next metalith with a skin of water, and I'm letting her go.'

Lerarus withdrew her hands neatly under the table. 'You've got most of it. Her name is Adelia, of House Manellus. She was seventeen when she was put into the vault. She was raised from birth to operate the Great Machine. Each of the Great Families provided similar talismans, in the days of Achromian glory. A girl or a boy from their most magically talented members. She lived a good life before she reached her majority, and she would have been feted after she took her place in the machine.'

'Not much of a choice though, is it, if she was taken into this club of yours as a child.'

'She had even less than that,' admitted Lerarus. 'She was bred for it. Generations of selective breeding.'

Drekki glared at her. 'I said I'll have no truck with slavery!'

'It is not slavery,' she said. 'How much choice did you have in your life, Captain Flynt? You were pushed into apprenticeship with Throkk.'

'I ran away.'

'Which further cut down your choices. Do you really want this vagabond life, roaming the skies with no master and no real home?'

'What I wanted or did not want is not the issue here,' he said.

'I think it is. You can't apply one set of rules to her and another to yourself. You have no choice. I have no choice. My father sent me on this mission. I must serve my house. It is fate. The gods decide what we must do.'

'No god chooses my path!'

'Is that right? Then think further, did you want to be a duardin?'

'That's preposterous. How could I be anything else?'

'Indeed. And the same goes for her, and for me. How can we be anything else than what we are? You didn't want to help me on this quest, and yet here you are now seeking to speak up for this girl that you first clapped eyes on a day ago.'

'Get to the point,' said Drekki.

She gave him a pitying look. 'None of us have much of a choice, Drekki. We make the best of what path we're put on.' Lerarus sat back. 'Whether or not the Azyrites tricked my ancestors, she knew what was going to happen to her when they took her into that vault. She is a loyal subject of the Achromian Empire, and so am I. You're just a mercenary.' Lerarus stood.

'Oh, right, so point made, you're just going to leave?' said Drekki. 'It doesn't work like that in real life, madam, only in stories and plays. I want to speak to her. I want to hear from her own lips that she is going freely to Bastion.'

'What if she isn't going there freely?'

'Then she'll be going wherever she wants. Damn whatever Throkk or you say.'

Lerarus gave a brief laugh.

'What is it now?'

'I'm just surprised,' she said. 'It seems you do have an interest in matters other than money after all.'

'When will she awaken?'

'She's already awake.'

'And you didn't tell me.'

'Only because I was gently bringing her round, and filling her in on the last five hundred years. It's a delicate process. I did say she could be volatile if woken abruptly, didn't I? I'm sure you'd not want the *Aelsling* blasted apart for no good reason.'

'Then I demand to speak to her now.'

'Captain, you're free to speak to her whenever you please. It is your ship, as you've mentioned several times. I was going to take her some food, but perhaps you would like to instead? It'll be her first meal in five centuries, then you can ask her all the questions you like, and we can put this foolishness of yours behind us.'

Lerarus stalked out.

'A deception and no mistake,' Drekki said. He drummed his fingers upon his desk and scowled. 'Nobody talks to me like that on my ship.'

Drekki went to the galley and ladled some soup into a bowl. Velunti did most of the cooking – thinking about it, Velunti did most of everything. A veritable smoother of wrinkles. An *underpaid* smoother of wrinkles.

That was the second time money and Velunti had come to mind. He thought back to the night of the harkraken attack. Velunti was only sort of joking about the money, wasn't he? It might be something to talk to him about. Raise the issue before Velunti could again. Drekki decided then and there to raise the fellow's share. The last thing he needed was trouble from that quarter…

He composed himself before knocking on the door, smoothing his beard down, then wondered mutteringly why he was fussing so for an umgi. He couldn't help it. Lerarus had a refined air that made him feel scruffy, and lacking. He'd be damned if he let another of them look at him that way.

That wasn't everything, though. Something about this really wasn't right, Lerarus' explanations could go hang.

He knocked. 'Miss Adelia?' he said through the door. 'I've brought you some soup.'

Khenna opened up.

'All is well, arkanaut?' he asked her in Kharadrid. 'I hear she's awake.'

Khenna nodded. 'She is. She's a bit hard for me to follow, that human talk has never sat right in my ears. But she seems fine. Disoriented, mostly.'

'I can speak for myself,' said Adelia, though she couldn't possibly know any of the duardin tongues. She spoke the high speech of Azyr with an archaic accent.

'Then I shall speak to you shortly, madam,' Drekki said to her. He then returned to Kharadrid, and to Khenna.

'Get yourself some soup,' he said. 'Take a turn on the deck. Have a break. Then I want you back in here keeping watch on our human guests.'

She nodded, a little miserably.

Drekki dropped his voice. 'Don't look downcast, lass. I've no less faith in you as an arkanaut than I have in any of the others. You've got a bit of refinement. You're not doing this because you're new. You're doing it because you're the best for the job. Least likely to cause her distress, got that? Poor thing's been asleep for five hundred years. Imagine being confronted with Umherth when you woke up, instead of you.'

Khenna tried a grin. 'I'd rather not.'

'That's right. Now get on out, get fed and get rested.'

Drekki went in. Adelia was sitting on the bed, her knees by necessity drawn up, because she was even taller than Lerarus.

'Apologies for the cramped nature of the accommodation,' he said, with a gallant little bow. Drekki spoke the language of Azyr well, pompous little flourishes and all. 'The *Aelsling* isn't designed for passengers. I haven't had the adaptations made. The money is good in transporting folk, but I find each one brings a host of problems.'

Adelia raised an elegant eyebrow at him. 'Am I, then, a problem?'

'That remains to be seen.' He shut the door behind him. 'Here, I brought you soup.'

She looked at it doubtfully, but took it anyway, and while they talked she ate it in small, methodical mouthfuls.

'What is this?' she said. 'Some sort of fish? Feels a bit too firm in the mouth for that.' She chewed thoughtfully. She had a very calm, somewhat unnerving air about her. Not like a young human at all.

'It's harkraken,' said Drekki.

'And that is?'

'A sort of a big squid that lives in the air, not in the sea,' he explained. 'I suppose they didn't have those in your day.'

'It appears there are a lot of things we did not have in my day.' She looked around her room. 'Like this vessel. You are taking me to Bastion?'

'I see Lerarus has told you something of our business.'

'She did,' Adelia said. 'And of the time that has passed since the Azyrites entombed me.'

Drekki leaned against the wall. 'How do you feel about that?'

'I was made for one purpose. I was an honour to my family.

My ancestors underwent four generations of arranged, loveless marriages so that I could be born to protect my people. Sigmar's kind stopped me from fulfilling my destiny. On the other hand, they said I was needed for the future. A strange future, that I see through your window here,' she said.

'Porthole,' Drekki corrected. He was a pedant for proper aeronautical terms.

She raised an eyebrow.

'Window on a ship,' he explained.

'Forgive me. I sailed only once before, on the Erulan Sea to come to the city when I was a child. I have never sailed in the sky. Now when I look out of this porthole, as you say, I see only sky. Tell me what happened to my country.'

'Has Lerarus not said?'

'She did, but these are legends to you, I gather, and legends differ with the teller. I want to know what you have to say,' she said, in her calm, unnerving way.

Drekki huffed a little, folded his arms, raised his eyebrows up and down. 'Well,' he said. 'Well, a question and a half to be sure. Nobody really knows. There's the legend, and the counterargument.'

'Tell me both.'

'Right,' said Drekki. 'In that case, legend first. The short version is, godbeasts did it. Do you remember Testudinous?'

'The divine draconic turtle,' she said. 'Patron of Achromia. His celestial form watched over us from the night sky. He was our patron beast.'

'Not any more he doesn't,' said Drekki. 'He died, they say, in the fighting. Chaos rose, drowned seven of the Eight Realms in blood and violence, all except for Azyr. When the Great Changer came for the Realm of Metal, his hordes brought war to every land. The fastnesses of my kind were destroyed. But here, out on the edge, Achromia stood against him. Yours was the strongest nation in these parts. Tzeentch faced many heroes, many mages of power, and the empire held. So Tzeentch unleashed a most terrible weapon, a corrupted godbeast dragged from some other realm. Testudinous gave up his position in the sky to fight against it.' Drekki shrugged. 'The world burned as a result, because that's what happens when gods get involved.'

His eyes took on a faraway look. He'd been told this story since he was a beardling, like all the young of Barak-Thrund, and he'd heard it so many times he could almost see Tzeentch's enslaved monster fighting the noble Testudinous.

'Nine hundred days this battle went on, the story goes. Testudinous dealt the monster many grievous wounds, but his armour was broken, and fragments of his shell rained down upon the lands, wreaking destruction. Until, finally, Testudinous dealt the decisive blow, and died in the doing, for as it perished Tzeentch's monster bit out the throat of the godbeast. Locked together in death, they fell through the heart of Achromia, shattering the lands into a hundred million parts with their impact.' He chuckled. 'The counterargument is that the godbeasts do not truly exist, and never did, and all that I told you is a poet's fancy. Our khemists say that what fell was a moon, or a continent, and that was what broke your homeland so badly.'

'Did you see it?'

'It happened centuries before I was born.'

'But your people are long-lived. Surely you must know the truth.'

'What is the truth? Only a score of generations of duardin have been born since the Days of Myth, and my kind keep good records, but much was lost, all was confusion, gods fought and died. Legends were born in that time, not facts.'

'What do you believe?'

'I've seen some strange things in my life, so if someone tells me a world-sized turtle fell from the sky and destroyed an empire, then I'm inclined to half believe it.'

'Lerarus tells me Bastion survived,' said Adelia. 'The machine I was made to empower kept it safe, so the mage says. Strange to think. Once Bastion was just a fortress to house the weapon out on the edge of the empire, but now she says it is a city floating in the sky.'

'This is true,' he said. 'It is a fine city, too.'

'And who are your people? I have seen the ingenuity of the duardin. Never something like this flying ship.'

'We duardin suffered a lot in the Age of Chaos. Some of us, my people, escaped into the sky. We've been there ever since. Kharadron Overlords, our rulers call us.' He grinned and dropped into a stage whisper. 'I tend to drop the "Overlords" part, makes us seem insufferably arrogant. Now times are changing. Sigmar's back, demigods popping up like weeds on a dungpile, gods moving.'

'And war.'

'War everywhere, all of the time. But it's not as bad as it was when Chaos gripped the realms. Lerarus says that your return will usher in a new era of peace and speed the return of the Achromian Empire.'

'That is what I was made to do.'

'It doesn't sound like much of a life, being locked into a machine.'

'We were not to be locked into it,' she said. 'It is a lifelong role, and restrictive, but it would have been a great honour to serve, and when not operating the machine in Achromia's defence, we would have lived as lords.'

Drekki was uncomfortable with that. It sounded too much like imprisonment to him. 'Not much choice, though.'

'None at all,' she said. 'No love, no children, no freedom. But it was necessary. It is necessary.'

'Then you'll go to Bastion freely?'

'I will go gladly. My time has come, finally.' She looked him curiously in the eye. Hers were the most startling green. 'You didn't know that I was a person, did you? Lerarus did not tell you. Were you told I was jewel, or some other thing?'

'I made an assumption.' He cleared his throat and fidgeted. 'Overconfidence can lead me to foolishness, sometimes.'

'You have a kind heart. I sense it.'

Drekki tugged his beard in embarrassment.

'Well, maybe.' He stood up straight. 'If you wish, you may leave this cabin and walk the deck. It is a glorious day. It will help you acclimatise to our world. Achromia is gone, but the shoals can be beautiful, and wondrous. If this is your time, you should get to know it.'

'Lerarus told me to stay in here.'

'You're only a little safer in here than you would be out and about,' said Drekki. 'Anyway, it's my ship, not hers. You want out of this room, then be my guest, because you are my guest.'

'Your guest, until we reach Bastion.'

'Until then.'

'Thank you for the soup.'

She held out the empty bowl. Drekki nodded and took it.

'You know,' said Drekki, as he opened the door, 'you shouldn't let anyone tell you what you have to be. That happened to me. I didn't like it, so I changed it. It's not too late for you, either. If you want, you can change your destiny.'

'You are still going to return me to Bastion, are you not?'

'A contract is a contract,' said Drekki. 'I have to take you, but I'll only do it if you're willing.'

She smiled at him. 'I'm not sure it would make any difference if I told you I didn't want to go. Do you see, if you can't choose your own path with complete freedom, how can I?'

'It's not that simple,' Drekki protested, but only half-heartedly. The girl was right. Contracts. Throkk. Damn it.

'If that is so, then your advice is of little use.' A change came over her. She became more regal. 'That will be all, captain.'

Drekki, thoughtful, departed.

CHAPTER TWENTY-FOUR

DUKE LERARUS

Bastion decorated the sky like a tasteful ornament, the Chaos-repellent barrier projected by the machine shimmering palely around it, almost too faint to see. They were at the edge of the shoals there, and the great, world-sized continent of Prosperis was a hazy bar across the sky. Drekki could fly over it, or under it, and he had, but that didn't alter his perception of the continent. It was a world of solid ground, and Sigmar's influence put it at odds with the fluid opportunities the Skyshoals offered. Bastion was the start of all that, a keep on the borderlands.

Drekki stood by Aelsling's brazen statue, watching the city getting bigger, reaching out to him, commanding him to obey, to conform, to – and this really made his spine go weak – pay his taxes. His beard roots crawled as he contemplated that. How long until Bastion's laws and ways were laid iron-hard over all the shoals, unbreakable as the chains that tethered her together?

Bastion occupied seventeen major metaliths and dozens of smaller isles. The largest supported districts as big as cities in their own right, the smallest might carry a single mansion or isolated temple. They were staggering in their diversity, but they all had their moorings in common. Each one was linked to its fellows by lengths of heavy bronze chains, with the links being a vast enlargement of the barred type used for anchors. Except for the smallest isles, which were held in place by single lines and free to drift a little, the chains were doubled up on every island, tripled and quadrupled for the larger, locking the group into a solid web that shifted only a little on the wind blowing ceaselessly off the mainland. Gargantuan staples sunk into the bedrock of the isles were the attachment points, the stone around them dyed a bright and virulent turquoise by verdigris. Whole colonies of birds made their homes on some of the chains, and the links were hairy with their nests, especially on the Parksisle.

None of this, not the isles nor their chains, were as imposing as the Anchor.

From the outer edge of the isle of Innermost, the Anchor ran, dipping under its own weight then rising up again to the edge of Prosperis, attaching the city forever to the coast, twenty-five miles away. Thousands upon thousands of tons of bronze. This was the work of Achromian duardin, who dwelled alongside the humans and aelves of Bastion. The Anchor rivalled the greatest feats of the olden karaks, and came close to matching the accomplishments of the Kharadron Overlords.

Individual buildings emerged from the maddening lines of urban sprawl. Lerarus came to the prow. Wordlessly, Drekki made space for her.

Bastion's walls were solid, brutish things. The fortifications were duardin designed, built by men, and adorned by aelves. They represented the best of all three races. There was none of the slapdash quality of human work apparent, but the umgi's innovative, clever ways of thinking were clear in the fort layout. Towers jutted far out so that no part of the high wall was left uncovered. There were no docks on the Citadel Isle, save a sole jetty by the Airgate. The base of the walls went right up to the edge, with not so much space for a razorbeak to land. Large engines of destruction topped every tower, magical weapons of great antiquity and incredible power. So imposing were the walls that the triple spires of the Palace of the Triumvirs only shyly poked over them, even though the palace was the largest building in that part of Chamon.

'Bastion by name and nature,' he said, breaking his silence. 'I've always thought it quite impressive.

'It's nothing,' the wizard said. 'Once we were masters of half a world, now all we have are a group of islands floating around in their own filth, beholden to a distant god.' She spoke so softly it was hard to hear her over the headwind.

'Well, times are changing, that's for sure,' said Drekki lamely. He had no clue how to deal with the emotions of kvinn, and that went doubly for umgi ones. If they weren't laughing at his jests or shouting at him, he was lost. He cleared his throat. 'Where are we to put in?'

'I care not. Where do you usually go?'

'Eyeward's my preference, no customs men that way.'

'Then go there. Our plan was to be quiet, to deliver her unknown. We were supposed to be here days ago, but we should stick to the plan. My father is very particular about his arrangements.'

'If you say.' He paused. 'I did run into a bit of trouble at Eyeward last time. There was a small matter of a fire at the Eldershell pub...'

'Just pick somewhere, and make it quick,' she said tiredly. 'We're late. My father will not be happy.'

Drekki looked back at the city. For all its bustle and excitement, there was something stifling about it: it was an ants' nest, too full of individuals and their activity. He had mixed feelings about Bastion, and mixed feelings about this business.

'Captain.' Tordis was behind him, stray hair from her long grey plaits shifting in the wind.

'Hrunki,' said Drekki. What can I do for you?'

'It's Ildrin. He wants to see you, and he's not taking no for an answer.'

Drekki rubbed at his shaved scalp. Now? 'Fair enough,' he said, because it was. 'I'll be right down.'

Duardin tolerate bodily odour well. Millennia of close confines, first in tunnels, then in airships, and a healthy respect for physical toil, means the stink of sweat and dirty cloth does little to offend them, but the smell coming out of Ildrin's cell made Drekki's eyes water.

'I think we'll look at getting you a bath,' said Drekki.

'I wouldn't be stinking so bad if you'd not locked me up,' said Ildrin. The brig looked a bit like Lerarus' cabin, only the brig's door locked from the outside, and had a grilled window set into it that could be closed by a hatch. A wide slot tall enough to accommodate the smallest mug of ale allowed feeding.

Ildrin had his hands hanging through this. They were dirty, like the rest of him, the scars on his right hand blacker streaks amid the filth.

'You wanted to see me,' said Drekki.

Ildrin seemed calm, none of his usual shouting and singing. 'Aye, captain. Listen to me. You've made a terrible mistake. It wasn't me, I swear.'

'Can you prove it?'

'No, otherwise why would I be locked up down here?' he hissed. His nose pressed close to the bars. 'But I know you're not convinced either.'

Drekki said nothing.

'Listen, captain. This is all done between you and me. I don't want anything off you. I just want you to let me go. You know what the witchfinders in Bastion will do to me if they believe all this *zhunfor-draz*[39] about me. Let me off in the slums, and we'll call it bygones. I'll vanish and you'll not see me again.'

'Ildrin, there's been no other incident since I put you in here,' said Drekki. 'I did have my doubts, you're right, but evidence says I was probably wrong.'

'You weren't wrong!' said Ildrin through gritted teeth. 'I'm innocent. Innocent!'

'If you're just going to keep saying that, Ildrin, I'll be going, because we're at an impasse, you and I. If you are innocent, I'm sorry, you're going to have to wait in here. I promise I won't hand you over to the Bastion authorities. But our own people will deal with you.'

Ildrin glowered. 'If you want thanks for that pathetic concession, you'll get none.'

Drekki nodded. 'I understand.' He got up to leave.

'Captain!' Ildrin called.

Drekki stopped. 'What?'

'Can I at least have some ale? I've not had any for days, and I've a fearsome thirst on me.'

'All right.' Drekki went into the cramped galley that Velunti kept so neat, got a pot that would fit through the feeding slot, and filled it to the brim. When he took it back, Ildrin's mouth was watering. Drekki handed it to him. Ildrin took it. In his left hand.

Drekki frowned a touch. 'Are your burns all right?' he asked, wondering if pain forced the arkanaut to take the ale in that hand.

'Why?' Ildrin clenched and unclenched his right fist. 'They're fine. That runesmith did a grand job. He said that I was lucky not to be tainted forever. If I ever find who did this to me, I'll–'

---

39 | Khazalid/Kharadrid: Dragon dung.

'Then you favour your left as habit?' Drekki interrupted.

'Aye,' said Ildrin. 'Been left-handed all my life. Baruz-drengi beardlings used to call me hammer-wrong when I was a brat. It's a curse.' He slurped his ale noisily.

'Is it, now,' said Drekki thoughtfully. A feeling of wrongness was filling his chest, smooth and chill as an air plume sinking from the higher airs. 'Is it, now.'

A whistle peeped.

'Captain!' Adrimm called down below. 'Ship coming in. She's asking us to stop.'

'We'll talk later,' Drekki said to Ildrin. 'I'll get Hrunki to bring you more ale.'

Ildrin gestured in thanks. Drekki stamped away, full of disquiet.

'Well, who is it, Adrimm?' Drekki said, coming up onto the deck. 'That bit of information I'll be needing to know!' Adrimm was no Evtorr, that was for sure. He found himself missing the poet. Bad verse aside, he'd been good at his actual job. 'What colours are they flying?'

Adrimm took a look through his telescope, lowered it, and frowned.

'Um, two hippogryphs fighting over a mace?' he said.

'The pennant of House Lerarus,' said Drekki.

Drekki pushed Adrimm aside and took out his own glass to survey the approaching vessel. It was an umgi sky-ship of similar design to the one that had pursued them: wooden, sailed, held aloft by two slender bags of woven aerite taut with captured gases. Signal winks from a heliograph employing Kharadron codes repeatedly requested that the *Aelsling* stop. A small, triangular flag fluttered at the top of the foremast: a golden crown on black.

'And that there flag is the duke's insignia. Tricky,' said Drekki.

'Tricky how?' asked Adrimm.

'Politics tricky.' Drekki collapsed his scope. 'Lerarus!' he called. 'Get yourself shipshape. It looks like your father's paying us a visit.'

Drekki had little time for pomp and ceremony, but he had a good idea of when it was useful, so he had his crew smarten themselves up and line up. He marched up and down the single rank of them, checking their gear and adjusting their stances. There were duardin more inclined to discipline than those of Barak-Mhornar, and privateers were among the most slovenly of their kind, but the *Aelsling's* complement put on a good show, he had to admit. Even Gord.

Shouts from the tops carried across the air between the *Aelsling* and the human ship. Scrawny umgi swung about as agile as apes, doing aeronautical things with bits of rope. Sailing ships were all so complicated, and to work they needed to be crammed with crew, yet it was effective, for the vessel pulled smoothly to a stop. Ropes were cast over. Adrimm and Khenna caught them, and the two vessels were drawn alongside.

Adrimm opened the rails. A gangplank slapped down onto the gunwales. Next to Drekki, Lerarus tensed. Whistles blew, and a guard of humans armed with blackpowder guns formed two lines, with a path down the middle.

A drum beat Duke Lerarus aboard.

He was tall, loftier than his daughter, with the pale skin of a man who spends too much time indoors. He wore a large, floppy hat of the sort fashionable in Bastion that season. Feathers were always in fashion among umgi of Bastion, it was how you wore them that counted, and Lerarus had his in the latest style, with a brooch keeping them together at the front, and a heavy gold chain looping back over one ear.

Beneath an all-weather airsailor's cloak, heavy with waxing, Duke Lerarus dressed flamboyantly, but if his garb was a dandy's, his face was an advocate's: a blade of a nose, long chin, thin, guarded mouth and eyes narrowed in permanent suspicion.

He arrived with two guards. They came no further onto the deck than was necessary for them to stand at attention. That was something at least. Drekki had no time for strangers lording it about on his ship.

'Daughter,' said Duke Lerarus. He leaned in for a rigid embrace. Their bodies never actually touched.

'Father,' she said coldly.

Grungni, thought Drekki. I thought my family interactions were bad. You could cut a tree down with these two, they're so stiff and sharp.

Duke Lerarus turned to look upon Adelia. The talisman stared back. Lerarus inclined his head by a precise degree before looking back to his daughter.

'You were successful, I see,' he said. 'Well done.'

'I was, no thanks to you.'

'I found you this ship to convey you, did I not?' Duke Lerarus said.

'A bare minimum, father. The task was harder than you told me.'

I've had enough of this, thought Drekki, and moved into action. 'I'm Captain Drekki Flynt!' he boomed, and thrust out his hand to grab Duke Lerarus'. He pumped at it. 'A pleasure to make your acquaintance, my duke. Not much actual aristocracy comes aboard this boat of mine.'

'Speak for yourself,' grumbled Kedren, who was of noble lineage himself.

Duke Lerarus extricated his hand with as much decorum as he could muster.

'Captain, I thank you for keeping my daughter safe. I am glad she has returned to us intact.' He considered his words, each one released only after careful vetting. 'If you would give us some privacy, you would only be providing more service to me, and I shall take that as a personal kindness.'

Courtly words fill no pint pots, Drekki thought. Can't trust these beggars.

'The captain stays,' said Lerarus firmly. Her head trembled a little. It was difficult standing up to her father, it appeared, even for this powerful mage. 'Anything you want to discuss with me, father, you must say in front of Captain Flynt.'

'If you would repair with me to the master cabin of the *Kaestris*...' Duke Lerarus said, gesturing back over the gangplank.

'I'm not getting on your ship,' she said. 'If you want to talk to me, talk to me here.'

Duke Lerarus' eyes flashed. Though it lacked the magical might of his daughter's displeasure, it was an altogether more dangerous signal.

Drekki coughed into his fist. 'Velunti, everyone back to their business, if you please.'

The duardin line broke up.

'Well?' said Sanasha Lerarus to her father.

The duke considered a moment.

'Very well. I see no harm in it. He is party to the pertinent facts, I suppose. Captain, if we might use your cabin, as a courtesy?'

'Of course, of course, follow me,' said Drekki. He shot the duke a grin. 'You'll have to duck a bit, tall fellow like you.'

They went inside. Duke Lerarus did indeed have to duck.

The three of them sat at Drekki's table, Drekki more comfortably than the Family Lerarus. Sanasha Lerarus could just about get her knees under the table, but the duke had to sit side-on, straddling the bench, a position below his dignity. He wasn't drinking the ale Drekki had given him either, but sniffed at it dubiously and poked at the froth.

Can't have good ale without a froth, Drekki thought. Humans would remain forever mysterious to him. They were worse than aelves sometimes, and that was saying something.

Duke Lerarus put his pint down, untouched. Typical, Drekki thought, and took an aggressive swig of his.

'Right then, to what do we owe this pleasure of a personal visit, my lord?' Drekki said.

'You were successful, Sanasha, captain,' Duke Lerarus said. 'Congratulations are due. Alas, you return with the talisman at the worst possible time and that is why I am here.' The look the duke gave his daughter was altogether emotionless. 'We were expecting you a week ago. Matters are moving quickly. This will not do.'

Drekki wiped foam from his beard. 'I'm sorry, your lordship, but it was not exactly easy.'

'You didn't expect me to succeed at all,' said Sanasha Lerarus.

'That is not so, daughter,' said the duke.

'I'm still the most expendable, aren't I?' she said. 'The youngest, no good as a successor, too mighty for a dynastic marriage.'

'You are a talented mage, my dear. You are an asset to our family.' The duke had all the warmth of a stone lodged in ice. 'You are valuable beyond compare.'

She laughed. 'Still expendable.'

The duke sighed. 'My dear, you are being melodramatic. I am glad you are home, I really am. I am proud that you have succeeded. This task was difficult. Know that it tortured my heart to give it to you.'

You don't look tortured, thought Drekki.

'As much as I enjoy a good family squabble, we should return to the matter at hand here,' he said. 'Why is the timing bad? Why does it matter?'

'The embassy from Azyr arrived yesterday.' The duke's thin mouth nearly vanished. 'Our intention was to have the talisman installed before the Azyrites arrived, so we could present them with a fully functioning machine. Installing the talisman in front of them will appear a calculated snub. Timing is everything in diplomacy.'

'Ah,' said Drekki, 'like with a good joke.'

'The stakes are rather higher,' said Duke Lerarus.

'Wait, then,' said Drekki. He took a slug of beer. 'Ahh,' he gasped. 'That's good. Really good. You should try yours.'

'We can't wait,' said Sanasha Lerarus. 'The last talisman is very old, and on the verge of death. If it is not replaced soon, then the machine will fail. When that happens, the machine will never function again. It was made to be always manned, by at least one of the talismans.'

'So one of them has been stuck in there for centuries, and Adelia will be too?'

The wizard had the grace to look a little ashamed. 'The situation is not ideal. Hopefully we'll find the others. We're investigating recreating the bloodlines. She won't be–'

The duke held up his hand.

'The fate of the talisman is of no consequence. The fate of the city, and of Achromia, is all. We will be forced to install Adelia Manellus in the machine while the Azyrites look on, or we will lose it.'

'The problem with that being, let me guess... politics?' said Drekki.

The duke nodded. 'The Integrationists. Arguments may see the ritual postponed. If that happens, we lose the machine. The Azyrites might intervene directly. If that happens, we lose the machine.' He leaned forward, his thin back arching under his cloak like a vulture's wings. 'And if we lose the machine, we lose our liberty.'

The duke looked upon them each in turn, long and hard, his gaze more chilling than a deep-winter breeze. Lerarus shrank from her father's displeasure. Drekki raised his eyebrows and took another pointed gulp of ale.

'You were ordered, daughter, to bring the talisman back before the fifteenth of Wanderfauld. You are a week late. You, captain, are at risk of breaching your contract.'

'I was never actually shown my contract,' Drekki said.

'Rogi Throkk assured me this would be done to my design,' said the duke.

'Throkk,' said Drekki. He twitched his head dismissively, and poured more ale.

'But, father, where is the harm in being late? We resisted four gods for half a millennium,' Sanasha Lerarus said. 'One god should be of no concern, especially with the machine's function guaranteed for yet more generations.'

'You mistake Sigmar for a gentler deity than the four great powers,' said the duke harshly. 'He is nothing of the sort. He will use these events as an excuse to conquer us, for he is blinded by his desire for revenge on the gods that humiliated him. If you had arrived on time, we could have presented a position of strength, and rebuilt Achromia while keeping Azyr at arm's length. Now we show them all our cards, we must undertake the ritual in front of their eyes. This is a delicate phase. Sigmar's legions are the great powers of our time. We risk everything by your tardiness.'

'It's all naught but bluff and appearances,' Drekki said.

'Both are important,' said Duke Lerarus. 'I have it on good authority that in other cities of the realms, the Stormcasts are losing their patience. They cite possible threats as reason for swift integration, and use it as a pretext for subjugation. They are not above using force.'

'They will take the talisman, then?'

'Who knows the will of a god, truly?' said Lerarus. 'But he acts like a man, and we must treat him as one, or else we must simply submit.' The duke rubbed his chin. The rasp of stubble surprised Drekki. 'Gods are the ultimate despots. They respect only worship and strength. I propose a judicious display of the two, in balance.'

He paused a moment, thinking. 'Bring the talisman direct to the main docks. Daughter, you must present her to me as if I knew nothing of this venture. We will not sneak, but welcome her home with all due fanfare. Let the Azyrites see our pride. Let the craven Integrationists dare to suggest openly then that we abandon our machine in favour of Sigmar's protection. That is my command to you. We must go openly now. We must be bold. Maybe it is time we challenged this absent god.' Lerarus turned to Drekki. 'You must help us, captain.'

'What's in it for me?'

'Freedom,' the duke said. 'Imagine a sky full of powerful vessels riding storm fronts, and lightning bolts delivering armies wherever Sigmar decrees. A privateer's life under such circumstances would prove untenable.'

'And can you guarantee it would be better under the rule of Bastion?'

'It might be, for those with the right friends. Be bold, master duardin. Show the realms that there are other forces of Order yet, and they need not bend the knee to Azyr to be counted among the good.'

Drekki tipped his beer back, gulping steadily, not stopping until he had drained the pot dry.

'That sounds interesting, I'll grant you.' He pointed a finger at Duke Lerarus. 'I'd need some guarantees, mind.'

'You will have them.'

'Very well.' He nodded, spread his hands on the table, examined the stitching in his gloves. 'But technically,' he said very carefully, as if he were thinking hard, 'my contract is with your daughter here.' He grinned at Lerarus. 'And technically, I am bound to do as she says, not you.'

'It is I who is paying you,' said the duke.

'It is you who is paying Throkk,' said Drekki. 'Only, it doesn't say that anywhere on any document, I'll bet, on account of you wanting to keep your nose clean.'

The duke simply stared at him. When Drekki looked into Duke Lerarus' eyes he saw all he hated in the world. He saw the arrogance of wealthy men. He saw Throkk in there. Everyone around the duke were pieces to be moved on some drengi game board, including his own daughter.

'Thought so. I can't break contract, and I reckon your lass here needs a chance to make up her own mind, don't you? Well then,' Drekki said. 'What say you, Sanasha? I'm on your wage. What's your command?'

Duke Lerarus kept his expression neutral, but there was a flintiness in his eyes, and his muscles were hard, like his face was silk draped over iron. His daughter did her best to stay firm in the face of his glare, but she was wilting like wax before a fire. Amazing, thought Drekki, the power your parents have over you. The wizard could have broken her father with a word. But she feared the duke.

'We shall do as my father says,' said Lerarus, 'for the greater good of Achromia.'

The duke stood, satisfied. 'Good. Perhaps you shall redeem yourself, my dear. We have nothing more to discuss. Daughter, I presume you shall present yourself at home?'

'I shall attend you and mother when I have the time,' said Lerarus.

With a bow Duke Lerarus was gone through the cabin's steel door.

Lerarus was white. She trembled almost imperceptibly. Umgi or dawi, bad relations were bad relations.

'It's not just me with family problems, I see,' Drekki said.

'I did it. I got the talisman, and he still isn't happy. I'm sick of living in his shadow,' she whispered. 'I'm sick of him pushing me around.' Her words were hot wounds on the air, licks of fire that sliced at time and space.

'Steady. Keep that magic under check. Don't fall prey to your own emotions, or you'll be a problem as well,' said Drekki. He got up. 'If we stay the course, we could all come up rich and smiling, but we're going to have to be very careful here, and by we, I mean you, wizard.'

CHAPTER TWENTY-FIVE

BASTION

The *Aelsling* visited Bastion often, but when it did, it was Drekki's habit to avoid the major docks. They came with all kinds of inconveniences, like forms and officials, bribes and fees, more forms, and taxes.

Drekki hated taxes.

Better to dodge all that, he held. Hence his favouring the Eyeward slums, where questions were supposed to be asked and dockets stamped, but rarely were.

This time, however, they were heading for Portsisle.

The majesty of the Portsisle Docks were a novelty to Drekki. He'd been there precisely once, never in the *Aelsling*, and his visit had proven a costly mistake. He'd forgotten how huge the wharfs were, more like fortifications, and once you'd absorbed them there were the actual fortifications at their backs to snatch your breath anew, although protecting the town was of secondary importance; the walls had found new purpose as a customs barrier.

Make that reason fifty-six to steer clear of this place, Drekki thought. He had a written list. He'd add to it later.

Several arrangements of nested spheres whirling around arrays of crystalline lenses topped towers on the walls, each manned by a lesser mage. Not weapons as they might first appear, their purpose was scrying incoming ships for traces of illicit sorcery, and that included old Achromian artefacts.

Out in the shanties, such devices did not exist; rubbing elbows here with the high and mighty meant subjecting the ship to the sweepers. Drekki watched them closely. One of the devices zeroed in on a cutter out of Barak-Nar. The lights inside the crystals pulsed rapidly. Someone up there would be jotting things down in a little book and costing some poor bugger a lot of money.

The others were sweeping back and forth. Their twinkling snouts passed over his ship and back again.

'Come on, come on, don't point at me,' he muttered. 'Stay away.'

Inevitably, they locked onto the *Aelsling*. There was a bone-deep thrill of magic as their spells passed through Drekki. His heart sank as he thought of the rune axe in the hold. Another source of profit went 'poof!' in his mind, and there were precious few to begin with.

'That'll be the wizard's daddy, that will,' Drekki said to Kedren. 'He's picked us out for a reading. I should have dropped off that axe somewhere out of the way.'

'It would have done no good, lad,' said Kedren. 'We're sure to be watched. Duke Lerarus knew we were coming. They'd know if you tried to bilk them out of the tax, and they'd use it against you. We're too high profile for the usual funny business.'

Drekki grumbled wordlessly.

'Heliograph coming in!' Adrimm shouted. He bent to a telescope fixed to the rail. 'They're asking us to go to the Hool's Duck.' Adrimm stood up and scratched his beard. 'I don't know that one.'

Adrimm needed more training as a signalduardin, Drekki thought.

'Could they by any chance mean the Hero's Dock, Adrimm?' Drekki shouted back.

'Oh yeah!' said Adrimm. 'That's it.'

'I sense someone making a statement,' growled Kedren. 'Hero's Dock is the place for showing off.' He'd grown up in Bastion, and knew such things.

'Aye,' said Drekki. 'We're up to the roots of our beards in this umgi nonsense, that's for sure.'

Evrokk piloted the ship through the crowded airlanes of the city. Juvenile whaleens scudded past with weary swipes of their flippers, bearing barges upon their backs. Wooden airships glided overhead. The smell of aether-fallout was ever present, for the Kharadron were there in numbers.

The way to the Hero's Dock was guarded by a pair of piers that reached out like arms to embrace the sky. They were supported on complicated arrangements of iron girders, and their ends bore huge braziers. Arrangements of cellular wind baffles shook in the breeze. The *Aelsling* passed between the fires into a lagoon of still air.

The Hero's Dock was sparsely occupied, and the few ships there were dwarfed by the Azyrite schooner at the wharf. It was a sleek, golden vessel with a single hull of fine lines and two tall masts amply provisioned with sails. Wind obviously propelled it, but how it stayed aloft, or what it was made of, was unclear.

At the back of the dock was a colossal silver statue depicting three warriors, one for each of Bastion's principal races of human, duardin and aelf. They were arranged in heroic poses, weapons held aloft, the foot of the man, who was central to the group, planted upon the broken breastplate of a bestial warrior of Chaos.

Some of the worst of the fighting of the Five Hundred Year

Siege had occurred in that part of the city. The statue gaudily commemorated it.

A dock marshal appeared on the wharf. Uniformed lackeys brought up a wheeled tower. The marshal clambered up to a small platform, took up a pair of flags and began the stiff-armed dance of semaphore.

Adrimm read off the instructions. Drekki put a hand on his backpack and pulled him gently from the rail.

'Best let me do this, eh?' he said. 'Don't want to pile into that fancy goldbug they got there. Last thing we need.' He grasped the stays and leaned out into the air. The flags fluttered around the marshal. He was a pompous sort, maintaining the kind of ridiculous, uncomfortable pose the rich like their flunkies to strike.

If he sticks his chest out any further, his ribs will break, Drekki thought.

In somewhat florid terms, he was telling them to put in next to the Sigmarite vessel.

'Arkanaut Bjarnisson!' Drekki ordered. 'Prepare to bring us in! Five degrees to edgeboard! One-sixteenth power. Steady as she goes!'

Drekki leapt down off the gunwales and went to join Otherek and Kedren.

'Quite a crowd has come to meet us on the dock,' he said to Kedren, as the *Aelsling* came to a stop.

Blocks of Achromian troops waited for them, what little wind the baffles let through stirring their pennants and crests. Delegations from each of Achromia's Great Houses added more colour to an already garish display. Most of these smaller parties were headed up by humans in such eye-watering dress they could only be senior members of their families.

Lord Lerarus was at the front of his household troop.

'Here we go again,' said Drekki.

'Theatre, theatre. I don't like the look of this one bit,' said the runesmith.

'And there are the Stormcast Eternals,' said Otherek.

There were nine of them in purple and white, stood in two perfectly straight ranks of four, with their shields and hammers held at attention. The ninth stood at their front. She carried a long, two-handed sword, and her helm sported a flamboyant crest.

'What's all the worry about? There's not very many of them,' said Gord. 'Six, er, ten, er, um, well…'

'There are nine, Gord. Three Stormcasts would have us all dead in a minute,' said Drekki. 'Nine is a lot.'

The *Aelsling* tied up. Before Drekki could order the gangplank rolled out, Sanasha Lerarus strode across the deck, leapt down from ship to wharf and went to her father.

'Daughter! How marvellous to see you home after your long absence.' The duke held up his hands to the wizard. He put a damn sight more warmth into his voice than he had when they were on the ship, but the embrace was just as awkward. 'Were you successful in your mission? Did you bring her home?'

Drekki and Kedren shared a sidelong look. 'He's a terrible actor,' said Drekki.

'I did, father,' said Lerarus. 'Might I present to you the Lady Adelia Manellus, talisman of Old Achromia, returned to us now so that the empire might rise again!'

She gestured at the ship.

'Gord?' she called. 'If you would please roll out the gangplank?'

Without so much as a backward look at Drekki, Gord hurried to obey, unclipping the plank from its storage position and pushing it out onto the wharfside. Its small metal wheels scraped over the cobbles.

Adelia walked serenely out onto the dock. The duardin looked on as she went to the delegations of the Great Houses, stopped, and made a complex bow.

'I return to Bastion to perform the duty I was made for,' Adelia said. 'I do this with all my heart, for the glory of our people.'

Duke Lerarus smiled as if he had witnessed the most marvellous miracle. Close to tears, he slowly clapped his hands and shook his head.

'My dear, my dear!' he cried. 'You come to us now at our hour of need. How marvellous.'

'What's he playing at?' Otherek asked quietly.

'Politics,' said Drekki.

The duke took Adelia's hand and held it up.

'See what my daughter has achieved. See what House Lerarus has done for our city! All hail the talisman! All hail Achromia!'

Adelia inclined her head graciously. The welcoming party got down on their knees, except the Stormcasts, the duke and the other leading nobles, then gave out a deafening cheer, punching the air with clenched fists.

'Achromia! Achromia! Achromia!'

The leaders of the families approached the talisman, each trying not to appear to be hurrying, each trying to get there before their fellows. They kissed her hand, they bowed. They welcomed her with great respect and courtesy, so it was impossible to see who was pleased she was there and who was not. Only one man was obviously furious, and even he was polite.

The Achromians got back to their feet. The soldiers wheeled about smartly and opened a path to the customs gates in the walls backing the docks.

'The triumvirs await,' Duke Lerarus said. 'Come with us, please, my daughter. Favour them with the talisman's presence.'

If it seemed like a request, it was not. Drekki was alive to polite orders.

'A moment, father. I must assemble my guard.'

'But we have our family guard, here.' Only then did the duke's facade crack a little.

'These duardin are my guard, mine and the talisman's,' she said, gesturing at the *Aelsling*.

Drekki pointed at his chest. 'Us?' he mouthed.

An awkward pause. Glances were shot back and forth like pucks on a *zhuftee*[40] table.

Lerarus came back to the side of the ship. 'A word, if you please, Captain Flynt.'

Drekki clambered down. 'Got a new deal for me, wizard?' he asked quietly.

Lerarus bent down to speak into his ear. 'Five hundred Achromisia if you accompany me to the triumvirs as my bodyguard,' said Lerarus. 'Five thousand if it goes sour. Ten thousand if you get me away.'

'Done,' he said. That amount of money would make the trip worthwhile, besides, he wanted to get to the bottom of who the spy was. 'Otherek, Kedren, Velunti, Umherth, Adrimm and Gord, you're with me. Tordis, you're in charge of the ship. Evrokk!'

The helmsduardin hurried over.

'Keep an eye on things, dockside,' Drekki said quietly. He dropped his voice even further. 'And don't let Urdi out of your sight.'

Evrokk shot him a questioning look.

'Later,' Drekki said.

'Aye, captain,' said Evrokk.

Weapons were passed down from the ship to Drekki's party. Lerarus gave her father an openly defiant look. The duardin were not challenged.

---

40 | Kharadrid: Popular bar game in Overlord ports played by two teams of two with a hollow puck of highly polished stone, levitated off the surface of the gaming table by the off-gassing of unstable aether fragments.

'Shoulder! Arms!' Drekki said, putting on the parade-ground bellow of a sergeant-at-arms. 'Assemble about the client!'

The crew took up guard position around the wizard and Adelia. Gord walked directly behind her, suitably menacing; Drekki and the rest made a little formation behind him, which had the advantage of putting some space between dawi and umgi, allowing them to talk among themselves.

'I am ready, father,' said Lerarus. She was emboldened by her guard of duardin and their ogor.

Drekki grinned to himself. 'Customer satisfaction,' he said.

One by one, the guards of the Great Houses filed out. There was a hierarchy to the order they left in. Duke Lerarus was third, the others waited for Sanasha Lerarus to fall in behind her father.

The Stormcasts remained motionless throughout, like statues of gods. As Drekki swaggered past the heroine, he jerked his thumb over his shoulder.

'Nice-looking ship you got there, madam,' he said.

Her eyes shone in the blackness of her mask when she tilted her head down to look at him, but she offered no words in reply. When the procession was already snaking its way through the custom's gate, the Stormcasts finally joined.

'I'll be glad when this is over,' said Kedren.

'I won't. I'll miss the wizard. She's a funny little thing, like a gnoblar, but she smells better, and with more fire,' said Gord wistfully. He'd developed quite an attachment to Lerarus. 'Can't we keep her, Drekki, please?'

Gord was not a quiet creature. He bellowed more often than spoke. Lerarus must have heard his plea. What she made of his devotion was anyone's guess.

'Shush, Gord, she's not a pet and you're undermining your menace,' said Drekki. 'We've talked about that. What's the use of a soppy Maneater?'

The tramp of boots on paving echoed off buildings. Warehouses and the secretive mansions of mercantile clans lined the road, their few outer windows watchfully slitted and barred. Above them, tall roofs of scalloped tiles teetered like the scaled helmets of palace guards.

Welcoming was not a word that could be applied easily to the core. The Citadel Isle's fortifications were immense, dominating everything. A massive bridge led over the short air channel between Portsisle and the Citadel. A high arch leapt from the walls, planting itself in a square on the Portsisle side. From this hung dozens of steel cables, each as thick through as a duardin. The deck was built onto the anchor chains tying the islands together. The procession marched onto the bridge, joining an endless stream of people and animals crossing to the other side. The whole thing flexed, chains, arch, boards and all.

'Bit flimsy, ain't it?' muttered Adrimm mistrustfully.

'My people built this,' said Kedren. 'Fine engineering, takes into account metalith movement in three dimensions and all the rest, so shut up.'

'This is risky ground, and I'm not just talking about this bridge. What's our angle here, captain?' Otherek asked. 'Maybe we should just cut and run?'

'We're going to find out what's going on,' said Drekki. They all spoke quietly enough that they weren't overheard. 'We're in this up to our beards, and we will be forever if we don't see it through.'

'This ain't about your principles is it?' Umherth said. 'That wizard maybe, or that there talisman. You and your principles have got us in bother more than once, captain.'

'We'll do the right thing and be richer for it,' said Drekki.

'So long as we're paid in coin and not just in worthy feelings!' Umherth growled.

Drekki looked back at him. 'Don't you want to know who's

been messing with us? I prefer to know who my enemies are, Umherth. You can't mow them down with aethershot if you don't know who they are.'

The bridge reached the Citadel wall, which plunged sheer into the Third Air without lip or ledge to interrupt it. Three gates were punched through the masonry; no gatehouses, just circular tunnels leading fifty or more raadfathoms to the other side. Inside the tunnels the cacophony of feet, voices and animal cries blended into a disorienting roar that discouraged talking.

They were in there long enough for their eyes to get used to the dark, and emerged squinting against the sun on the far side.

The Citadel was divided into concentric rings. The first was irregular, for it followed the path of the walls, which followed the outline of the island, but past the first ward a circular order was imposed. Three roads ringed the Citadel's heart, the blocks between them divided up by straight boulevards, all of them well tended, well surfaced and open. The maze of stinking alleys the duardin associated with human settlements were conspicuous by their absence.

The barred paranoia of Portsisle was lacking on the Citadel. Every mansion gleamed with huge windows. People watched from them. Rich, sleek people: aelves, duardin and men.

'I have, I confess, often dreamed of robbing this place,' Umherth said, apropos of nothing.

The gate roads led to the central plaza, and at the centre of that was the Palace of the Triumvirs. The larger part was a massive, shallow dome held up on thick fluted pillars. Some of these were in the process of being replaced; Drekki heard they were bringing in the masonry from their new colonies so that the colonnade would represent Bastion's holdings. An expression of reborn Achromian power.

Three huge towers reached up over the dome, one for each

member of the triumvirate, so tall they cast sundial shadows out into the wider city beyond.

The procession entered the palace by way of the main gate, saluting guards and all. Trumpets blew. Flags unfurled. Complicated presentations of arms were accomplished. There were a lot of soldiers in there.

Huge marble halls, rammed full of gilt, mirrors and lamps led to the senate. Outside, the Stormcasts were politely prevented from entering, but the crew and Lerarus were ushered within.

There, under the dome of the House of Assembly, Drekki was given an audience with the triumvirs of Bastion.

The triumvirate comprised a human, an aelf and a duardin. Bastion had been ruled in this manner since the beginning of the Age of Chaos.

The procession marched to the centre of the hall, where the triumvirs waited upon thrones of creamy ivory set atop small floating platforms. The aelf, Helithin, stood as they approached.

'Welcome home, Sanasha Lerarus,' she said. 'I hear you bring news of a great triumph for our city. Glory is yours for your efforts.'

It was said that Helithin had been captain of the castle garrison the day the lands had shattered. That was old even for an aelf, so old her skin had grown translucent, allowing a glimpse of the soul shining within. Fine traceries of veins showed up against the glow of her spirit. Her hair was soft, fine, sparse as the filaments of airborne seeds. She dressed simply, only a plain diadem upon her brow. Her arms were thin as switches. She seemed to be comprised more of light than matter, daunting to see, yet her eyes held a deep empathy. She was as ethereal as a gheist, as unyielding as the earth, and her voice was loud and clear as a ship's bell.

The human, Lhorine Diphellius, was ancient, wrinkly as an ironcone pine left to grow in isolation upon a parched rock, its determination to live fired to a steely hardness by an unforgiving sun. A tree that takes root against the odds, and survives by tenacity alone. Bleached, hunched, and creased by time, Lhorine was a mummy draped in finery. Even so, she was centuries younger than both the duardin and aelf, two races which enjoyed a more leisurely rate of decay. Since the fall, one aelf had ruled on the council, only a handful of duardin. Eighteen short-lived humans had taken their turn on the third throne in the same time.

'You return a talisman to us. That is a matter of import,' Lhorine said. Her voice was thin, a candle on the verge of going out, yet it remained shrewd.

The left-hand throne cradled Drunderin Khazdok, patriarch of House Khazdok, Achromia's richest Dispossessed clan, and the only duardin Great House. He was by far the fattest duardin Drekki had ever seen, so fat that he lay in a sprawl upon his cushions, gut thrust up so high he had to peer over the top to see. His beard was long as a yard-arm, brushed till it shone like silver. Jewelled cinches gathered the hair into thick ropes, which were curled decoratively around his limbs. His hands were so covered in rings he would have struggled to make a fist. One gnarled hand rested on a diamond big as Drekki's head that topped a cane. His ostentation extended to a tall crown.

'You bring us opportunities and problems, cousin,' he said to Drekki. 'And much to think about.'

'Talisman of the old empire, step forward,' said Helithin.

Adelia moved to the front.

'You are Adelia Manellus, of House Manellus,' said Helithin.

'I am, your highness,' said Adelia. She knelt.

'I remember you. You were only a child when I met you, long ago. We were not sure which talisman was in the vault of Erulu,'

Helithin said. 'The fates of your generation were lost to time. It pleases me it is you. Your father was a good friend.'

'You have come back at a difficult moment, many forces are at work in this world,' said Drunderin. 'The reality we face is fraught with delicate questions of sovereignty and power, survival and ascendance. The time of the siege was simpler,' he concluded with a low chuckle.

'You are a great boon to us, child,' said Lhorine. 'Your return brings opportunity.'

'It is arguable that her return brings difficulty,' said Helithin.

'Nevertheless, we three alone must choose what is to be done,' said Lhorine.

'You are ready to resume your sacred duty, to take upon you the tasks that you were born for?' asked Drunderin.

'Yes,' said Adelia. 'With all my heart.'

The triumvirs looked to one another.

'What is our judgement?' Helithin said.

'Let us have her take her place in the machine now. The talisman we have is failing,' said Lhorine. 'He is old. The negotiations with Azyr will take time. Should he die while we wait for them to depart, the machine will never be reawakened.'

'It must be so,' said Drunderin. 'With the machine guaranteed, we shall have more bargaining power with Azyr. Thanks to Duke Lerarus, Azyr knows we have the talisman. We use her, and make our stand, or we do not, and effectively submit. Matters have come to a head. Helithin, what is your judgement?'

'I would have preferred this reunion to have taken place after our negotiations were settled,' said the aelf. 'I fear the Restoration Party will feel empowered, and that brings dangers to the balance of our rule, but what can we do? Adelia's presence here is enough to shift the balance of the argument among the houses towards the Restorationists. We will appear weak if we do not make immediate use of her. A fact I am sure Duke Lerarus took into account when he announced the success of his daughter's mission.' Her radiant face turned to the duke and she stared at him with an imperious sadness. 'With a heavy heart, I concur.'

Duke Lerarus stepped forward. He could barely conceal his triumph.

'Lords and lady triumvir. My daughter risked all to embark on this mission for House Lerarus,' he said. 'I feared for her safety, yet such is her courage, her devotion to her city.'

'You've stirred us all right up, young Lady Sanasha, and no mistake,' said Drunderin.

'You are seeking reward for your daughter's actions?' said Lhorine.

'For my house, not for myself,' said the duke.

'She shall be rewarded,' said Helithin. 'You have played the game well, duke, and we are forced to look as if this were our intention all along. Despite the fact you acted against our wishes. Despite the fact you force us into a course of action we might not have taken. Seeming is all. Let there be an elevation in office for the wizard, but no further reward for House Lerarus.'

'I must protest,' said the duke. 'This is an historic occasion.'

'We have made our judgement,' said Lhorine.

Duke Lerarus bowed. 'Of course.'

'Go now, begin preparations for the ritual to install Adelia Manellus in her rightful place,' Helithin said. Adelia got up.

'I do so gladly,' said Adelia. 'It is my fate.'

The audience concluded, the triumvirate's guards began their elaborate twirling of arms and stamping of feet that was really just a way of sweeping the chamber clear.

A loudly cleared throat stopped them. Drekki's throat.

'You have something to say, Kharadron?' Lhorine said.

'I do, your worships,' said Drekki. 'I apologise for being indelicate, but what do we gain for our service to this fine city? Without us, you'd have no talisman.'

Helithin looked upon Drekki. The light of her soul changed hue, becoming colder. 'You would demand remuneration?'

'What else does a fellow like me yearn for, but treasure and beer? Offices and titles are of no use to me.' He bowed. 'It's the treasure I'm after specifically, though.'

'Very well. Twenty thousand Achromisia.' She crooked a finger at a court official. He bowed and came forward with a chest. Another courtier opened it. Inside was a pile of Bastion's currency: tiny five-pointed gems formed in the magic-washed hinterlands of the shoals. Drekki nodded. The chest snapped shut. Otherek took it.

'You will stay, of course, captain,' said Helithin. 'For the ritual of the machine.'

'Naturally,' Drekki bowed.

Helithin inclined her head in response.

'I believe you retrieved other artefacts from the vault.'

'Only one, madam,' said Drekki.

'One or a hundred, the law dictates that all magical artefacts recovered from the ruins of the old empire be presented to the Retrievals Guild for evaluation,' Helithin said. 'Though you already know this, is that not the case, Drekki Flynt?'

Drekki bowed again. 'I do.'

'Then go to the guild, and pay your dues.'

Drekki shot a look at Lerarus. She nodded slightly. The duardin bowed again and departed.

'Oh, we've been royally stuffed here,' said Umherth under his breath on their way out. 'Though twenty thousand takes the sting out of it a bit.'

'Aye,' said Drekki. 'And it's going to get worse before it gets better.' They walked quickly, keeping their voices low. 'No matter what happens, trust me, all right?'

The crew nodded and made noises of affirmation, but Drekki detected notes of disgruntlement. What choice did they have? None at all, that's what.

CHAPTER TWENTY-SIX

THE RETRIEVALS GUILD

The Bastion Artefacts Retrievals Guild was one of the least popular institutions in Bastion. Its job was singular: every magical artefact taken from the broken lands of the old empire was required, by law, to be presented for examination. The best were confiscated, though a finder's fee was paid. Everything else was taxed heavily. The way the triumvirate put it in their law codes, the material belonged to the Bastionites anyway, or the Achromians or whatever they were calling themselves. There was no mercy in its ironclad walls, no exceptions. All must pay the taxes. All must bear the punishments if they refused. The guild's judgements could not be challenged. In a city known for its bureaucracy, it was loathed for being especially bureaucratic. Back-alley trading was so much simpler. The guild's existence encouraged a hearty black market trade in Old Achromian artefacts, which is why Drekki had managed ten years in the sky without having to deal with the guild once.

They had to go back to the ship, then get their loot. Velunti,

Adrimm and Gord remained behind. Drekki took Umherth, Kedren and Otherek with him to the guild bank, which dominated a crag on Calliostro's Island, way out to edgeward. So it was Drekki found himself on a gondola slung beneath a silk bag of magic-warmed air, being conveyed to the one place in Bastion he had always striven to avoid.

'Do we have to go there?' Otherek said, looking miserably ahead.

'There' was the guild up ahead. 'There' was the place dreams of fortunes went to die. 'There' was a huge, rust-red building with complicated, expensive-looking windows paid for by unfair levies on honest treasure hunters.

Umherth nodded vigorously, sending his plaited beard and nose ring dancing. 'Just hide it, captain. Stick it away. Drop it wrapped in rags on a rock somewhere, retrieve it later. Don't show it to them. The tax will be horrible.'

'We are going to have to give it up,' said Drekki. 'They've got it marked and logged. Funti search sweepers. Drengi wizards. Blasted triumvirs. We ain't got no choice.'

'What about the gems and coins we got in the vault, captain. We're keeping them, right?' said Umherth, ever so slightly desperately.

'Shhhh,' said Drekki out of the corner of his mouth. He waggled a meaningful eyebrow in the gondolier's direction. 'Shut up about those, or we'll be out of pocket entirely. They've taxes for everything here.'

The gondola docked at one of many piers cut into the guild's lowest floor, like individual teeth in a mouth ready to gobble up money. People arrived and departed in constant motion. The passengers looked glum on arrival, furious when they departed. A few hard-bitten sky-dogs were stifling tears.

Drekki's heart, already in his boots, dropped through his soles. He imagined it falling forever. Much like his balance of wealth.

'Come on, lads, let's get this over with.'

An extravagantly decorated hall led to a row of counters set into an equally lavish wall. Close inspection revealed it was also heavily reinforced. Assessors occupied each of the cubbyholes, protected by sheets of thick glass. Serious-looking drawers were located in the base of each window, all the better to accommodate treasure.

Guards in thick padded armour prodded guild 'clients', as the signs called those about to be fleeced, into queues. Conversation was muted. When voices could be heard, they were raised.

Drekki's gang shuffled forward, burdened by the inevitability of loss.

'Hey!' said Kedren, elbowing Drekki when they neared the front. 'We've got one of our own,' he said. 'Look. Our assessor is a duardin.'

'So he is. A good sign,' said Otherek.

It was, predictably, not.

The fellow behind the glass was a skinny type with a scruffy grey beard going yellow at the edges. Disreputable traits in any one of the duardin nations. He scratched away in a fat ledger with a greasy griffin quill. Behind him a door led through to a corridor. Surrounding it were a mass of packages and literal pots of gold. Seeing how much money these bloodsuckers took made Drekki's blood simmer.

'Present the property of Achromia,' said the clerk. He had a nasal whine of a voice.

'Let me handle this,' said Kedren confidently.

Drekki, disconsolate, shrugged. Umherth reluctantly handed the wrapped axe to Kedren.

'Here we are,' said Kedren. The axe went into the drawer reluctantly. The assessor gave him a slow look. He hardly glanced at the axe.

'Rune axe, one. Single-handed. Runes of fire, smiting and biting.

Late pre-Chaos vintage.' He jotted down his pronouncements. 'State location of recovery.'

'Erulu. The city, not the islands.'

To have been to those grot-infested lands and return was no mean feat. Many would have called Kedren a liar.

The assessor's pen kept the same busybody's pace.

'One rune axe, returned,' he said. His hand went for a stamp hanging in a wire rack.

'Now hang on a minute,' said Kedren. 'That there is duardin rune work. It belongs to the duardin. Not to Bastion. Y'see, longbeard, I know because I'm a runesmith.' He said so very importantly. There was a special, down-the-nose look that accompanied the revelation of his craft.

Although Kedren's status carried a lot of weight in duardin society, whether Dispossessed, Fyreslayer, or Kharadron, that did not appear to be the case in the guild. The assessor was completely uncaring.

'The axe is of Achromian origin,' he said. 'Bastion is the current capital of Achromia. This artefact was made by an Achromian duardin, in service of the Achromian Empire. Therefore, this axe is the property of the sovereign government of Bastion.'

'Now just you wait there, you little office grobi. I found that axe, it's mine!' Umherth started. Drekki swung out his arm to stop his advance.

'Ours. 'It's ours. We get to keep the axe, Umherth,' said Drekki, hoping to calm the oldbeard. 'There'll just be tax to pay, that's all.' He spoke with loud confidence.

The duardin turned his beady little eyes on Drekki.

'Not so. As a treasure of Old Achromia, the axe will be retained.' He yanked the drawer back.

Umherth roared. 'This isn't fair!'

Round holes opened in the wall above the glass. Small mechanical arms emerged, each bearing a businesslike aether-pistol, all of which swivelled on smooth bearings to point at the crew.

'At least we get to keep our cash. No tax, right, if you'll be keeping it?' said Drekki.

'Well,' said the old duardin, who was just about to get to that. 'No. A finding tax is due on this item of twenty thousand Achromisia…'

'But… but… that's about as much as we were just given,' said Umherth. His face was going that purply colour that preceded Umherthian mayhem.

'You will be recompensed,' the assessor droned on. 'For the return of said axe.'

'I suppose that's something!' said Drekki. 'How much?'

'Forty-five thousand.'

There were expressions of delight, and back slappings, and a little jig from Umherth.

'Forty-five thousand Achromisia!' Kedren whistled. 'Not bad, Drekki, not bad.'

'Not Achromisia. Trade tokens,' the assessor corrected.

'What? Trade tokens? They're worthless!' said Drekki.

'Tokens may be exchanged for goods and services. Supplies, food, other useful goods.'

'Useless is about funti right!' Drekki said. 'They can be exchanged with people that take the bloody things, and nobody bloody does, because the bloody things are bloody worthless!'

'I may provide a list of vendors,' said the assessor. The whiny drone of his voice did not vary by a semitone.

'Written on the back of a smoke weed packet, is it?' Drekki said. 'Short, is it? Three greengrocers who don't know better and that bloody annoying shop in Eyeward that sells nothing but glass figurines of aelven princesses?'

The assessor kept his eyes on the ledger. His pen stopped moving. He laid it carefully aside, reached up, and yanked a lever.

A heavy, three-sided copper ingot clanged out of a tube into a shallow bowl at the front of the desk.

'Take your chit.'

'Excuse me?'

'Take your chit. You may exchange it for trade tokens at the exchange booth.'

'You mean, you're giving us a worthless token for worthless tokens?'

'The triumvirs of Bastion thank you for your service.'

'I'll bet they funti drekking do!' said Drekki. 'This is why we don't do business here! You bunch of shiftless, cheating, no-good...'

The assessor blinked rheumy eyes at Drekki. 'I shall note here that you rejected your chit,' said the assessor. His pen moved with purpose to a box in the ledger, a box marked 'payment rejected'.

'Just you hang on a minute, laddo,' said Drekki, and snatched the copper from the dish. 'What's mine is mine, even if it is worth nothing.'

All of them started shouting then, Umherth loudest of all. The assessor let them rage for half a minute or so, then pressed a button on his desk. Hammers clicked on the pistols.

'We find that these aethermatic weapons you Kharadron make are exceptionally good at resolving disputes,' the assessor said archly.

Drekki's eyes focused on the manufacturer's plate. *Throkk and Co.* it said, in a jauntily expressive typeface. Typical. He bet the Achromian government didn't pay for *those* with trade tokens.

Calm returned. Enforced, but calm nonetheless.

'The triumvirs thank you for your–' said the assessor.

'Yeah yeah,' said Drekki. 'Get stuffed.'

Umherth bared his teeth at the official. The skinny duardin pulled another lever. A set of sturdy bars dropped down over his window. He cocked his head, then went back to his ledger.

'Cheating bozdok,' Drekki muttered.

'This trip has cost us a fortune,' said Otherek.

'At least there's the money Lerarus will pay,' said Umherth sarcastically. 'Only there isn't, because we're not getting any!'

Umherth harrumphed. He folded his arms, hugging imagined treasures to his chest.

'Come on,' said Drekki. 'Let's get this worthless lump of troggoth dung changed and see what wonders we can buy with forty-five thousand pointless trade tokens. From three greengrocers. A lot of apples, I expect. I hate apples.'

They didn't even get to pick up the tokens. As they were leaving the hall, the crowds parted. A number of armed humans and duardin in black uniforms ringed Drekki's little group.

'Ah, another shining moment to add to the pile of *zhakust*[41] today brings,' Drekki said.

The troop's leader stepped forward. 'Are you Drekki Flynt?'

'You have me mistaken,' Drekki said with dangerous cheer. 'I'm Grand Admiral Brokk Grungsson of Barak-Nar, on my way to the milliner to buy a new top hat. Good day.'

Drekki was halted by a hand to the chest.

'You're Drekki Flynt all right. I heard you had a mouth on you. By the order of Lord Marsden Crave, Witchfinder-General of Bastion, you are to come with us. Do it freely, or be compelled.'

For the second time in as many minutes, guns were pointed in Drekki's direction.

'Marvellous,' he said with a huge and insincere grin, 'more funti-dreng aristocrats.'

---

41 | Kharadrid: Droppings.

CHAPTER TWENTY-SEVEN

HOUSE CRAVE

House Crave occupied a forbidding castle on a rock all of its own. Drekki's lot docked in front and were hustled in through a side gate. Guards marched them into a hall and withdrew, barring the doors behind them.

The hall was tall and square, decorated modestly, with a timber gallery running around three sides. Ale tankards and jugs for each duardin had been set at the table. Lord Crave was already present, sitting in a high wooden chair not quite grand enough to be a throne, a little too big not to be.

Crave was a short, slight man, saturnine in appearance and manner, clad in furs though the day was warm outside, as if all he had seen in his life had frozen some fundamental part of his soul. His face was ruddy and dry, as if chapped by ill winds. He looked a little feeble, but he was watchful, still in a dangerous way. Drekki could imagine him moving unexpectedly to strike.

Two duardin sat at the long table in front of the lord's not-quite-throne. Seeing Urdi was not much of a surprise. Seeing Evrokk was.

Both the duardin seemed to be there of their own volition, as neither was restrained. Only Evrokk attempted to stand when Drekki entered, and he was dismayed.

'Captain!' he said.

Urdi grasped his wrist and pulled him back into his chair.

'Well, well,' said Drekki. 'Looks like I have a serpent in the nest after all. I've had my eye on you since Bavardia, Urdi. I'm surprised at you, Evrokk.'

'It's not what it looks like, captain!' said Evrokk.

'He's done nothing,' said Urdi, who was making a show of confidence, but was only a little more composed than his shipmate. 'Evrokk followed me when I left the ship to meet my contact. He was apprehended. It's me who you should be angry with. Lord Crave don't mean him any harm. He don't mean you any either, captain. You have to listen to him, please.'

Crave cleared his throat. A dry, raspy sound, like grit rolling round a polishing barrel.

'Perhaps "no harm" is a little disingenuous,' Crave said. 'But it is certainly nothing personal. Sit and take refreshment with us, and we shall see if we can resolve this issue together.' He extended his hand towards the chairs.

'Refreshment,' said Drekki. 'Not going to do us in? Or are you one of those types who likes to play nice before torturing his guests to death?'

'Don't be ridiculous,' said Crave. 'We are servants of Order, the opponents of evil.'

Drekki shrugged. 'A lot of people do a lot of inexplicable things.' He gave Urdi a hard stare.

'Captain–' said Urdi pleadingly.

'You be quiet now, Urdi Duntsson – whichever way you dice it, you're a traitor.'

Urdi looked down, ashamed.

'All right then,' said Drekki. 'Let's hear what you have to say, Crave.' He drew Karon and put her down meaningfully on the table. 'Lads, weapons down. Helms and packs off.'

The crew sat. Drekki took the place at the end facing Lord Crave.

'I reckon time's getting a little tight, if I'm right about what's going on,' said Drekki. 'So how about I'll tell you what I know, and you tell me what you know. Deal?'

Crave raised a hand. 'Let us judge the quality of your information first.'

'Whatever,' said Drekki. 'First up, you've been watching me. That was your man in Bavardia my khemist saw. You had one of your ships follow me and attack, because you wanted to stop us getting the talisman. Having failed to destroy the *Aelsling*, your nephew decided to go for the talisman before me. But when he got there, members of his own crew turned on him, and his ship was caught by the grots, so we got it after all. That about it?' He took a gulp of his drink. 'Nice beer, by the way.'

'The attack on you was an unfortunate business,' said Crave. 'I strive to uphold the responsibilities of my house, which are protecting this city against Chaos. That is my duty. I regret your inconvenience.'

'Inconvenience? Bombing innocent skyfarers?' said Drekki.

'A life is of little consequence in the war against Chaos. If you were the most innocent creature in all the realms, and your death would keep this city safe, then I would kill you without hesitation. Regrettable, but necessary.'

'More regrettable for me than for you, I'll warrant,' said Drekki. He scratched his beard. Gold jewellery clicked. 'Then there's that other thing, the markings on the ship that drew in the daemons to attack us. At the time, I thought it was all part and parcel. Funny thing is, I thought it was Urdi here.' He gave Urdi an insincere smile. 'No offence, Urdi.'

Urdi was having a hard time looking Drekki in the eye.

'But Urdi's not working for them, he's working for you.'

'You are correct,' said Crave. 'We have been following the actions of a traitor in Bastion for several months. His cult have their agents everywhere, including, as you have pointed out, within the crew of my nephew's ship. We learned not long after Duke Lerarus contacted Rogi Throkk that there was also an agent among your crew. My man in Bastion was to observe you, to see what you knew. Urdi agreed to act as our operative aboard your ship.'

'For a small fee no doubt,' said Drekki. 'We could have worked together, Crave. You could have told me.'

'I could not trust you,' said Crave. 'I could not trust Sanasha Lerarus. Not knowing your allegiances or hers, and unable to contact your man here, our priority was to stop the talisman falling into your hands, a task my nephew singularly failed at.' He showed a touch of emotion, but it was fleeting.

'What's your game then?' Drekki said. 'You want the talisman for yourself? Is this about prestige? Who brings Adelia back and who gets the biggest pat on the head?'

Crave shook his head.

'Our goal was to return the talisman to Achromia, the same as yours.'

'Urdi, why didn't you just come clean?'

'I couldn't tell you, captain,' said Urdi. 'Lord Crave, the younger Lord Crave, begging your pardon, your lordship, said we needed to catch whoever the agent was on the *Aelsling*. That they needed him because they need proof to catch their traitor, and Ildrin *is* the proof.'

'I assume also your pay was dependent on this?' said Drekki.

Urdi wriggled with shame. 'I only did it for a bit of extra money. We've been unsuccessful the last few times out. I've got expenses.'

'Crew's more important than cash, Urdi.'

'I'm sorry!'

'Then it was you I saw at the prow,' said Drekki.

Urdi nodded. 'I saw someone doing something there,' he babbled, a rush of guilty words. 'Putting that mark on the ship, I suppose, but when I went to look I found nothing. That's when you saw me. If I'd have seen what it was, I would have told you about it, I swear. I didn't know what was going to happen.'

He looked desperately from Crave to Drekki and back again.

'Why call in daemons to attack?' asked Drekki. 'That's the only part that foxes me.'

'The plans of the enemy are never transparent, and rarely comprehensible,' said Crave. 'I can only assume that attacking you set in motion events that pushed you to beat the odds and retrieve the talisman. By doing so, you have put us all in grave danger. Bravo,' he concluded.

'But the captain has him, Lord Crave. Don't you, captain?' said Urdi desperately. 'Ildrin's in the brig. It's all going to be fine, isn't it?'

'It is a beginning,' said Crave. 'We can question this Ildrin, and he might give us the proof I need to arrest the traitor. If so, the day will be saved and you will be rewarded.'

Drekki grinned bitterly and drank.

'I would bring Ildrin to you like a shot, because I do like money,' said Drekki. 'But I'm not going to.'

'Do you dare to hold this city to ransom?' said Crave. 'I will not dicker over the fate of my people.'

'I'm not holding you to ransom. The reason I'm not going to bring you Ildrin is because it weren't him,' said Drekki.

This news was a surprise to everyone.

'How can you be sure?' asked Kedren.

'It's the paint on Ildrin's hand. It was put there to look like he'd smudged himself when steadying a brush. You know, when you don't have a painter's rest, you use the fat of your palm to keep the lines straight.'

'Aye,' said Kedren. 'I tended the burns myself when he got that stuff on him.'

'A good job you did of it. I went to see Ildrin the other day, had a little chat. He said his hand was as right as rain.'

'And what is the significance of this?' Crave said.

'Someone put the mark on him while he was asleep. Ildrin was a recent recruit. An easy distraction. But whoever did it didn't know him well enough to know one crucial thing, and neither did any of the rest of us. Thing is, Ildrin's left-handed,' said Drekki. 'I only found out this morning.'

'How can you be sure?' said Crave. 'That can be faked.'

'He took his ale with his left hand, you umgi drengi. That's a hard instinct for a duardin to override.'

'Then who is the traitor on your ship?' Crave said.

Drekki hunkered down over his beer and shrugged. 'I don't know. I do wonder if anybody on my bloody ship is actually working for me, to be honest. Velunti's losing his touch. He should be stricter vetting the crew.'

'Nothing else has happened after we locked up Ildrin,' said Kedren.

'That's because the plan came to fruition,' said Drekki. 'They have what they need now, don't they? The talisman is in the city, where the enemy wanted her all along. I think I know who this traitor is.' Drekki slugged back some more ale. 'It's Duke Lerarus, isn't it?'

Otherek bristled. 'And we delivered the talisman directly into his hands!'

'Well, fine, but that's not the end of the world,' said Kedren. 'Can't you arrest him?'

'I would have done months ago, but I need proof,' said Crave.

'Lord Lerarus is a powerful man. If I move on him now, I risk my own position, and that means the city will be without its most diligent protector. His cult is well hidden. Your traitor offered me the greatest chance at gaining said proof.'

'You should let Ildrin out!' said Otherek, who was by now a little outraged.

'We can't,' said Drekki. 'If we do that, the enemy will know that we know.'

'The conspiracy will go to ground. We will lose them. The machine might be safe, but the danger will remain, and Duke Lerarus will still be in power. You give me no choice but to arrest you all,' said Crave. 'I regret this, but you must all be questioned until the traitor is revealed. I apologise for the unpleasantness that is to come.'

The crew leapt to their feet, but men appeared on the gallery above them, and trained their weapons on the room.

Only Drekki remained seated, and very carefully poured himself another beer. He held the jug up high, letting the brown liquid fall in a long, silken stream. 'You're not going to do that,' he said.

'And why is that?' said Crave.

'Because we're going to help you bring this whole thing down. Tomorrow the talisman will be installed in your machine. I'll bet that is when Duke Lerarus will make his move, and what better proof will you get than catching him red-handed? The machine will be vulnerable, and the chances are his cult will be there to witness his victory. You can prepare and grab them all. Of course, that will only happen if you don't toss us all into your dungeons and tip them off.'

Crave appeared thoughtful. 'It's a risk.'

'It's a better choice than the one you have right now,' said Drekki. 'I'd guess he'd just kill the talisman if he got wind of our disappearance, then you'd have no arrests, and no machine. If you do nothing, he'll win. If you got ready and no ill befalls your talisman or the machine, then what's the harm? This is your best option. We need to work together. You know we do. And if I'm wrong, what do you really lose?'

Crave put long fingers to his cracked, dry chin. 'You'll be performing this service for free, no doubt,' said Crave sarcastically. 'For the love of Achromia.'

'There you are wrong.' Drekki grinned. 'I'm Drekki Flynt,' he said. 'And I don't come cheap.'

CHAPTER TWENTY-EIGHT

THE GREAT MACHINE

The government of Bastion decided to make a big deal about the return of the talisman.

Drekki had his whole crew with him, except Evrokk and Bokko, who were left on the *Aelsling* with orders to keep the endrins running. As far as Drekki was concerned they were beyond reproach. Fair enough, he couldn't completely rule out that one of them was the traitor, but then risk was a big part of Drekki's world. If it turned out Evrokk or, Grungni forfend, Bokko had turned on him, he'd deal with it later. He wasn't going to get stuck in Bastion once all this was over, and they represented the best chance to get free. And once he was gone, he expected he wouldn't be coming back for a very long time.

That's me, he thought, making friends all over the place.

Trumpets wailed. Drums drummed. Troops marched. Batons twirled. By Grungni, not only was it a big deal they were making of this, but a *very* big deal. The mood was joyous. People hung out of their windows, dressing in their finery, casting long ribbons of coloured paper onto the marching columns of troops and dignitaries, shouting Adelia's name. What the Azyrites made of this was anyone's guess. Drekki had yet to hear them speak. The triumvirs were absent, apparently they rarely left their palace, but the heads of the noble houses strutted along, soaking up the cheers of the crowds, seemingly oblivious to the seven-foot-tall demigods armoured head to toe treading behind them. Many of the nobles had come with their entire families, making gaudy phalanxes of the rich, all of them armed and armoured in gear so overdecorated as to be useless for fighting.

There were exceptions. Crave's equipment was noticeably sturdy looking, as was that of Duke Lerarus. Crave came without family members, while the duke was accompanied only by Sanasha. It was as if both sides had given up pretence. Surely the Stormcasts must have noticed this, Drekki thought. He wondered if they were in on Crave's plan. He tried very hard to ignore Crave, Duke Lerarus and the Azyrites as they made their way to the tower, for fear of provoking events. The whole thing made him feel unaccustomedly nervous.

The machine was housed in a round tower at the rear of the Citadel Isle which was over a hundred raadfathoms across, the biggest building on the metalith except the palace. As they approached, he saw tiny figures up the top, and what looked like dainty ornaments, but were in fact enormous magical war machines. They were soon lost to view as the tower climbed up and up. Its shadow was deep and cold. Hysh itself could not best the tower, and the ground beneath it never saw the sun.

In through a huge gate, then up round a spiral stairway inside the walls wide enough to carry the entire parade. They emerged at last, with many brassy trumpet blares and stampings of feet, into the chamber of the machine. The stair came to a circular platform that jutted out over a long drop before continuing up on the inside of the chamber to the roof access, a simple slot in the ceiling that let the stairs out and slice of daylight in.

The platform was big enough for them all to get onto. The floor was fretted, with coiling beasts and suchlike, decorative cut-outs that allowed them to see right down the hollow tower, and to the machine that it protected. The air was heavy with magic, the same thick-aired, prickly sensation that you find in the presence of aethermatic machinery.

'It's all right I suppose,' said Kedren grudgingly. 'I've seen bigger, probably better too, but it's not bad for umgi and elgi work.' It was a half-hearted dismissal; the machine was an impressive thing.

The machine floated upon a disc that plugged the shaft like a floor. Greased wheels running in grooves kept it in the same orientation, but unless there was a massive piston beneath, it was magic for sure holding the thing up. Carvings of constellations and godbeasts decorated the machine's deck, over which trickles of light ran, bringing them to disturbing life. Griffons roared. Comets glared. Stylised representations of Hysh flared and wavered.

The machine itself was a complicated series of metal spheres that orbited each other on circular tracks. Once more, magic provided the motive force.

There were nine little pulpits, almost like cockpits, situated around the edges of the platform. They were sized for humans, free of any sort of control mechanism, except for two silver prongs pointing up at their fronts like the antennae on an insect's brow.

All these were empty, save one. An ancient human occupied it, a solitary guard against all of Chaos, the last of the talismans bred in Adelia's time. Drekki shuddered. He didn't look like he'd been living it up between bouts of sorcery. He looked like he'd been shut in there for five centuries straight.

A priest moved out from the procession. A choir sang him to his position in the middle of the deck.

'Bring forth the talisman!' he cried.

Adelia walked into the centre of the group. She moved in a stagey kind of way; she'd probably rehearsed this ritual a thousand times. There were, he saw now, nine little discs set into the platform, and she took her place on one of them. As soon as she did, blue light shone up around her.

The priest began a rambling speech about responsibility, the gods, and the power of the ancients. Drekki listened with less than half an ear. He looked around the room, at the representatives of the Great Families. What was going on in their little umgi heads, he could not begin to speculate. He wondered how many of them were in Duke Lerarus' pay.

The duke stood beside his daughter, his face studiously neutral. From Drekki's position he seemed like all the rest within the room, worshipful, though cultivating an air of aristocratic disdain. He dared hope they'd got it all wrong and the duke was simply a wazzock, not a villain.

If they were right, then Crave's troops were ready in a hidden gallery at the top of the chamber. There were guns that could be aimed at the duke.

It was his crew that concerned Drekki the most. Not knowing which of his surrogate family had betrayed him ate at his heart like troggoth acid. Standing to attention behind him, they were so smart, guns and gear polished, a credit to his ship. He valued them all, and yet one of them would have gladly seen him dead. Assuming it wasn't either Evtorr or Gunterr...

Otherek and Kedren were unlikely candidates, though Drekki had reached a high enough level of paranoia not to be able to discount them completely. Umherth hated Chaos more than any of them, so he was probably out. Hrunki didn't have an evil bone in her body, for all her love of fighting. Adrimm? A possibility. He moaned enough, that was true, and a handsome payoff might tempt him away. Khenna was still an unknown quantity, but he could tell she had monsters of her own to slay that were nothing to do with him or Bastion. Bokko loved the ship too much to hurt her. Evrokk was as solid a duardin as could be. So was Velunti, the duardin of many roles. Not just cargo-master, but purser, third mate, surgeon, cook. So diffident, so hard-working. What would he do without Velunti? He'd suffered on this voyage. Drekki had to make it up to him. His gaze moved onto the humans standing so solemnly around him, but something drew it back to Velunti.

Velunti. Good old Velunti. He hardly had to get involved at all when Velunti took charge.

'Do you solemnly swear to uphold the rites and responsibilities of a talisman of Achromia, binding your life to the Great Machine to ward and protect us, to keep us from harm, and to allow our people to prosper?' The priest was reaching the climax. Adelia knelt before him on her glowing disc.

'I do. I will. I shall,' said Adelia.

What would he do without Velunti?

'Then be it known that you are the talisman, you are our shield and our sword. Welcome home, Adelia Manellus.' The priest waved his arm about in commanding fashion. 'Bring up the machine!'

The wheels on the platforms squealed. The air vibrated with magic and the Great Machine crept up the shaft. Weird lights played over the gathering, distorting their outlines. A pressure grew in Drekki's head. But all he could think about was Velunti.

Velunti's face, mild and tipsy in the lamplight of the great cabin, where the ale flowed as quick as the laughter.

'I'll fetch a cask, if it's all right with you, captain?'

Drekki had barely noticed that Velunti left the room that night. Why would he? Velunti was always bustling about, doing one of his many jobs. But that was the night the mark was made.

That blow he took from that daemon should've killed him. Drekki had seen that with his own eyes. But it didn't.

The machine came to a stop, its deck locking into the platform edge with a series of bangs. The sense of magic dwindled. The priest drew in a lungful of breath to speak. He never got the chance.

'Stop!' Drekki shouted. He drew Karon. From all around him came the sharp, unmistakable clicks of blackpowder hammers being pulled back. If he had been pointing his gun at any of the Achromians, Drekki would have been dead. But he wasn't.

Karon's three barrels were pointing at Velunti.

'This is an outrage!' spluttered the priest. 'You interrupt a most holy ceremony!'

A good number of nobles' household troops moved forward.

'Hold!' commanded Lord Crave. 'This is the business of the city witchfinders.' He nodded at Drekki. There was an unpleasant gleam of triumph in his eyes.

'Take your helmet off, Velunti,' Drekki said. The room was quiet. Four hundred humans, aelves and duardin held their breath. The machine hummed sonorously behind them.

'Captain?' Velunti said.

'You heard. Take it off. I need to see your face. I pray to Grungni that I'm wrong, but just take it off.'

Velunti reached up. He undid the clasps. Air mix hissed as the seals came apart. He tucked it under his arm.

'Why?' said Velunti. 'What have I done?' His expression of bewilderment was almost enough to fool Drekki. He seemed stricken.

Then a single trickle of sweat slipped down his face, and Drekki knew. He just knew.

'It was you,' said Drekki.

'Captain...'

'You were the only one who was out of the room besides the others that night the harkraken attacked,' Drekki said.

'It was Ildrin!' Velunti laughed. He was trying to be reasonable, but the sweat was running freely now.

'You've never once complained on a voyage when every other one of the crew has been moaning fit to burst. Not a single mutter beyond that not-quite-joke about not being paid enough. Not once, even though I have wrung every last drop of labour out of you. What kind of duardin would never moan?'

'Why would I grumble? Captain, I've been with you for years! Come on, Drekki, it's me, good old Velunti!'

'You *should* grumble,' said Drekki. His voice caught in his throat. 'You should grumble because you've given the *Aelsling* everything, and what have you got in return?'

'Adventure. Friendship. Comrades,' said Velunti.

'It's not enough, is it? It's not enough for any of us. It's the gold fever, Velunti. It's in us all. It's in you.'

'I didn't–'

'Don't lie!' Drekki shouted. His voice echoed fiercely round the tower. 'How much did he offer you?'

Halfway through another excuse, Velunti's voice faltered. He looked to his friends. He looked ready to lie, but something in his face changed.

'A lot,' he said. 'More than a lot. Enough to buy five ships like the *Aelsling*, more. I didn't get into this to be your lackey, Drekki. I had my own ambitions. My own dreams. Where are they? Seven years I've been with you. I've heard every promise, every boast. What have I got to show for it?' His voice dropped to a poisonous hiss. 'Nothing.'

'I was going to give you a raise!' said Drekki.

'After all you've put me through, it would never have been enough.'

'You don't know what you've done,' said Drekki. 'Tell us who paid you, Velunti. It might go a bit easier for you.'

Velunti made another strangled laugh. 'Drekki!'

'I mean it, Velunti,' said Drekki. He pulled the hammer back on Karon.

Velunti's expression turned to a snarl. 'Very well,' he said. With a deliberate swagger, he walked over to the duke. Lerarus Family soldiers parted to let him through. A good many of them seemed shocked, but others were noticeably calm, as if ready for this turn of events. At that moment Drekki knew for certain that Crave had the right man. He also suspected things weren't going to go all their own way. He had a nose for trouble, and it itched like mad.

The duke did nothing, but nodded to Velunti, and allowed him to take his place at his side.

A gloating expression settled on Lord Crave's face. He held up his hand. Shutters of stone swivelled open noiselessly in the top of the tower, A hundred guns emerged from behind.

'So the traitor is revealed,' said Lord Crave. His voice was now strong and loud, his movements decisive. 'I've waited for this moment, Lerarus.'

'Traitor?' said Duke Lerarus quizzically, but he was smiling in a way Drekki didn't like. He was smiling like a man who thought he had won.

'What's going on?' Umherth hissed.

'Let's just say you were right about Urdi,' said Drekki from the corner of his mouth. 'More or less.'

Murmurs spread through the crowd of nobles.

'What is the meaning of this?' one called. Or maybe two. That's what nobles tended to say when confronted by unknown circumstances, which was generally whenever people didn't do exactly as they demanded. It made them panic.

'Stand aside, loyal servants of Achromia. Duke Lerarus is under arrest!' Crave said.

'You had better be very sure of your sources, my lord,' said Duke Lerarus. 'You do not wish to anger me.'

'Do you deny that you have sold yourself to our greatest enemy?' Crave said. 'Do you deny that you have abandoned sense and Order for the lure of Chaos, that you have thrown in your lot with the Great Changer?' His voice rose, becoming a shout that could be heard over the consternation spreading through the nobles. 'Do you deny that you are a servant of Tzeentch?'

Duke Lerarus' smile broadened, becoming something hideous, an inhuman leer with more than a touch of madness to it, and yet triumph shone there still.

'I deny nothing,' he said. 'Why would I deny the truth?'

'Father?' said Lerarus. She backed away.

'Get away from him, lass,' Drekki said. He moved Karon to point at the duke.

'Let her go,' Crave said to his men. 'Keep your weapons on the duke!'

The duke turned his pitiless smile on his daughter. 'You wouldn't understand,' he said. 'I was going to tell you, in good time. It's still not too late for you to be saved. I did it for us, my dear. I did it for our family.'

Drekki's eyes slid nervously to the Stormcast Eternals. They stood there motionless, useless gods.

Duke Lerarus looked around at the assembled people. 'You're all fools. We cannot beat the Great Changer. We sit in this city congratulating ourselves like dogs that have barked at the sun until it has gone down, feeling ourselves to be brave, not seeing that our success in driving it away is nothing of the sort, but a trick played by our inadequate minds. We resisted for five hundred years. We believe that to be impressive. Yet the gods hunger for all eternity!

They will find ways to destroy us that you cannot even dream of. Do you think I wanted to do this? Do you think it pleases me to become a traitor to my own? But I have seen the truth of the world and know how it will end. You are deluded, arguing with yourselves about bending the knee to Sigmar when the true gods watch and laugh at us, already sure of our downfall. Better to take power from the Great Changer when it is freely offered.'

'Father!' Lerarus said again, anguished.

'He's right,' Velunti said. 'At the end of the voyage when the Dark Gods return, will cleaving to Order make a blind bit of difference? They're coming for all of you. At least I tried. I could have been rich for a while. Better that than to slave forever for nothing.'

'Condemned out of your own mouths,' Crave said. He lifted his hand. 'By the powers invested in me by the most holy and ancient office of Witchfinder-General, you are hereby sentenced to die.'

Velunti stood tall, facing his end as a duardin should.

'Sorry, Drekki, it weren't nothing personal. Just business, is all.'

Duke Lerarus smiled wider. 'This will solve nothing. You're already too late.' He began to laugh, a mad, booming cackle that sent shivers down Drekki's spine.

Some of Duke Lerarus' troops, seeing what was about to happen, tried to run, screaming their innocence. It did not save them.

'Fire!' Crave shouted.

Drekki could not bring himself to shoot. He pointed Karon at the ceiling as gunshots cracked from every quarter. Some of Lerarus' men fired back. All were felled whether they ran or fought. Duke Lerarus dropped, laughing, his body full of bloody holes.

Drekki watched Velunti. He watched rounds skidding off his armour plates, ringing from his backpack. Red circles opened in his flight suit where the bullets found their way past metal, enough to have killed him, but he stood proudly for longer than he should. Even a Kharadron cannot survive such a fusillade, and he finally fell, the last in the group to die. His gear hitting the machine deck made a hollow boom.

'Cease fire!' Lord Crave commanded.

Gun smoke drifted.

'What the drukk just happened?' Adrimm ventured. Gord scratched himself and yawned. The lack of reaction from that ogor astonished Drekki sometimes.

Troops of House Crave ran onto the platform. House Manellus stood firm, as did the aelven house of Aenlus, and the duardin house of Khazdok. The nobles of the other four Great Houses acted less than valorously, hightailing it for the stairs. The crowd on the platform thinned.

Velunti had died with his eyes facing Lerarus, whose body had been pounded to bloody mince by the attack. Velunti's expression was one of horror, as if the truth of what he had done had come to him at the last.

'Unfortunate that we could not interrogate them,' said Crave to Drekki.

'Aye, I suppose it is,' said Drekki. A deadened feeling had him by the heart. He felt like he was speaking through a thick blanket.

'Remove their bodies,' Lord Crave ordered. 'Take the duardin and the duke back to Castle Crave. Burn the rest.' Soldiers ran forward to drag the dead off the platform. They struggled with Velunti. Two tried and failed. A third didn't help. Four got him rolling.

'Still, it is not a total loss,' said Crave. 'As we speak, their families are being arrested. We may yet find evidence upon their corpses, and my wizards may make their spirits talk.'

'That's my friend you're talking about,' said Drekki.

'They are always somebody's friend,' said Crave. He turned on his heel. 'Which is why we must be vigilant. Guards, arrest these duardin.'

'Now just hang on a minute!' said Drekki. His crew bunched up in the face of Crave's advancing men.

'You don't think I was actually going to pay you, do you? I did tell you, you greedy duardin, that I would kill you without hesitation if I felt that you imperilled my city. You have, and so your life is forfeit. You will be executed once I have the whole truth of this matter out of you.'

'You'll have to get past us first, you lanky man-bastard!' Umherth shouted. His volley gun was braced and ready.

Drekki brought Karon up again. Duardin aetherguns pointed back at human rifles.

'I advise you to let us go, or we will fight our way out of here, and you won't be able to stop us.'

'Crave, stop this,' the priest called. 'You're risking the machine.'

An argument commenced, dragging in all of the nobles still present. These people never stopped arguing.

'Just try it, tall boy, just try it!' Umherth was shouting.

The row almost drowned out the small, strange noise that came from Velunti's corpse. A sort of squealing, high-pitched moan.

'Shut up!' Drekki shouted. 'Shut up, all of you!'

The soldiers holding the corpse dropped it, and stepped back. Velunti was moving, bonelessly, like rubber or gelatine shaken hard. The squeal rose. The violent shudders rippling through the corpse culminated in a wet, gristly *pop*, and Velunti stopped moving.

The Stormcast Eternals reacted then, metal grinding on metal as they adopted a combat stance.

'Funti drukk,' said Drekki. He backed up. 'Get ready,' he whispered to his crew.

Shock froze the company into a dramatic tableau. They stared at Velunti's corpse.

And nothing happened.

One of the soldiers who had borne the cargo-master's body began to laugh in relief. His mirth spread to his fellows, until they were all laughing. He was stopped, immediately and fatally, by a tentacle that shot out of Velunti's back right through his heart.

There was screaming. The other three corpse bearers stumbled back, fumbling for their weapons. They too were slain by gristly spines shooting from Velunti's back. As this happened, Duke Lerarus rose up from between the two men carrying him, his body cracking and twitching as broken bones rearranged themselves. Bravely, the men struggled to constrain him, but he threw them off, until he stood, hunched, monstrous, less than human, horribly mutilated by the dozens of bullet wounds he had taken, yet somehow alive, and somehow, horribly, still able to smile.

'I did say it was too late,' Duke Lerarus said through bloodied teeth. Daggers appeared in his hands, and the two men by his side fell back even as they went for their swords, blood spraying from their opened throats.

Sanasha Lerarus yelled words of power. A fireball roared from her outstretched hand towards her father. There was a brilliant purple flash and Lerarus vanished; the fireball passed through empty air and slammed into the tower wall.

Chaos burst from Velunti's body.

CHAPTER TWENTY-NINE

BASTION IN PERIL

A thick column of flesh erupted from Velunti, as if he were a decoy, a rag of flesh laid over a trapdoor, hiding unfathomed spaces where huge and terrible creatures swam slow circles. The trick was revealed, the door opened, and one of those things was emerging, right into the machine tower. Drekki followed the flesh up. It grew like a monstrous tree, with outrageously patterned fish skin for bark. A wet smacking ran up the limb, like dozens of appreciative lips parting at once, and a thousand golden eyes glared upon the Realm of Metal hungrily.

'Drekki!'

Gord launched himself, cannonball-hard, tackling Drekki from the side, knocking the wind out of him, loosening his teeth in his jaws. Duardin and ogor sailed through the air as the living pillar fell down, right on the spot where Drekki had been standing, and commenced a violent writhing.

Guns banged from every quarter, both aether and blackpowder. Blue and gold striped the air. Belches of smoky fire flashed from musket muzzles. Neither had much effect. Small, pathetic craters popped open on the thing's hide, and it continued to roll about unhindered. Throwing stones at it would probably have had as much effect.

The thing had a crown of flailing tentacles atop its head, like an anemone, or deep-water medusa. Eyes randomly popped into existence on the tips, not so much opening as manifesting briefly and then turning back into mucus-slick flesh.

Gord got up, helped Drekki stand, and dusted him off.

A man flew overhead, screaming.

'Funti drengi drukk!' Drekki said. 'What by Grungni's beards is that?'

'Dunno,' said Gord. 'But I wouldn't want to eat it.'

Gord never could grasp the concept of rhetorical questions.

'Daemon beast. They tricked him!' Drekki shook his head. 'Poor Velunti. Whatever they paid him wasn't enough.'

Spells flared. Lightning and fire crashed into the flesh-tower's flanks. It was like an eel, or a snake, its tail still inside a burrow dug deep into another reality. It seemed to focus: the fleshy crown's many eyes swivelled about, fixing on the machine, and the desiccated living corpse who operated it and Adelia standing beside it. It began then to heave itself forward, not as a serpent might, with smooth ease, but with undulating difficultly. Each whip-flick of flesh sent its belly crashing into the platform. Everyone on it was thrown upward with each blow, as if engaged in a strange game of simultaneous leaping. The metal squealed, bent in the middle. The fitments holding it to the tower's stone were scraping free.

By this time, Drekki was running, Gord at his side. He saw how little use guns were against the creature. He had no wish to hang about. Drekki had but one thing on his mind, and that was a rapid departure.

'We're leaving!' he shouted at his crew. Some of them were on the way to the stairs already, dashing past the flopping beast. Drekki reached Adrimm as he stumbled, catching him, saving him from a long fall and a quick death. 'Stay on your feet, eh, Fair-weather?'

There was thunder, the fury of caged storms raging against imprisonment. The Stormcasts attacked like a series of lightning strikes, relentlessly, each one engaging, withdrawing, while the next was already landing his blow. Their hammers hit with the sound of tempests in high mountains, sheet lightning accompanying every impact leaving searing after-images, knocking wide chunks from the beast's flesh and showering their armour in oily, rainbow-hued blood. Their leader, the Knight-whatever-she-was, leapt onto the thing's back, and plunged her sword through the hide up to the quillions. This pained the daemon-beast, and it flicked itself about, knocking mortals and Stormcasts flying. The female warrior rode its fury, her sword carving long furrows in the thing's flesh like a drunkenly directed plough.

Drekki reached the edge of the rocking platform, leaping past the root of the beast onto the stone. Velunti's remains circled the bottom of the thing, a half-discarded snakeskin. It was so stretched, it could have been any sort of dross were it not for the flat, empty limbs that flapped about on the metal. They looked alive. Drekki didn't like to think about that.

'Adrimm, Otherek, Kedren, Hrunki...' He counted off his crew as they ran off the platform. Umherth was reluctant in coming. He had some berserker blood in him, that one, and preferred to fight every time. His volley gun blatted loudly, stitching bright lines up the side of the monster. It only made it angry. It was sprouting extra arms, bladed limbs, and extra heads on nodding stalks, which fell forward with snapping teeth and acid spit, fending off the Stormcasts and the peoples of Bastion while the main body continued to crawl slowly forward.

Another duardin ran up. Drekki counted him off aloud.

'Urdi... Urdi?' Drekki said warily.

'Please, captain,' panted Urdi. 'I've learned my lesson. Let me come with you.'

Drekki dithered for but a second. 'Gah! On up the stairs with you! I'll deal with you later.' He gave him a push to send him on his way.

The crew gathered on a landing a few feet up from the mayhem, where they shot down at the creature. Khenna and Kedren were the last on the platform with Umherth.

'Grab him, Khenna!' Drekki shouted. 'Get the mad old bozdok away from that thing!'

She didn't hear the detail, but she got the gist. She hooked her arm through the oldbeard's elbow and hauled him backward. He kept firing, laughing.

The runesmith hopped up off the platform. He thumped Drekki, trying to make himself heard over the battle.

'Where's Lerarus?' Kedren was saying. 'Where's Adelia?'

'Not my problem,' said Drekki, but he looked anyway. The mage Drekki could not see, though the flash of fireballs suggested she yet lived. Drekki had quite forgotten about Adelia in all the commotion, and was surprised to see she was still on the edge of the platform near the machine. She hadn't moved, and the thing was getting closer.

'There,' he said, and pointed.

'Poor lass,' said Kedren.

'Aye, well, someone will save her,' said Drekki. 'Meanwhile, we need to save ourselves.'

The creature had Adelia under some sort of spell. Its frills were pulsing, dancing, entrancing. She looked at it slack-jawed. Swaying hypnotically, it advanced on her.

'Who will save her?' said Kedren.

'What? Oh no, no no no, I've had it with this lot.'

Other heads on the beast roared, and it swung its hideous length from side to side, trying to dislodge the Knight. It smashed into one of her men, lifting him up off the platform and into the wall of the tower. He moved still, but the creature pushed, grinding sparks, then flesh, from the warrior.

A giant thunderclap and a burst of upward lightning punching through the roof announced the slaying of the first of the Stormcast Eternals.

The creature slammed back down, all the while its head continuing to entrance Adelia.

'Look at that thing, Drekki, who's going to save her?'

'Get on! Get on!' Drekki shouted, trying to usher Kedren after the others.

The runesmith shook him. 'The way is blocked to everyone, except you.' He was right. The platform was full of holes. The monster sprouted tentacles all over its sides that wrapped themselves round human and Stormcast, and pulled the creature's body tight to the metal. Kedren gave Drekki's harpoon a meaningful look.

'Grimnir burn you, Kedren! Everyone, up the tower!'

'Not... down?' said Adrimm.

'No, not down! Up! To the roof, you nitwit!'

The crew set off, firing behind them. A warrior of House Crave made a foolish attempt to arrest them. He got as far as 'Halt!' before Gord hoisted him up by the seat of his trousers and flung him over the edge. There were more soldiers coming down the stairs from the roof. The entire garrison had been drawn in by the fighting. It looked like Drekki's crew were going to have to shoot their way out, but the warriors surged past, towards the platform.

Drekki took his axe in two hands, and levelled the harpoon built into the top.

'If I die, Kedren, I'm going to be mightily annoyed.'

Kedren growled. It was almost a laugh. 'Don't worry, if you die, I'll die, because I'm coming with you.'

'No you're not,' said Drekki. 'You're going to make sure the others get away.'

'Drekki…'

'That's an order, Kedren.'

Kedren hesitated, then nodded. 'Aye, captain. Good luck.' Kedren hurried on up the stairs, the runes burning in his axe head trailing fire behind him.

Drekki squeezed the trigger handle on his axe. Aether puffed and the hook shot out, dragging line. The grapnel sank deep into rubbery flesh. Limbs slapped at it, but the wire was strong, duardin woven.

'See you in Shyish, runesmith,' Drekki muttered, and released the trigger.

The small winch in the axe head whirred hard. The line went taut, yanking Drekki off his feet. He flew towards the head of the monster, through the disorienting blur of battle. Someone was shouting, 'It's going for the talisman!' Lots of people were screaming. Magic crackled and gunfire roared. This was not the way the harpoon was supposed to be used, and the chances of failure were high. He whipped past the Stormcast hero, who was struggling against flat, ribbon-like extrusions growing out of the monster. All over the platform the number of combatants was much reduced.

It was a frightening ride, brought to an abrupt halt on the creature's back. He hit, bounced, and rolled onto the platform. The drop knocked the wind out of him, and his axe fell to the floor. The monster nearly crushed him. He rolled out of the way, snatching up his weapon. Runes glowed in the head, ready to unleash their might, but Drekki was not there for fighting. He cut the harpoon line, leaving the barb sunk in the daemon.

There was little thinking to do, and less time to waste. The next part of his improvised plan flashed into place. Drekki ran in front of the swaying thing, finding Adelia taking sluggish steps forward, arms held out.

'Oh no you don't,' said Drekki. He ran at her, picked her up. She was barely any burden at all to a stocky duardin, and he didn't stop until he was on the deck of the machine. Drekki turned to fight the Velunti-thing, axe ready, meaning to yell at Adelia to get into a pulpit while he held it off. But it had stopped short of the machine, where it bobbed about uncertainly. From inside, Drekki saw the machine deck was protected by a faint magical shield, a lesser version of the great energy barrier it projected around Bastion. The daemon couldn't do the machine harm while that was in place. The thing shrieked and warbled, approaching the shield closely then rearing back afraid, then repeated the motion, as blind and unthinking as the wrigglings of a worm.

'Right, then,' said Drekki. He turned.

The mummified umgi was motionless in his control pod. If Drekki didn't know otherwise he would have thought the human dead. Perhaps he was, in most senses. The man was disturbing, something that went beyond the dreadful way he looked, all sunken flesh and stretched-tight features, a corpse wrapped in the tarpaulin of its own skin. He projected a sense of suffering and of sorrow that Drekki could practically taste.

The Velunti-thing screeched, reared up, and slammed like a flail into the barrier. Light blazed. The monster's skin blackened, but lurched back for another attempt, ignoring the men and Stormcasts hewing at its flanks.

The shield was dimming.

Drekki went to Adelia. 'Adelia,' he said. 'Adelia.' He shook her. Her eyes cleared.

'The creature...'

'It can't get in,' said Drekki.

'No,' she said. She got up. 'The machine's purpose is to bar all things of Chaos.' She watched it slam into the barrier again. 'It is failing.' She glanced back at the other human, the near-corpse, and her resolve faltered a little. 'He cannot last. He has little strength. It will get through.' Her eyes clouded with tears. 'It was never supposed to be like this. He was a boy when they brought him here, not a man. I think he never became one,' said Adelia. 'He was my friend.'

Drekki really wished he could afford to be more sympathetic.

'If you take control of the machine, you'll be able to slay the thing, correct?'

'Yes,' she said. 'I am young. My soul is strong.'

'Well, we're in dire straits,' he said. 'I'd say fulfilling your destiny is the only thing that will keep us alive, lass.' He paused. The next question was hard. 'Can you get out if you go in?'

She didn't answer but smiled wanly. 'Are you asking me to choose my own fate?'

'You still have a choice,' he said. 'We can run.' He elected to ignore the thing scraping at the barrier around the machine, the mayhem that went on behind it, the impassable platform that led to the only way out.

'There is no choice. If this machine is destroyed, the city will die. Chaos will rise in the Skyshoals again. It is vulnerable only now, while I hesitate. I know what I must do.' She gently removed his hands from her shoulders. 'Do not step off the platform. Stay inside the shield.'

'I'm sorry.'

'Don't be,' she said. 'It's destiny, remember? This is what I was made for.'

She went to one of the other pulpits and climbed in, took a deep breath and grasped the two smooth silver handles project-ing from the front. Drekki kept watching her, kept his back to the creature so he didn't have to look, but when it spoke, he could not help but turn.

'Help me, Drekki, help me.'

The words sank like hooks into his mind. He felt some malign influence draw tight as angling cord, pull on his soul and turn him against his will.

'Help me, Drekki, help me.'

The voice came from the swaying crown of tentacles. The frill parted. In the very middle, framed like the stamen of a flower, Velunti's face gaped like an idiot fish: rolling, bulging eyes, lips working out of synchronisation with his mouth. His voice was nevertheless clear, and so, so enticing.

'Velunti?' said Drekki. 'Velunti? Is that you?'

The little fronds danced prettily. His mind dulled. It was relaxing. Very relaxing. He felt like lying down to watch.

'Help me, Drekki, help me,' said Velunti. 'Come closer, please, help me. I'm afraid.'

Drekki reached out his hand, unaware of the building sense of power coming off the machine. The spheres on their orbital tracks ran faster, emitting a growing light.

'Help me, Drekki, help me.'

Drekki's vision shifted. He was back on the *Aelsling*. Velunti was hanging off the shrouds, up near the top where they joined to the endrin.

'Velunti, what are you doing up there?'

Drekki approached the magical barrier. The thing swayed, drawing him out. He didn't see any of that, only his crewmate, good old Velunti.

He lifted up his hand.

'Kill her, Drekki, stop her. She's going to kill me, Drekki. Help me, Drekki, help me. Drekki, you're my friend!'

With limbs as slow as those of a dreamer, Drekki turned. There she was, the talisman. She gripped the small horns tightly. She would never let go. Light played around her, from within her, showing up her bones. But though he saw her, he did not really see. Instead he saw a woman holding a gun trained on Velunti. The machine was shaking. The pitch rising. He felt the deck of the *Aelsling* throbbing under full power.

'Quickly, Drekki, now, now,' said the Velunti-thing. 'Stop her! She means to kill me!'

The voice was in his head. In his limbs. Without knowing how it had happened, Karon was in his hand, pointing at the girl.

'Drekki! Drekki, no!' Adelia shouted through gritted teeth. An arc of power cracked from her pulpit, connected with his helm. It was just enough to shake him out of it. The *Aelsling* swam, and melted away. He staggered back.

'Funti drukk!' Drekki swore. 'What am I doing?' He tried to move his hand. He could not. It took all his willpower not to squeeze the trigger and send a spray of bullets into her.

'Drekki! Drekki! Drekki!' wailed Velunti.

Some resolve within aided his arm. He swung his aim away from Adelia as his treacherous finger contracted. Triple bullets thrummed through the air over Adelia's head, blue streaks of death leaving watery shockwaves.

Adelia screamed. The light shone out of her mouth and eyes. She was changing, and for a moment he saw her as something other than a young woman; he saw her as something transcendent.

The sight freed his mind. He threw himself to the floor.

'Dreeeekkkkkkkkiiiiiiii!'

The machine shook, once. A surge of magical energy burst outward. It sliced through the daemon-monster, more fundamentally wounding than any knife, cutting through its very essence, turning it at once from a solid, dangerous being to a translucent slime that dropped in one, slapping fall onto the platform.

Drekki got up. His body felt like rock. His flight gear dragged at him. Dazedly, he realised the aether-reactor had gone out, and he was bearing the full weight. He wasn't too dazed to restart it.

Adelia was slumped over the pulpit. She seemed slimmer, drained, a touch ghostly. The machine was sucking her life away. She lifted her head with great difficulty.

'Run,' she said.

There were many things Drekki thought to say. They were all inadequate. He nodded once at her, grabbed his weapons, turned on his wobbly heels, and fled.

Humans, aelves and duardin were lying all over the platform. The emission of the machine had done for them all. Most were unconscious. A few gave out feeble groans. Drekki thought some of them might have been dead.

Being at the epicentre must have shielded him.

Duardin can move fast when required. Arms and legs pumping, Drekki raced over the platform, praying to the brother gods that he wouldn't slip in the mess left behind by the beast. He barged past a man who was less affected than most, knocking him back to the floor. Then he was up the stairs, running for the roof.

Groans were giving way to shouts.

'Stop him!' Crave called. It figured that he'd be the first to recover.

A musket ball cracked off the wall. Splinters of rock pinged off his armour. Another followed. Drekki cursed human resilience. They looked so delicate too.

The exit to the roof was ahead. He cleared the steps two at a time, and hurled himself out into daylight.

All of the humans and aelves stationed on the roof had come down because of the fighting. That was a stroke of luck. Unfortunately, the Stormcast Eternals had beaten him up the stairs. Worse than that, his crew were nowhere to be seen.

There were only four of the Azyrites left, including their leader, but four demigods were still an insurmountable proposition. Drekki had the choice to bargain or run. He opted for running.

Drekki charged at the battlements. What he was going to do when he got there, he wasn't rightly sure. He was making this up on the fly.

A warrior in purple and white stepped in his way. His livery was scraped, showing dull gold sigmarite beneath. Huge dents marked his plating, and he'd lost his shield. None of this made him any less daunting. Drekki skidded, and scrambled out of the way. Another one stepped in at him. They were coming from nowhere. How did they move so silently and so fast? But they were there, around him, boxing him in, until he had nowhere left to go.

Shouts and running feet were approaching from below. The Stormcast hero stepped in front of him. Drekki held up his hands.

'Can we at least talk about this?' he said.

The woman stared down at him, the sole sign of humanity the eyes just visible through the vision holes of her mask. They were a steady grey.

The shouts were drawing closer. They were nearly on the roof.

There was another sound. The sound of aether-endrins working hard, and airscrews chopping the air. Then the sweet, sweet sound of Trokwi trilling, his secret song letting Drekki know the *Aelsling* was near.

'Let me go,' he said. 'You know what I did. You know what they'll do to me. I'll repay you one day, I swear.'

The woman held his eyes, then nodded wordlessly.

The Stormcasts stepped back, and clashed their hammers on their shields.

'Thank you,' Drekki said.

He hopped onto a crenel. Lord Crave's troops were spilling onto the roof. Crave followed them.

'Stop him!' Crave shouted at the Stormcasts. 'Stop him!'

The warriors of Azyr did not move. They had made their position clear.

'You can't stop me, you honourless bozdoks,' said Drekki. 'Because I'm Drekki Flynt!'

He waved flamboyantly, and he jumped. Guns banged all over the roof.

A second later the *Aelsling* rose over the parapet. Endrin portholes glaring, she swung around in the air, and made all speed from Bastion.

Drekki bent double, heaving fiery breaths.

'I don't mind the odd daring escape, but that was too close,' he panted.

'Sorry, captain,' said Bokko. 'We couldn't hold station once we'd picked everyone up. The weapons on the other towers got a bead on us. A moving target is harder to hit.'

'No mind, lad,' said Drekki. He stood up and slapped Bokko on the shoulder. 'You always come right in the end.'

The Citadel Isle fell behind the stern, the rest of the islands of Bastion dropping into place around it like puzzle pieces. Evrokk had the ship on a steep climb, taking them out of the range of the city's weaponry. The barrier was ahead, brighter and stronger than before. He held his breath as they approached, but they sped through freely.

'Chaos free,' said Drekki. He had a feeling this revived barrier wouldn't have let Velunti through.

Bokko tugged his arm.

'Sorry again, captain, but there's something else needs dealing with…'

'Damn right,' said Drekki. He set himself against the pitch of the deck and marched up to Urdi. 'You've a bloody cheek coming on this boat, my lad,' said Drekki.

'Captain, I–'

Drekki talked right over him. 'But I'm willing to let this lapse go. You'll take a fifty per cent cut in shares, and if there's so much as a whiff of you working for someone else while you're on my roster, I'll toss you over the side myself. Is that clear?'

Urdi nodded shamefacedly. 'Thank you, captain, I don't deserve it.'

'Funti dreng you don't, Urdi. You've got a long road ahead of you before you'll win back our trust. You might never. You might want to think about a new ship to join.'

'No, captain,' he said, downcast. 'I belong here. I know that now.'

'That remains to be seen,' said Drekki. 'Get to work.'

'Erm, sorry, captain,' said Bokko for the third time. 'But that's not the something else I meant.' He stepped aside. Sitting against the door into Drekki's cabin was Sanasha Lerarus. Bokko pointed at her. 'She is.'

The ship was levelling off. Drekki went and sat down beside her. He suddenly felt very tired.

'I'm not surprised to see you here, given what just happened,' he said. 'I suppose you don't have that ten thousand Achromisia you offered me?'

She snorted. 'No.'

'And I suppose you don't want to go home. I don't blame you for that, so...' He spread his hands. 'Do you want that job? I really could use you,' he said. 'The mage position is still open.'

She tried a smile. It didn't really fit.

'Maybe one day, but not now. Your life is a bit too unpredictable for me.' She turned her head to look at him. She was exhausted, shattered, full of sorrow, but there was a new steeliness to her. 'But you could do me a favour.'

CHAPTER THIRTY

DREKKI FLIES AGAIN

'Are you sure you don't want to stay with us?' asked Drekki.

'Aye,' said Kedren. 'You're not a bad lass, for an umgi.'

'I need to decide what I'm going to do with the rest of my life,' she said. 'My father left me with some questions, and I don't think I'll find the answers with you.'

They were at a quayside shiny with new construction. Drekki and Kedren stood on the ship, Lerarus had already disembarked. Behind her rose the free city of Tabar, Sigmar's new outpost on the coast of the mainland. Heroic statues lined the docks and walls, looking out over the interior and the Skyshoals both. Their eyes glowed with protective magics, and yet they seemed eager to survey. A little too eager. There was something of the conqueror to them.

Several nexus syphons shone like captured suns, draining corruption from the land. Already the town had overspilled its initial set of defensive walls. There was scaffolding everywhere, and the sounds of chisels and hammers made a constant, asynchronous beat. Beyond, the wide open spaces of the continent of Prosperis, rich with peril and opportunity. The shoals ended at Tabar for real. Past it was solid ground, and a different set of dangers.

'A lot of opportunities for a canny thing like you,' Drekki said. He bent low and extended a hand. 'I guess this is it.'

She took his hand, and shook it.

'I'll be seeing you, captain,' she said.

Drekki grinned. 'If you can find me.'

She smiled back. 'You're Drekki Flynt. Your legend precedes you. I'll find you if I need you.'

Sanasha Lerarus shouldered her knapsack, gave him a tight nod, turned on her heel and walked away, losing herself in the crowds.

'Poor lass,' said Kedren. 'She's some hard years ahead.'

'I think she'll be fine,' said Drekki.

Adrimm and Otherek were down on the quay, haggling with a duardin merchant over the value of the cargo Velunti had picked up in Bavardia. That was heaped neatly on the dock. New cargo was being craned in; Drekki had a packet job from an umgi armourer. Swords and guns for the outlying colonies of Bastion. Umherth was nearby, frightening the replacement crew Hrunki and Khenna had rounded up from Tabar's two taverns. The others attended to their tasks, weary, battle-scarred, but content. Drekki looked on the scene with calm satisfaction. The events of Bastion already seemed a long way away; just another day in the shoals.

'Looks like business as usual, thank the brothers,' he said.

There was some huffing and puffing by the gate in the rails as Ildrin Gothrik threw his duffel bag onto the dock and jumped down after it. He followed his belongings with about as much grace, and pushed off without a backward glance, scowl fixed. He'd taken his share then demanded release. Drekki had granted it. He didn't speak to anyone beyond that.

'Don't suppose we'll be seeing him again,' said Kedren.

'Can you blame him?'

Kedren grunted with laughter. 'He blames you, lad.'

'The pains of being a captain,' said Drekki. 'Can't keep everyone happy all of the time. Speaking of which,' he continued, 'at least this voyage was not a total loss.' He reached into a pouch on his belt, and pulled out one of the bags of gems they'd taken from Erulu. 'With this, the navigational data Otherek scraped from the Eye, and the profits from that cargo, we should pull in a tidy sum.'

'Pfft! You've hardly covered our living expenses. There's the water, the food, the fuel...' Kedren said, poking his thick fingers into his palm.

'Kedren, Kedren, shh!' said Drekki. Trokwi peeped admonishingly at the smith, on Drekki's side for once. 'I'll be avoiding the awkward moment of telling our arkanauts that they aren't getting paid. That is something. A small something, but from small, positive somethings are worthwhile lives constructed, my friend.'

'That's as may be, but they're not getting paid *enough* for all that bother. With Duke Lerarus gone, there'll be no money, so Throkk's still going to be after you. You've broken contract with Rikko Riksson into the bargain, we'll not be welcome in Bavardia again, so we'll have to be careful in its colonies. Not to mention the duke getting away in a puff of smoke. I don't like it when our enemies are hidden, Drekki.'

'We did save the day,' said Drekki. 'Be happy with that!'

'Days saved buy no bacon,' said Kedren.

'Has anyone ever told you that you grumble a lot?' said Drekki. 'One thing at a time, runesmith. One at a time.'

The ship's whistle hooted. The cargo hatch was shut up. Evening was coming and the rising off-wind was blowing from the land, stirring Drekki's beard. He could scent adventure.

Otherek Zhurafon joined them.

'Get a good price for the cargo?' Drekki asked.

'Nearly a fair one, I don't know about good,' said the aether-khemist.

'You don't seem happy.'

Otherek sniffed the air. 'It's this wind. The stink of corruption. It's on everything. I've a feeling Bastion was only the start.'

'Nah, it's just the mainland. Wasteland most of it, full of evil.'

'It's more than that,' said Otherek. 'Grungni break me on his anvil if I can tell from which direction, but something bad is coming.'

'Let's worry about that tomorrow, Otherek, and tomorrow is another day,' said Drekki. 'Arkanaut Adrimmsson! Prepare to cast off!' he shouted. 'Endrinrigger Dwindonsson, warm the endrins!'

A shiver of energy passed through the crew and the ship. They went at their tasks with renewed gusto. For all they enjoyed their time ashore, they were skyfarers all, and the sky was where they belonged.

The whistle blew again. Khenna and Adrimm gathered in the ropes. Evrokk threw levers, and the screws began to bite.

Gracefully, the *Aelsling* came about, prow pointed to the outer edges of the realm of Chamon, and pulled out into the evening.

ABOUT THE AUTHOR

Guy Haley is the author of the Siege of Terra novel *The Lost and the Damned*, as well as the Horus Heresy novels *Titandeath*, *Wolfsbane* and *Pharos*, and the Primarchs novels *Konrad Curze: The Night Haunter*, *Corax: Lord of Shadows* and *Perturabo: The Hammer of Olympia*. He has also written many Warhammer 40,000 novels, including the Dawn of Fire titles *Avenging Son* and *Throne of Light*, as well as *Belisarius Cawl: The Great Work*, the Dark Imperium trilogy, *The Devastation of Baal*, *Dante*, *Darkness in the Blood* and *Astorath: Angel of Mercy*. He has also written stories set in the Age of Sigmar, included in *War Storm*, *Ghal Maraz* and *Call of Archaon*. He lives in Yorkshire with his wife and son.

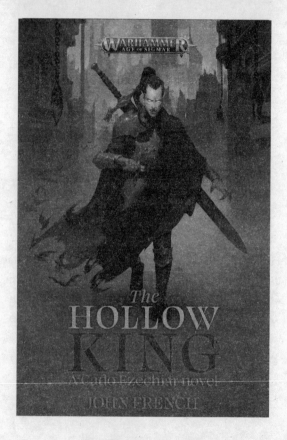